I0785676

Mary Roberts Rinehart

A Poor Wise Man

OK Publishing 2021

Mary Roberts Rinehart

A POOR WISE MAN

Political Thriller

Published by

MUSAICUM

Books

- Advanced Digital Solutions & High-Quality book Formatting -

musaicumbooks@okpublishing.info

2021 OK Publishing

ISBN 978-80-272-7769-8

Contents

Chapter I

The city turned its dreariest aspect toward the railway on blackened walls, irregular and ill-paved streets, gloomy warehouses, and over all a gray, smoke-laden atmosphere which gave it mystery and often beauty. Sometimes the softened towers of the great steel bridges rose above the river mist like fairy towers suspended between Heaven and earth. And again the sun tipped the surrounding hills with gold, while the city lay buried in its smoke shroud, and white ghosts of river boats moved spectrally along.

Sometimes it was ugly, sometimes beautiful, but always the city was powerful, significant, important. It was a vast melting pot. Through its gates came alike the hopeful and the hopeless, the dreamers and those who would destroy those dreams. From all over the world there came men who sought a chance to labor. They came in groups, anxious and dumb, carrying with them their pathetic bundles, and shepherded by men with cunning eyes.

Raw material, for the crucible of the city, as potentially powerful as the iron ore which entered the city by the same gate.

The city took them in, gave them sanctuary, and forgot them. But the shepherds with the cunning eyes remembered.

Lily Cardew, standing in the train shed one morning early in March, watched such a line go by. She watched it with interest. She had developed a new interest in people during the year she had been away. She had seen, in the army camp, similar shuffling lines of men, transformed in a few hours into ranks of uniformed soldiers, beginning already to be actuated by the same motive. These aliens, going by, would become citizens. Very soon now they would appear on the streets in new American clothes of extraordinary cut and color, their hair cut with clippers almost to the crown, and surmounted by derby hats always a size too small.

Lily smiled, and looked out for her mother. She was suddenly unaccountably glad to be back again. She liked the smoke and the noise, the movement, the sense of things doing. And the sight of her mother, small, faultlessly tailored, wearing a great bunch of violets, and incongruous in that work-a-day atmosphere, set her smiling again.

How familiar it all was! And heavens, how young she looked! The limousine was at the curb, and a footman as immaculately turned out as her mother stood with a folded rug over his arm. On the seat inside lay a purple box. Lily had known it would be there. They would be ostensibly from her father, because he had not been able to meet her, but she knew quite well that Grace Cardew had stopped at the florist's on her way downtown and bought them.

A little surge of affection for her mother warmed the girl's eyes. The small attentions which in the Cardew household took the place of loving demonstrations had always touched her. As a family the Cardews were rather loosely knitted together, but there was something very lovable about her mother.

Grace Cardew kissed her, and then held her off and looked at her.

"Mercy, Lily!" she said, "you look as old as I do."

"Older, I hope," Lily retorted. "What a marvel you are, Grace dear." Now and then she called her mother "Grace." It was by way of being a small joke between them, but limited to their moments alone. Once old Anthony, her grandfather, had overheard her, and there had been rather a row about it.

"I feel horribly old, but I didn't think I looked it."

They got into the car and Grace held out the box to her. "From your father, dear. He wanted so to come, but things are dreadful at the mill. I suppose you've seen the papers." Lily opened the box, and smiled at her mother.

"Yes, I know. But why the subterfuge about the flowers, mother dear? Honestly, did he send them, or did you get them? But never mind about that; I know he's worried, and you're sweet to do it. Have you broken the news to grandfather that the last of the Cardews is coming home?"

"He sent you all sorts of messages, and he'll see you at dinner."

Lily laughed out at that.

"You darling!" she said. "You know perfectly well that I am nothing in grandfather's young life, but the Cardew women all have what he likes to call savoir faire. What would they do, father and grandfather, if you didn't go through life smoothing things for them?"

Grace looked rather stiffly ahead. This young daughter of hers, with her directness and her smiling ignoring of the small subterfuges of life, rather frightened her. The terrible honesty of youth! All these years of ironing the wrinkles out of life, of smoothing the difficulties between old Anthony and Howard, and now a third generation to contend with. A pitilessly frank and unconsciously cruel generation. She turned and eyed Lily uneasily.

"You look tired," she said, "and you need attention. I wish you had let me send Castle to you."

But she thought that lily was even lovelier than she had remembered her. Lovely rather than beautiful, perhaps. Her face was less childish than when she had gone away; there was, in certain of her expressions, an almost alarming maturity. But perhaps that was fatigue.

"I couldn't have had Castle, mother. I didn't need anything. I've been very happy, really, and very busy."

"You have been very vague lately about your work."

Lily faced her mother squarely.

"I didn't think you'd much like having me do it, and I thought it would drive grandfather crazy."

"I thought you were in a canteen."

"Not lately. I've been looking after girls who had followed soldiers to camps. Some of them were going to have babies, too. It was rather awful. We married quite a lot of them, however."

The curious reserve that so often exists between mother and daughter held Grace Cardew dumb. She nodded, but her eyes had slightly hardened. So this was what war had done to her. She had had no son, and had thanked God for it during the war, although old Anthony had hated her all her married life for it. But she had given her daughter, her clear-eyed daughter, and they had shown her the dregs of life.

Her thoughts went back over the years. To Lily as a child, with Mademoiselle always at her elbow, and life painted as a thing of beauty. Love, marriage and birth were divine accidents. Death was a quiet sleep, with heaven just beyond, a sleep which came only to age, which had wearied and would rest. Then she remembered the day when Elinor Cardew, poor unhappy Elinor, had fled back to Anthony's roof to have a baby, and after a few rapturous weeks for Lily the baby had died.

"But the baby isn't old," Lily had persisted, standing in front of her mother with angry, accusing eyes.

Grace was not an imaginative woman, but she turned it rather neatly, as she told Howard later.

"It was such a nice baby," she said, feeling for an idea. "I think probably God was lonely without it, and sent an angel for it again."

"But it is still upstairs," Lily had insisted. She had had a curious instinct for truth, even then. But there Grace's imagination had failed her, and she sent for Mademoiselle. Mademoiselle was a good Catholic, and very clear in her own mind, but what she left in Lily's brain was a confused conviction that every person was two persons, a body and a soul. Death was simply a split-up, then. One part of you, the part that bathed every morning and had its toe-nails cut, and went to dancing school in a white frock and thin black silk stockings and carriage boots over pumps, that part was buried and would only came up again at the Resurrection. But the other part was all the time very happy, and mostly singing.

Lily did not like to sing.

Then there was the matter of tears. People only cried when they hurt themselves. She had been told that again and again when she threatened tears over her music lesson. But when Aunt Elinor had gone away she had found Mademoiselle, the deadly antagonist of tears, weeping. And here again Grace remembered the child's wide, insistent eyes.

"Why?"

"She is sorry for Aunt Elinor."

"Because her baby's gone to God? She ought to be glad, oughtn't she?"

"Not that," said Grace, and had brought a box of chocolates and given her one, although they were not permitted save one after each meal.

Then Lily had gone away to school. How carefully the school had been selected! When she came back, however, there had been no more questions, and Grace had sighed with relief. That bad time was over, anyhow. But Lily was rather difficult those days. She seemed, in some vague way, resentful. Her mother found her, now and then, in a frowning, half-defiant mood. And once, when Mademoiselle had ventured some jesting remark about young Alston Denslow, she was stupefied to see the girl march out of the room, her chin high, not to be seen again for hours.

Grace's mind was sub-consciously remembering those things even when she spoke.

"I didn't know you were having to learn about that side of life," she said, after a brief silence.

"That side of life is life, mother," Lily said gravely. But Grace did not reply to that. It was characteristic of her to follow her own line of thought.

"I wish you wouldn't tell your grandfather. You know he feels strongly about some things. And he hasn't forgiven me yet for letting you go."

Rather diffidently Lily put her hand on her mother's. She gave her rare caresses shyly, with averted eyes, and she was always more diffident with her mother than with her father. Such spontaneous bursts of affection as she sometimes showed had been lavished on Mademoiselle. It was Mademoiselle she had hugged rapturously on her small feast days, Mademoiselle who never demanded affection, and so received it.

"Poor mother!" she said, "I have made it hard for you, haven't I? Is he as bad as ever?"

She had not pinned on the violets, but sat holding them in her hands, now and then taking a luxurious sniff. She did not seem to expect a reply. Between Grace and herself it was quite understood that old Anthony Cardew was always as bad as could be.

"There is some sort of trouble at the mill. Your father is worried."

And this time it was Lily who did not reply. She said, inconsequentially:

"We're saved, and it's all over. But sometimes I wonder if we were worth saving. It all seems such a mess, doesn't it?" She glanced out. They were drawing up before the house, and she looked at her mother whimsically.

"The last of the Cardews returning from the wars!" she said. "Only she is unfortunately a she, and she hasn't been any nearer the war than the State of Ohio."

Her voice was gay enough, but she had a quick vision of the grim old house had she been the son they had wanted to carry on the name, returning from France.

The Cardews had fighting traditions. They had fought in every war from the Revolution on. There had been a Cardew in Mexico in '48, and in that upper suite of rooms to which her grandfather had retired in wrath on his son's marriage, she remembered her sense of awe as a child on seeing on the wall the sword he had worn in the Civil War. He was a small man, and the scabbard was badly worn at the end, mute testimony to the long forced marches of his youth. Her father had gone to Cuba in '98, and had almost died of typhoid fever there, contracted in the marshes of Florida.

Yes, they had been a fighting family. And now —

Her mother was determinedly gay. There were flowers in the dark old hall, and Grayson, the butler, evidently waiting inside the door, greeted her with the familiarity of the old servant who had slipped her sweets from the pantry after dinner parties in her little-girl years.

"Welcome home, Miss Lily," he said.

Mademoiselle was lurking on the stairway, in a new lace collar over her old black dress. Lily recognized in the collar a great occasion, for Mademoiselle was French and thrifty. Suddenly a wave of warmth and gladness flooded her. This was home. Dear, familiar home. She had come back. She was the only young thing in the house. She would bring them gladness and youth. She would try to make them happy. Always before she had taken, but now she meant to give.

Not that she formulated such a thought. It was an emotion, rather. She ran up the stairs and hugged Mademoiselle wildly.

"You darling old thing!" she cried. She lapsed into French. "I saw the collar at once. And think, it is over! It is finished. And all your nice French relatives are sitting on the boulevards in the sun, and sipping their little glasses of wine, and rising and bowing when a pretty girl passes. Is it not so?"

"It is so, God and the saints be praised!" said Mademoiselle, huskily.

Grace Cardew followed them up the staircase. Her French was negligible, and she felt again, as in days gone by, shut from the little world of two which held her daughter and governess. Old Anthony's doing, that. He had never forgiven his son his plebeian marriage, and an early conversation returned to her. It was on Lily's first birthday and he had made one of his rare visits to the nursery. He had brought with him a pearl in a velvet case.

"All our women have their own pearls," he had said. "She will have her grandmother's also when she marries. I shall give her one the first year, two the second, and so on." He had stood looking down at the child critically. "She's a Cardew," he said at last. "Which means that she will be obstinate and self-willed." He had paused there, but Grace had not refuted the statement. He had grinned. "As you know," he added. "Is she talking yet?"

"A word or two," Grace had said, with no more warmth in her tone than was in his.

"Very well. Get her a French governess. She ought to speak French before she does English. It is one of the accomplishments of a lady. Get a good woman, and for heaven's sake arrange to serve her breakfast in her room. I don't want to have to be pleasant to any chattering French woman at eight in the morning."

"No, you wouldn't," Grace had said.

Anthony had stamped out, but in the hall he smiled grimly. He did not like Howard's wife, but she was not afraid of him. He respected her for that. He took good care to see that the Frenchwoman was found, and at dinner, the only meal he took with the family, he would now and then send for the governess and Lily to come in for dessert. That, of course, was later on, when the child was nearly ten. Then would follow a three-cornered conversation in rapid French, Howard and Anthony and Lily, with Mademoiselle joining in timidly, and with Grace, at the side of the table, pretending to eat and feeling cut off, in a middle-class world of her own, at the side of the table. Anthony Cardew had retained the head of his table, and he had never asked her to take his dead wife's place.

After a time Grace realized the consummate cruelty of those hours, the fact that Lily was sent for, not only because the old man cared to see her, but to make Grace feel the outsider that she was. She made desperate efforts to conquer the hated language, but her accent was atrocious. Anthony would correct her suavely, and Lily would laugh in childish, unthinking mirth. She gave it up at last.

She never told Howard about it. He had his own difficulties with his father, and she would not add to them. She managed the house, checked over the bills and sent them to the office, put up a cheerful and courageous front, and after a time sheathed herself in an armor of smiling indifference. But she thanked heaven when the time came to send Lily away to school. The effort of concealing the armed neutrality between Anthony and herself was growing more wearing. The girl was observant. And Anthony had been right, she was a Cardew. She would have fought her grandfather out on it, defied him, accused him, hated him. And Grace wanted peace.

Once again as she followed Lily and Mademoiselle up the stairs she felt the barrier of language, and back of it the Cardew pride and traditions that somehow cut her off.

But in Lily's rooms she was her sane and cheerful self again. Inside the doorway the girl was standing, her eyes traveling over her little domain ecstatically.

"How lovely of you not to change a thing, mother!" she said. "I was so afraid —I know how you hate my stuff. But I might have known you wouldn't. All the time I've been away, sleeping in a dormitory, and taking turns at the bath, I have thought of my own little place." She wandered around, touching her familiar possessions with caressing hands. "I've a good notion," she declared, "to go to bed immediately, just for the pleasure of lying in linen sheets again." Suddenly she turned to her mother. "I'm afraid you'll find I've made some queer friends, mother."

"What do you mean by 'queer'?"

"People no proper Cardew would care to know." She smiled. "Where's Ellen? I want to tell her I met somebody she knows out there, the nicest sort of a boy." She went to the doorway and called lustily: "Ellen! Ellen!" The rustling of starched skirts answered her from down the corridor.

"I wish you wouldn't call, dear." Grace looked anxious. "You know how your grandfather—there's a bell for Ellen."

"What we need around here," said Lily, cheerfully, "is a little more calling. And if grandfather thinks it is unbefitting the family dignity he can put cotton in his ears. Come in, Ellen. Ellen, do you know that I met Willy Cameron in the camp?"

"Willy!" squealed Ellen. "You met Willy? Isn't he a fine boy, Miss Lily?"

"He's wonderful," said Lily. "I went to the movies with him every Friday night." She turned to her mother. "You would like him, mother. He couldn't get into the army. He is a little bit lame. And —" she surveyed Grace with amused eyes, "you needn't think what you are thinking. He is tall and thin and not at all good-looking. Is he, Ellen?"

"He is a very fine young man," Ellen said rather stiffly. "He's very highly thought of in the town I come from. His father was a doctor, and his buggy used to go around day, and night. When he found they wouldn't take him as a soldier he was like to break his heart."

"Lame?" Grace repeated, ignoring Ellen.

"Just a little. You forget all about it when you know him. Don't you, Ellen?"

But at Grace's tone Ellen had remembered. She stiffened, and became again a housemaid in the Anthony Cardew house, a self-effacing, rubber-heeled, pink-uniformed lower servant. She glanced at Mrs. Cardew, whose eyebrows were slightly raised.

"Thank you, miss," she said. And went out, leaving Lily rather chilled and openly perplexed.

"Well!" she said. Then she glanced at her mother. "I do believe you are a little shocked, mother, because Ellen and I have a mutual friend in Mr. William Wallace Cameron! Well, if you want the exact truth, he hadn't an atom of use for me until he heard about Ellen." She put an arm around Grace's shoulders. "Brace up, dear," she said, smilingly. "Don't you cry. I'll be a Cardew bye-and-bye."

"Did you really go to the moving pictures with him?" Grace asked, rather unhappily. She had never been inside a moving picture theater. To her they meant something a step above the corner saloon, and a degree below the burlesque houses. They were constituted of bad air and unchaperoned young women accompanied by youths who dangled cigarettes from a lower lip, all obviously of the lower class, including the cigarette; and of other women, sometimes drab, dragged of breast and carrying children who should have been in bed hours before; or still others, wandering in pairs, young, painted and predatory. She was not imaginative, or she could not have lived so long in Anthony Cardew's house. She never saw, in the long line waiting outside even the meanest of the little theaters that had invaded the once sacred vicinity of the Cardew house, the cry of every human heart for escape from the sordid, the lure of romance, the call of adventure and the open road.

"I can't believe it," she added.

Lily made a little gesture of half-amused despair.

"Dearest," she said, "I did. And I liked it. Mother, things have changed a lot in twenty years. Sometimes I think that here, in this house, you don't realize that —" she struggled for a phrase —"that things have changed," she ended, lamely. "The social order, and that sort of thing. You know. Caste." She hesitated. She was young and inarticulate, and when she saw Grace's face, somewhat frightened. But she was not old Anthony's granddaughter for nothing. "This idea of being a Cardew," she went on, "that's ridiculous, you know. I'm only half Cardew, anyhow. The rest is you, dear, and it's got being a Cardew beaten by quite a lot."

Mademoiselle was deftly opening the girl's dressing case, but she paused now and turned. It was to Grace that she spoke, however.

"They come home like that, all of them," she said. "In France also. But in time they see the wisdom of the old order, and return. It is one of the fruits of war."

Grace hardly heard her.

"Lily," she asked, "you are not in love with this Cameron person, are you?"

But Lily's easy laugh reassured her.

"No, indeed," she said. "I am not. I shall probably marry beneath me, as you would call it, but not William Wallace Cameron. For one thing, he wouldn't have grandfather in his family."

Some time later Mademoiselle tapped at Grace's door, and entered. Grace was reclining on a chaise longue, towels tucked about her neck and over her pillows, while Castle, her elderly English maid, was applying ice in a soft cloth to her face. Grace sat up. The towel, pinned around her hair like a coif, gave a placid, almost nun-like appearance to her still lovely face.

"Well?" she demanded. "Go out for a minute, Castle."

Mademoiselle waited until the maid had gone.

"I have spoken to Ellen," she said, her voice cautious. "A young man who does not care for women, a clerk in a country pharmacy. What is that, Mrs. Cardew?"

"It would be so dreadful, Mademoiselle. Her grandfather —"

"But not handsome," insisted Mademoiselle, "and lame! Also, I know the child. She is not in love. When that comes to her we shall know it."

Grace lay back, relieved, but not entirely comforted.

"She is changed, isn't she, Mademoiselle?"

Mademoiselle shrugged her shoulders.

"A phase," she said. She had got the word from old Anthony, who regarded any mental attitude that did not conform with his own as a condition that would pass. "A phase, only. Now that she is back among familiar things, she will become again a daughter of the house."

"Then you think this talk about marrying beneath her —"

"She 'as had liberty," said Mademoiselle, who sometimes lost an aspirate. "It is like wine to the young. It intoxicates. But it, too, passes. In my country —"

But Grace had, for a number of years, heard a great deal of Mademoiselle's country. She settled herself on her pillows.

"Call Castle, please," she said. "And-do warn her not to voice those ideas of hers to her grandfather. In a country pharmacy, you say?"

"And lame, and not fond of women," corroborated Mademoiselle. "Ca ne pourrait pas etre mieux, n'est-ce pas?"

Chapter II

Shortly after the Civil War Anthony Cardew had left Pittsburgh and spent a year in finding a location for the investment of his small capital. That was in the very beginning of the epoch of steel. The iron business had already laid the foundations of its future greatness, but steel was still in its infancy.

Anthony's father had been an iron-master in a small way, with a monthly pay-roll of a few hundred dollars, and an abiding faith in the future of iron. But he had never dreamed of steel. But "sixty-five" saw the first steel rail rolled in America, and Anthony Cardew began to dream. He went to Chicago first, and from there to Michigan, to see the first successful Bessemer converter. When he started east again he knew what he was to make his life work.

He was very young and his capital was small. But he had an abiding faith in the new industry. Not that he dreamed then of floating steel battleships. But he did foresee steel in new and various uses. Later on he was experimenting with steel cable at the very time Roebling made it a commercial possibility, and with it the modern suspension bridge and the elevator. He never quite forgave Roebling. That failure of his, the difference only of a month or so, was one of the few disappointments of his prosperous, self-centered, orderly life. That, and Howard's marriage. And, at the height of his prosperity, the realization that Howard's middle-class wife would never bear a son.

The city he chose was a small city then, yet it already showed signs of approaching greatness. On the east side, across the river, he built his first plant, a small one, with the blast heated by passing through cast iron pipes, with the furnaceman testing the temperature with strips of lead and zinc, and the skip hoist a patient mule.

He had ore within easy hauling distance, and he had fuel, and he had, as time went on, a rapidly increasing market. Labor was cheap and plentiful, too, and being American-born, was willing and intelligent. Perhaps Anthony Cardew's sins of later years were due to a vast impatience that the labor of the early seventies was no longer to be had.

The Cardew fortune began in the seventies. Up to that time there was a struggle, but in the seventies Anthony did two things. He went to England to see the furnaces there, and brought home a wife, a timid, tall Englishwoman of irreproachable birth, who remained always an alien in the crude, busy new city. And he built himself a house, a brick house in lower East Avenue, a house rather like his tall, quiet wife, and run on English lines. He soon became the leading citizen. He was one of the committee to welcome the Prince of Wales to the city, and from the very beginning he took his place in the social life.

He found it very raw at times, crude and new. He himself lived with dignity and elegant simplicity. He gave now and then lengthy, ponderous dinners, making out the lists himself, and handing them over to his timid English wife in much the manner in which he gave the wine list and the key to the wine cellar to the butler. And, at the head of his table, he let other men talk and listened. They talked, those industrial pioneers, especially after the women had gone. They saw the city the center of great business and great railroads. They talked of its coal, its river, and the great oil fields not far away which were then in their infancy. All of them dreamed a dream, saw a vision. But not all of them lived to see their dream come true.

Old Anthony lived to see it.

In the late eighties, his wife having been by that time decorously interred in one of the first great mausoleums west of the mountains, Anthony Cardew found himself already wealthy. He owned oil wells and coal mines. His mines supplied his coke ovens with coal, and his own river boats, as well as railroads in which he was a director, carried his steel.

He labored ably and well, and not for wealth alone. He was one of a group of big-visioned men who saw that a nation was only as great as its industries. It was only in his later years that he loved power for the sake of power, and when, having outlived his generation, he had developed a rigidity of mind that made him view the forced compromises of the new regime as pusillanimous.

He considered his son Howard's quiet strength weakness. "You have no stamina," he would say. "You have no moral fiber. For God's sake, make a stand, you fellows, and stick to it."

He had not mellowed with age. He viewed with endless bitterness the passing of his own day and generation, and the rise to power of younger men; with their "shilly-shallying," he would say. He was an aristocrat, an autocrat, and a survival. He tied Howard's hands in the management of the now vast mills, and then blamed him for the results.

But he had been a great man.

He had had two children, a boy and a girl. The girl had been the tragedy of his middle years, and Howard had been his hope.

On the heights outside the city and overlooking the river he owned a farm, and now and then, on Sunday afternoons in the eighties, he drove out there, with Howard sitting beside him, a rangy boy in his teens, in the victoria which Anthony considered the proper vehicle for Sunday afternoons. The farmhouse was in a hollow, but always on those excursions Anthony, fastidiously dressed, picking his way half-irritably through briars and cornfields, would go to the edge of the cliffs and stand there, looking down. Below was the muddy river, sluggish always, but a thing of terror in spring freshets. And across was the east side, already a sordid place, its steel mills belching black smoke that killed the green of the hillsides, its furnaces dwarfed by distance and height, its rows of unpainted wooden structures which housed the mill laborers.

Howard would go with him, but Howard dreamed no dreams. He was a sturdy, dependable, unimaginative boy, watching the squirrels or flinging stones over the palisades. Life for Howard was already a thing determined. He would go to college, and then he would come back and go into the mill offices. In time, he would take his father's place. He meant to do it well and honestly. He had but to follow. Anthony had broken the trail, only by that time it was no longer a trail, but a broad and easy way.

Only once or twice did Anthony Cardew give voice to his dreams. Once he said: "I'll build a house out here some of these days. Good location. Growth of the city is bound to be in this direction."

What he did not say was that to be there, on that hill, overlooking his activities, his very own, the things he had builded with such labor, gave him a sense of power. "This below," he felt, with more of pride than arrogance, "this is mine. I have done it. I, Anthony Cardew."

He felt, looking down, the pride of an artist in his picture, of a sculptor who, secure from curious eyes, draws the sheet from the still moist clay of his modeling, and now from this angle, now from that, studies, criticizes, and exults.

But Anthony Cardew never built his house on the cliff. Time was to come when great houses stood there, like vast forts, overlooking, almost menacing, the valley beneath. For, until the nineties, although the city distended in all directions, huge, ugly, powerful, infinitely rich, and while in the direction of Anthony's farm the growth was real and rapid, it was the plain people who lined its rapidly extending avenues with their two-story brick houses; little homes of infinite tenderness and quiet, along tree-lined streets, where the children played on the cobble-stones, and at night the horse cars, and later the cable system, brought home tired clerks and storekeepers to small havens, already growing dingy from the smoke of the distant mills.

Anthony Cardew did not like the plain people. Yet in the end, it was the plain people, those who neither labored with their hands nor lived by the labor of others-it was the plain people who vanquished him. Vanquished him and tried to protect him. But could not. A smallish man, hard and wiry, he neither saved himself nor saved others. He had one fetish, power. And one pride, his line. The Cardews were iron masters. Howard would be an iron master, and Howard's son.

But Howard never had a son.

Chapter III

All through her teens Lily had wondered about the mystery concerning her Aunt Elinor. There was an oil portrait of her in the library, and one of the first things she had been taught was not to speak of it.

Now and then, at intervals of years, Aunt Elinor came back. Her mother and father would look worried, and Aunt Elinor herself would stay in her rooms, and seldom appeared at meals. Never at dinner. As a child Lily used to think she had two Aunt Elinors, one the young girl in the gilt frame, and the other the quiet, soft-voiced person who slipped around the upper corridors like a ghost.

But she was not to speak of either of them to her grandfather.

Lily was not born in the house on lower East Avenue.

In the late eighties Anthony built himself a home, not on the farm, but in a new residence portion of the city. The old common, grazing ground of family cows, dump and general eye-sore, had become a park by that time, still only a potentially beautiful thing, with the trees that were to be its later glory only thin young shoots, and on the streets that faced it the wealthy of the city built their homes, brick houses of square solidity, flush with brick pavements, which were carefully reddened on Saturday mornings. Beyond the pavements were cobble-stoned streets. Anthony Cardew was the first man in the city to have a rubber-tired carriage. The story of Anthony Cardew's new home is the story of Elinor's tragedy. Nor did it stop there. It carried on to the third generation, to Lily Cardew, and in the end it involved the city itself. Because of the ruin of one small home all homes were threatened. One small house, and one undying hatred.

Yet the matter was small in itself. An Irishman named Doyle owned the site Anthony coveted. After years of struggle his small grocery had begun to put him on his feet, and now the new development of the neighborhood added to his prosperity. He was a dried-up, sentimental little man, with two loves, his wife's memory and his wife's garden, which he still tended religiously between customers; and one ambition, his son. With the change from common to park, and the improvement in the neighborhood, he began to flourish, and he, too, like Anthony, dreamed a dream. He would make his son a gentleman, and he would get a shop assistant and a horse and wagon. Poverty was still his lot, but there were good times coming. He saved carefully, and sent Jim Doyle away to college.

He would not sell to Anthony. When he said he could not sell his wife's garden, Anthony's agents reported him either mad or deeply scheming. They kept after him, offering much more than the land was worth. Doyle began by being pugnacious, but in the end he took to brooding.

"He'll get me yet," he would mutter, standing among the white phlox of his little back garden. "He'll get me. He never quits."

Anthony Cardew waited a year. Then he had the frame building condemned as unsafe, and Doyle gave in. Anthony built his house. He put a brick stable where the garden had been, and the night watchman for the property complained that a little man, with wild eyes, often spent half the night standing across the street, quite still, staring over. If Anthony gave Doyle a thought, it was that progress and growth had their inevitable victims. But on the first night of Anthony's occupancy of his new house Doyle shot himself beside the stable, where a few stalks of white phlox had survived the building operations.

It never reached the newspapers, nor did a stable-boy's story of hearing the dying man curse Anthony and all his works. But nevertheless the story of the Doyle curse on Anthony Cardew spread. Anthony heard it, and forgot it. But two days later he was dragged from his carriage by young Jim Doyle, returned for the older Doyle's funeral, and beaten insensible with the stick of his own carriage whip.

Young Doyle did not run away. He stood by, a defiant figure full of hatred, watching Anthony on the cobbles, as though he wanted to see him revive and suffer.

"I didn't do it to revenge my father," he said at the trial. "He was nothing to me —I did it to show old Cardew that he couldn't get away with it. I'd do it again, too."

Any sentiment in his favor died at that, and he was given five years in the penitentiary. He was a demoralizing influence there, already a socialist with anarchical tendencies, and with the gift of influencing men. A fluent, sneering youth, who lashed the guards to fury with his unctuous, diabolical tongue.

The penitentiary had not been moved then. It stood in the park, a grim gray thing of stone. Elinor Cardew, a lonely girl always, used to stand in a window of the new house and watch the walls. Inside there were men who were shut away from all that greenery around them. Men who could look up at the sky, or down at the ground, but never out and across, as she could.

She was always hoping some of them would get away. She hated the sentries, rifle on shoulder, who walked their monotonous beats, back and forward, along the top of the wall.

Anthony's house was square and substantial, with high ceilings. It was paneled with walnut and furnished in walnut, in those days. Its tables and bureaus were of walnut, with cold white marble tops. And in the parlor was a square walnut piano, which Elinor hated because she had to sit there three hours each day, slipping on the top of the horsehair-covered stool, to practice. In cold weather her German governess sat in the frigid room, with a shawl and mittens, waiting until the onyx clock on the mantel-piece showed that the three hours were over.

Elinor had never heard the story of old Michael Doyle, or of his son Jim. But one night-she was seventeen then, and Jim Doyle had served three years of his sentence-sitting at dinner with her father, she said:

"Some convicts escaped from the penitentiary today, father."

"Don't believe it," said Anthony Cardew. "Nothing about it in the newspapers."

"Fraulein saw the hole."

Elinor had had an Alsatian governess. That was one reason why Elinor's niece had a French one.

"Hole? What do you mean by hole?"

Elinor shrank back a little. She had not minded dining with her father when Howard was at home, but Howard was at college. Howard had a way of good-naturedly ignoring his father's asperities, but Elinor was a suppressed, shy little thing, romantic, aloof, and filled with undesired affections. "She said a hole," she affirmed, diffidently. "She says they dug a tunnel and got out. Last night."

"Very probably," said Anthony Cardew. And he repeated, thoughtfully, "Very probably."

He did not hear Elinor when she quietly pushed back her chair and said "good-night." He was sitting at the table, tapping on the cloth with finger-tips that were slightly cold. That evening Anthony Cardew had a visit from the police, and considerable fiery talk took place in his library. As a result there was a shake-up in city politics, and a change in the penitentiary management, for Anthony Cardew had a heavy hand and a bitter memory. And a little cloud on his horizon grew and finally settled down over his life, turning it gray. Jim Doyle was among those who had escaped. For three months Anthony was followed wherever he went by detectives, and his house was watched at night. But he was a brave man, and the espionage grew hateful. Besides, each day added to his sense of security. There came a time when he impatiently dismissed the police, and took up life again as before.

Then one day he received a note, in a plain white envelope. It said: "There are worse things than death." And it was signed: "J. Doyle."

Doyle was not recaptured. Anthony had iron gratings put on the lower windows of his house after that, and he hired a special watchman. But nothing happened, and at last he began to forget. He was building the new furnaces up the river by that time. The era of structural steel for tall buildings was beginning, and he bought the rights of a process for making cement out of his furnace slag. He was achieving great wealth, although he did not change his scale of living.

Now and then Fraulein braved the terrors of the library, small neatly-written lists in her hands. Miss Elinor needed this or that. He would check up the lists, sign his name to them, and Elinor and Fraulein would have a shopping excursion. He never gave Elinor money.

On one of the lists one day he found the word, added in Elinor's hand: "Horse."

"Horse?" he said, scowling up at Fraulein. "There are six horses in the stable now."

"Miss Elinor thought —a riding horse —"

"Nonsense!" Then he thought a moment. There came back to him a picture of those English gentlewomen from among whom he had selected his wife, quiet-voiced, hard-riding, high-colored girls, who could hunt all day and dance all night. Elinor was a pale little thing. Besides, every gentlewoman should ride.

"She can't ride around here."

"Miss Elinor thought-there are bridle paths near the riding academy."

It was odd, but at that moment Anthony Cardew had an odd sort of vision. He saw the little grocer lying stark and huddled among the phlox by the stable, and the group of men that stooped over him.

"I'll think about it," was his answer.

But within a few days Elinor was the owner of a quiet mare, stabled at the academy, and was riding each day in the tan bark ring between its white-washed fences, while a mechanical piano gave an air of festivity to what was otherwise rather a solemn business.

Within a week of that time the riding academy had a new instructor, a tall, thin young man, looking older than he was, with heavy dark hair and a manner of repressed insolence. A man, the grooms said among themselves, of furious temper and cold eyes.

And in less than four months Elinor Cardew ran away from home and was married to Jim Doyle. Anthony received two letters from a distant city, a long, ecstatic but terrified one from his daughter, and one line on a slip of paper from her husband. The one line read: "I always pay my debts."

Anthony made a new will, leaving Howard everything, and had Elinor's rooms closed. Fraulein went away, weeping bitterly, and time went on. Now and then Anthony heard indirectly from Doyle. He taught in a boys' school for a time, and was dismissed for his radical views. He did brilliant editorial work on a Chicago newspaper, but now and then he intruded his slant-eyed personal views, and in the end he lost his position. Then he joined the Socialist party, and was making speeches containing radical statements that made the police of various cities watchful. But he managed to keep within the letter of the law.

Howard Cardew married when Elinor had been gone less than a year. Married the daughter of a small hotel-keeper in his college town, a pretty, soft-voiced girl, intelligent and gentle, and because Howard was all old Anthony had left, he took her into his home. But for many years he did not forgive her. He had one hope, that she would give Howard a son to carry on the line. Perhaps the happiest months of Grace Cardew's married life were those before Lily was born, when her delicate health was safeguarded in every way by her grim father-in-law. But Grace bore a girl child, and very nearly died in the bearing. Anthony Cardew would never have a grandson.

He was deeply resentful. The proud fabric of his own weaving would descend in the fullness of time to a woman. And Howard himself-old Anthony was pitilessly hard in his judgments-Howard was not a strong man. A good man. A good son, better than he deserved. But amiable, kindly, without force.

Once the cloud had lifted, and only once. Elinor had come home to have a child. She came at night, a shabby, worn young woman, with great eyes in a chalk-white face, and Grayson had not recognized her at first. He got her some port from the dining-room before he let her go into the library, and stood outside the door, his usually impassive face working, during the interview which followed. Probably that was Grayson's big hour, for if Anthony turned her out he intended to go in himself, and fight for the woman he had petted as a child.

But Anthony had not turned her out. He took one comprehensive glance at her thin face and distorted figure. Then he said:

"So this is the way you come back."

"He drove me out," she said dully. "He sent me here. He knew I had no place else to go. He knew you wouldn't want me. It's revenge, I suppose. I'm so tired, father."

Yes, it was revenge, surely. To send back to him this soiled and broken woman, bearing the mark he had put upon her-that was deviltry, thought out and shrewdly executed. During the next hour Anthony Cardew suffered, and made Elinor suffer, too. But at the end of that time he found himself confronting a curious situation. Elinor, ashamed, humbled, was not contrite. It began to dawn on Anthony that Jim Doyle's revenge was not finished. For-Elinor loved the man.

She both hated him and loved him. And that leering Irish devil knew it.

He sent for Grace, finally, and Elinor was established in the house. Grace and little Lily's governess had themselves bathed her and put her to bed, and Mademoiselle had smuggled out of the house the garments Elinor had worn into it. Grace had gone in the motor-one of the first in the city-and had sent back all sorts of lovely garments for Elinor to wear, and quantities of fine materials to be made into tiny garments. Grace was a practical woman, and she disliked the brooding look in Elinor's eyes.

"Do you know," she said to Howard that night, "I believe she is quite mad about him still."

"He ought to be drawn and quartered," said Howard, savagely.

Anthony Cardew gave Elinor sanctuary, but he refused to see her again. Except once.

"Then, if it is a boy, you want me to leave him with you?" she asked, bending over her sewing.

"Leave him with me! Do you mean that you intend to go back to that blackguard?"

"He is my husband. He isn't always cruel."

"Good God!" shouted Anthony. "How did I ever happen to have such a craven creature for a daughter?"

"Anyhow," said Elinor, "it will be his child, father."

"When he turned you out, like any drab of the streets!" bellowed old Anthony. "He never cared for you. He married you to revenge himself on me. He sent you back here for the same reason. He'll take your child, and break its spirit and ruin its body, for the same reason. The man's a maniac."

But again, as on the night she came, he found himself helpless against Elinor's quiet impassivity. He knew that, let Jim Doyle so much as raise a beckoning finger, and she would go to him. He did not realize that Elinor had inherited from her quiet mother the dog-like quality of love in spite of cruelty. To Howard he stormed. He considered Elinor's infatuation indecent. She was not a Cardew. The Cardew women had some pride. And Howard, his handsome figure draped negligently against the library mantel, would puzzle over it, too.

"I'm blessed if I understand it," he would say.

Elinor's child had been a boy, and old Anthony found some balm in Gilead. Jim Doyle had not raised a finger to beckon, and if he knew of his son, he made no sign. Anthony still ignored Elinor, but he saw in her child the third generation of Cardews. Lily he had never counted. He took steps to give the child the Cardew name, and the fact was announced in the newspapers. Then one day Elinor went out, and did not come back. It was something Anthony Cardew had not counted on, that a woman could love a man more than her child.

"I simply had to do it, father," she wrote. "You won't understand, of course. I love him, father. Terribly. And he loves me in his way, even when he is unfaithful to me. I know he has been that. Perhaps if you had wanted me at home it would have been different. But it kills me to leave the baby. The only reason I can bring myself to do it is that, the way things are, I cannot give him the things he ought to have. And Jim does not seem to want him. He has never seen him, for one thing. Besides—I am being honest—I don't think the atmosphere of the way we live would be good for a boy."

There was a letter to Grace, too, a wild hysterical document, filled with instructions for the baby's care. A wet nurse, for one thing. Grace read it with tears in her eyes, but Anthony saw in it only the ravings of a weak and unbalanced woman.

He never forgave Elinor, and once more the little grocer's curse thwarted his ambitions. For, deprived of its mother's milk, the baby died. Old Anthony sometimes wondered if that, too, had been calculated, a part of the Doyle revenge.

Chapter IV

While Grace rested that afternoon of Lily's return, Lily ranged over the house. In twenty odd years the neighborhood had changed, and only a handful of the old families remained. Many of the other large houses were prostituted to base uses. Dingy curtains hung at their windows, dingy because of the smoke from the great furnaces and railroads. The old Osgood residence, nearby, had been turned into apartments, with bottles of milk and paper bags on its fire-escapes, and a pharmacy on the street floor. The Methodist Church, following its congregation to the vicinity of old Anthony's farm, which was now cut up into city lots, had abandoned the building, and it had become a garage. The penitentiary had been moved outside the city limits, and near its old site was a small cement-lined lake, the cheerful rendezvous in summer of bathing children and thirsty dogs.

Lily was idle, for the first time in months. She wandered about, even penetrating to those upper rooms sacred to her grandfather, to which he had retired on Howard's marriage. How strangely commonplace they were now, in the full light of day, and yet, when he was in them, the doors closed and only Burton, his valet, in attendance, how mysterious they became!

Increasingly, in later years, Lily had felt and resented the domination of the old man. She resented her father's acquiescence in that domination, her mother's good-humored tolerance of it. She herself had accepted it, although unwillingly, but she knew, rather vaguely, that the Lily Cardew who had gone away to the camp and the Lily Cardew who stood that day before her grandfather's throne-like chair under its lamp, were two entirely different people.

She was uneasy rather than defiant. She meant to keep the peace. She had been brought up to the theory that no price was too great to pay for peace. But she wondered, as she stood there, if that were entirely true. She remembered something Willy Cameron had said about that very thing.

"What's wrong with your grandfather," he had said, truculently, and waving his pipe, "is that everybody gets down and lets him walk on them. If everybody lets a man use them as doormats, you can't blame him for wiping his feet on them. Tell him that sometime, and see what happens."

"Tell him yourself!" said Lily.

He had smiled cheerfully. He had an engaging sort of smile.

"Maybe I will," he said. "I am a rising young man, and my voice may some day be heard in the land. Sometimes I feel the elements of greatness in me, sweet child. You haven't happened to notice it yourself, have you?"

He had gazed at her with solemn anxiety through the smoke of his pipe, and had grinned when she remained silent.

Lily drew a long breath. All that delightful fooling was over; the hard work was over. The nights were gone when they would wander like children across the parade grounds, or past the bayonet school, with its rows of tripods upholding imitation enemies made of sacks stuffed with hay, and showing signs of mortal injury with their greasy entrails protruding. Gone, too, were the hours when Willy sank into the lowest abyss of depression over his failure to be a fighting man.

"But you are doing your best for your country," she would say.

"I'm not fighting for it, or getting smashed up for it. I don't want to be a hero, but I'd like to have had one good bang at them before I quit."

Once she had found him in the hut, with his head on a table. He said he had a toothache.

Well, that was all over. She was back in her grandfather's house, and —

"He'll get me too, probably," she reflected, as she went down the stairs, "just as he's got all the others."

Mademoiselle was in Lily's small sitting room, while Castle was unpacking under her supervision. The sight of her uniforms made Lily suddenly restless.

"How you could wear these things!" cried Mademoiselle. "You, who have always dressed like a princess!"

"I liked them," said Lily, briefly. "Mademoiselle, what am I going to do with myself, now?"

"Do?" Mademoiselle smiled. "Play, as you deserve, Cherie. Dance, and meet nice young men. You are to make your debut this fall. Then a very charming young man, and marriage."

"Oh!" said Lily, rather blankly. "I've got to come out, have I? I'd forgotten people did such things. Please run along and do something else, Castle. I'll unpack."

"That is very bad for discipline," Mademoiselle objected when the maid had gone. "And it is not necessary for Mr. Anthony Cardew's granddaughter."

"It's awfully necessary for her," Lily observed, cheerfully. "I've been buttoning my own shoes for some time, and I haven't developed a spinal curvature yet." She kissed Mademoiselle's perplexed face lightly. "Don't get to worrying about me," she added. "I'll shake down in time, and be just as useless as ever. But I wish you'd lend me your sewing basket."

"Why?" asked Mademoiselle, suspiciously.

"Because I am possessed with a mad desire to sew on some buttons."

A little later Lily looked up from her rather awkward but industrious labors with a needle, and fixed her keen young eyes on Mademoiselle.

"Is there any news about Aunt Elinor?" she asked.

"She is with him," said Mademoiselle, shortly. "They are here now, in the city. How he dared to come back!"

"Does mother see her?"

"No. Certainly not."

"Why 'certainly' not? He is Aunt Elinor's husband. She isn't doing anything wicked."

"A woman who would leave a home like this," said Mademoiselle, "and a distinguished family. Position. Wealth. For a brute who beats her. And desert her child also!"

"Does he really beat her? I don't quite believe that, Mademoiselle."

"It is not a subject for a young girl."

"Because really," Lily went on, "there is something awfully big about a woman who will stick to one man like that. I am quite sure I would bite a man who struck me, but-suppose I loved him terribly —" her voice trailed off. "You see, dear, I have seen a lot of brutality lately. An army camp isn't a Sunday school picnic. And I like strong men, even if they are brutal sometimes."

Mademoiselle carefully cut a thread.

"This-you were speaking to Ellen of a young man. Is he a —what you term brutal?"

Suddenly Lily laughed.

"You poor dear!" she said. "And mother, too, of course! You're afraid I'm in love with Willy Cameron. Don't you know that if I were, I'd probably never even mention his name?"

"But is he brutal?" persisted Mademoiselle.

"I'll tell you about him. He is a thin, blond young man, tall and a bit lame. He has curly hair, and he puts pomade on it to take the curl out. He is frightfully sensitive about not getting in the army, and he is perfectly sweet and kind, and as brutal as a June breeze. You'd better tell mother. And you can tell her he isn't in love with me, or I with him. You see, I represent what he would call the monied aristocracy of America, and he has the most fearful ideas about us."

"An anarchist, then?" asked. Mademoiselle, extremely comforted.

"Not at all. He says he belongs to the plain people. The people in between. He is rather oratorical about them. He calls them the backbone of the country."

Mademoiselle relaxed. She had been too long in old Anthony's house to consider very seriously the plain people. Her world, like Anthony Cardew's, consisted of the financial aristocracy, which invested money in industries and drew out rich returns, while providing employment for the many; and of the employees of the magnates, who had recently shown strong tendencies toward upsetting the peace of the land, and had given old Anthony one or two attacks of irritability when it was better to go up a rear staircase if he were coming down the main one.

"Wait a moment," said Lily, suddenly. "I have a picture of him somewhere."

She disappeared, and Mademoiselle heard her rummaging through the drawers of her dressing table. She came back with a small photograph in her hand.

It showed a young man, in a large apron over a Red Cross uniform, bending over a low field range with a long-handled fork in his hand.

"Frying doughnuts," Lily explained. "I was in this hut at first, and I mixed them and cut them, and he fried them. We made thousands of them. We used to talk about opening a shop somewhere, Cardew and Cameron. He said my name would be fine for business. He'd fry them in the window, and I'd sell them. And a coffee machine-coffee and doughnuts, you know."

"Not-seriously?"

At the expression on Mademoiselle's face Lily laughed joyously.

"Why not?" she demanded. "And you could be the cashier, like the ones in France, and sit behind a high desk and count money all day. I'd rather do that than come out," she added.

"You are going to be a good girl, Lily, aren't you?"

"If that means letting grandfather use me for a doormat, I don't know."

"Lily!"

"He's old, and I intend to be careful. But he doesn't own me, body and soul. And it may be hard to make him understand that."

Many times in the next few months Mademoiselle was to remember that conversation, and turn it over in her shrewd, troubled mind. Was there anything she could have done, outside of warning old Anthony himself? Suppose she had gone to Mr. Howard Cardew?

"And how," said Mademoiselle, trying to smile, "do you propose to assert this new independence of spirit?"

"I am going to see Aunt Elinor," observed Lily. "There, that's eleven buttons on, and I feel I've earned my dinner. And I'm going to ask Willy Cameron to come here to see me. To dinner. And as he is sure not to have any evening clothes, for one night in their lives the Cardew men are going to dine in mufti. Which is military, you dear old thing, for the everyday clothing that the plain people eat in, without apparent suffering!"

Mademoiselle got up. She felt that Grace should be warned at once. And there was a look in Lily's face when she mentioned this Cameron creature that made Mademoiselle nervous.

"I thought he lived in the country."

"Then prepare yourself for a blow," said Lily Cardew, cheerfully. "He is here in the city, earning twenty-five dollars a week in the Eagle Pharmacy, and serving the plain people perfectly preposterous patent potions-which is his own alliteration, and pretty good, I say."

Mademoiselle went out into the hall. Over the house, always silent, there had come a death-like hush. In the lower hall the footman was hanging up his master's hat and overcoat. Anthony Cardew had come home for dinner.

Chapter V

Mr. William Wallace Cameron, that evening of Lily's return, took a walk. From his boarding house near the Eagle Pharmacy to the Cardew residence was a half-hour's walk. There were a number of things he had meant to do that evening, with a view to improving his mind, but instead he took a walk. He had made up a schedule for those evenings when he was off duty, thinking it out very carefully on the train to the city. And the schedule ran something like this:

Monday: 8-11. Read History. Wednesday: 8-11. Read Politics and Economics. Friday: 8-9:30. Travel. 9:30-11. French. Sunday: Hear various prominent divines.

He had cut down on the travel rather severely, because travel was with him an indulgence rather than a study. The longest journey he had ever taken in his life was to Washington. That was early in the war, when it did not seem possible that his country would not use him, a boy who could tramp incredible miles in spite of his lameness and who could shoot a frightened rabbit at almost any distance, by allowing for a slight deflection to the right in the barrel of his old rifle.

But they had refused him.

"They won't use me, mother," he had said when he got home, home being a small neat house on a tidy street of a little country town. "I tried every branch, but the only training I've had-well, some smart kid said they weren't planning to serve soda water to the army. They didn't want cripples, you see."

"I wish you wouldn't, Willy."

He had been frightfully sorry then and had comforted her at some length, but the fact remained.

"And you the very best they've ever had for mixing prescriptions!" she had said at last. "And a graduate in chemistry!"

"Well," he said, "that's that, and we won't worry about it. There's more than one way of killing a cat."

"What do you mean, Willy? More than one way?"

There was no light of prophecy in William Wallace Cameron's gray eyes, however, when he replied: "More than one way of serving my country. Don't you worry. I'll find something."

So he had, and he had come out of his Red Cross work in the camp with one or two things in his heart that had not been there before. One was a knowledge of men. He could not have put into words what he felt about men. It was something about the fundamental simplicity of them, for one thing. You got pretty close to them at night sometimes, especially when the homesick ones had gone to bed, and the phonograph was playing in a corner of the long, dim room. There were some shame-faced tears hidden under army blankets those nights, and Willy Cameron did some blinking on his own account.

Then, under all the blasphemy, the talk about women, the surface sordidness of their daily lives and thoughts, there was one instinct common to all, one love, one hidden purity. And the keyword to those depths was "home."

"Home," he said one day to Lily Cardew. "Mostly it's the home they've left, and maybe they didn't think so much of it then. But they do now. And if it isn't that, it's the home they want to have some day." He looked at Lily. Sometimes she smiled at things he said, and if she had not been grave he would not have gone on. "You know," he continued, "there's mostly a girl some place. All this talk about the nation, now —" He settled himself on the edge of the pine table where old Anthony Cardew's granddaughter had been figuring up her week's accounts, and lighted his pipe, "the nation's too big for us to understand. But what is the nation, but a bunch of homes?"

"Willy dear," said Lily Cardew, "did you take any money out of the cigar box for anything this week?"

"Dollar sixty-five for lard," replied Willy dear. "As I was saying, we've got to think of this country in terms of homes. Not palaces like yours —"

"Good gracious!" said Lily, "I don't live in a palace. Get my pocket-book, will you? I'm out three dollars somehow, and I'd rather make it up myself than add these figures over again. Go on and talk, Willy. I love hearing you."

"Not palaces like yours," repeated Mr. Cameron, "and not hovels. But mostly self-respecting houses, the homes of the plain people. The middle class, Miss Cardew. My class. The people who never say anything, but are squeezed between capital, represented by your grandfather, with its parasites, represented by you, and —"

"You represent the people who never say anything," observed the slightly flushed parasite of capital, "about as adequately as I represent the idle rich."

Yet not even old Anthony could have resented the actual relationship between them. Lily Cardew, working alone in her hut among hundreds of men, was as without sex consciousness as a child. Even then her flaming interest was in the private soldiers. The officers were able to amuse themselves; they had money and opportunity. It was the doughboys she loved and mothered. For them she organized her little entertainments. For them she played and sang in the evenings, when the field range in the kitchen was cold, and her blistered fingers stumbled sometimes over the keys of the jingling camp piano.

Gradually, out of the chaos of her early impressions, she began to divide the men in the army into three parts. There were the American born; they took the war and their part in it as a job to be done, with as few words as possible. And there were the foreigners to whom America was a religion, a dream come true, whose flaming love for their new mother inspired them to stuttering eloquence and awkward gestures. And then there was a third division, small and mostly foreign born, but with a certain percentage of native malcontents, who hated the war and sneered among themselves at the other dupes who believed that it was a war for freedom. It was a capitalists' war. They considered the state as an instrument of oppression, as a bungling interference with liberty and labor; they felt that wealth inevitably brought depravity. They committed both open and overt acts against discipline, and found in their arrest and imprisonment renewed grievances, additional oppression, tyranny. And one day a handful of them, having learned Lily's identity, came into her hut and attempted to bait her.

"Gentlemen," said one of them, "we have here an example of one of the idle rich, sacrificing herself to make us happy. Now, boys, be happy. Are we all happy?" He surveyed the group. "Here, you," he addressed a sullen-eyed squat Hungarian. "Smile when I tell you. You're a slave in one of old Cardew's mills, aren't you? Well, aren't you grateful to him? Here he goes and sends his granddaughter —"

Willy Cameron had entered the room with a platter of doughnuts in his hand, and stood watching, his face going pale. Quite suddenly there was a crash, and the gang leader went down in a welter of porcelain and fried pastry. Willy Cameron was badly beaten up, in the end, and the beaters were court-martialed. But something of Lily's fine faith in humanity was gone.

"But," she said to him, visiting him one day in the base hospital, where he was still an aching, mass of bruises, "there must be something behind it. They didn't hate me. They only hated my-well, my family."

"My dear child," said Willy Cameron, feeling very old and experienced, and, it must be confessed, extremely happy, "of course there's something behind it. But the most that's behind it is a lot of fellows who want without working what the other fellow's worked to get."

It was about that time that Lily was exchanged into the town near the camp, and Willy Cameron suddenly found life a stale thing, and ashes in the mouth. He finally decided that he had not been such a hopeless fool as to fall in love with her, but that it would be as well not to see her too much.

"The thing to do," he reasoned to himself, "is, first of all, not to see her. Or only on Friday nights, because she likes the movies, and it would look queer to stop." Thus Willy Cameron speciously to himself, and deliberately ignoring the fact that some twenty-odd officers stood ready to seize those Friday nights. "And then to work hard, so I'll sleep better, and not lie awake making a fool of myself. And when I get a bit of idiocy in the daytime, I'd better just walk it off. Because I've got to live with myself a long time, probably, and I'm no love-sick Romeo."

Which excellent practical advice had cost him considerable shoe-leather at first. In a month or two, however, he considered himself quite cured, and pretended to himself that he was surprised to find it Friday again. But when, after retreat, the band marched back again to its quarters playing, for instance, "There's a Long, Long Trail," there was something inside him that insisted on seeing the years ahead as a long, long trail, and that the trail did not lead to the lands of his dreams.

He got to know that very well indeed during the winter that followed the armistice. Because there was work to do he stayed and finished up, as did Lily Cardew. But the hut was closed and she was working in the town, and although they kept up their Friday evenings, the old intimacy was gone. And one night she said:

"Isn't it amazing, when you are busy, how soon Friday night comes along?"

And on each day of the preceding week he had wakened and said to himself: "This is Monday —" —or whatever it might be —"and in four more days it will be Friday."

In February he was sent home. Lily stayed on until the end of March. He went back to his little village of plain people, and took up life again as best he could. But sometimes it seemed to him that from behind every fire-lit window in the evenings-he was still wearing out shoe-leather, particularly at nights-somebody with a mandolin was wailing about the long, long trail.

His mother watched him anxiously. He was thinner than ever, and oddly older, and there was a hollow look about his eyes that hurt her.

"Why don't you bring home a bottle of tonic from the store, Willy," she said, one evening when he had been feverishly running through the city newspaper. He put the paper aside hastily.

"Tonic!" he said. "Why, I'm all right, mother. Anyhow, I wouldn't take any of that stuff." He caught her eye and looked away. "It takes a little time to get settled again, that's all, mother."

"The Young People's Society is having an entertainment at the church to-night, Willy."

"Well, maybe I'll go," he agreed to her unspoken suggestion. "If you insist on making me a society man —"

But some time later he came downstairs with a book.

"Thought I'd rather read," he explained. "Got a book here on the history of steel. Talk about romances! Let me read some of it to you. You sit there and close your eyes and just listen to this: 'The first Cardew furnace was built in 1868. At that time —'"

Some time later he glanced up. His mother was quietly sleeping, her hands folded in her lap. He closed the book and sat there, fighting again his patient battle with himself. The book on his knee seemed to symbolize the gulf between Lily Cardew and himself. But the real gulf, the unbridgeable chasm, between Lily and himself, was neither social nor financial.

"As if that counted, in America," he reflected scornfully.

No. It was not that. The war had temporarily broken down the old social barriers. Some of them would never be erected again, although it was the tendency of civilization for men to divide themselves, rather than to be divided, into the high, the middle and the low. But in his generation young Cameron knew that there would be no uncrossable bridge between old Anthony's granddaughter and himself, were it not for one thing.

She did not love him. It hurt his pride to realize that she had never thought of him in any terms but that of a pleasant comradeship. Hardly even as a man. Men fought, in war time. They did not fry doughnuts and write letters home for the illiterate. Any one of those boys in the ranks was a better man than he was. All this talk about a man's soul being greater than his body, that was rot. A man was as good as the weakest part of him, and no more.

His sensitive face in the lamplight was etched with lines of tragedy. He put the book on the table, and suddenly flinging his arms across it, dropped his head on them. The slight movement wakened his mother.

"Why, Willy!" she said.

After a moment he looked up. "I was almost asleep," he explained, more to protect her than himself. "I —I wish that fool Nelson kid would break his mandolin-or his neck," he said irritably. He kissed her and went upstairs. From across the quiet street there came thin, plaintive, occasionally inaccurate, the strains of the long, long trail.

There was the blood of Covenanters in Willy Cameron's mother, a high courage of sacrifice, and an exceedingly shrewd brain. She lay awake that night, carefully planning, and when everything was arranged in orderly fashion in her mind, she lighted her lamp and carried it to the door of Willy's room. He lay diagonally across his golden-oak bed, for he was very long, and sleep had rubbed away the tragic lines about his mouth. She closed his door and went back to her bed.

"I've seen too much of it," she reflected, without bitterness. She stared around the room. "Too much of it," she repeated. And crawled heavily back into bed, a determined little figure, rather chilled.

The next morning she expressed a desire to spend a few months with her brother in California.

"I coughed all last winter, after I had the flu," she explained, "and James has been wanting me this long time. I don't want to leave you, that's all, Willy. If you were in the city it would be different."

He was frankly bewildered and a little hurt, to tell the truth. He no more suspected her of design than of crime.

"Of course you are going," he said, heartily. "It's the very thing. But I like the way you desert your little son!"

"I've been thinking about that, too," she said, pouring his coffee. "I —if you were in the city, now, there would always be something to do."

He shot her a suspicious glance, but her face was without evidence of guile.

"What would I do in the city?"

"They use chemists in the mills, don't they?"

"A fat chance I'd have for that sort of job," he scoffed. "No city for me, mother."

But she knew. She read his hesitation accurately, the incredulous pause of the bird whose cage door is suddenly opened. He would go.

"I'd think about it, anyhow, Willy."

But for a long time after he had gone she sat quietly rocking in her rocking chair in the bay window of the sitting room. It was a familiar attitude of hers, homely, middle-class, and in a way symbolic. Had old Anthony Cardew ever visualized so imaginative a thing as a Nemesis, he would probably have summoned a vision of a huddled figure in his stable-yard, dying, and cursing him as he died. Had Jim Doyle, cunningly plotting the overthrow of law and order, been able in his arrogance to conceive of such a thing, it might have been Anthony Cardew he saw. Neither of them, for a moment, dreamed of it as an elderly Scotch Covenanter, a plain little womanly figure, rocking in a cane-seated rocking chair, and making the great sacrifice of her life.

All of which simply explains how, on a March Wednesday evening of the great year of peace after much tribulation, Mr. William Wallace Cameron, now a clerk at the Eagle Pharmacy, after an hour of Politics, and no Economics at all, happened to be taking a walk toward the Cardew house. Such pilgrimages has love taken for many years, small uncertain ramblings where the fancy leads the feet and far outstrips them, and where heart-hunger hides under various flimsy pretexts; a fine night, a paper to be bought, a dog to be exercised.

Not that Willy Cameron made any excuses to himself. He had a sort of idea that if he saw the magnificence that housed her, it would through her sheer remoteness kill the misery in him. But he regarded himself with a sort of humorous pity, and having picked up a stray dog, he addressed it now and then.

"Even a cat can look at a king," he said once. And again, following some vague train of thought, on a crowded street: "The People's voice is a queer thing. 'It is, and it is not, the voice of God.' The people's voice, old man. Only the ones that count haven't got a voice."

There were, he felt, two Lily Cardews. One lived in an army camp, and wore plain clothes, and got a bath by means of calculation and persistency, and went to the movies on Friday nights, and was quite apt to eat peanuts at those times, carefully putting the shells in her pocket.

And another one lived inside this great pile of brick, —he was standing across from it, by the park railing, by that time-where motor cars drew up, and a footman with an umbrella against a light rain ushered to their limousines draped women and men in evening clothes, their strong blacks and whites revealed in the light of the street door. And this Lily Cardew lived in state, bowed to by flunkeys in livery, dressed and undressed-his Scotch sense of decorum resented this-by serving women. This Lily Cardew would wear frivolous ball-gowns, such things as he saw in the shop windows, considered money only as a thing of exchange, and had traveled all over Europe a number of times.

He took his station against the park railings and reflected that it was a good thing he had come, after all. Because it was the first Lily whom he loved, and she was gone, with the camp and the rest, including war. What had he in common with those lighted windows, with their heavy laces and draperies?

"Nothing at all, old man," he said cheerfully to the dog, "nothing at all."

But although the ache was gone when he turned homeward, the dog still at his heels, he felt strangely lonely without it. He considered that very definitely he had put love out of his life. Hereafter he would travel the trail alone. Or accompanied only by History, Politics, Economics, and various divines on Sunday evenings.

Chapter VI

"Well, grandfather," said Lily Cardew, "the last of the Cardews is home from the wars."

"So I presume," observed old Anthony. "Owing, however, to your mother's determination to shroud this room in impenetrable gloom, I can only presume. I cannot see you."

His tone was less unpleasant than his words, however. He was in one of the rare moods of what passed with him for geniality. For one thing, he had won at the club that afternoon, where every day from four to six he played bridge with his own little group, reactionaries like himself, men who viewed the difficulties of the younger employers of labor with amused contempt. For another, he and Howard had had a difference of opinion, and he had, for a wonder, made Howard angry.

"Well, Lily," he inquired, "how does it seem to be at home?"

Lily eyed him almost warily. He was sometimes most dangerous in these moods.

"I'm not sure, grandfather."

"Not sure about what?"

"Well, I am glad to see everybody, of course. But what am I to do with myself?"

"Tut." He had an air of benignantly forgiving her. "You'll find plenty. What did you do before you went away?"

"That was different, grandfather."

"I'm blessed," said old Anthony, truculently, "if I understand what has come over this country, anyhow. What is different? We've had a war. We've had other wars, and we didn't think it necessary to change the Constitution after them. But everything that was right before this war is wrong after it. Lot of young idiots coming back and refusing to settle down. Set of young Bolshevists!"

He had always managed to arouse a controversial spirit in the girl.

"Maybe, if it isn't right now, it wasn't right before." Having said it, Lily immediately believed it. She felt suddenly fired with an intense dislike of anything that her grandfather advocated.

"Meaning what?" He fixed her with cold but attentive eyes.

"Oh-conditions," she said vaguely. She was not at all sure what she meant. And old Anthony realized it, and gave a sardonic chuckle.

"I advise you to get a few arguments from your father, Lily. He is full of them. If he had his way I'd have a board of my workmen running my mills, while I played golf in Florida."

Dinner was a relatively pleasant meal. In her gradual rehabilitation of the house Grace had finally succeeded in doing over the dining room. Over the old walnut paneling she had hung loose folds of faded blue Italian velvet, with old silver candle sconces at irregular intervals along the walls. The great table and high-backed chairs were likewise Italian, and the old-fashioned white marble fireplace had been given an over-mantel, also white, enclosing an old tapestry. For warmth of color there were always flowers, and that night there were red roses.

Lily liked the luxury of it. She liked the immaculate dinner dress of the two men; she liked her mother's beautiful neck and arms; she liked the quiet service once more; she even liked herself, moderately, in a light frock and slippers. But she watched it all with a new interest and a certain detachment. She felt strange and aloof, not entirely one of them. She felt very keenly that no one of them was vitally interested in this wonder-year of hers. They asked her perfunctory questions, but Grace's watchful eyes were on the service, Anthony was engrossed with his food, and her father —

Her father was changed. He looked older and care-worn. For the first time she began to wonder about her father. What was he, really, under that calm, fastidiously dressed, handsome exterior? Did he mind the little man with the sardonic smile and the swift unpleasant humor, whose glance reduced the men who served into terrified menials? Her big, blond father, with his rather slow speech, his honest eyes, his slight hesitation before he grasped some of the finer nuances of his father's wit. No, he was not brilliant, but he was real, real and kindly. Perhaps he was strong, too. He looked strong.

With the same pitiless judgment she watched her mother. Either Grace was very big, or very indifferent to the sting of old Anthony's tongue. Sometimes women suffered much in silence, because they loved greatly. Like Aunt Elinor. Aunt Elinor had loved her husband more than she had loved her child. Quite calmly Lily decided that, as between her husband and herself, her mother loved her husband. Perhaps that was as it should be, but it added to her sense of aloofness. And she wondered, too, about these great loves that seemed to feed on sacrifice.

Anthony, who had a most unpleasant faculty of remembering things, suddenly bent forward and observed to her, across the table:

"I should be interested to know, since you regard present conditions as wrong, and, I inferred, wrong because of my mishandling of them, just what you would propose to do to right them."

"But I didn't say they were wrong, did I?"

"Don't answer a question with a question. It's a feminine form of evasion, because you have no answer and no remedy. Yet, heaven save the country, women are going to vote!" He pushed his plate away and glanced at Grace. "Is that the new chef's work?"

"Yes. Isn't it right?"

"Right? The food is impossible."

"He came from the club."

"Send him back," ordered Anthony. And when Grace observed that it was difficult to get servants, he broke into a cold fury. What had come over the world, anyhow? Time was when a gentleman's servants stayed with the family until they became pensioners, and their children took their places. Now —!

Grace said nothing. Her eyes sought Howard's, and seemed to find some comfort there. And Lily, sorry for her mother, said the first thing that came into her head.

"The old days of caste are gone, grandfather. And service, in your sense of the word, went with them."

"Really?" he eyed her. "Who said that? Because I daresay it is not original."

"A man I knew at camp."

"What man?"

"His name was Willy Cameron."

"Willy Cameron! Was this-er-person qualified to speak? Does he know anything about what he chooses to call caste?"

"He thinks a lot about things."

"A little less thinking and more working wouldn't hurt the country any," observed old Anthony. He bent forward. "As my granddaughter, and the last of the Cardews," he said, "I have a certain interest in the sources of your political opinions. They will probably, like your father's, differ from mine. You may not know that your father has not only opinions, but ambitions." She saw Grace stiffen, and Howard's warning glance at her. But she saw, too, the look in her mother's eyes, infinitely loving and compassionate. "Dear little mother," she thought, "he is her baby, really. Not I."

She felt a vague stirring of what married love at its best must be for a woman, its strange complex of passion and maternity. She wondered if it would ever come to her. She rather thought not. But she was also conscious of a new attitude among the three at the table, her mother's tense watchfulness, her father's slightly squared shoulders, and across from her her grandfather, fingering the stem of his wineglass and faintly smiling.

"It's time somebody went into city politics for some purpose other than graft," said Howard. "I am going to run for mayor, Lily. I probably won't get it."

"You can see," said old Anthony, "why I am interested in your views, or perhaps I should say, in Willy Cameron's. Does your father's passion for uplift, for instance, extend to you?"

"Why won't you be elected, father?"

"Partly because my name is Cardew."

Old Anthony chuckled.

"What!" he exclaimed, "after the bath-house and gymnasium you have built at the mill? And the laundries for the women-which I believe they do not use. Surely, Howard, you would not accuse the dear people of ingratitude?"

"They are beginning to use them, sir." Howard, in his forties, still addressed his father as "Sir!"

"Then you admit your defeat beforehand."

"You are rather a formidable antagonist."

"Antagonist!" Anthony repeated in mock protest. "I am a quiet onlooker at the game. I am amused, naturally. You must understand," he said to Lily, "that this is a matter of a principle with your father. He believes that he should serve. My whole contention is that the people don't want to be served. They want to be bossed. They like it; it's all they know. And they're suspicious of a man who puts his hand into his own pocket instead of into theirs."

He smiled and sipped his wine.

"Good wine, this," he observed. "I'm buying all I can lay my hands on, against the approaching drought."

Lily's old distrust of her grandfather revived. Why did people sharpen like that with age? Age should be mellow, like old wine. And-what was she going to do with herself? Already the atmosphere of the house began to depress and worry her; she felt a new, almost violent impatience with it. It was so unnecessary.

She went to the pipe organ which filled the space behind the staircase, and played a little, but she had never been very proficient, and her own awkwardness annoyed her. In the dining room she could hear the men talking, Howard quietly, his father in short staccato barks. She left the organ and wandered into her mother's morning room, behind the drawing room, where Grace sat with the coffee tray before her.

"I'm afraid I'm going to be terribly on your hands, mother," she said, "I don't know what to do with myself, so how can you know what to do with me?"

"It is going to be rather stupid for you at first, of course," Grace said. "Lent, and then so many of the men are not at home. Would you like to go South?"

"Why, I've just come home!"

"We can have some luncheons, of course. Just informal ones. And there will be small dinners. You'll have to get some clothes. I saw Suzette yesterday. She has some adorable things."

"I'd love them. Mother, why doesn't he want father to go into politics?"

Grace hesitated.

"He doesn't like change, for one thing. But I don't know anything about politics. Suzette says —"

"Will he try to keep him from being elected?"

"He won't support him. Of course I hardly think he would oppose him. I really don't understand about those things."

"You mean you don't understand him. Well, I do, mother. He has run everything, including father, for so long —"

"Lily!"

"I must, mother. Why, out at the camp —" She checked herself. "All the papers say the city is badly governed, and that he is responsible. And now he is going to fight his own son! The more I think about it, the more I understand about Aunt Elinor. Mother, where do they live?"

Grace looked apprehensively toward the door. "You are not allowed to visit her."

"You do."

"That's different. And I only go once or twice a year."

"Just because she married a poor man, a man whose father —"

"Not at all. That is all dead and buried. He is a very dangerous man. He is running a Socialist newspaper, and now he is inciting the mill men to strike. He is preaching terrible things. I haven't been there for months."

"What do you mean by terrible things, mother?"

"Your father says it amounts to a revolution. I believe he calls it a general strike. I don't really know much about it."

Lily pondered that.

"Socialism isn't revolution, mother, is it? But even then-is all this because grandfather drove his father to —"

"I wish you wouldn't, Lily. Of course it is not that. I daresay he believes what he preaches. He ought to be put into jail. Why the country lets such men go around, preaching sedition, I don't understand."

Lily remembered something else Willy Cameron had said, and promptly repeated it.

"We had a muzzled press during the war," she said, "and now we've got free speech. And one's as bad as the other. She must love him terribly, mother," she added.

But Grace harked back to Suzette, and the last of the Cardews harked with her. Later on people dropped in, and Lily made a real attempt to get back into her old groove, but that night, when she went upstairs to her bedroom, with its bright fire, its bed neatly turned down, her dressing gown and slippers laid out, the shaded lamps shining on the gold and ivory of her dressing table, she was conscious of a sudden homesickness. Homesickness for her bare little room in the camp barracks, for other young lives, noisy, chattering, often rather silly, occasionally unpleasant, but young. Radiantly, vitally young. The great house, with its stillness and decorum, oppressed her. There was no youth in it, save hers.

She went to her window and looked out. Years ago, like Elinor, she had watched the penitentiary walls from that window, with their endlessly pacing sentries, and had grieved for those men who might look up at the sky, or down at the earth, but never out and across, to see the spring trees, for instance, or the children playing on the grass. She remembered the story about Jim Doyle's escape, too. He had dug a perilous way to freedom. Vaguely she wondered if he were not again digging a perilous way to freedom.

Men seemed always to be wanting freedom, only they had so many different ideas of what freedom was. At the camp it had meant breaking bounds, balking the Military Police, doing forbidden things generally. Was that, after all, what freedom meant, to do the forbidden thing? Those people in Russia, for instance, who stole and burned and appropriated women, in the name of freedom. Were law and order, then, irreconcilable with freedom?

After she had undressed she rang her bell, and Castle answered it.

"Please find out if Ellen has gone to bed," she said. "If she has not, I would like to talk to her."

The maid looked slightly surprised.

"If it's your hair, Miss Lily, Mrs. Cardew has asked me to look after you until she has engaged a maid for you."

"Not my hair," said Lily, cheerfully. "I rather like doing it myself. I just want to talk to Ellen."

It was a bewildered and rather scandalized Castle who conveyed the message to Ellen.

Chapter VII

"I wish you'd stop whistling that thing," said Miss Boyd, irritably. "It makes me low in my mind."

"Sorry," said Willy Cameron. "I do it because I'm low in my mind."

"What are you low about?" Miss Boyd had turned toward the rear of the counter, where a mirror was pasted to a card above a box of chewing gum, and was carefully adjusting her hair net. "Lady friend turned you down?"

Willy Cameron glanced at her.

"I'm low because I haven't got a lady friend, Miss Boyd." He held up a sheet of prescription paper and squinted at it. "Also because the medical profession writes with its feet, apparently. I've done everything to this but dip it in acid. I've had it pinned to the wall, and tried glancing at it as I went past. Sometimes you can surprise them that way. But it does no good. I'm going to take it home and dream on it, like bride's cake."

"They're awful, aren't they?"

"When I get into the Legislature," said Willy Cameron, "I'm going to have a bill passed compelling doctors to use typewriters. Take this now. Read upside down, its horse liniment. Read right side up, it's poison. And it's for internal use."

"What d'you mean you haven't got a lady friend?"

"The exact and cruel truth." He smiled at her, and had Miss Boyd been more discerning she might have seen that the smile was slightly forced. Also that his eyes were somewhat sunken in his head. Which might, of course, have been due to too much political economy and history, and the eminent divines on Sunday evenings. Miss Boyd, however, was not discerning, and moreover, she was summoning her courage to a certain point.

"Why don't you ask me to go to the movies some night?" she said. "I like the movies, and I get sick of going alone."

"My dear child," observed Willy Cameron, "if that young man in the sack suit who comes in to see you every day were three inches shorter and twenty pounds lighter, I'd ask you this minute."

"Oh, him!" said Miss Boyd, with a self-conscious smile. "I'm through with him. He's a Bolshevik!"

"He has the Bolshevist possessive eye," agreed Willy Cameron, readily. "Does he know you are through with him? Because that's important, too. You may know it, and I may know it, but if he doesn't know it —"

"Why don't you say right out you don't want to take me?" Willy Cameron's chivalrous soul was suddenly shocked. To his horror he saw tears in Miss Boyd's eyes.

"I'm just a plain idiot, Miss Edith," he said. "I was only fooling. It will mean a lot to me to have a nice girl go with me to the movies, or anywhere else. We'll make it to-night, if that suits you, and I'll take a look through the neighborhood at noon and see what's worth while."

The Eagle Pharmacy was a small one in a quiet neighborhood. During the entire day, and for three evenings a week, Mr. William Wallace Cameron ran it almost single-handed, having only the preoccupied assistance of Miss Boyd in the candy and fancy goods. At the noon and dinner hours, and four evenings a week, he was relieved by the owner, Mr. Davis, a tired little man with large projecting ears and worried, child-like eyes, who was nursing an invalid wife at home. A pathetic little man, carrying home with unbounded faith day after day bottles of liquid foods and beef capsules, and making wistful comments on them when he returned.

"She couldn't seem to keep that last stuff down, Mr. Cameron," he would say. "I'll try something else."

And he would stand before his shelves, eyes upturned, searching, eliminating, choosing.

Miss Boyd attended to the general merchandise, sold stationery and perfumes, candy and fancy soaps, and in the intervals surveyed the world that lay beyond the plate glass windows with shrewd, sophisticated young eyes.

"That new doctor across the street is getting busier," she would say. Or, "The people in 42 have got a Ford. They haven't got room for a garage, either. Probably have to leave it out at nights."

Her sophistication was kindly in the main. She combined it with an easy tolerance of weakness, and an invincible and cheery romanticism, as Willy Cameron discovered the night they first went to a moving picture theater together. She frankly wept and joyously laughed, and now and then, delighted at catching some film subtlety and fearful that he would miss it, she would nudge him with her elbow.

"What d'you think of that?" she would say. "D'you get it? He thinks he's getting her-Alice Joyce, you know-on the telephone, and it's a private wire to the gang." She was rather quiet after that particular speech. Then she added: "I know a place that's got a secret telephone." But he was absorbed in the picture, and made no comment on that. She seemed rather relieved.

Once or twice she placed an excited hand on his knee. He was very uncomfortable until she removed it, because he had a helpless sort of impression that she was not quite so unconscious of it as she appeared. Time had been, and not so long ago, when he might have reciprocated her little advance in the spirit in which it was offered, might have taken the hand and held it, out of the sheer joy of youth and proximity. But there was nothing of the philanderer in the Willy Cameron who sat beside Edith Boyd that night in body, while in spirit he was in another state, walking with his slight limp over crisp snow and sodden mud, but through magic lands, to the little moving picture theater at the camp.

Would he ever see her again? Ever again? And if he did, what good would it be? He roused himself when they started toward her home. The girl was chattering happily. She adored Douglas Fairbanks. She knew a girl who had written for his picture but who didn't get one. She wouldn't do a thing like that. "Did they really say things when they moved their lips?"

"I think they do," said Willy Cameron. "When that chap was talking over the telephone I could tell what he was saying by-Look here, what did you mean when you said you knew of a place that has a secret telephone?"

"I was only talking."

"No house has any business with a secret telephone," he said virtuously.

"Oh, forget it. I say a lot of things I don't mean." He was a little puzzled and rather curious, but not at all disturbed.

"Well, how did you get to know about it?"

"I tell you I was only talking."

He let it drop at that. The street crowds held and interested him. He liked to speculate about them; what life meant to them, in work and love and play; to what they were going on such hurrying feet. A country boy, the haste of the city impressed him.

"Why do they hurry so?" he demanded, almost irritably.

"Hurrying home, most of them, because they've got to get up in the morning and go to work."

"Do you ever wonder about the homes they are hurrying to?"

"Me? I don't wonder. I know. Most of them have to move fast to keep up with the rent."

"I don't mean houses," he explained, patiently. "I mean —A house isn't a home."

"You bet it isn't."

"It's the families I'm talking about. In a small town you know all about people, who they live with, and all that." He was laboriously talking down to her. "But here —"

He saw that she was not interested. Something he had said started an unpleasant train of thought in her mind. She was walking faster, and frowning slightly. To cheer her he said:

"I am keeping an eye out for the large young man in the sack suit, you know. If he jumps me, just yell for the police, will you? Because I'll probably not be able to."

"I wish you'd let me forget him."

"I will. The question is, will he?" But he saw that the subject was unpleasant.

"We'll have to do this again. It's been mighty nice of you to come."

"You'll have to ask me, the next time."

"I certainly will. But I think I'd better let your family look me over first, just so they'll know that I don't customarily steal the silver spoons when I'm asked out to dinner. Or anything like that."

"We're just-folks."

"So am I, awfully-folks! And pretty lonely folks at that. Something like that pup that has adopted me, only worse. He's got me, but I haven't anybody."

"You'll not be lonely long." She glanced up at him.

"That's cheering. Why?"

"Well, you are the sort that makes friends," she said, rather vaguely. "That crowd that drops into the shop on the evenings you're there-they're crazy about you. They like to hear you talk."

"Great Scott! I suppose I've been orating all over the place!"

"No, but you've got ideas. You give them something to think about when they go home. I wish I had a mind like yours."

He was so astonished that he stopped dead on the pavement. "My Scottish blood," he said despondently. "A Scot is always a reformer and a preacher, in his heart. I used to orate to my mother, but she liked it. She is a Scot, too. Besides, it put her to sleep. But I thought I'd outgrown it."

"You don't make speeches. I didn't mean that."

But he was very crestfallen during the remainder of the way, and rather silent. He wondered, that night before he went to bed, if he had been didactic to Lily Cardew. He had aired his opinions to her at length, he knew. He groaned as he took off his coat in his cold little room at the boarding house which lodged and fed him, both indifferently, for the sum of twelve dollars per week.

Jinx, the little hybrid dog, occupied the seat of his one comfortable chair. He eyed the animal somberly.

"Hereafter, old man," he said, "when I feel a spell of oratory coming on, you will have to be the audience." He took his dressing gown from a nail behind the door, and commenced to put it on. Then he took it off again and wrapped the dog in it.

"I can read in bed, which you can't," he observed. "Only, I can't help thinking, with all this town to pick from, you might have chosen a fellow with two dressing gowns and two chairs."

He was extremely quiet all the next day. Miss Boyd could hear him, behind the partition with its "Please Keep Out" sign, fussing with bottles and occasionally whistling to himself. Once it was the "Long, Long Trail," and a moment later he appeared in his doorway, grinning.

"Sorry," he said. "I've got in the habit of thinking to the fool thing. Won't do it again."

"You must be thinking hard."

"I am," he replied, grimly, and disappeared. She could hear the slight unevenness of his steps as he moved about, but there was no more whistling. Edith Boyd leaned both elbows on the top of a showcase and fell into a profound and troubled thought. Mostly her thoughts were of Willy Cameron, but some of them were for herself. Up dreary and sordid by-paths her mind wandered; she was facing ugly facts for the first time, and a little shudder of disgust shook her. He wanted to meet her family. He was a gentleman and he wanted to meet her family. Well, he could meet them all right, and maybe he would understand then that she had never had a chance. In all her young life no man had ever proposed letting her family look him over. Hardly ever had they visited her at home, and when they did they seemed always glad to get away. She had met them on street corners, and slipped back alone, fearful of every creak of the old staircase, and her mother's querulous voice calling to her:

"Edie, where've you been all this time?" And she had lied. How she had lied!

"I'm through with all that," she resolved. "It wasn't any fun anyhow. I'm sick of hating myself."

Some time later Willy Cameron heard the telephone ring, and taking pad and pencil started forward. But Miss Boyd was at the telephone, conducting a personal conversation.

"No....No, I think not....Look here, Lou, I've said no twice."

There was a rather lengthy silence while she listened. Then: "You might as well have it straight, Lou. I'm through....No, I'm not sick. I'm just through....I wouldn't....What's the use?"

Willy Cameron, retreating into his lair, was unhappily conscious that the girl was on the verge of tears. He puzzled over the situation for some time. His immediate instinct was to help any troubled creature, and it had dawned on him that this composed young lady who manicured her nails out of a pasteboard box during the slack portion of every day was troubled. In his abstraction he commenced again his melancholy refrain, and a moment later she appeared in the doorway:

"Oh, for mercy's sake, stop," she said. She was very pale.

"Look here, Miss Edith, you come in here and tell me what's wrong. Here's a chair. Now sit down and talk it out. It helps a lot to get things off your chest."

"There's nothing the matter with me. And if the boss comes in here and finds me —"

Quite suddenly she put her head down on the back of the chair and began to cry. He was frightfully distressed. He poured some aromatic ammonia into a medicine glass and picking up her limp hand, closed her fingers around it.

"Drink that," he ordered.

She shook her head.

"I'm not sick," she said. "I'm only a fool."

"If that fellow said anything over the telephone —!"

She looked up drearily.

"It wasn't him. He doesn't matter. It's just — I got to hating myself." She stood up and carefully dabbed her eyes. "Heavens, I must be a sight. Now don't you get to thinking things, Mr. Cameron. Girls can't go out and fight off a temper, or get full and sleep it off. So they cry."

Some time later he glanced out at her. She was standing before the little mirror above the chewing gum, carefully rubbing her cheeks with a small red pad. After that she reached into the show case, got out a lip pencil and touched her lips.

"You're pretty enough without all that, Miss Edith."

"You mind your own business," she retorted acidly.

Chapter VIII

Lily had known Alston Denslow most of her life. The children of that group of families which formed the monied aristocracy of the city knew only their own small circle. They met at dancing classes, where governesses and occasionally mothers sat around the walls, while the little girls, in handmade white frocks of exquisite simplicity, their shining hair drawn back and held by ribbon bows, made their prim little dip at the door before entering, and the boys, in white Eton collars and gleaming pumps, bowed from the waist and then dived for the masculine corner of the long room.

No little girl ever intruded on that corner, although now and then a brave spirit among the boys would wander, with assumed unconsciousness but ears rather pink, to the opposite corner where the little girls were grouped like white butterflies milling in the sun.

The pianist struck a chord, and the children lined up, the girls on one side, the boys on the other, a long line, with Mrs. Van Buren in the center. Another chord, rather a long one. Mrs. Van Buren curtsied to the girls. The line dipped, wavered, recovered itself. Mrs. Van Buren turned. Another chord. The boys bent, rather too much, from the waist, while Mrs. Van Buren swept another deep curtsey. The music now, very definite as to time. Glide and short step to the right. Glide and short step to the left. Dancing school had commenced. Outside were long lines of motors waiting. The governesses chatted, and sometimes embroidered. Mademoiselle tatted.

Alton Denslow was generally known as Pink, but the origin of the name was shrouded in mystery. As "Pink" he had learned to waltz at the dancing class, at a time when he was more attentive to the step than to the music that accompanied it. As Pink Denslow he had played on a scrub team at Harvard, and got two broken ribs for his trouble, and as Pink he now paid intermittent visits to the Denslow Bank, between the hunting season in October and polo at eastern fields and in California. At twenty-three he was still the boy of the dancing class, very careful at parties to ask his hostess to dance, and not noticeably upset when she did, having arranged to be cut in on at the end of the second round.

Pink could not remember when he had not been in love with Lily Cardew. There had been other girls, of course, times when Lily seemed far away from Cambridge, and some other fair charmer was near. But he had always known there was only Lily. Once or twice he would have become engaged, had it not been for that. He was a blond boy, squarely built, good-looking without being handsome, and on rainy Sundays when there was no golf he went quite cheerfully to St. Peter's with his mother, and watched a pretty girl in the choir.

He wished at those times that he could sing.

A pleasant cumberer of the earth, he had wrapped his talents in a napkin and buried them by the wayside, and promptly forgotten where they were. He was to find them later on, however, not particularly rusty, and he increased them rather considerably before he got through.

It was this pleasant cumberer of the earth, then, who on the morning after Lily's return, stopped his car before the Cardew house and got out. Immediately following his descent he turned, took a square white box from the car, ascended the steps, settled his neck in his collar and his tie around it, and rang the bell.

The second man, hastily buttoned into his coat and with a faint odor of silver polish about him, opened the door. Pink gave him his hat, but retained the box firmly.

"Mrs. Cardew and Miss Cardew at home?" he asked. "Yes? Then you might tell Grayson I'm here to luncheon-unless the family is lunching out."

"Yes, sir," said the footman. "No, sir, they are lunching at home."

Pink sauntered into the library. He was not so easy as his manner indicated. One never knew about Lily. Sometimes she was in a mood when she seemed to think a man funny, and not to be taken seriously. And when she was serious, which was the way he liked her-he rather lacked humor-she was never serious about him or herself. It had been religion once, he remembered. She had wanted to know if he believed in the thirty-nine articles, and because he had seen them in the back of the prayer-book, where they certainly would not be if there was not authority for them, he had said he did.

"Well, I don't," said Lily. And there had been rather a bad half-hour, because he had felt that he had to stick to his thirty-nine guns, whatever they were. He had finished on a rather desperate note of appeal.

"See here, Lily," he had said. "Why do you bother your head about such things, anyhow?"

"Because I've got a head, and I want to use it."

"Life's too short."

"Eternity's pretty long. Do you believe in eternity?" And there they were, off again, and of course old Anthony had come in after that, and had wanted to know about his Aunt Marcia, and otherwise had shown every indication of taking root on the hearth rug.

Pink was afraid of Anthony. He felt like a stammering fool when Anthony was around. That was why he had invited himself to luncheon. Old Anthony lunched at his club.

When he heard Lily coming down the stairs, Pink's honest heart beat somewhat faster. A good many times in France, but particularly on the ship coming back, he had thought about this meeting. In France a fellow had a lot of distractions, and Lily had seemed as dear as ever, but extremely remote. But once turned toward home, and she had filled the entire western horizon. The other men had seen sunsets there, and sometimes a ship, or a school of porpoises. But Pink had seen only Lily.

She came in. The dear old girl! The beautiful, wonderful, dear old girl! The —

"Pink!"

"H —hello, Lily."

"Why, Pink-you're a man!"

"What'd you think I'd be? A girl?"

"You've grown."

"Oh, now see here, Lily. I quit growing years ago."

"And to think you are back all right. I was so worried, Pink."

He flushed at that.

"Needn't have worried," he said, rather thickly. "Didn't get to the front until just before the end. My show was made a labor division in the south of France. If you laugh, I'll take my flowers and go home."

"Why, Pink dear, I wouldn't laugh for anything. And it was the man behind the lines who —"

"Won the war," he finished for her, rather grimly. "All right, Lily. We've heard it before. Anyhow, it's all done and over, and —I brought gardenias and violets. You used to like 'em."

"It was dear of you to remember."

"Couldn't help remembering. No credit to me. I —you were always in my mind."

She was busily unwrapping the box.

"Always," he repeated, unsteadily.

"What gorgeous things!" she buried her face in them.

"Did you hear what I said, Lily?"

"Yes, and it's sweet of you. Now sit down and tell me about things. I've got a lot to tell you, too."

He had a sort of quiet obstinacy, however, and he did not sit down. When she had done so he stood in front of her, looking down at her.

"You've been in a camp. I know that. I heard it over there. Anne Devereaux wrote me. It worried me because-we had girls in the camps over there, and every one of them had a string of suitors a mile long."

"Well, I didn't," said Lily, spiritedly. Then she laughed. He had been afraid she would laugh. "Oh, Pink, how dear and funny and masculine you are! I have a perfectly uncontrollable desire to kiss you."

Which she did, to his amazement and consternation. Nothing she could have done would more effectually have shown him the hopelessness of his situation than that sisterly impulse.

"Good Lord," he gasped, "Grayson's in the hall."

"If he comes in I shall probably do it again. Pink, you darling child, you are still the little boy at Mrs. Van Buren's and if you would only purse your lips and count one-two-three-Are you staying to luncheon?"

He was suffering terribly. Also he felt strangely empty inside, because something that he had carried around with him for a long time seemed to have suddenly moved out and left a vacancy.

"Thanks. I think not, Lily; I've got a lot to do to-day."

She sat very still. She had had to do it, had had to show him, somehow, that she loved him without loving him as he wanted her to. She had acted on impulse, on an impulse born of intention, but she had hurt him. It was in every line of his rigid body and set face.

"You're not angry, Pink dear?"

"There's nothing to be angry about," he said, stolidly. "Things have been going on, with me, and staying where they've always been, with you. That's all. I'm not very keen, you know, and I used to think-Your people like me. I mean, they wouldn't —"

"Everybody likes you, Pink."

"Well, I'll trot along." He moved a step, hesitated. "Is there anybody else, Lily?"

"Nobody."

"You won't mind if I hang around a bit, then? You can always send me off when you are sick of me. Which you couldn't if you were fool enough to marry me."

"Whoever does marry you, dear, will be a lucky woman."

In the end he stayed to luncheon, and managed to eat a very fair one. But he had little lapses into silence, and Grace Cardew drew her own shrewd conclusions.

"He's such a nice boy, Lily," she said, after he had gone. "And your grandfather would like it. In a way I think he expects it."

"I'm not going to marry to please him, mother."

"But you are fond of Alston."

"I want to marry a man, mother. Pink is a boy. He will always be a boy. He doesn't think; he just feels. He is fine and loyal and honest, but I would loathe him in a month."

"I wish," said Grace Cardew unhappily, "I wish you had never gone to that camp."

All afternoon Lily and Grace shopped. Lily was fitted into shining evening gowns, into bright little afternoon frocks, into Paris wraps. The Cardew name was whispered through the shops, and great piles of exotic things were brought in for Grace's critical eye. Lily's own attitude was joyously carefree. Long lines of models walked by, draped in furs, in satins and velvet and chiffon, tall girls, most of them, with hair carefully dressed, faces delicately tinted and that curious forward thrust at the waist and slight advancement of one shoulder that gave them an air of languorous indifference.

"The only way I could get that twist," Lily confided to her mother, "would be to stand that way and be done up in plaster of paris. It is the most abandoned thing I ever saw."

Grace was shocked, and said so.

Sometimes, during the few hours since her arrival, Lily had wondered if her year's experiences had coarsened her. There were so many times when her mother raised her eyebrows. She knew that she had changed, that the granddaughter of old Anthony Cardew who had come back from the war was not the girl who had gone away. She had gone away amazingly ignorant; what little she had known of life she had learned away at school. But even there she had not realized the possibility of wickedness and vice in the world. One of the girls had run away with a music master who was married, and her name was forbidden to be mentioned. That was wickedness, like blasphemy, and a crime against the Holy Ghost.

She had never heard of prostitution. Near the camp there was a district with a bad name, and the girls of her organization were forbidden to so much as walk in that direction. It took her a long time to understand, and she suffered horribly when she did. There were depths of wickedness, then, and of abasement like that in the world. It was a bad world, a cruel, sordid world. She did not want to live in it.

She had had to reorganize all her ideas of life after that. At first she was flamingly indignant. God had made His world clean and beautiful, and covered it with flowers and trees that grew, cleanly begotten, from the earth. Why had He not stopped there? Why had He soiled it with passion and lust?

It was a little Red Cross nurse who helped her, finally.

"Very well," she said. "I see what you mean. But trees and flowers are not God's most beautiful gift to the world."

"I think they are."

"No. It is love."

"I am not talking about love," said Lily, flushing.

"Oh, yes, you are. You have never loved, have you? You are talking of one of the many things that go to make up love, and out of that one phase of love comes the most wonderful thing in the world. He gives us the child."

And again:

"All bodies are not whole, and not all souls. It is wrong to judge life by its exceptions, or love by its perversions, Lily."

It had been the little nurse finally who cured her, for she secured Lily's removal to that shady house on a by-street, where the tragedies of unwise love and youth sought sanctuary. There were prayers there, morning and evening. They knelt, those girls, in front of their little wooden chairs, and by far the great majority of them quite simply laid their burdens before God, and with an equal simplicity, felt that He would help them out.

"We have erred, and strayed from Thy ways like lost sheep. We have followed too much the devices and desires of our own hearts. We have offended against Thy holy laws....Restore Thou those who are penitent, according to Thy promises....And grant, Oh most merciful Father, that we may hereafter live a godly, righteous and sober life."

After a time Lily learned something that helped her. The soul was greater and stronger than the body and than the mind. The body failed. It sinned, but that did not touch the unassailable purity and simplicity of the soul. The soul, which lived on, was always clean. For that reason there was no hell.

Lily rose and buttoned her coat. Grace was fastening her sables, and making a delayed decision in satins.

"Mother, I've been thinking it over. I am going to see Aunt Elinor."

Grace waited until the saleswoman had moved away.

"I don't like it, Lily."

"I was thinking, while we were ordering all that stuff. She is a Cardew, mother. She ought to be having that sort of thing. And just because grandfather hates her husband, she hasn't anything."

"That is rather silly, dear. They are not in want. I believe he is quite flourishing."

"She is father's sister. And she is a good woman. We treat her like a leper."

Grace was weakening. "If you take the car, your grandfather may hear of it."

"I'll take a taxi."

Grace followed her with uneasy eyes. For years she paid a price for peace, and not a small price. She had placed her pride on the domestic altar, and had counted it a worthy sacrifice for Howard's sake. And she had succeeded. She knew Anthony Cardew had never forgiven her and would never like her, but he gave her, now and then, the tribute of a grudging admiration.

And now Lily had come home, a new and different Lily, with her father's lovableness and his father's obstinacy. Already Grace saw in the girl the beginning of a passionate protest against things as they were. Perhaps, had Grace given to Lily the great love of her life, instead of to Howard, she might have understood her less clearly. As it was, she shivered slightly as she got into the limousine.

Chapter IX

Lily Cardew inspected curiously the east side neighborhood through which the taxi was passing. She knew vaguely that she was in the vicinity of one of the Cardew mills, but she had never visited any of the Cardew plants. She had never been permitted to do so. Perhaps the neighborhood would have impressed her more had she not seen, in the camp, that life can be stripped sometimes to its essentials, and still have lost very little. But the dinginess depressed her. Smoke was in the atmosphere, like a heavy fog. Soot lay on the window-sills, and mingled with street dust to form little black whirlpools in the wind. Even the white river steamers, guiding their heavy laden coal barges with the current, were gray with soft coal smoke. The foam of the river falling in broken cataracts from their stern wheels was oddly white in contrast.

Everywhere she began to see her own name. "Cardew" was on the ore hopper cars that were moving slowly along a railroad spur. One of the steamers bore "Anthony Cardew" in tall black letters on its side. There was a narrow street called "Cardew Way."

Aunt Elinor lived on Cardew Way. She wondered if Aunt Elinor found that curious, as she did. Did she resent these ever-present reminders of her lost family? Did she have any bitterness because the very grayness of her skies was making her hard old father richer and more powerful?

Yet there was comfort, stability and a certain dignity about Aunt Elinor's house when she reached it. It stood in the district, but not of it, withdrawn from the street in a small open space which gave indication of being a flower garden in summer. There were two large gaunt trees on either side of a brick walk, and that walk had been swept to the last degree of neatness. The steps were freshly scoured, and a small brass door-plate, like a doctor's sign, was as bright as rubbing could make it. "James Doyle," she read.

Suddenly she was glad she had come. The little brick house looked anything but tragic, with its shining windows, its white curtains and its evenly drawn shades. Through the windows on the right came a flickering light, warm and rosy. There must be a coal fire there. She loved a coal fire.

She had braced herself to meet Aunt Elinor at the door, but an elderly woman opened it.

"Mrs. Doyle is in," she said; "just step inside."

She did not ask Lily's name, but left her in the dark little hall and creaked up the stairs. Lily hesitated. Then, feeling that Aunt Elinor might not like to find her so unceremoniously received, she pushed open a door which was only partly closed, and made a step into the room. Only then did she see that it was occupied. A man sat by the fire, reading. He was holding his book low, to get the light from the fire, and he turned slowly to glance at Lily. He had clearly expected some one else. Elinor, probably.

"I beg your pardon," Lily said. "I am calling on Mrs. Doyle, and when I saw the firelight —"

He stood up then, a tall, thin man, with close-cropped gray mustache and heavy gray hair above a high, bulging forehead. She had never seen Jim Doyle, but Mademoiselle had once said that he had pointed ears, like a satyr. She had immediately recanted, on finding Lily searching in a book for a picture of a satyr. This man had ears pointed at the top. Lily was too startled then to analyze his face, but later on she was to know well the high, intellectual forehead, the keen sunken eyes, the full but firmly held mouth and pointed, satyr-like ears of that brilliant Irishman, cynic and arch scoundrel, Jim Doyle.

He was inspecting her intently.

"Please come in," he said. "Did the maid take your name?"

"No. I am Lily Cardew."

"I see." He stood quite still, eyeing her. "You are Anthony's granddaughter?"

"Yes."

"Just a moment." He went out, closing the door behind him, and she heard him going quickly up the stairs. A door closed above, and a weight settled down on the girl's heart. He was not going to let her see Aunt Elinor. She was frightened, but she was angry, too. She would not run away. She would wait until he came down, and if he was insolent, well, she could be haughty. She moved to the fire and stood there, slightly flushed, but very straight.

She heard him coming down again almost immediately. He was outside the door. But he did not come in at once. She had a sudden impression that he was standing there, his hand on the knob, outlining what he meant to say to her when he showed the door to a hated Cardew. Afterwards she came to know how right that impression was. He was never spontaneous. He was a man who debated everything, calculated everything beforehand.

When he came in it was slowly, and with his head bent, as though he still debated within himself. Then:

"I think I have a right to ask what Anthony Cardew's granddaughter is doing in my house."

"Your wife's niece has come to call on her, Mr. Doyle."

"Are you quite sure that is all?"

"I assure you that is all," Lily said haughtily. "It had not occurred to me that you would be here."

"I dare say. Still, strangely enough, I do spend a certain amount of time in my home."

Lily picked up her muff.

"If you have forbidden her to come down, I shall go."

"Wait," he said slowly. "I haven't forbidden her to see you. I asked her to wait. I wanted a few moments. You see, it is not often that I have a Cardew in my house, and I am a selfish man."

She hated him. She loathed his cold eyes, his long, slim white hands. She hated him until he fascinated her.

"Sit down, and I will call Mrs. Doyle."

He went out again, but this time it was the elderly maid who went up the stairs. Doyle himself came back, and stood before her on the hearth rug. He was slightly smiling, and the look of uncertainty was gone.

"Now that you've seen me, I'm not absolutely poisonous, am I, Miss Lily? You don't mind my calling you that, do you? You are my niece. You have been taught to hate me, of course."

"Yes," said Lily, coldly.

"By Jove, the truth from a Cardew!" Then: "That's an old habit of mine, damning the Cardews. I'll have to try to get over it, if they are going to reestablish family relations." He was laughing at her, Lily knew, and she flushed somewhat.

"I wouldn't make too great an effort, then," she said.

He smiled again, this time not unpleasantly, and suddenly he threw into his rich Irish voice an unexpected softness. No one knew better than Jim Doyle the uses of the human voice.

"You mustn't mind me, Miss Lily. I have no reason to love your family, but I am very happy that you came here to-day. My wife has missed her people. If you'll run in like this now and then it will do her worlds of good. And if my being here is going to keep you away I can clear out."

She rather liked him for that speech. He was totally unlike what she had been led to expect, and she felt a sort of resentment toward her family for misleading her. He was a gentleman, on the surface at least. He had not been over-cordial at first, but then who could have expected cordiality under the circumstances? In Lily's defense it should be said that the vicissitudes of Elinor's life with Doyle had been kept from her always. She had but two facts to go on: he had beaten her grandfather as a young man, for a cause, and he held views as to labor which conflicted with those of her family.

Months later, when she learned all the truth, it was too late.

"Of course you're being here won't keep me away, if you care to have me come."

He was all dignity and charm then. They needed youth in that quiet place. They ought all to be able to forget the past, which was done with, anyhow. He showed the first genuine interest she had found in her work at the camp, and before his unexpected geniality the girl opened like a flower.

And all the time he was watching her with calculating eyes. He was a gambler with life, and he rather suspected that he had just drawn a valuable card.

"Thank you," he said gravely, when she had finished. "You have done a lot to bridge the gulf that lies —I am sure you have noticed it-between the people who saw service in this war and those who stayed at home."

Suddenly Lily saw that the gulf between her family and herself was just that, which was what he had intended.

When Elinor came in they were absorbed in conversation, Lily flushed and eager, and her husband smiling, urbane, and genial.

To Lily, Elinor Doyle had been for years a figure of mystery. She had not seen her for many years, and she had, remembered a thin, girlish figure, tragic-eyed, which eternally stood by a window in her room, looking out. But here was a matronly woman, her face framed with soft, dark hair, with eyes like her father's, with Howard Cardew's ease of manner, too, but with a strange passivity, either of repression or of fires early burned out and never renewed.

Lily was vaguely disappointed. Aunt Elinor, in soft gray silk, matronly, assured, unenthusiastically pleased to see her; Doyle himself, cheerful and suave; the neat servant; the fire lit, comfortable room, —there was no drama in all that, no hint of mystery or tragedy. All the hatred at home for an impulsive assault of years ago, and-this!

"Lily, dear!" Elinor said, and kissed her. "Why, Lily, you are a woman!"

"I am twenty, Aunt Elinor."

"Yes, of course. I keep forgetting. I live so quietly here that the days go by faster than I know." She put Lily back in her chair, and glanced at her husband.

"Is Louis coming to dinner, Jim?"

"Yes."

"I suppose you cannot stay, Lily?"

"I ought to tell you, Aunt Elinor. Only mother knows that I am here."

Aunt Elinor smiled her quiet smile.

"I understand, dear. How are they all?"

"Grandfather is very well. Father looks tired. There is some trouble at the mill, I think."

Elinor glanced at Doyle, but he said nothing.

"And your mother?"

"She is well."

Lily was commencing to have an odd conviction, which was that her Aunt Elinor was less glad to have her there than was Jim Doyle. He seemed inclined to make up for Elinor's lack of enthusiasm by his own. He built up a larger fire, and moved her chair near it.

"Weather's raw," he said. "Sure you are comfortable now? And why not have dinner here? We have an interesting man coming, and we don't often have the chance to offer our guests a charming young lady."

"Lily only came home yesterday, Jim," Elinor observed. "Her own people will want to see something of her. Besides, they do no know she is here."

Lily felt slightly chilled. For years she had espoused her Aunt Elinor's cause; in the early days she had painfully hemstitched a small handkerchief each fall and had sent it, with much secrecy, to Aunt Elinor's varying addresses at Christmas. She had felt a childish resentment of Elinor Doyle's martyrdom. And now —

"Her father and grandfather are dining out to-night." Had Lily looked up she would have seen Doyle's eyes fixed on his wife, ugly and menacing.

"Dining out?" Lily glanced at him in surprise.

"There is a dinner to-night, for the —" He checked himself "The steel manufacturers are having a meeting," he finished. "I believe to discuss me, among other things. Amazing the amount of discussion my simple opinions bring about."

Elinor Doyle, unseen, made a little gesture of despair and surrender.

"I hope you will stay, Lily," she said. "You can telephone, if you like. I don't see you often, and there is so much I want to ask you."

In the end Lily agreed. She would find out from Grayson if the men were really dining out, and if they were Grayson would notify her mother that she was staying. She did not quite know herself why she had accepted, unless it was because she was bored and restless at home. Perhaps, too, the lure of doing a forbidden thing influenced her sub-consciously, the thought that her grandfather would detest it. She had not forgiven him for the night before.

Jim Doyle left her in the back hall at the telephone, and returned to the sitting room, dosing the door behind him. His face was set and angry.

"I thought I told you to be pleasant."

"I tried, Jim. You must remember I hardly know her." She got up and placed her hand on his arm, but he shook it off. "I don't understand, Jim, and I wish you wouldn't. What good is it?"

"I've told you what I want. I want that girl to come here, and to like coming here. That's plain, isn't it? But if you're going to sit with a frozen face-She'll be useful. Useful as hell to a preacher."

"I can't use my family that way."

"You and your family! Now listen, Elinor. This isn't a matter o the Cardews and me. It may be nothing, but it may be a big thing. I hardly know yet —" His voice trailed off; he stood with his head bent, lost in those eternal calculations with which Elinor Doyle was so familiar.

The doorbell rang, and was immediately followed by the opening and closing of the front door.

From her station at the telephone Lily Cardew saw a man come in, little more than a huge black shadow, which placed a hat on the stand and then, striking a match, lighted the gas overhead. In the illumination he stood before the mirror, smoothing back his shining black hair. Then he saw her, stared and retreated into the sitting room.

"Got company, I see."

"My niece, Lily Cardew," said Doyle, dryly.

The gentleman seemed highly amused. Evidently he considered Lily's presence in the house in the nature of a huge joke. He was conveying this by pantomime, in deference to the open door, when Doyle nodded toward Elinor.

"It's customary to greet your hostess, Louis."

"Easiest thing I do," boasted the new arrival cheerily. "'Lo, Mrs. Doyle. Is our niece going to dine with us?"

"I don't know yet, Mr. Akers," she said, without warmth. Louis Akers knew quite well that Elinor did not like him, and the thought amused him, the more so since as a rule women liked him rather too well. Deep in his heart he respected Jim Doyle's wife, and sometimes feared her. He respected her because she had behind her traditions of birth and wealth, things he professed to despise but secretly envied. He feared her because he trusted no woman, and she knew too much.

She loved Jim Doyle, but he had watched her, and he knew that sometimes she hated Doyle also. He knew that could be, because there had been women he had both loved and hated himself.

Elinor had gone out, and Akers sat down.

"Well," he said, in a lowered tone. "I've written it."

Doyle closed the door, and stood again with his head lowered, considering.

"You'd better look over it," continued Lou. "I don't want to be jailed. You're better at skating over thin ice than I am. And I've been thinking over the Prohibition matter, Jim. In a sense you're right. It will make them sullen and angry. But they won't go the limit without booze. I'd advise cache-ing a lot of it somewhere, to be administered when needed."

Doyle returned to his old place on the hearth-rug, still thoughtful. He had paid no attention to Aker's views on Prohibition, nor to the paper laid upon the desk in the center of the room.

"Do you know that that girl in the hall will be worth forty million dollars some day?"

"Some money," said Akers, calmly. "Which reminds me, Jim, that I've got to have a raise. And pretty soon."

"You get plenty, if you'd leave women alone."

"Tell them to leave me alone, then," said Akers, stretching out his long legs. "All right. We'll talk about that, after dinner. What about this forty millions?"

Doyle looked at him quickly. Akers' speech about women had crystallized the vague plans which Lily's arrival had suddenly given rise to. He gave the young man a careful scrutiny, from his handsome head to his feet, and smiled. It had occurred to him that the Cardew family would loathe a man of Louis Akers' type with an entire and whole-hearted loathing.

"You might try to make her have a pleasant evening," he suggested dryly. "And, to do that, it might be as well to remember a number of things, one of which is that she is accustomed to the society of gentlemen."

"All right, old dear," said Akers, without resentment.

"She hates her grandfather like poison," Doyle went on. "She doesn't know it, but she does. A little education, and it is just possible —"

"Get Olga. I'm no kindergarten teacher."

"You haven't seen her in the light yet."

Louis Akers smiled and carefully settled his tie.

Like Doyle, Akers loved the game of life, and he liked playing for high stakes. He had joined forces with Doyle because the game was dangerous and exciting, rather than because of any real conviction. Doyle had a fanatic faith, with all his calculation, but Louis Akers had only calculation and ambition. A practicing attorney in the city, a specialist in union law openly, a Red in secret, he played his triple game shrewdly and with zest.

Doyle turned to go, then stopped and came back. "I was forgetting something," he said, slowly. "What possessed you to take that Boyd girl to the Searing Building the other night?"

"Who told you that?"

"Woslosky saw you coming out."

"I had left something there," Akers said sullenly. "That's the truth, whether you believe it or not. I wasn't there two minutes."

"You're a fool, Louis," Doyle said coldly. "You'll play that game once too often. What happens to you is your own concern, but what may happen to me is mine. And I'll take mighty good care it doesn't happen."

Doyle was all unction and hospitality when he met Lily in the hall. At dinner he was brilliant, witty, the gracious host. Akers played up to him. At the foot of the table Elinor sat, outwardly passive, inwardly puzzled, and watched Lily. She knew the contrast the girl must be drawing, between the bright little meal, with its simple service and clever talk, and those dreary formal dinners at home when old Anthony sometimes never spoke at all, or again used his caustic tongue like a scourge. Elinor did not hate her father; he was simply no longer her father. As for Howard, she had had a childish affection for him, but he had gone away early to school, and she hardly knew him. But she did not want his child here, drinking in as she was, without clearly understanding what they meant, Doyle's theories of unrest and revolution.

"You will find that I am an idealist, in a way," he was saying. "That is, if you come often. I hope you will, by the way. I am perpetually dissatisfied with things as they are, and wanting them changed. With the single exception of my wife"—he bowed to Elinor, "and this little party, which is delightful."

"Are you a Socialist?" Lily demanded, in her direct way.

"Well, you might call it that. I go a bit further."

"Don't talk politics, Jim," Elinor hastily interposed. He caught her eye and grinned.

"I'm not talking politics, my dear." He turned to Lily, smiling.

"For one thing, I don't believe that any one should have a lot of money, so that a taxicab could remain ticking away fabulous sums while a charming young lady dines at her leisure." He smiled again.

"Will it be a lot?" Lily asked. "I thought I'd better keep him, because —" She hesitated.

"Because this neighborhood is unlikely to have a cab stand? You were entirely right. But I can see that you won't like my idealistic community. You see, in it everybody will have enough, and nobody will have too much."

"Don't take him too seriously, Miss Cardew," said Akers, bending forward. "You and I know that there isn't such a thing as too much."

Elinor changed the subject; as a girl she had drawn rather well, and she had retained her interest in that form of art. There was an exhibition in town of colored drawings. Lily should see them. But Jim Doyle countered her move.

"I forgot to mention," he said, "that in this ideal world we were discussing the arts will flourish. Not at once, of course, because the artists will be fighting—"

"Fighting?"

"Per aspera ad astra," put in Louis Akers. "You cannot change a world in a day, without revolution —"

"But you don't believe that revolution is ever worth while, do you?"

"If it would drive starvation and wretchedness from the world, yes."

Lily found Louis Akers interesting. Certainly he was very handsome. And after all, why should there be misery and hunger in the world? There must be enough for all. It was hardly fair, for instance, that she should have so much, and others scarcely anything. Only it was like thinking about religion; you didn't get anywhere with it. You wanted to be good, and tried to be. And you wanted to love God, only He seemed so far away, mostly. And even that was confusing, because you prayed to God to be forgiven for wickedness, but it was to His Son our Lord one went for help in trouble.

One could be sorry for the poor, and even give away all one had, but that would only help a few. It would have to be that every one who had too much would give up all but what he needed.

Lily tried to put that into words.

"Exactly," said Jim Doyle. "Only in my new world we realize that there would be a few craven spirits who might not willingly give up what they have. In that case it would be taken from them."

"And that is what you call revolution?"

"Precisely."

"But that's not revolution. It is a sort of justice, isn't it?"

"You think very straight, young lady," said Jim Doyle.

He had a fascinating theory of individualism, too; no man should impose his will and no community its laws, on the individual. Laws were for slaves. Ethics were better than laws, to control.

"Although," he added, urbanely, "I daresay it might be difficult to convert Mr. Anthony Cardew to such a belief."

While Louis Akers saw Lily to her taxicab that night Doyle stood in the hall, waiting. He was very content with his evening's work.

"Well?" he said, when Akers returned.

"Merry as a marriage bell. I'm to show her the Brunelleschi drawings to-morrow."

Slightly flushed, he smoothed his hair in front of the mirror over the stand.

"She's a nice child," he said. In his eyes was the look of the hunting animal that scents food.

Chapter X

Lily did not sleep very well that night. She was repentant, for one thing, for her mother's evening alone, and for the anxiety in her face when she arrived.

"I've been so worried," she said, "I was afraid your grandfather would get back before you did."

"I'm sorry, mother dear. I know it was selfish. But I've had a wonderful evening."

"Wonderful?"

"All sorts of talk," Lily said, and hesitated. After all, her mother would not understand, and it would only make her uneasy. "I suppose it is rank hearsay to say it, but I like Mr. Doyle."

"I detest him."

"But you don't know him, do you?"

"I know he is stirring up all sorts of trouble for us. Lily, I want you to promise not to go back there."

There was a little silence. A small feeling of rebellion was rising in the girl's heart.

"I don't see why. She is my own aunt."

"Will you promise?"

"Please don't ask me, mother. I—oh, don't you understand? It is interesting there, that's all. It isn't wrong to go. And the moment you forbid it you make me want to go back."

"Were there any other people there to dinner?" Grace asked, with sudden suspicion.

"Only one man. A lawyer named Akers."

The name meant nothing to Grace Cardew.

"A young man?"

"Not very young. In his thirties, I should think," Lily hesitated again. She had meant to tell her mother of the engagement for the next day, but Grace's attitude made it difficult. To be absolutely forbidden to meet Louis Akers at the gallery, and to be able to give no reason beyond the fact that she had met him at the Doyle house, seemed absurd.

"A gentleman?"

"I hardly know," Lily said frankly. "In your sense of the word, perhaps not, mother. But he is very clever."

Grace Cardew sighed and picked up her book. She never retired until Howard came in. And Lily went upstairs, uneasy and a little defiant. She must live her own life, somehow; have her own friends; think her own thoughts. The quiet tyranny of the family was again closing down on her. It would squeeze her dry, in the end, as it had her mother and Aunt Elinor.

She stood for a time by her window, looking out at the city. Behind her was her warm, luxurious room, her deep, soft bed. Yet all through the city there were those who did not sleep warm and soft. Close by, perhaps, in that deteriorated neighborhood, there were children that very night going to bed hungry.

Because things had always been like that, should they always be so? Wasn't Mr. Doyle right, after all? Only he went very far. You couldn't, for instance, take from a man the thing he had earned. What about the people who did not try to earn?

She rather thought she would be clearer about it if she talked to Willy Cameron.

She went to bed at last, a troubled young thing in a soft white night-gown, passionately in revolt against the injustice which gave to her so much and to others so little. And against that quiet domestic tyranny which was forcing her to her first deceit.

Yet the visit to the gallery was innocuous enough. Louis Akers met her there, and carefully made the rounds with her. Then he suggested tea, and chose a quiet tea-room, and a corner.

"I'll tell you something, now it's over," he said, his bold eyes fixed on hers. "I loathe galleries and pictures. I wanted to see you again. That's all. You see, I am starting in by being honest with you."

She was rather uncomfortable.

"Why don't you like pictures?"

"Because they are only imitations of life. I like life." He pushed his teacup away. "I don't want tea either. Tea was an excuse, too." He smiled at her. "Perhaps you don't like honesty," he said. "If you don't you won't care for me."

She was too inexperienced to recognize the gulf between frankness and effrontery, but he made her vaguely uneasy. He knew so many things, and yet he was so obviously not quite a gentleman, in her family's sense of the word. He had a curious effect on her, too, one that she resented. He made her insistently conscious of her sex.

And of his. His very deference had something of restraint about it. She thought, trying to drink her tea quietly, that he might be very terrible if he loved any one. There was a sort of repressed fierceness behind his suavity.

But he interested her, and he was undeniably handsome, not in her father's way but with high-colored, almost dramatic good looks. There could be no doubt, too, that he was interested in her. He rarely took his eyes off hers. Afterwards she was to know well that bold possessive look of his.

It was just before they left that he said:

"I am going to see you again, you know. May I come in some afternoon?"

Lily had been foreseeing that for some moments, and she raised frank eyes to his.

"I am afraid not," she said. "You see, you are a friend of Mr. Doyle's, and you must know that my people and Aunt Elinor's husband are on bad terms."

"What has that got to do with you and me?" Then he laughed. "Might be unpleasant, I suppose. But you go to the Doyles'."

She was very earnest.

"My mother knows, but my grandfather wouldn't permit it if he knew."

"And you put up with that sort of thing?" He leaned closer to her. "You are not a baby, you know. But I will say you are a good sport to do it, anyhow."

"I'm not very comfortable about it."

"Bosh," he said, abruptly. "You go there as often as you can. Elinor Doyle's a lonely woman, and Jim is all right. You pick your own friends, my child, and live your own life. Every human being has that right."

He helped her into a taxi at the door of the tea shop, giving her rather more assistance than she required, and then standing bare-headed in the March wind until the car had moved away. Lily, sitting back in her corner, was both repelled and thrilled. He was totally unlike the men she knew, those carefully repressed, conventional clean-cut boys, like Pink Denslow. He was raw, vigorous and possibly brutal. She did not quite like him, but she found herself thinking about him a great deal.

The old life was reaching out its friendly, idle hands toward her. The next day Grace gave a luncheon for her at the house, a gay little affair of color, chatter and movement. But Lily found herself with little to say. Her year away had separated her from the small community of interest that bound the others together, and she wondered, listening to them in her sitting room later, what they would all talk about when they had exchanged their bits of gossip, their news of this man and that. It would all be said so soon. And what then?

Here they were, and here they would always be, their own small circle, carefully guarded. They belonged together, they and the men who likewise belonged. Now and then there would be changes. A new man, of irreproachable family connections would come to live in the city, and cause a small flurry. Then in time he would be appropriated. Or a girl would come to visit, and by the same system of appropriation would come back later, permanently. Always the same faces, the same small talk. Orchids or violets at luncheons, white or rose or blue or yellow frocks at dinners and dances. Golf at the country club. Travel, in the Cardew private car, cut off from fellow travelers who might prove interesting. Winter at Palm Beach, and a bit of a thrill at seeing moving picture stars and theatrical celebrities playing on the sand. One never had a chance to meet them.

And, in quiet intervals, this still house, and grandfather shut away in his upstairs room, but holding the threads of all their lives as a spider clutches the diverging filaments of its web.

"Get in on this, Lily," said a clear young voice. "We're talking about the most interesting men we met in our war work. You ought to have known a lot of them."

"I knew a lot of men. They were not so very interesting. There was a little nurse —"

"Men, Lily dear."

"There was one awfully nice boy. He wasn't a soldier, but he was very kind to the men. They adored him."

"Did he fall in love with your?"

"Not a particle."

"Why wasn't he a soldier?"

"He is a little bit lame. But he is awfully nice."

"But what is extraordinary about him, then?"

"Not a thing, except his niceness."

But they were surfeited with nice young men. They wanted something dramatic, and Willy Cameron was essentially undramatic. Besides, it was quite plain that, with unconscious cruelty, his physical handicap made him unacceptable to them.

"Don't be ridiculous, Lily. You're hiding some one behind this kind person. You must have met somebody worth while."

"Not in the camp. I know a perfectly nice Socialist, but he was not in the army. Not a Socialist, really. Much worse. He believes in having a revolution."

That stirred them somewhat. She saw their interested faces turned toward her.

"With a bomb under his coat, of course, Lily."

"He didn't bulge."

"Good-looking?"

"Well, rather."

"How old is he, Lily?" one of them asked, suspiciously.

"Almost fifty, I should say."

"Good heavens!"

Their interest died. She could have revived it, she knew, if she mentioned Louis Akers; he would have answered to their prime requisite in an interesting man. He was both handsome and young. But she felt curiously disinclined to mention him.

The party broke up. By ones and twos luxuriously dressed little figures went down the great staircase, where Grayson stood in the hall and the footman on the doorstep signaled to the waiting cars. Mademoiselle, watching from a point of vantage in the upper hall, felt a sense of comfort and well-being after they had all gone. This was as it should be. Lily would take up life again where she had left it off, and all would be well.

It was now the sixth day, and she had not yet carried out that absurd idea of asking Ellen's friend to dinner.

Lily was, however, at that exact moment in process of carrying it out.

"Telephone for you, Mr. Cameron."

"Thanks. Coming," sang out Willy Cameron.

Edith Boyd sauntered toward his doorway.

"It's a lady."

"Woman," corrected Willy Cameron. "The word 'lady' is now obsolete, since your sex has entered the economic world." He put on his coat.

"I said 'lady' and that's what I mean," said Edith. "'May I speak to Mr. Cameron?'" she mimicked. "Regular Newport accent."

Suddenly Willy Cameron went rather pale. If it should be Lily Cardew-but then of course it wouldn't be. She had been home for six days, and if she had meant to call —

"Hello," he said.

It was Lily. Something that had been like a band around his heart suddenly loosened, to fasten about his throat. His voice sounded strangled and strange.

"Why, yes," he said, in the unfamiliar voice. "I'd like to come, of course."

Edith Boyd watched and listened, with a slightly strained look in her eyes.

"To dinner? But—I don't think I'd better come to dinner."

"Why not, Willy?"

Mr. William Wallace Cameron glanced around. There was no one about save Miss Boyd, who was polishing the nails of one hand on the palm of the other.

"May I come in a business suit?"

"Why, of course. Why not?"

"I didn't know," said Willy Cameron. "I didn't know what your people would think. That's all. To-morrow at eight, then. Thanks."

He hung up the receiver and walked to the door, where he stood looking out and seeing nothing. She had not forgotten. He was going to see her. Instead of standing across the street by the park fence, waiting for a glimpse of her which never came, he was to sit in the room with her. There would be-eight from eleven was three-three hours of her.

What a wonderful day it was! Spring was surely near. He would like to be able to go and pick up Jinx, and then take a long walk through the park. He needed movement. He needed to walk off his excitement or he felt that he might burst with it.

"Eight o'clock!" said Edith. "I wish you joy, waiting until eight for supper."

He had to come back a long, long way to her.

"'May I come in a business suit?'" she mimicked him. "My evening clothes have not arrived yet. My valet's bringing them up to town to-morrow."

Even through the radiant happiness that surrounded him like a mist, he caught the bitterness under her raillery. It puzzled him.

"It's a young lady I knew at camp. I was in an army camp, you know."

"Is her name a secret?"

"Why, no. It is Cardew. Miss Lily Cardew."

"I believe you-not."

"But it is," he said, genuinely concerned. "Why in the world should I give you a wrong name?"

Her eyes were fixed on his face.

"No. You wouldn't. But it makes me laugh, because-well, it was crazy, anyhow."

"What was crazy?"

"Something I had in my mind. Just forget it. I'll tell you what will happen, Mr. Cameron. You'll stay here about six weeks. Then you'll get a job at the Cardew Mills. They use chemists there, and you will be —"

She lifted her finger-tips and blew along them delicately.

"Gone—like that," she finished.

Sometimes Willy Cameron wondered about Miss Boyd. The large young man, for instance, whose name he had learned was Louis Akers, did not come any more. Not since that telephone conversation. But he had been distinctly a grade above that competent young person, Edith Boyd, if there were such grades these days; fluent and prosperous-looking, and probably able to offer a girl a good home. But she had thrown him over. He had heard her doing it, and when he had once ventured to ask her about Akers she had cut him off curtly.

"I was sick to death of him. That's all," she had said.

But on the night of Lily's invitation he was to hear more of Louis Akers.

It was his evening in the shop. One day he came on at seven-thirty in the morning and was off at six, and the next he came at ten and stayed until eleven at night. The evening business was oddly increasing. Men wandered in, bought a tube of shaving cream or a tooth-brush, and sat or stood around for an hour or so; clerks whose families had gone to the movies, bachelors who found their lodging houses dreary, a young doctor or two, coming in after evening office hours to leave a prescription, and remaining to talk and listen. Thus they satisfied their gregarious instinct while within easy call of home.

The wealthy had their clubs. The workmen of the city had their balls and sometimes their saloons. But in between was that vast, unorganized male element which was neither, and had neither. To them the neighborhood pharmacy, open in the evening, warm and bright, gave them a rendezvous. They gathered there in thousands, the country over. During the war they fought their daily battles there, with newspaper maps. After the war the League of Nations, local politics, a bit of neighborhood scandal, washed down with soft drinks from the soda fountain, furnished the evening's entertainment.

The Eagle Pharmacy had always been the neighborhood club, but with the advent of Willy Cameron it was attaining a new popularity. The roundsman on the beat dropped in, the political boss of the ward, named Hendricks, Doctor Smalley, the young physician who lived across the street, and others. Back of the store proper was a room, with the prescription desk at one side and reserve stock on shelves around the other three. Here were a table and a half dozen old chairs, a war map, still showing with colored pins the last positions before the great allied advance, and an ancient hat-rack, which had held from time immemorial an umbrella with three broken ribs and a pair of arctics of unknown ownership.

"Going to watch this boy," Hendricks confided to Doctor Smalley a night or two after Lily's return, meeting him outside. "He sure can talk."

Doctor Smalley grinned.

"He can read my writing, too, which is more than I can do myself. What do you mean, watch him?"

But whatever his purposes Mr. Hendricks kept them to himself. A big, burly man, with a fund of practical good sense a keen knowledge of men, he had gained a small but loyal following. He was a retired master plumber, with a small income from careful investments, and he had a curious, almost fanatic love for the city.

"I was born here," he would say, boastfully. "And I've seen it grow from fifty thousand to what it's got now. Some folks say it's dirty, but it's home to me, all right."

But on the evening of Lily's invitation the drug store forum found Willy Cameron extremely silent. He had been going over his weaknesses, for the thought of Lily always made him humble, and one of them was that he got carried away by things and talked too much. He did not intend to do that the next night, at the Cardew's.

"Something's scared him off," said Mr. Hendricks to Doctor Smalley, after a half hour of almost taciturnity, while Willy Cameron smoked his pipe and listened. "Watch him rise to this, though." And aloud:

"Why don't you fellows drop the League of Nations, which none of you knows a damn about anyhow, and get to the thing that's coming in this country?"

"I'll bite," said Mr. Clarey, who sold life insurance in the daytime and sometimes utilized his evenings in a similar manner. "What's coming to this country?"

"Revolution."

The crowd laughed.

"All right," said Mr. Hendricks. "Laugh while you can. I saw the Chief of Police to-day, and he's got a line of conversation that makes a man feel like taking his savings out of the bank and burying them in the back yard."

Willy Cameron took his pipe out of his mouth, but remained dumb.

Mr. Hendricks nudged Doctor Smalley, who rose manfully to the occasion. "What does he say?"

"Says the Russians have got a lot of paid agents here. Not all Russians either. Some of our Americans are in it. It's to begin with a general strike."

"In this town?"

"All over the country. But this is a good field for them. The crust's pretty thin here, and where that's the case there is likely to be earthquakes and eruptions. The Chief says they're bringing in a bunch of gunmen, wobblies and Bolshevists from every industrial town on the map. Did you get that, Cameron? Gunmen!"

"Any of you men here dissatisfied with this form of government?" inquired Willy, rather truculently.

"Not so you could notice it," said Mr. Clarey. "And once the Republican party gets in —"

"Then there will never be a revolution."

"Why?"

"That's why," said Willy Cameron. "Of course you are worthless now. You aren't organized. You don't know how many you are or how strong you are. You can't talk. You sit back and listen until you believe that this country is only capital and labor. You get squeezed in between them. You see labor getting more money than you, and howling for still more. You see both capital and labor raising prices until you can't live on what you get. There are a hundred times as many of you as represent capital and labor combined, and all you do is loaf here and growl about things being wrong. Why don't you do something? You ought to be running this country, but you aren't. You're lazy. You don't even vote. You leave running the country to men like Mr. Hendricks here."

Mr. Hendricks was cheerfully unirritated.

"All right, son," he said, "I do my bit and like it. Go on. Don't stop to insult me. You can do that any time."

"I've been buying a seditious weekly since I came," said Willy Cameron. "It's preaching a revolution, all right. I'd like to see its foreign language copies. They'll never overthrow the government, but they may try. Why don't you fellows combine to fight them? Why don't you learn how strong you are? Nine-tenths of the country, and milling like sheep with a wolf around!"

Mr. Hendricks winked at the doctor.

"What'd I tell you?" whispered Hendricks. "Got them, hasn't he? If he'd suggest arming them with pop bottles and attacking that gang of anarchists at the cobbler's down the street, they'd do it this minute."

"All right, son," he offered. "We'll combine. Anything you say goes. And we'll get the Jim Doyle-Woslosky-Louis Akers outfit first. I know a first-class brick wall —"

"Akers?" said Willy Cameron. "Do you know him?"

"I do," said Hendricks. "But that needn't prejudice you against me any. He's a bad actor, and as smooth as butter. D'you know what their plan is? They expect to take the city. This city! The —" Mr. Hendrick's voice was lost in fury.

"Talk!" said the roundsman. "Where'd the police be, I'm asking?"

"The police," said Mr. Hendricks, evidently quoting, "are as filled with sedition as a whale with corset bones. Also the army. Also the state constabulary."

"The hell they are," said the roundsman aggressively. But Willy Cameron was staring through the smoke from his pipe at the crowd.

"They might do it, for a while," he said thoughtfully. "There's a tremendous foreign population in the mill towns around, isn't there? Does anybody in the crowd own a revolver? Or know how to use it if he has one."

"I've got one," said the insurance agent. "Don't know how it would work. Found my wife nailing oilcloth with it the other day."

"Very well. If we're a representative group, they wouldn't need a battery of eight-inch guns, would they?"

A little silence fell on the group. Around them the city went about its business; the roar of the day had softened to muffled night sounds, as though one said: "The city sleeps. Be still." The red glare of the mills was the fire on the hearth. The hills were its four protecting walls. And the night mist covered it like a blanket.

"Here's one representative of the plain people," said Mr. Hendricks, "who is going home to get some sleep. And tomorrow I'll buy me a gun, and if I can keep the children out of the yard I'll learn to use it."

For a long time after he went home that night Willy Cameron paced the floor of his upper room, paced it until an irate boarder below hammered on his chandelier. Jinx followed him, moving sedately back and forth, now and then glancing up with idolatrous eyes. Willy Cameron's mind was active and not particularly coordinate. The Cardews and Lily; Edith Boyd and Louis Akers; the plain people; an army marching to the city to loot and burn and rape, and another army meeting it, saying: "You shall not pass"; Abraham Lincoln, Russia, Lily.

His last thought, of course, was of Lily Cardew. He had neglected to cover Jinx, and at last the dog leaped on the bed and snuggled close to him. He threw an end of the blanket over him and lay there, staring into the darkness. He was frightfully lonely. At last he fell asleep, and the March wind, coming in through the open window, overturned a paper leaning against his collar box, on which he had carefully written:

Have suit pressed.

Buy new tie.

Shirts from laundry.

Chapter XI

Going home that night Mr. Hendricks met Edith Boyd, and accompanied her for a block or two. At his corner he stopped.

"How's your mother, Edith?"

It was Mr. Hendricks' business to know his ward thoroughly.

"About the same. She isn't really sick, Mr. Hendricks. She's just low spirited, but that's enough. I hate to go home."

Hendricks hesitated.

"Still, home's a pretty good place," he said. "Especially for a pretty girl." There was unmistakable meaning in his tone, and she threw up her head.

"I've got to get some pleasure out of life, Mr. Hendricks."

"Sure you have," he agreed affably. "But playing around with Louis Akers is like playing with a hand-grenade, Edith." She said nothing. "I'd cut him out, little girl. He's poor stuff. Mind, I'm not saying he's a fool, but he's a bad actor. Now if I was a pretty girl, and there was a nice fellow around like this Cameron, I'd be likely to think he was all right. He's got brains." Mr. Hendricks had a great admiration for brains.

"I'm sick of men."

He turned at her tone and eyed her sharply.

"Well, don't judge them all by Akers. This is my corner. Good-night. Not afraid to go on by yourself, are you?"

"If I ever was I've had a good many chances to get over it."

He turned the corner, but stopped and called after her.

"Tell Dan I'll be in to see him soon, Edith. Haven't seen him since he came back from France."

"All right."

She went on, her steps lagging. She hated going home. When she reached the little house she did not go in at once. The March night was not cold, and she sat the step, hoping to see her mother's light go out in the second-story front windows. But it continued to burn steadily, and at last, with a gesture of despair, she rose and unlocked the door.

Almost at once she heard footsteps above, and a peevish voice.

"That you, Edie?"

"Yes."

"D'you mind bringing up the chloroform liniment and rubbing my back?"

"I'll bring it, mother."

She found it on the wainscoting in the untidy kitchen. She could hear the faint scurrying of water beetles over the oilcloth-covered floor, and then silence. She fancied myriads of tiny, watchful eyes on her, and something crunched under her foot. She felt like screaming. That new clerk at the store was always talking about homes. What did he know of squalid city houses, with their insects and rats, their damp, moldy cellars, their hateful plumbing? A thought struck her. She lighted the gas and stared around. It was as she had expected. The dishes had not been washed. They were piled in the sink, and a soiled dish-towel had been thrown over them.

She lowered the gas and went upstairs. The hardness had, somehow, gone out of her when she thought of Willy Cameron.

"Back bad again, is it?" she asked.

"It's always bad. But I've got a pain in my left shoulder and down my arm that's driving me crazy. I couldn't wash the dishes."

"Never mind the dishes. I'm not tired. Now crawl into bed and let me rub you."

Mrs. Boyd complied. She was a small, thin woman in her early fifties, who had set out to conquer life and had been conquered by it. The hopeless drab of her days stretched behind her, broken only by the incident of her widowhood, and stretched ahead hopelessly. She had accepted Dan's going to France resignedly, with neither protest nor undue anxiety. She had never been very close to Dan, although she loved him more than she did Edith. She was the sort of woman who has no fundamental knowledge of men. They had to be fed and mended for, and they had strange physical wants that made a great deal of trouble in the world. But mostly they ate and slept and went to work in the morning, and came home at night smelling of sweat and beer.

There had been one little rift in the gray fog of her daily life, however. And through it she had seen Edith well married, with perhaps a girl to do the house work, and a room where Edith's mother could fold her hands and sit in the long silences without thought that were her sanctuary against life.

"Is that the place, mother?"

"Yes." Edith's unwonted solicitude gave her courage.

"Edie, I want to ask you something."

"Well?" But the girl stiffened.

"Lou hasn't been round, lately."

"That's all over, mother."

"You mean you've quarreled? Oh, Edie, and me planning you'd have a nice home and everything."

"He never meant to marry me, if that's what you mean."

Mrs. Boyd turned on her back impatiently.

"You could have had him. He was crazy about you. Trouble is with you, you think you've got a fellow hard and fast, and you begin acting up. Then, first thing you know —"

Some of that strange new tolerance persisted in the girl. "Listen, mother," she said. "I give you my word, Lou'd run a mile if he thought any girl wanted to marry him. I know him better than you do. If any one ever does rope him in, he'll stick about three months, and then beat it."

"I don't know why we have to have men, anyhow. Put out the gas, Edie. No, don't open the window. The night air makes me cough."

Edith started downstairs and set to work in the kitchen. Something would have to be done about the house. Dan was taking to staying out at nights, because the untidy rooms repelled him. And there was the question of food. Her mother had never learned to cook, and recently more and more of the food had been something warmed out of a tin. If only they could keep a girl, one who would scrub and wash dishes. There was a room on the third floor, an attic, full now of her mother's untidy harborings of years, that might be used for a servant. Or she could move up there, and they could get a roomer. The rent would pay a woman to come in now and then to clean up.

She had played with that thought before, and the roomer she had had in mind was Willy Cameron. But the knowledge that he knew the Cardews had somehow changed all that. She couldn't picture him going from this sordid house to the Cardew mansion, and worse still, returning to it afterwards. She saw him there, at the Cardews, surrounded by bowing flunkies — a picture of wealth gained from the movies-and by women who moved indolently, trailing through long vistas of ball room and conservatory in low gowns without sleeves, and draped with ropes of pearls. Women who smoked cigarettes after dinner and played bridge for money.

She hated the Cardews.

On her way to her room she paused at her mother's door.

"Asleep yet, mother?"

"No. Feel like I'm not going to sleep at all."

"Mother," she said, with a desperate catch in her voice, "we've got to change things around here. It isn't fair to Dan, for one thing. We've got to get a girl to do the work. And to do that we'll have to rent a room."

She heard the thin figure twist impatiently.

"I've never yet been reduced to taking roomers, and I'm not going to let the neighbors begin looking down on me now."

"Now, listen, mother —"

"Go on away, Edie."

"But suppose we could get a young man, a gentleman, who would be out all but three evenings a week. I don't know, but Mr. Cameron at the store isn't satisfied where he is. He's got a dog, and they haven't any yard. We've got a yard."

"I won't be bothered with any dog," said the querulous voice, from the darkness.

With a gesture of despair the girl turned away. What was the use, anyhow? Let them go on, then, her mother and Dan. Only let them let her go on, too. She had tried her best to change herself, the house, the whole rotten mess. But they wouldn't let her.

Her mood of disgust continued the next morning. When, at eleven o'clock, Louis Akers sauntered in for the first time in days, she looked at him somberly but without disdain. Lou or somebody else, what did it matter? So long as something took her for a little while away from the sordidness of home, its stale odors, its untidiness, its querulous inmates.

"What's got into you lately, Edith?" he inquired, lowering his voice. "You used to be the best little pal ever. Now the other day, when I called up —"

"Had the headache," she said laconically. "Well?"

"Want to play around this evening?"

She hesitated. Then she remembered where Willy Cameron would be that night, and her face hardened. Had any one told Edith that she was beginning to care for the lame young man in the rear room, with his exaggerated chivalry toward women, his belief in home, and his sentimental whistling, she would have laughed. But he gave her something that the other men she knew robbed her of, a sort of self-respect. It was perhaps not so much that she cared for him, as that he enabled her to care more for herself.

But he was going to dinner with Lily Cardew.

"I might, depending on what you've got to offer."

"I've got a car now, Edith. I'm not joking. There was a lot of outside work, and the organization came over. I've been after it for six months. We can have a ride, and supper somewhere. How's the young man with the wooden leg?"

"If you want to know I'll call him out and let him tell you."

"Quick, aren't you?" He smiled down at where she stood, firmly entrenched behind a show case. "Well, don't fall in love with him. That's all. I'm a bad man when I'm jealous."

He sauntered out, leaving Edith gazing thoughtfully after him. He did not know, nor would have cared had he known, that her acceptance of his invitation was a complex of disgust of home, of the call of youth, and of the fact that Willy Cameron was dining at the Cardews that night.

Chapter XII

Howard Cardew was in his dressing room, sitting before the fire. His man had put out his dinner clothes and retired, and Howard was sitting before the fire rather listlessly.

In Grace's room, adjoining, he could hear movements and low voices. Before Lily's return, now and then when he was tired Grace and he had dined by the fire in her boudoir. It had been very restful. He was still in love with his wife, although, as in most marriages, there was one who gave more than the other. In this case it was Grace who gave, and Howard who received. But he loved her. He never thought of other women. Only his father had never let him forget her weaknesses.

Sometimes he was afraid that he was looking at Grace with his father's eyes, rather than his own.

He had put up a hard fight with his father. Not about Grace. That was over and done with, although it had been bad while it lasted. But his real struggle had been to preserve himself, to keep his faiths and his ideals, and even his personality. In the inessentials he had yielded easily, and so bought peace. Or perhaps a truce, of a sort. But for the essentials he was standing with a sort of dogged conviction that if he lowered his flag it would precipitate a crisis. He was not brilliant, but he was intelligent, progressive and kindly. He knew that his father considered him both stupid and obstinate.

There was going to be a strike. The quarrel now was between Anthony's curt "Let them strike," and his own conviction that a strike at this time might lead to even worse things. The men's demands were exorbitant. No business, no matter how big, could concede them and live. But Howard was debating another phase of the situation.

Not all the mills would go down. A careful canvass of some of the other independent concerns had shown the men eighty, ninety, even one hundred per cent, loyal. Those were the smaller plants, where there had always been a reciprocal good feeling between the owners and the men; there the men knew the owners, and the owners knew the men, who had been with them for years.

But the Cardew Mills would go down. There had been no liaison between the Cardews and the workmen. The very magnitude of the business forbade that. And for many years, too, the Cardews had shown a gross callousness to the welfare of the laborers. Long ago he had urged on his father the progressive attitude of other steel men, but Anthony had jeered, and when Howard had forced the issue and gained concessions, it was too late. The old grievances remained in too many minds. To hate the Cardews bad become a habit. Their past sins would damn them now. The strike was wrong, a wicked thing. It was without reason and without aim. The men were knocking a hole in the boat that floated them. But —

There was a tap at his door, and he called "Come in." From her babyhood Lily had had her own peculiar method of signaling that she stood without, a delicate rapid tattoo of finger nails on the panel. He watched smilingly for her entrance.

"Well!" she said. "Thank goodness you haven't started to dress. I tried to get here earlier, but my hair wouldn't go up, I want to make a good impression to-night."

"Is there a dinner on? I didn't know it."

"Not a dinner. A young man. I came to see what you are going to wear."

"Really! Well, I haven't a great variety. The ordinary dinner dress of a gentleman doesn't lend itself to any extraordinary ornamentation. If you like, I'll pin on that medal from the Iron and Steel—Who's coming, Lily?"

"Grayson says grandfather's dining out."

"I believe so."

"What a piece of luck! I mean—you know what he'd say if I asked him not to dress for dinner."

"Am I to gather that you are asking me?"

"You wouldn't mind, would you? He hasn't any evening clothes."

"Look here, Lily," said her father, sitting upright. "Who is coming here to-night? And why should he upset the habits of the entire family?"

"Willy Cameron. You know, father. And he has the queerest ideas about us. Honestly. And I want him to like us, and it's such a good chance, with grandfather out."

He ignored that.

"How about our liking him?"

"Oh, you'll like him. Everybody does. You will try to make a good impression, won't you, father?"

He got up, and resting his hands on her shoulders, smiled down into her upturned face. "I will," he said. "But I think I should tell you that your anxiety arouses deep and black suspicions in my mind. Am I to understand that you have fixed your young affections on this Willy Cameron, and that you want your family to help you in your dark designs?"

Lily laughed.

"I love him," she said. "I really do. I could listen to him for hours. But people don't want to marry Willy Cameron. They just love him."

There was born in Howard's mind a vision of a nice pink and white young man, quite sexless, whom people loved but did not dream of marrying.

"I see," he said slowly. "Like a puppy."

"Not at all like a puppy."

"I'm afraid I'm not subtle, my dear. Well, ring for Adams, and—you think he wouldn't care for the medal?"

"I think he'd love it. He'd probably think some king gave it to you. I'm sure he believes that you and grandfather habitually hobnob with kings." She turned to go out. "He doesn't approve of kings."

"You are making me extremely uneasy," was her father's shot. "I only hope I acquit myself well."

"Hurry, then. He is sure to be exactly on the hour." Howard was still smiling slightly to himself when, a half-hour later, he descended the staircase. But he had some difficulty first in reconciling his preconceived idea of Willy with the tall young man, with the faint unevenness of step, who responded to his greeting so calmly and so easily. "We are always glad to see any of Lily's friends."

"It is very good of you to let me come, sir."

Why, the girl was blind. This was a man, a fine, up-standing fellow, with a clean-cut, sensitive face, and honest, almost beautiful eyes. How did women judge men, anyhow?

And, try as he would, Howard Cardew could find no fault with Willy Cameron that night. He tried him out on a number of things. In religion, for instance, he was orthodox, although he felt that the church had not come up fully during the war.

"Religion isn't a matter only of churches any more," said Mr. Cameron. "It has to go out into the streets, I think, sir. It's a—well, Christ left the tabernacle, you remember."

That was all right. Howard felt that himself sometimes. He was a vestryman at Saint Peter's, and although he felt very devout during the service, especially during the offertory, when the music filled the fine old building, he was often conscious that he shed his spirituality at the door, when he glanced at the sky to see what were the prospects for an afternoon's golf.

In politics Willy Cameron was less satisfactory.

"I haven't decided, yet," he said. "I voted for Mr. Wilson in 1916, but although I suppose parties are necessary, I don't like to feel that I am party-bound. Anyhow, the old party lines are gone. I rather look —"

He stopped. That terrible speech of Edith Boyd's still rankled.

"Go on, Willy," said Lily. "I told them they'd love to you talk."

"That's really all, sir," said Willy Cameron, unhappily. "I am a Scot, and to start a Scot on reform is fatal."

"Ah, you believe in reform?"

"We are not doing very well as we are, sir."

"I should like extremely to know how you feel about things," said Howard, gravely.

"Only this: So long as one party is, or is considered, the representative of capital, the vested interests, and the other of labor, the great mass of the people who are neither the one nor the other cannot be adequately represented."

"And the solution?"

"Perhaps a new party. Or better still, a liberalizing of the Republican."

"Before long," said Lily suddenly, "there will be no state. There will be enough for everybody, and nobody will have too much."

Howard smiled at her indulgently.

"How do you expect to accomplish this ideal condition?"

"That's the difficulty about it," said Lily, thoughtfully. "It means a revolution. It would be peaceful, though. The thing to do is to convince people that it is simple justice, and then they will divide what they have."

"Why, Lily!" Grace's voice was anxious. "That's Socialism."

But Howard only smiled tolerantly, and changed the subject. Every one had these attacks of idealism in youth. They were the exaggerated altruism of adolescence; a part of its dreams and aspirations. He changed the subject.

"I like the boy," he said to Grace, later, over the cribbage board in the morning room. "He has character, and a queer sort of magnetism. It mightn't be a bad thing —"

Grace was counting.

"I forgot to tell you; I think she refused Pink Denslow the other day."

"I rather gathered, from the way she spoke of young Cameron, that she isn't interested there either."

"Not a bit," said Grace, complacently. "You needn't worry about him."

Howard smiled. He was often conscious that after all the years of their common life, his wife's mind and his traveled along parallel lines that never met.

Willy Cameron was extremely happy. He had brought his pipe along, although without much hope, but the moment they were settled by the library fire Lily had suggested it.

"You know you can't talk unless you have it in your hand to wave around," she said. "And I want to know such a lot of things. Where you live, and all that."

"I live in a boarding house. More house than board, really. And the work's all right. I'm going to study metallurgy some day. There are night courses at the college, only I haven't many nights."

He had lighted his pipe, and kept his eyes on it mostly, or on the fire. He was afraid to look at Lily, because there was something he could not keep out of his eyes, but must keep from her. It had been both better and worse than he had anticipated, seeing her in her home. Lily herself had not changed. She was her wonderful self, in spite of her frock and her surroundings. But the house, her people, with their ease of wealth and position, Grace's slight condescension, the elaborate simplicity of dining, the matter-of-course-ness of the service. It was not that Lily was above him. That was ridiculous. But she was far removed from him.

"There is something wrong with you, Willy," she said unexpectedly. "You are not happy, or you are not well. Which is it? You are awfully thin, for one thing."

"I'm all right," he said, evading her eyes.

"Are you lonely? I don't mean now, of course."

"Well, I've got a dog. That helps. He's a helpless sort of mutt. I carry his meat home from the shop in my pocket, and I feel like a butcher's wagon, sometimes. But he's taken a queer sort of liking to me, and he is something to talk to."

"Why didn't you bring him along?"

Dogs were forbidden in the Cardew house, by old Anthony's order, as were pipes, especially old and beloved ones, but Lily was entirely reckless.

"He did follow me. He's probably sitting on the doorstep now. I tried to send him back, but he's an obstinate little beast."

Lily got up.

"I am going to bring him in," she said. "And if you'll ring that bell we'll get him some dinner."

"I'll get him, while you ring."

Half an hour later Anthony Cardew entered his house. He had spent a miserable evening. Some young whipper snapper who employed a handful of men had undertaken to show him where he, Anthony Cardew, was a clog in the wheel of progress. Not in so many words, but he had said: "Tempora mutantur, Mr. Cardew. And the wise employer meets those changes half-way."

"You young fools want to go all the way."

"Not at all. We'll meet them half-way, and stop."

"Bah!" said Anthony Cardew, and had left the club in a temper. The club was going to the dogs, along with the rest of the world. There was only a handful of straight-thinking men like himself left in it. Lot of young cravens, letting their men dominate them and intimidate them.

So he slammed into his house, threw off his coat and hat, and-sniffed. A pungent, acrid odor was floating through a partly closed door. Anthony Cardew flung open the door and entered.

Before the fire, on a deep velvet couch, sat his granddaughter. Beside her was a thin young man in a gray suit, and the thin young man was waving an old pipe about, and saying:

"Tempora mutantur, Lily. The wise employer —"

"I am afraid, sir," said Anthony, in a terrible voice, "that you are not acquainted with the rules of my house. I object to pipes. There are cigars in the humidor behind you."

"Very sorry, Mr. Cardew," Willy Cameron explained. "I didn't know. I'll put it away, sir."

But Anthony was not listening. His eyes had traveled from an empty platter on the hearth-rug to a deep chair where Jinx, both warm and fed at the same time, and extremely distended with meat, lay sleeping. Anthony put out a hand and pressed the bell beside him.

"I want you to meet Mr. Cameron, grandfather." Lily was rather pale, but she had the Cardew poise. "He was in the camp when I was."

Grayson entered on that, however, and Anthony pointed to Jinx.

"Put that dog out," he said, and left the room, his figure rigid and uncompromising.

"Grayson," Lily said, white to the lips, "that dog is to remain here. He's perfectly quiet. And, will you find Ellen and ask her to come here?"

"Haven't I made enough trouble?" asked Willy Cameron, unhappily. "I can see her again, you know."

"She's crazy to see you, Willy. And besides —"

Grayson had gone, after a moment's hesitation.

"Don't you see?" she said. "The others have always submitted. I did, too. But I can't keep it up, Willy. I can't live here and let him treat me like that. Or my friends. I know what will happen. I'll run away, like Aunt Elinor."

"You must not do that, Lily." He was very grave.

"Why not? They think she is unhappy. She isn't. She ran away and married a man she cared about. I may call you up some day and ask you to marry me!" she added, less tensely. "You would be an awfully good husband, you know."

She looked up at him, still angry, but rather amused with this new conceit.

"Don't!"

She was startled by the look on his face.

"You see," he said painfully, "what only amuses you in that idea is-well, it doesn't amuse me, Lily."

"I only meant —" she was very uncomfortable. "You are so real and dependable and kind, and I —"

"I know what you mean. Like Jinx, there. I'm sorry! I didn't mean that. But you must not talk about marrying me unless you mean it. You see, I happen to care."

"Willy!"

"It won't hurt you to know, although I hadn't meant to tell you. And of course, you know, I am not asking you to marry me. Only I'd like you to feel that you can count on me, always. The one person a woman can count on is the man who loves her."

And after a little silence:

"You see, I know you are not in love with me. I cared from the beginning, but I always knew that."

"I wish I did." She was rather close to tears. She had not felt at all like that with Pink. But, although she knew he was suffering, his quietness deceived her. She had the theory of youth about love, that it was a violent thing, tempestuous and passionate. She thought that love demanded, not knowing that love gives first, and then asks. She could not know how he felt about his love for her, that it lay in a sort of cathedral shrine in his heart. There were holy days when saints left their niches and were shown in city streets, but until that holy day came they remained in the church.

"You will remember that, won't you?"

"I'll remember, Willy."

"I won't be a nuisance, you know. I've never had any hope, so I won't make you unhappy. And don't be unhappy about me, Lily. I would rather love you, even knowing I can't have you, than be loved by anybody else."

Perhaps, had he shown more hurt, he would have made it seem more real to her. But he was frightfully anxious not to cause her pain.

"I'm really very happy, loving you," he added, and smiled down at her reassuringly. But he had for all that a wild primitive impulse which almost overcame him for a moment, to pick her up in his arms and carry her out the door and away with him. Somewhere, anywhere. Away from that grim old house, and that despotic little man, to liberty and happiness and-William Wallace Cameron.

Ellen came in, divided between uneasiness and delight, and inquired painstakingly about his mother, and his uncle in California, and the Presbyterian minister. But she was uncomfortable and uneasy and refused to sit down, and Willy watched her furtively slipping out again with a slight frown. It was not right, somehow, this dividing of the world into classes, those who served and those who were served. But he had an idea that it was those below who made the distinction, nowadays. It was the masses who insisted on isolating the classes. They made kings, perhaps that they might some day reach up and pull them off their thrones. At the top of the stairs Ellen found Mademoiselle, who fixed her with cold eyes.

"What were you doing down there," she demanded.

"Miss Lily sent for me, to see that young man I told you about."

"How dare you go down? And into the library?"

"I've just told you," said Ellen, her face setting. "She sent for me."

"Why didn't you say you were in bed?"

"I'm no liar, Mademoiselle. Besides, I guess it's no crime to see a boy I've known all his life, and his mother and me like sisters."

"You are a fool," said Mademoiselle, and turning clumped back in her bedroom slippers to her room.

Ellen went up to her room. Heretofore she had given her allegiance to Mademoiselle and Mrs. Cardew, and in a more remote fashion, to Howard. But Ellen, crying angry tears in her small white bed that night, sensed a new division in the family, with Mademoiselle and Anthony and Howard and Grace on one side, and Lily standing alone, fighting valiantly for the right to live her own life, to receive her own friends, and the friends of her friends, even though one of these latter might be a servant in her own house.

Yet Ellen, with the true snobbishness of the servants' hall, disapproved of Lily's course while she admired it.

"But they're all against her," Ellen reflected. "The poor thing! And just because of Willy Cameron. Well, I'll stand by her, if they throw me out for it."

In her romantic head there formed strange, delightful visions. Lily eloping with Willy Cameron, assisted by herself. Lily in the little Cameron house, astounding the neighborhood with her clothes and her charm, and being sponsored by Ellen. The excitement of the village, and the visits to Ellen to learn what to wear for a first call, and were cards necessary?

Into Ellen's not very hard-working but monotonous life had comes its first dream of romance.

Chapter XIII

For three weeks Lily did not see Louis Akers, nor did she go back to the house on Cardew Way. She hated doing clandestine or forbidden things, and she was, too, determined to add nothing to the tenseness she began to realize existed at home. She went through her days, struggling to fit herself again into the old environment, reading to her mother, lending herself with assumed enthusiasm to such small gayeties as Lent permitted, and doing penance in a dozen ways for that stolen afternoon with Louis Akers.

She had been forbidden to see him again. It had come about by Grace's confession to Howard as to Lily's visit to the Doyles. He had not objected to that.

"Unless Doyle talks his rubbish to her," he said. "She said something the other night that didn't sound like her. Was any one else there?"

"An attorney named Akers," she said.

And at that Howard had scowled.

"She'd better keep away altogether," he observed, curtly. "She oughtn't to meet men like that."

"Shall I tell her?"

"I'll tell her," he said. And tell her he did, not too tactfully, and man-like shielding her by not telling her his reasons.

"He's not the sort of man I want you to know," he finished. "That ought to be sufficient. Have you seen him since?"

Lily flushed, but she did not like to lie.

"I had tea with him one afternoon. I often have tea with men, father. You know that."

"You knew I wouldn't approve, or you would have mentioned it."

Because he felt that he had been rather ruthless with her, he stopped in at the jeweler's the next morning and sent her a tiny jeweled watch. Lily was touched and repentant. She made up her mind not to see Louis Akers again, and found a certain relief in the decision. She was conscious that he had a peculiar attraction for her, a purely emotional appeal. He made her feel alive. Even when she disapproved of him, she was conscious of him. She put him resolutely out of her mind, to have him reappear in her dreams, not as a lover, but as some one dominant and insistent, commanding her to do absurd, inconsequential things.

Now and then she saw Willy Cameron, and they had gone back, apparently, to the old friendly relationship. They walked together, and once they went to the moving pictures, to Grace's horror. But there were no peanuts to eat, and instead of the jingling camp piano there was an orchestra, and it was all strangely different. Even Willy Cameron was different. He was very silent, and on the way home he did not once speak of the plain people.

Louis Akers had both written and telephoned her, but she made excuses, and did not see him, and the last time he had hung up the receiver abruptly. She felt an odd mixture of relief and regret.

Then, about the middle of April, she saw him again.

Spring was well on by that time. Before the Doyle house on Cardew Way the two horse-chestnuts were showing great red-brown buds, ready to fall into leaf with the first warm day, and Elinor, assisted by Jennie, the elderly maid, was finishing her spring house-cleaning. The Cardew mansion showed window-boxes at each window, filled by the florist with spring flowers, to be replaced later by summer ones. A potted primrose sat behind the plate glass of the Eagle Pharmacy, among packets of flower seeds and spring tonics, its leaves occasionally nibbled by the pharmacy cat, out of some atavistic craving survived through long generations of city streets.

The children's playground near the Lily furnace was ready; Howard Cardew himself had overseen the locations of the swings and chute-the-chutes. And at Friendship an army of workers was sprinkling and tamping the turf of the polo field. After two years of war, there was to be polo again that spring and early summer. The Cherry Hill Hunt team was still intact, although some of the visiting outfits had been badly shot to pieces by the war. But the war was over. It lay behind, a nightmare to be forgotten as soon as possible. It had left its train of misery and debt, but-spring had come.

On a pleasant Monday, Lily motored out to the field with Pink Denslow. It had touched her that he still wanted her, and it had offered an escape from her own worries. She was fighting a sense of failure that day. It seemed impossible to reconcile the warring elements at home. Old Anthony and his son were quarreling over the strike, and Anthony was jibing constantly at Howard over the playground. It was not so much her grandfather's irritability that depressed her as his tyranny over the household, and his attitude toward her mother roused her to bitter resentment.

The night before she had left the table after one of his scourging speeches, only to have what amounted to a scene with her mother afterward.

"But I cannot sit by while he insults you, mother."

"It is just his way. I don't mind, really. Oh, Lily, don't destroy what I have built up so carefully. It hurts your father so."

"Sometimes," Lily said slowly, "he makes me think Aunt Elinor's husband was right. He believes a lot of things —"

"What things?" Grace had asked, suspiciously.

Lily hesitated.

"Well, a sort of Socialism, for one thing, only it isn't exactly that. It's individualism, really, or I think so; the sort of thing that this house stifles." Grace was too horrified for speech. "I don't want to hurt you, mother, but don't you see? He tyrannizes over all of us, and it's bad for our souls. Why should he bellow at the servants? Or talk to you the way he did to-night?" She smiled faintly. "We're all drowning, and I want to swim, that's all. Mr. Doyle —"

"You are talking nonsense," said Grace sharply. "You have got a lot of ideas from that wretched house, and now you think they are your own. Lily, I warn you, if you insist on going back to the Doyles I shall take you abroad."

Lily turned and walked out of the room, and there was something suggestive of old Anthony in the pitch of her shoulders. Her anger did not last long, but her uneasiness persisted. Already she knew that she was older in many ways than Grace; she had matured in the past year more than her mother in twenty, and she felt rather like a woman obeying the mandates of a child.

But on that pleasant Monday she was determined to be happy.

"Old world begins to look pretty, doesn't it?" said Pink, breaking in on her thoughts.

"Lovely."

"It's not a bad place to live in, after all," said Pink, trying to cheer his own rather unhappy humor. "There is always spring to expect, when we get low in winter. And there are horses and dogs, and-and blossoms on the trees, and all that." What he meant was, "If there isn't love."

"You are perfectly satisfied with things just as they are, aren't you?" Lily asked, half enviously.

"Well, I'd change some things." He stopped. He wasn't going to go round sighing like a furnace. "But it's a pretty good sort of place. I'm for it."

"Have you sent your ponies out?"

"Only two. I want to show you one I bought from the Government almost for nothing. Remount man piped me off. Light in flesh, rather, but fast. Handy, light mouth-all he needs is a bit of training."

They had been in the open country for some time, but now they were approaching the Cardew's Friendship plant. The furnaces had covered the fields with a thin deposit of reddish ore dust. Such blighted grass as grew had already lost its fresh green, and the trees showed stunted blossoms. The one oasis of freshness was the polo field itself, carefully irrigated by underground pipes. The field, with its stables and grandstand, had been the gift of Anthony Cardew, thereby promoting much discussion with his son. For Howard had wanted the land for certain purposes of his own, to build a clubhouse for the men at the plant, with a baseball field. Finding his father obdurate in that, he had urged that the field be thrown open to the men and their families, save immediately preceding and during the polo season. But he had failed there, too. Anthony Cardew had insisted, and with some reason, that to use the grounds for band concerts and baseball games, for picnics and playgrounds, would ruin the turf for its legitimate purpose.

Howard had subsequently found other land, and out of his own private means had carried out his plans, but the location was less desirable. And he knew what his father refused to believe, that the polo ground, taking up space badly needed for other purposes, was a continual grievance.

Suddenly Pink stared ahead.

"I say," he said, "have they changed the rule about that sort of thing?"

He pointed to the field. A diamond had been roughly outlined on it with bags of sand, and a ball-game was in progress, boys playing, but a long line of men watching from the side lines.

"I don't know, but it doesn't hurt anything."

"Ruins the turf, that's all." He stopped the car and got out. "Look at this sign. It says 'ball-playing or any trespassing forbidden on these grounds.' I'll clear them off."

"I wouldn't, Pink. They may be ugly."

But he only smiled at her reassuringly, and went off. She watched him go with many misgivings, his sturdy young figure, his careful dress, his air of the young aristocrat, easy, domineering, unconsciously insolent. They would resent him, she knew, those men and boys. And after all, why should they not use the field? There was injustice in that sign.

Yet her liking and real sympathy were with Pink.

"Pink!" she called, "Come back here. Let them alone."

He turned toward her a face slightly flushed with indignation and set with purpose.

"Sorry. Can't do it, Lily. This sort of thing's got to be stopped."

She felt, rather hopelessly, that he was wrong, but that he was right, too. The grounds were private property. She sat back and watched.

Pink was angry. She could hear his voice, see his gestures. He was shooing them off like a lot of chickens, and they were laughing. The game had stopped, and the side lines were pressing forward. There was a moment's debate, with raised voices, a sullen muttering from the crowd, and the line closing into a circle. The last thing she saw before it closed was a man lunging at Pink, and his counter-feint. Then some one was down. If it was Pink he was not out, for there was fighting still going on. The laborers working on the grounds were running.

Lily stood up in the car, pale and sickened. She was only vaguely conscious of a car that suddenly left the road, and dashed recklessly across the priceless turf, but she did see, and recognize, Louis Akers as he leaped from it and flinging men this way and that disappeared into the storm center. She could hear his voice, too, loud and angry, and see the quick dispersal of the crowd. Some of the men, foreigners, passed quite near to her, and eyed her either sullenly or with mocking smiles. She was quite oblivious of them. She got out and ran with shaking knees across to where Pink lay on the grass, his profile white and sharply chiseled, with two or three men bending over him.

Pink was dead. Those brutes had killed him. Pink.

He was not dead. He was moving his arms.

Louis Akers straightened when he saw her and took off his hat.

"Nothing to worry about, Miss Cardew," he said. "But what sort of idiocy—! Hello, old man, all right now?"

Pink sat up, then rose stiffly and awkwardly. He had a cut over one eye, and he felt for his handkerchief.

"Fouled me," he said. "Filthy lot, anyhow. Wonder they didn't walk on me when I was down." He turned to the grounds-keeper, who had come up. "You ought to know better than to let those fellows cut up this turf," he said angrily. "What're you here for anyhow?"

But he was suddenly very sick. He looked at Lily, his face drawn and blanched.

"Got me right," he muttered. "I—"

"Get into my car," said Akers, not too amiably. "I'll drive you to the stables. I'll be back, Miss Cardew."

Lily went back to the car and sat down. She was shocked and startled, but she was strangely excited. The crowd had beaten Pink, but it had obeyed Louis Akers like a master. He was a man. He was a strong man. He must be built of iron. Mentally she saw him again, driving recklessly over the turf, throwing the men to right and left, hoarse with anger, tall, dominant, powerful.

It was more important that a man be a man than that he be a gentleman.

After a little he drove back across the field, sending the car forward again at reckless speed. Some vision of her grandfather, watching the machine careening over the still soft and spongy turf and leaving deep tracks behind it, made her smile. Akers leaped out.

"No need to worry about our young friend," he said cheerfully. "He is alternately being very sick at his stomach and cursing the poor working man. But I think I'd better drive you back. He'll be poor company, I'll say that."

He looked at her, his bold eyes challenging, belying the amiable gentleness of his smile.

"I'd better let him know."

"I told him. He isn't strong for me. Always hate the fellow who saves you, you know. But he didn't object."

Lily moved into his car obediently. She felt a strange inclination to do what this man wanted. Rather, it was an inability to oppose him. He went on, big, strong, and imperious. And he carried one along. It was easy and queer. But she did, unconsciously, what she had never done with Pink or any other man; she sat as far away from him on the wide seat as she could.

He noticed that, and smiled ahead, over the wheel. He had been infuriated over her avoidance of him, but if she was afraid of him—

"Bully engine in this car. Never have to change a gear."

"You certainly made a road through the field."

"They'll fix that, all right. Are you warm enough?"

"Yes, thank you."

"You have been treating me very badly, you know, Miss Cardew."

"I have been frightfully busy."

"That's not true, and you know it. You've been forbidden to see me, haven't you?"

"I have been forbidden to go back to Cardew Way."

"They don't know about me, then?"

"There isn't very much to know, is there?"

"I wish you wouldn't fence with me," he said impatiently. "I told you once I was frank. I want you to answer one question. If this thing rested with you, would you see me again?"

"I think I would, Mr. Akers," she said honestly.

Had she ever known a man like the one beside her, she would not have given him that opportunity. He glanced sharply around, and then suddenly stopped the car and turned toward her.

"I'm crazy about you, and you know it," he said. And roughly, violently, he caught her to him and kissed her again and again. Her arms were pinned to her sides, and she was helpless. After a brief struggle to free herself she merely shut her eyes and waited for him to stop.

"I'm mad about you," he whispered.

Then he freed her. Lily wanted to feel angry, but she felt only humiliated and rather soiled. There were men like that, then, men who gave way to violent impulses, who lost control of themselves and had to apologize afterwards. She hated him, but she was sorry for him, too. He would have to be so humble. She was staring ahead, white and waiting for his explanation, when he released the brake and started the car forward slowly.

"Well?" he said, with a faint smile.

"You will have to apologize for that, Mr. Akers."

"I'm damned if I will. That man back there, Denslow-he's the sort who would kiss a girl and then crawl about it afterwards. I won't. I'm not sorry. A strong man can digest his own sins. I kissed you because I wanted to. It wasn't an impulse. I meant to when we started. And you're only doing the conventional thing and pretending to be angry. You're not angry. Good God, girl, be yourself once in a while."

"I'm afraid I don't understand you." Her voice was haughty. "And I must ask you to stop the car and let me get out."

"I'll do nothing of the sort, of course. Now get this straight, Miss Cardew. I haven't done you any harm. I may have a brutal way of showing that I'm crazy about you, but it's my way. I'm a man, and I'm no hand kisser."

And when she said nothing:

"You think I'm unrestrained, and I am, in a way. But if I did what I really want to do, I'd not take you home at all. I'd steal you. You've done something to me, God knows what."

"Then I can only say I'm sorry," Lily said slowly.

She felt strangely helpless and rather maternal. With all his strength this sort of man needed to be protected from himself. She felt no answering thrill whatever to his passion, but as though, having told her he loved her, he had placed a considerable responsibility in her hands.

"I'll be good now," he said. "Mind, I'm not sorry. But I don't want to worry you."

He made no further overtures to her during the ride, but he was neither sulky nor sheepish. He feigned an anxiety as to the threatened strike, and related at great length and with extreme cleverness of invention his own efforts to prevent it.

"I've a good bit of influence with the A.F.L.," he said. "Doyle's in bad with them, but I'm still solid. But it's coming, sure as shooting. And they'll win, too."

He knew women well, and he saw that she was forgiving him. But she would not forget. He had a cynical doctrine, to the effect that a woman's first kiss of passion left an ineradicable mark on her, and he was quite certain that Lily had never been so kissed before.

Driving through the park he turned to her:

"Please forgive me," he said, his mellow voice contrite and supplicating. "You've been so fine about it that you make me ashamed."

"I would like to feel that it wouldn't happen again: That's all."

"That means you intend to see me again. But never is a long word. I'm afraid to promise. You go to my head, Lily Cardew." They were halted by the traffic, and it gave him a chance to say something he had been ingeniously formulating in his mind. "I've known lots of girls. I'm no saint. But you are different. You're a good woman. You could do anything you wanted with me, if you cared to."

And because she was young and lovely, and because he was always the slave of youth and beauty, he meant what he said. It was a lie, but he was lying to himself also, and his voice held unmistakable sincerity. But even then he was watching her, weighing the effect of his words on her. He saw that she was touched.

He was very well pleased with himself on his way home. He left the car at the public garage, and walked, whistling blithely, to his small bachelor apartment. He was a self-indulgent man, and his rooms were comfortable to the point of luxury. In the sitting room was a desk, as clean and orderly as Doyle's was untidy. Having put on his dressing gown he went to it, and with a sheet of paper before him sat for some time thinking.

He found his work irksome at times. True, it had its interest. He was the liaison between organized labor, which was conservative in the main, and the radical element, both in and out of the organization. He played a double game, and his work was always the same, to fan the discontent latently smoldering in every man's soul into a flame. And to do this he had not Doyle's fanaticism. Personally, Louis Akers found the world a pretty good place. He hated the rich because they had more than he had, but he scorned the poor because they had less. And he liked the feeling of power he had when, on the platform, men swayed to his words like wheat to a wind.

Personal ambition was his fetish, as power was Anthony Cardew's. Sometimes he walked past the exclusive city clubs, and he dreamed of a time when he, too, would have the entree to them. But time was passing. He was thirty-three years old when Jim Doyle crossed his path, and the clubs were as far away as ever. It was Doyle who found the weak place in his armor, and who taught him that when one could not rise it was possible to pull others down.

But it was Woslosky, the Americanized Pole; who had put the thing in a more appealing form.

"Our friend Doyle to the contrary," he said cynically, "we cannot hope to contend against the inevitable. The few will always govern the many, in the end. It will be the old cycle, autocracy, anarchy, and then democracy; but out of this last comes always the one man who crowns himself or is crowned. One of the people. You, or myself, it may be."

The Pole had smiled and shrugged his shoulders.

Akers did not go to work immediately. He sat for some time, a cigarette in his hand, his eyes slightly narrowed. He believed that he could marry Lily Cardew. It would take time and all his skill, but he believed he could do it. His mind wandered to Lily herself, her youth and charm, her soft red mouth, the feel of her warm young body in his arms. He brought himself up sharply. Where would such a marriage take him?

He pondered the question pro and con. On the one hand the Cardews, on the other, Doyle and a revolutionary movement. A revolution would be interesting and exciting, and there was strong in him the desire to pull down. But revolution was troublesome. It was violent and bloody. Even if it succeeded it would be years before the country would be stabilized. This other, now —

He sat low in his chair, his long legs stretched out in his favorite position, and dreamed. He would not play the fool like Doyle. He would conciliate the family. In the end he would be put up at the clubs; he might even play polo. His thoughts wandered to Pink Denslow at the polo grounds, and he grinned.

"Young fool!" he reflected. "If I can't beat his time —" He ordered dinner to be sent up, and mixed himself a cocktail, using the utmost care in its preparation. Drinking it, he eyed himself complacently in the small mirror over the mantel. Yes, life was not bad. It was damned interesting. It was a game. No, it was a race where a man could so hedge his bets that he stood to gain, whoever won.

When there was a knock at the door he did not turn. "Come in," he said.

But it was not the waiter. It was Edith Boyd. He saw her through the mirror, and so addressed her.

"Hello, sweetie," he said. Then he turned. "You oughtn't to come here, Edith. I've told you about that."

"I had to see you, Lou."

"Well, take a good look, then," he said. Her coming fitted in well with the complacence of his mood. Yes, life was good, so long as it held power, and drink, and women.

He stooped to kiss her, but although she accepted the caress, she did not return it.

"Not mad at me, Miss Boyd, are you?"

"No. Lou, I'm frightened!"

Chapter XIV

On clear Sundays Anthony Cardew played golf all day. He kept his religious observances for bad weather, but at such times as he attended service he did it with the decorum and dignity of a Cardew, who bowed to his God but to nothing else. He made the responses properly and with a certain unction, and sat during the sermon with a vigilant eye on the choir boys, who wriggled. Now and then, however, the eye wandered to the great stained glass window which was a memorial to his wife. It said beneath: "In memoriam, Lilian Lethbridge Cardew."

He thought there was too much yellow in John the Baptist. On the Sunday afternoon following her ride into the city with Louis Akers, Lily found herself alone. Anthony was golfing and Grace and Howard had motored out of town for luncheon. In a small office near the rear of the hall the second man dozed, waiting for the doorbell. There would be people in for tea later, as always on Sunday afternoons; girls and men, walking through the park or motoring up in smart cars, the men a trifle bored because they were not golfing or riding, the girls chattering about the small inessentials which somehow they made so important.

Lily was wretchedly unhappy. For one thing, she had begun to feel that Mademoiselle was exercising over her a sort of gentle espionage, and she thought her grandfather was behind it. Out of sheer rebellion she had gone again to the house on Cardew Way, to find Elinor out and Jim Doyle writing at his desk. He had received her cordially, and had talked to her as an equal. His deferential attitude had soothed her wounded pride, and she had told him something-very little-of the situation at home.

"Then you are still forbidden to come here?"

"Yes. As if what happened years ago matters now, Mr. Doyle."

He eyed her.

"Don't let them break your spirit, Lily," he had said. "Success can make people very hard. I don't know myself what success would do to me. Plenty, probably." He smiled. "It isn't the past your people won't forgive me, Lily. It's my failure to succeed in what they call success."

"It isn't that," she had said hastily. "It is-they say you are inflammatory. Of course they don't understand. I have tried to tell them, but —"

"There are fires that purify," he had said, smilingly.

She had gone home, discontented with her family's lack of vision, and with herself.

She was in a curious frame of mind. The thought of Louis Akers repelled her, but she thought of him constantly. She analyzed him clearly enough; he was not fine and not sensitive. He was not even kind. Indeed, she felt that he could be both cruel and ruthless. And if she was the first good woman he had ever known, then he must have had a hateful past.

The thought that he had kissed her turned her hot with anger and shame at such times, but the thought recurred.

Had she had occupation perhaps she might have been saved, but she had nothing to do. The house went on with its disciplined service; Lent had made its small demands as to church services, and was over. The weather was bad, and the golf links still soggy with the spring rains. Her wardrobe was long ago replenished, and that small interest gone.

And somehow there had opened a breach between herself and the little intimate group that had been hers before the war. She wondered sometimes what they would think of Louis Akers. They would admire him, at first, for his opulent good looks, but very soon they would recognize what she knew so well-the gulf between him and the men of their own world, so hard a distinction to divine, yet so real for all that. They would know instinctively that under his veneer of good manners was something coarse and crude, as she did, and they would politely snub him. She had no name and no knowledge for the urge in the man that she vaguely recognized and resented. But she had a full knowledge of the obsession he was becoming in her mind.

"If I could see him here," she reflected, more than once, "I'd get over thinking about him. It's because they forbid me to see him. It's sheer contrariness."

But it was not, and she knew it. She had never heard of his theory about the mark on a woman.

She was hating herself very vigorously on that Sunday afternoon. Mademoiselle and she had lunched alone in Lily's sitting-room, and Mademoiselle had dozed off in her chair afterwards, a novel on her knee. Lily was wandering about downstairs when the telephone rang, and she had a quick conviction that it was Louis Akers. It was only Willy Cameron, however, asking her if she cared to go for a walk.

"I've promised Jinx one all day," he explained, "and we might as well combine, if you are not busy."

She smiled at that.

"I'd love it," she said. "In the park?"

"Wait a moment." Then: "Yes, Jinx says the park is right."

His wholesome nonsense was good for her. She drew a long breath.

"You are precisely the person I need to-day," she said. "And come soon, because I shall have to be back at five."

When he came he was very neat indeed, and most scrupulous as to his heels being polished. He was also slightly breathless.

"Had to sew a button on my coat," he explained. "Then I found I'd sewed in one of my fingers and had to start all over again."

Lily was conscious of a change in him. He looked older, she thought, and thinner. His smile, when it came, was as boyish as ever, but he did not smile so much, and seen in full daylight he was shabby. He seemed totally unconscious of his clothes, however.

"What do you do with yourself, Willy?" she asked. "I mean when you are free?"

"Read and study. I want to take up metallurgy pretty soon. There's a night course at the college."

"We use metallurgists in the mill. When you are ready I know father would be glad to have you."

He flushed at that.

"Thanks," he said. "I'd rather get in, wherever I go, by what I know, and not who I know."

She felt considerably snubbed, but she knew his curious pride. After a time, while he threw a stick into the park lake and Jinx retrieved it, he said:

"What do you do with yourself these days, Lily?"

"Nothing. I've forgotten how to work, I'm afraid. And I'm not very happy, Willy. I ought to be, but I'm just-not."

"You've learned what it is to be useful," he observed gravely, "and now it hardly seems worth while just to live, and nothing else. Is that it?"

"I suppose."

"Isn't there anything you can do?"

"They won't let me work, and I hate to study."

There was a silence. Willy Cameron sat on the bench, bent and staring ahead. Jinx brought the stick, and, receiving no attention, insinuated a dripping body between his knees. He patted the dog's head absently.

"I have been thinking about the night I went to dinner at your house," he said at last. "I had no business to say what I said then. I've got a miserable habit of saying just what comes into my mind, and I've been afraid, ever since, that it would end in your not wanting to see me again. Just try to forget it happened, won't you?"

"I knew it was an impulse, but it made me very proud, Willy."

"All right," he said quietly. "And that's that. Now about your grandfather. I've had him on my mind, too. He is an old man, and sometimes they are peculiar. I am only sorry I upset him. And you are to forget that, too."

In spite of herself she laughed, rather helplessly.

"Is there anything I am to remember?"

He smiled too, and straightened himself, like a man who has got something off his chest.

"Certainly there is, Miss Cardew. Me. Myself. I want you to know that I'm around, ready to fetch and carry like Jinx here, and about as necessary, I suppose. We are a good bit alike, Jinx and I. We're satisfied with a bone, and we give a lot of affection. You won't mind a bone now and then?"

His cheerful tone reassured the girl. There was no real hurt, then.

"That's nice of you, you know."

"Well," he said slowly, "you know there are men who prefer a dream to reality. Perhaps I'm like that. Anyhow, that's enough about me. Do you know that there is a strike coming?"

"Yes. I ought to tell you, Willy. I think the men are right."

He stared at her incredulously.

"Right?" he said. "Why, my dear child, most of them want to strike about as much as I want delirium tremens. I've talked to them, and I know."

"A slave may be satisfied if he has never known freedom."

"Oh, fudge," said Willy Cameron, rudely. "Where do you get all that? You're quoting; aren't you? The strike, any strike, is an acknowledgment of weakness. It is a resort to the physical because the collective mentality of labor isn't as strong as the other side. Or labor thinks it isn't, which amounts to the same thing. And there is a fine line between the fellow who fights for a principle and the one who knocks people down to show how strong he is."

"This is a fight for a principle, Willy."

"Fine little Cardew you are!" he scoffed. "Don't make any mistake. There have been fights by labor for a principle, and the principle won, as good always wins over evil. But this is different. It's a direct play by men who don't realize what they are doing, into the hands of a lot of—well, we'll call them anarchists. It's Germany's way of winning the war. By indirection."

"If by anarchists you mean men like my uncle —"

"I do," he said grimly. "That's a family accident and you can't help it. But I do mean Doyle. Doyle and a Pole named Woslosky, and a scoundrel of an attorney here in town, named Akers, among others."

"Mr. Akers is a friend of mine, Willy."

He stared at her.

"If they have been teaching you their dirty doctrines, Lily," he said at last, "I can only tell you this. They can disguise it in all the fine terms they want. It is treason, and they are traitors. I know. I've had a talk with the Chief of Police."

"I don't believe it."

"How well do you know Louis Akers?"

"Not very well." But there were spots of vivid color flaming in her cheeks. He drew a long breath.

"I can't retract it," he said. "I didn't know, of course. Shall we start back?"

They were very silent as they walked. Willy Cameron was pained and anxious. He knew Akers' type rather than the man himself, but he knew the type well. Every village had one, the sleek handsome animal who attracted girls by sheer impudence and good humor, who made passionate, pagan love promiscuously, and put the responsibility for the misery they caused on the Creator because He had made them as they were.

He was agonized by another train of thought. For him Lily had always been something fine, beautiful, infinitely remote. There were other girls, girls like Edith Boyd, who were touched, some more, some less, with the soil of life. Even when they kept clean they saw it all about them, and looked on it with shrewd, sophisticated eyes. But Lily was-Lily. The very thought of Louis Akers looking at her as he had seen him look at Edith Boyd made him cold with rage.

"Do you mind if I say something?"

"That sounds disagreeable. Is it?"

"Maybe, but I'm going to anyhow, Lily. I don't like to think of you seeing Akers. I don't know anything against him, and I suppose if I did I wouldn't tell you. But he is not your sort."

An impulse of honesty prevailed with her.

"I know that as well as you do. I know him better than you do. But, he stands for something, at least," she added rather hotly. "None of the other men I know stand for anything very much. Even you, Willy."

"I stand for the preservation of my country," he said gravely. "I mean, I represent a lot of people who-well, who don't believe that change always means progress, and who do intend that the changes Doyle and Akers and that lot want they won't get. I don't believe-if you say you want what they want-that you know what you are talking about."

"Perhaps I am more intelligent than you think I am."

He was, of course, utterly wretched, impressed by the futility of arguing with her.

"Do your people know that you are seeing Louis Akers!"

"You are being rather solicitous, aren't you?"

"I am being rather anxious. I wouldn't dare, of course, if we hadn't been such friends. But Akers is wrong, wrong every way, and I have to tell you that, even if it means that you will never see me again. He takes a credulous girl —"

"Thank you!"

"And talks bunk to her and possibly makes love to her —"

"Haven't we had enough of Mr. Akers?" Lily asked coldly. "If you cannot speak of anything else, please don't talk."

The result of which was a frozen silence until they reached the house.

"Good-by," she said primly. "It was very nice of you to call me up. Good-by, Jinx." She went up the steps, leaving him bare-headed and rather haggard, looking after her.

He took the dog and went out into the country on foot, tramping through the mud without noticing it, and now and then making little despairing gestures. He was helpless. He had cut himself off from her like a fool. Akers. Akers and Edith Boyd. Other women. Akers and other women. And now Lily. Good God, Lily!

Jinx was tired. He begged to be carried, planting two muddy feet on his master's shabby trouser leg, and pleading with low whines. Willy Cameron stooped and, gathering up the little animal, tucked him under his arm. When it commenced to rain he put him under his coat and plunged his head through the mud and wet toward home.

Lily had entered the house in a white fury, but a moment later she was remorseful. For one thing, her own anger bewildered her. After all, he had meant well, and it was like him to be honest, even if it cost him something he valued.

She ran to the door and looked around for him, but he had disappeared. She went in again, remorseful and unhappy. What had come over her to treat him like that? He had looked almost stricken.

"Mr. Akers is calling, Miss Cardew," said the footman. "He is in the drawing-room."

Lily went in slowly.

Louis Akers had been waiting for some time. He had lounged into the drawing-room, with an ease assumed for the servant's benefit, and had immediately lighted a cigarette. That done, and the servant departed, he had carefully appraised his surroundings. He liked the stiff formality of the room. He liked the servant in his dark maroon livery. He liked the silence and decorum. Most of all, he liked himself in these surroundings. He wandered around, touching a bowl here, a vase there, eyeing carefully the ancient altar cloth that lay on a table, the old needle-work tapestry on the chairs.

He saw himself fitted into this environment, a part of it; coming down the staircase, followed by his wife, and getting into his waiting limousine; sitting at the head of his table, while the important men of the city listened to what he had to say. It would come, as sure as God made little fishes. And Doyle was a fool. He, Louis Akers, would marry Lily Cardew and block that other game. But he would let the Cardews know who it was who had blocked it and saved their skins. They'd have to receive him after that; they would cringe to him.

Then, unexpectedly, he had one of the shocks of his life. He had gone to the window and through it he saw Lily and Willy Cameron outside. He clutched at the curtain and cursed under his breath, apprehensively. But Willy Cameron did not come in; Akers watched him up the street with calculating, slightly narrowed eyes. The fact that Lily Cardew knew the clerk at the Eagle Pharmacy was an unexpected complication. His surprise was lost in anxiety. But Lily, entering the room a moment later, rather pale and unsmiling, found him facing the door, his manner easy, his head well up, and drawn to his full and rather overwhelming height. She found her poise entirely gone, and it was he who spoke first.

"I know," he said. "You didn't ask me, but I came anyhow."

She held out her hand rather primly.

"It is very good of you to come."

"Good! I couldn't stay away."

He took her outstretched hand, smiling down at her, and suddenly made an attempt to draw her to him.

"You know that, don't you?"

"Please!"

He let her go at once. He had not played his little game so long without learning its fine points. There were times to woo a woman with a strong arm, and there were other times that required other methods.

"Right-o," he said, "I'm sorry. I've been thinking about you so much that I daresay I have got farther in our friendship than I should. Do you know that you haven't been out of my mind since that ride we had together?"

"Really? Would you like some tea?"

"Thanks, yes. Do you dislike my telling you that?"

She rang the bell, and then stood facing him.

"I don't mind, no. But I am trying very hard to forget that ride, and I don't want to talk about it."

"When a beautiful thing comes into a man's life he likes to remember it."

"How can you call it beautiful?"

"Isn't it rather fine when two people, a man and a woman, suddenly find a tremendous attraction that draws them together, in spite of the fact that everything else is conspiring to keep them apart?"

"I don't know," she said uncertainly. "It just seemed all wrong, somehow."

"An honest impulse is never wrong."

"I don't want to discuss it, Mr. Akers. It is over."

While he was away from her, her attraction for him loomed less than the things she promised, of power and gratified ambition. But he found her, with her gentle aloofness, exceedingly appealing, and with the tact of the man who understands women he adapted himself to her humor.

"You are making me very unhappy; Miss Lily," he said. "If you'll only promise to let me see you now and then, I'll promise to be as mild as dish-water. Will you promise?"

She was still struggling, still remembering Willy Cameron, still trying to remember all the things that Louis Akers was not.

"I think I ought not to see you at all."

"Then," he said slowly, "you are going to cut me off from the one decent influence in my life."

She was still revolving that in her mind when tea came. Akers, having shot his bolt, watched with interest the preparation for the little ceremony, the old Georgian teaspoons, the Crown Derby cups, the bell-shaped Queen Anne teapot, beautifully chased, the old pierced sugar basin. Almost his gaze was proprietary. And he watched Lily, her casual handling of those priceless treasures, her taking for granted of service and beauty, her acceptance of quality because she had never known anything else, watched her with possessive eyes.

When the servant had gone, he said:

"You are being very nice to me, in view of the fact that you did not ask me to come. And also remembering that your family does not happen to care about me."

"They are not at home."

"I knew that, or I should not have come. I don't want to make trouble for you, child." His voice was infinitely caressing. "As it happens, I know your grandfather's Sunday habits, and I met your father and mother on the road going out of town at noon. I knew they had not come back."

"How do you know that?"

He smiled down at her. "I have ways of knowing quite a lot of things. Especially when they are as vital to me as this few minutes alone with you."

He bent toward her, as he sat behind the tea table.

"You know how vital this is to me, don't you?" he said. "You're not going to cut me off, are you?"

He stood over her, big, compelling, dominant, and put his hand under her chin.

"I am insane about you," he whispered, and waited.

Slowly, irresistibly, she lifted her face to his kiss.

Chapter XV

On the first day of May, William Wallace Cameron moved his trunk, the framed photograph of his mother, eleven books, an alarm clock and Jinx to the Boyd house. He went for two reasons. First, after his initial call at the dreary little house, he began to realize that something had to be done in the Boyd family. The second reason was his dog.

He began to realize that something had to be done in the Boyd family as soon as he had met Mrs. Boyd.

"I don't know what's come over the children," Mrs. Boyd said, fretfully. She sat rocking persistently in the dreary little parlor. Her chair inched steadily along the dull carpet, and once or twice she brought up just as she was about to make a gradual exit from the room. "They act so queer lately."

She hitched the chair into place again. Edith had gone out. It was her idea of an evening call to serve cakes and coffee, and a strong and acrid odor was seeping through the doorway. "There's Dan come home from the war, and when he gets back from the mill he just sits and stares ahead of him. He won't even talk about the war, although he's got a lot to tell."

"It takes some time for the men who were over to get settled down again, you know."

"Well, there's Edith," continued the querulous voice. "You'd think the cat had got her tongue, too. I tell you, Mr. Cameron, there are meals here when if I didn't talk there wouldn't be a word spoken."

Mr. Cameron looked up. It had occurred to him lately, not precisely that a cat had got away with Edith's tongue, but that something undeniably had got away with her cheerfulness. There were entire days in the store when she neglected to manicure her nails, and stood looking out past the fading primrose in the window to the street. But there were no longer any shrewd comments on the passers-by.

"Of course, the house isn't very cheerful," sighed Mrs. Boyd. "I'm a sick woman, Mr. Cameron. My back hurts most of the time. It just aches and aches."

"I know," said Mr. Cameron. "My mother has that, sometimes. If you like I'll mix you up some liniment, and Miss Edith can bring it to you."

"Thanks. I've tried most everything. Edith wants to rent a room, so we can keep a hired girl, but it's hard to get a girl. They want all the money on earth, and they eat something awful. That's a nice friendly dog of yours, Mr. Cameron."

It was perhaps Jinx who decided Willy Cameron. Jinx was at that moment occupying the only upholstered chair, but he had developed a strong liking for the frail little lady with the querulous voice and the shabby black dress. He had, indeed, insisted shortly after his entrance on leaping into her lap, and had thus sat for some time, completely eclipsing his hostess.

"Just let him sit," Mrs. Boyd said placidly. "I like a dog. And he can't hurt this skirt I've got on. It's on its last legs."

With which bit of unconscious humor Willy Cameron had sat down. Something warm and kindly glowed in his heart. He felt that dogs have a curious instinct for knowing what lies concealed in the human heart, and that Jinx had discovered something worth while in Edith's mother.

It was later in the evening, however, that he said, over Edith's bakery cakes and her atrocious coffee:

"If you really mean that about a roomer, I know of one." He glanced at Edith. "Very neat. Careful with matches. Hard to get up in the morning, but interesting, highly intelligent, and a clever talker. That's his one fault. When he is interested in a thing he spouts all over the place."

"Really?" said Mrs. Boyd. "Well, talk would be a change here. He sounds kind of pleasant. Who is he?"

"This paragon of beauty and intellect sits before you," said Willy Cameron.

"You'll have to excuse me. I didn't recognize you by the description," said Mrs. Boyd, unconsciously. "Well, I don't know. I'd like to have this dog around."

Even Edith laughed at that. She had been very silent all evening, sitting most of the time with her hands in her lap, and her eyes on Willy Cameron. Rather like Jinx's eyes they were, steady, unblinking, loyal, and with something else in common with Jinx which Willy Cameron never suspected.

"I wouldn't come, if I were you," she said, unexpectedly.

"Why, Edie, you've been thinking of asking him right along."

"We don't know how to keep a house," she persisted, to him. "We can't even cook-you know that's rotten coffee. I'll show you the room, if you like, but I won't feel hurt if you don't take it, I'll be worried if you do."

Mrs. Boyd watched them perplexedly as they went out, the tall young man with his uneven step, and Edith, who had changed so greatly in the last few weeks, and blew hot one minute and cold the next. Now that she had seen Willy Cameron, Mrs. Boyd wanted him to come. He would bring new life into the little house. He was cheerful. He was not glum like Dan or discontented like Edie. And the dog-She got up slowly and walked over to the chair where Jinx sat, eyes watchfully on the door.

"Nice Jinx," she said, and stroked his head with a thin and stringy hand. "Nice doggie."

She took a cake from the plate and fed it to him, bit by bit. She felt happier than she had for a long time, since her children were babies and needed her.

"I meant it," said Edith, on the stairs. "You stay away. We're a poor lot, and we're unlucky, too. Don't get mixed up with us."

"Maybe I'm going to bring you luck."

"The best luck for me would be to fall down these stairs and break my neck."

He looked at her anxiously, and any doubts he might have had, born of the dreariness, the odors of stale food and of the musty cellar below, of the shabby room she proceeded to show him, died in an impulse to somehow, some way, lift this small group of people out of the slough of despondency which seemed to be engulfing them all.

"Why, what's the matter with the room?" he said. "Just wait until I've got busy in it! I'm a paper hanger and a painter, and —"

"You're a dear, too," said Edith.

So on the first of May he moved in, and for some evenings Political Economy and History and Travel and the rest gave way to anxious cuttings and fittings of wall paper, and a pungent odor of paint. The old house took on new life and activity, the latter sometimes pernicious, as when Willy Cameron fell down the cellar stairs with a pail of paint in his hand, or Dan, digging up some bricks in the back yard for a border the seeds of which were already sprouting in a flat box in the kitchen, ran a pickaxe into his foot.

Some changes were immediate, such as the white-washing of the cellar and the unpainted fence in the yard, where Willy Cameron visualized, later on, great draperies of morning glories. He papered the parlor, and coaxed Mrs. Boyd to wash the curtains, although she protested that, with the mill smoke, it was useless labor.

But there were some changes that he knew only time would effect. Sometimes he went to his bed worn out both physically and spiritually, as though the burden of lifting three life-sodden souls was too much. Not that he thought of that, however. What he did know was that the food was poor. No servant had been found, and years of lack of system had left Mrs. Boyd's mind confused and erratic. She would spend hours concocting expensive desserts, while the vegetables boiled dry and scorched and meat turned to leather, only to bring pridefully to the table some flavorless mixture garnished according to a picture in the cook book, and totally unedible.

She would have ambitious cleaning days, too, starting late and leaving off with beds unmade to prepare the evening meal. Dan, home from the mill and newly adopting Willy Cameron's system of cleaning up for supper, would turn sullen then, and leave the moment the meal was over.

"Hell of a way to live," he said once. "I'd get married, but how can a fellow know whether a girl will make a home for him or give him this? And then there would be babies, too."

The relations between Dan and Edith were not particularly cordial. Willy Cameron found their bickering understandable enough, but he was puzzled, sometimes, to find that Dan was surreptitiously watching his sister. Edith was conscious of it, too, and one evening she broke into irritated speech.

"I wish you'd quit staring at me, Dan Boyd."

"I was wondering what has come over you," said Dan, ungraciously. "You used to be a nice kid. Now you're an angel one minute and a devil the next."

Willy spoke to him that night when they were setting out rows of seedlings, under the supervision of Jinx.

"I wouldn't worry her, Dan," he said; "it is the spring, probably. It gets into people, you know. I'm that way myself. I'd give a lot to be in the country just now."

Dan glanced at him quickly, but whatever he may have had in his mind, he said nothing just then. However, later on he volunteered:

"She's got something on her mind. I know her. But I won't have her talking back to mother."

A week or so after Willy Cameron had moved, Mr. Hendricks rang the bell of the Boyd house, and then, after his amiable custom, walked in.

"Oh, Cameron!" he bawled.

"Upstairs," came Willy Cameron's voice, somewhat thickened with carpet tacks. So Mr. Hendricks climbed part of the way, when he found his head on a level with that of the young gentleman he sought, who was nailing a rent in the carpet.

"Don't stop," said Mr. Hendricks. "Merely friendly call. And for heaven's sake don't swallow a tack, son. I'm going to need you."

"Whaffor?" inquired Willy Cameron, through his nose.

"Don't know yet. Make speeches, probably. If Howard Cardew, or any Cardew, thinks he's going to be mayor of this town, he's got to think again."

"I don't give a tinker's dam who's mayor of this town, so long as he gives it honest government."

"That's right," said Mr. Hendricks approvingly. "Old Cardew's been running it for years, and you could put all the honest government he's given us in a hollow tooth. If you'll stop that hammering, I'd like to make a proposition to you."

Willy Cameron took an admiring squint at his handiwork.

"Sorry to refuse you, Mr. Hendricks, but I don't want to be mayor."

Mr. Hendricks chuckled, as Willy Cameron led the way to his room. He wandered around the room while Cameron opened a window and slid the dog off his second chair.

"Great snakes!" he said. "Spargo's Bolshevism! Political Economy, History of—. What are you planning to be? President?"

"I haven't decided yet. It's a hard job, and mighty thankless. But I won't be your mayor, even for you."

Mr. Hendricks sat down.

"All right," he said. "Of course if you'd wanted it!" He took two large cigars from the row in his breast pocket and held one out, but Willy Cameron refused it and got his pipe.

"Well?" he said.

Mr. Hendrick's face became serious and very thoughtful. "I don't know that I have ever made it clear to you, Cameron," he said, "but I've got a peculiar feeling for this city. I like it, the way some people like their families. It's —well, it's home to me, for one thing. I like to go out in the evenings and walk around, and I say to myself: 'This is my town.' And we, it and me, are sending stuff all over the world. I like to think that somewhere, maybe in China, they are riding on our rails and fighting with guns made from our steel. Maybe you don't understand that."

"I think I do."

"Well, that's the way I feel about it, anyhow. And this Bolshevist stuff gets under my skin. I've got a home and a family here. I started in to work when I was thirteen, and all I've got I've made and saved right here. It isn't much, but it's mine."

Willy Cameron was lighting his pipe. He nodded. Mr. Hendricks bent forward and pointed a finger at him.

"And to govern this city, who do you think the labor element is going to put up and probably elect? We're an industrial city, son, with a big labor vote, and if it stands together-they're being swindled into putting up as an honest candidate one of the dirtiest radicals in the country. That man Akers."

He got up and closed the door.

"I don't want Edith to hear me," he said. "He's a friend of hers. But he's a bad actor, son. He's wrong with women, for one thing, and when I think that all he's got to oppose him is Howard Cardew —" Mr. Hendricks got up, and took a nervous turn about the room.

"Maybe you know that Cardew has a daughter?"

"Yes."

"Well, I hear a good many things, one way and another, and my wife likes a bit of gossip. She knows them both by sight, and she ran into them one day in the tea room of the Saint Elmo, sitting in a corner, and the girl had her back to the room. I don't like the look of that, Cameron."

Willy Cameron got up and closed the window. He stood there, with his back to the light, for a full minute. Then:

"I think there must be some mistake about that, Mr. Hendricks. I have met her. She isn't the sort of girl who would do clandestine things."

Mr. Hendricks looked up quickly. He had made it his business to study men, and there was something in Willy Cameron's voice that caught his attention, and turned his shrewd mind to speculation.

"Maybe," he conceded. "Of course, anything a Cardew does is likely to be magnified in this town. If she's as keen as the men in her family, she'll get wise to him pretty soon." Willy Cameron came back then, but Mr. Hendricks kept his eyes on the tip of his cigar.

"We've got to lick Cardew," he said, "but I'm cursed if I want to do it with Akers."

When there was no comment, he looked up. Yes, the boy had had a blow. Mr. Hendricks was sorry. If that was the way the wind blew it was hopeless. It was more than that; it was tragic.

"Sorry I said anything, Cameron. Didn't know you knew her."

"That's all right. Of course I don't like to think she is being talked about."

"The Cardews are always being talked about. You couldn't drop her a hint, I suppose?"

"She knows what I think about Louis Akers."

He made a violent effort and pulled himself together. "So it is Akers and Howard Cardew, and one's a knave and one's a poor bet."

"Right," said Mr. Hendricks. "And one's Bolshevist, if I know anything, and the other is capital, and has about as much chance as a rich man to get through the eye of a needle."

Which was slightly mixed, owing to a repressed excitement now making itself evident in Mr. Hendricks's voice.

"Why not run an independent candidate?" Willy Cameron asked quietly. "I've been shouting about the plain people. Why shouldn't they elect a mayor? There is a lot of them."

"That's the talk," said Mr. Hendricks, letting his excitement have full sway. "They could. They could run this town and run it right, if they'd take the trouble. Now look here, son, I don't usually talk about myself, but—I'm honest. I don't say I wouldn't get off a street-car without paying my fare if the conductor didn't lift it! But I'm honest. I don't lie. I keep my word. And I live clean-which you can't say for Lou Akers. Why shouldn't I run on an independent ticket? I mightn't be elected, but I'd make a damned good try."

He stood up, and Willy Cameron rose also and held out his hand.

"I don't know that my opinion is of any value, Mr. Hendricks. But I hope you get it, and I think you have a good chance. If I can do anything—"

"Do anything! What do you suppose I came here for? You're going to elect me. You're going to make speeches and kiss babies, and tell the ordinary folks they're worth something after all. You got me started on this thing, and now you've got to help me out."

The future maker of mayors here stepped back in his amazement, and Jinx emitted a piercing howl. When peace was restored the F.M. of M. had got his breath, and he said:

"I couldn't remember my own name before an audience, Mr. Hendricks."

"You're fluent enough in that back room of yours."

"That's different."

"The people we're going after don't want oratory. They want good, straight talk, and a fellow behind it who doesn't believe the country's headed straight for perdition. We've had enough calamity bowlers. You've got the way out. The plain people. The hope of the nation. And, by God, you love your country, and not for what you can get out of it. That's a thing a fellow's got to have inside him. He can't pretend it and get it over."

In the end the F.M. of M. capitulated.

It was late when Mr. Hendricks left. He went away with all the old envelopes in his pockets covered with memoranda.

"Just wait a minute, son," he would say. "I've got to make some speeches myself. Repeat that, now. 'Sins of omission are as great, even greater than sins of commission. The lethargic citizen throws open the gates to revolution.' How do you spell 'lethargic'?"

But it was not Hendricks and his campaign that kept the F.M. of M. awake until dawn. He sat in front of his soft coal fire, and when it died to gray-white ash he still sat there, unconscious of the chill of the spring night. Mostly he thought of Lily, and of Louis Akers, big and handsome, of his insolent eyes and his self-indulgent mouth. Into that curious whirlpool that is the mind came now and then other visions: His mother asleep in her chair; the men in the War Department who had turned him down; a girl at home who had loved him, and made him feel desperately unhappy because he could not love her in return. Was love always like that? If it was what He intended, why was it so often without reciprocation?

He took to walking about the room, according to his old habit, and obediently Jinx followed him.

It was four by his alarm clock when Edith knocked at his door. She was in a wrapper flung over her nightgown, and with her hair flying loose she looked childish and very small.

"I wish you would go to bed," she said, rather petulantly. "Are you sick, or anything?"

"I was thinking, Edith. I'm sorry. I'll go at once. Why aren't you asleep?"

"I don't sleep much lately." Their voices were cautious. "I never go to sleep until you're settled down, anyhow."

"Why not? Am I noisy?"

"It's not that."

She went away, a drooping, listless figure that climbed the stairs slowly and left him in the doorway, puzzled and uncomfortable.

At six that morning Dan, tip-toeing downstairs to warm his left-over coffee and get his own breakfast, heard a voice from Willy Cameron's room, and opened the door. Willy Cameron was sitting up in bed with his eyes closed and his arms extended, and was concluding a speech to a dream audience in deep and oratorical tones.

"By God, it is time the plain people know their power."

Dan grinned, and, his ideas of humor being rather primitive, he edged his way into the room and filled the orator's sponge with icy water from the pitcher.

"All right, old top," he said, "but it is also time the plain people got up."

Then he flung the sponge and departed with extreme expedition.

Chapter XVI

It was not until a week had passed after Louis Akers' visit to the house that Lily's family learned of it.

Lily's state of mind during that week had been an unhappy one. She magnified the incident until her nerves were on edge, and Grace, finding her alternating between almost demonstrative affection and strange aloofness, was bewildered and hurt. Mademoiselle watched her secretly, shook her head, and set herself to work to find out what was wrong. It was, in the end, Mademoiselle who precipitated the crisis.

Lily had not intended to make a secret of the visit, but as time went on she found it increasingly difficult to tell about it. She should, she knew, have spoken at once, and it would be hard to explain why she had delayed.

She meant to go to her father with it. It was he who had forbidden her to see Akers, for one thing. And she felt nearer to her father than to her mother, always. Since her return she had developed an almost passionate admiration for Howard, founded perhaps on her grandfather's attitude toward him. She was strongly partizan, and she watched her father, day after day, fighting his eternal battles with Anthony, sometimes winning, often losing, but standing for a principle like a rock while the seas of old Anthony's wrath washed over and often engulfed him.

She was rather wistful those days, struggling with her own perplexities, and blindly reaching out for a hand to help her. But she could not bring herself to confession. She would wander into her father's dressing-room before she went to bed, and, sitting on the arm of his deep chair, would try indirectly to get him to solve the problems that were troubling her. But he was inarticulate and rather shy with her. He had difficulty, sometimes, after her long absence at school and camp, in realizing her as the little girl who had once begged for his neckties to make into doll frocks.

Once she said:

"Could you love a person you didn't entirely respect, father?"

"Love is founded on respect, Lily."

She pondered that. She felt that he was wrong.

"But it does happen, doesn't it?" she had persisted.

He had been accustomed to her searchings for interesting abstractions for years. She used to talk about religion in the same way. So he smiled and said:

"There is a sort of infatuation that is based on something quite different."

"On what?"

But he had rather floundered there. He could not discuss physical attraction with her.

"We're getting rather deep for eleven o'clock at night, aren't we?"

After a short silence:

"Do you mind speaking about Aunt Elinor, father?"

"No, dear. Although it is rather a painful subject."

"But if she is happy, why is it painful?"

"Well, because Doyle is the sort of man he is."

"You mean-because he is unfaithful to her? Or was?"

He was very uncomfortable.

"That is one reason for it, of course. There are others."

"But if he is faithful to her now, father? Don't you think, whatever a man has been, if he really cares for a woman it makes him over?"

"Sometimes, not always." The subject was painful to him. He did not want his daughter to know the sordid things of life. But he added, gallantly: "Of course a good woman can do almost anything she wants with a man, if he cares for her."

She lay awake almost all night, thinking that over.

On the Sunday following Louis Akers' call Mademoiselle learned of it, by the devious route of the servants' hall, and she went to Lily at once, yearning and anxious, and in her best lace collar. She needed courage, and to be dressed in her best gave her moral strength.

"It is not," she said, "that they wish to curtail your liberty, Lily. But to have that man come here, when he knows he is not wanted, to force himself on you —"

"I need not have seen him. I wanted to see him."

Mademoiselle waved her hands despairingly.

"If they find it out!" she wailed.

"They will. I intend to tell them."

But Mademoiselle made her error there. She was fearful of Grace's attitude unless she forewarned her, and Grace, frightened, immediately made it a matter of a family conclave. She had not intended to include Anthony, but he came in on an excited speech from Howard, and heard it all.

The result was that instead of Lily going to them with her confession, she was summoned, to find her family a unit for once and combined against her. She was not to see Louis Akers again, or the Doyles.

They demanded a promise, but she refused. Yet even then, standing before them, forced to a defiance she did not feel, she was puzzled as well as angry. They were wrong, and yet in some strange way they were right, too. She was Cardew enough to get their point of view. But she was Cardew enough, too, to defy them.

She did it rather gently.

"You must understand," she said, her hands folded in front of her, "that it is not so much that I care to see the people you are talking about. It is that I feel I have the right to choose my own friends."

"Friends!" sneered old Anthony. "A third-rate lawyer, a —"

"That is not the point, grandfather. I went away to school when I was a little girl. I have been away for five years. You cannot seem to realize that I am a woman now, not a child. You bring me in here like a bad child."

In the end old Anthony had slammed out of the room. There were arguments after that, tears on Grace's part, persuasion on Howard's; but Lily had frozen against what she considered their tyranny, and Howard found in her a sort of passive resistance, that drove him frantic.

"Very well," he said finally. "You have the arrogance of youth, and its cruelty, Lily. And you are making us all suffer without reason."

"Don't you think I might say that too, father?"

"Are you in love with this man?"

"I have only seen him four times. If you would give me some reasons for all this fuss —"

"There are things I cannot explain to you. You wouldn't understand."

"About his moral character?"

Howard was rather shocked. He hesitated:

"Yes."

"Will you tell me what they are?"

"Good heavens, no!" he exploded. "The man's a radical, too. That in itself ought to be enough."

"You can't condemn a man for his political opinions."

"Political opinions!"

"Besides," she said, looking at him with her direct gaze, "isn't there some reason in what the radicals believe, father? Maybe it is a dream that can't come true, but it is rather a fine dream, isn't it?"

It was then that Howard followed his father's example, and flung out of the room.

After that Lily went, very deliberately and without secrecy, to the house on Cardew Way. She found a welcome there, not so marked on her Aunt Elinor's part as on Doyle's, but a welcome. She found approval, too, where at home she had only suspicion and a solicitude based on anxiety. She found a clever little circle there, and sometimes a cultured one; underpaid, disgruntled, but brilliant professors from the college, a journalist or two, a city councilman, even prosperous merchants, and now and then strange bearded foreigners who were passing through the city and who talked brilliantly of the vision of Lenine and the future of Russia.

She learned that the true League of Nations was not a political alliance, but a union of all the leveled peoples of the world. She had no curiosity as to how this leveling was to be brought about. All she knew was that these brilliant dreamers made her welcome, and that instead of the dinner chat at home, small personalities, old Anthony's comments on his food, her father's heavy silence, here was world talk, vast in its scope, idealistic, intoxicating.

Almost always Louis Akers was there; it pleased her to see how the other men listened to him, deferred to his views, laughed at his wit. She did not know the care exercised in selecting the groups she was to meet, the restraints imposed on them. And she could not know that from her visits the Doyle establishment was gaining a prestige totally new to it, an almost respectability.

Because of those small open forums, sometimes noted in the papers, those innocuous gatherings, it was possible to hold in that very room other meetings, not open and not innocuous, where practical plans took the place of discontented yearnings, and where the talk was more often of fighting than of brotherhood.

She was, by the first of May, frankly infatuated with Louis Akers, yet with a curious knowledge that what she felt was infatuation only. She would lie wide-eyed at night and rehearse painfully the weaknesses she saw so clearly in him. But the next time she saw him she would yield to his arms, passively but without protest. She did not like his caresses, but the memory of them thrilled her.

She was following the first uncurbed impulse of her life. Guarded and more or less isolated from other youth, she had always lived a strong inner life, purely mental, largely interrogative. She had had strong childish impulses, sometimes of pure affection, occasionally of sheer contrariness, but always her impulses had been curbed.

"Do be a little lady," Mademoiselle would say.

She had got, somehow, to feel that impulse was wrong. It ranked with disobedience. It partook of the nature of sin. People who did wicked things did them on impulse, and were sorry ever after; but then it was too late.

As she grew older, she added something to that. Impulses of the mind led to impulses of the body, and impulse was wrong. Passion was an impulse of the body. Therefore it was sin. It was the one sin one could not talk about, so one was never quite clear about it. However, one thing seemed beyond dispute; it was predominatingly a masculine wickedness. Good women were beyond and above it, its victims sometimes, like those girls at the camp, or its toys, like the sodden creatures in the segregated district who hung, smiling their tragic smiles, around their doorways in the late afternoons.

But good women were not like that. If they were, then they were not good. They did not lie awake remembering the savage clasp of a man's arms, knowing all the time that this was not love, but something quite different. Or if it was love, that it was painful and certainly not beautiful.

Sometimes she thought about Willy Cameron. He had had very exalted ideas about love. He used to be rather oratorical about it.

"It's the fundamental principle of the universe," he would say, waving his pipe wildly. "But it means suffering, dear child. It feeds on martyrdom and fattens on sacrifice. And as the h.c. of l. doesn't affect either commodity, it lives forever."

"What does it do, Willy, if it hasn't any martyrdom and sacrifice to feed on? Do you mean to say that when it is returned and everybody is happy, it dies?"

"Practically," he had said. "It then becomes domestic contentment, and expresses itself in the shape of butcher's bills and roast chicken on Sundays."

But that had been in the old care-free days, before Willy had thought he loved her, and before she had met Louis.

She made a desperate effort one day to talk to her mother. She wanted, somehow, to be set right in her own eyes. But Grace could not meet her even half way; she did not know anything about different sorts of love, but she did know that love was beautiful, if you met the right man and married him. But it had to be some one who was your sort, because in the end marriage was only a sort of glorified companionship.

The moral in that, so obviously pointed at Louis Akers, invalidated the rest of it for Lily.

She was in a state of constant emotional excitement by that time, and it was only a night or two after that she quarreled with her grandfather. There had been a dinner party, a heavy, pompous affair, largely attended, for although spring was well advanced, the usual May hegira to the country or the coast had not yet commenced. Industrial conditions in and around the city were too disturbed for the large employers to get away, and following Lent there had been a sort of sporadic gayety, covering a vast uneasiness. There was to be no polo after all.

Lily, doing her best to make the dinner a success, found herself contrasting it with the gatherings at the Doyle house, and found it very dull. These men, with their rigidity of mind, invited because they held her grandfather's opinions, or because they kept their own convictions to themselves, seemed to her of a bygone time. She did not see in them a safe counterpoise to a people which in its reaction from the old order, was ready to swing to anything that was new. She saw only a dozen or so elderly gentlemen, immaculate and prosperous, peering through their glasses after a world which had passed them by.

They were very grave that night. The situation was serious. The talk turned inevitably to the approaching strike, and from that to a possible attempt on the part of the radical element toward violence. The older men pooh-poohed that, but the younger ones were uncertain. Isolated riotings, yes. But a coordinated attempt against the city, no. Labour was greedy, but it was law-abiding. Ah, but it was being fired by incendiary literature. Then what were the police doing? They were doing everything. They were doing nothing. The governor was secretly a radical. Nonsense. The governor was saying little, but was waiting and watching. A general strike was only another word for revolution. No. It would be attempted, perhaps, but only to demonstrate the solidarity of labor.

After a time Lily made a discovery. She found that even into that carefully selected gathering had crept a surprising spirit, based on the necessity for concession; a few men who shared her father's convictions, and went even further. One or two, even, who, cautiously for fear of old Anthony's ears, voiced a belief that before long invested money would be given a fixed return, all surplus profits to be divided among the workers, the owners and the government.

"What about the lean years?" some one asked.

The government's share of all business was to form a contingent fund for such emergencies, it seemed.

Lily listened attentively. Was it because they feared that if they did not voluntarily divide their profits they would be taken from them? Enough for all, and to none too much. Was that what they feared? Or was it a sense of justice, belated but real?

She remembered something Jim Doyle had said:

"Labor has learned its weakness alone, its strength united. But capital has not learned that lesson. It will not take a loss for a principle. It will not unite. It is suspicious and jealous, so it fights its individual battles alone, and loses in the end."

But then to offset that there was something Willy Cameron had said one day, frying dough-nuts for her with one hand, and waving the fork about with the other.

"Don't forget this, oh representative of the plutocracy," he had said. "Capital has its side, and a darned good one, too. It's got a sense of responsibility to the country, which labor may have individually but hasn't got collectively."

These men at the table were grave, burdened with responsibility. Her father. Even her grandfather. It was no longer a question of profit. It was a question of keeping the country going. They were like men forced to travel, and breasting a strong head wind. There were some there who would turn, in time, and travel with the gale. But there were others like her grandfather, obstinate and secretly frightened, who would refuse. Who would, to change the figure, sit like misers over their treasure, an eye on the window of life for thieves.

She went upstairs, perplexed and thoughtful. Some time later she heard the family ascending, the click of her mother's high heels on the polished wood of the staircase, her father's sturdy tread, and a moment or two later her grandfather's slow, rather weary step. Suddenly she felt sorry for him, for his age, for his false gods of power and pride, for the disappointment she was to him. She flung open her door impulsively and confronted him.

"I just wanted to say good-night, grandfather," she said breathlessly. "And that I am sorry."

"Sorry for what?"

"Sorry —" she hesitated. "Because we see things so differently."

Lily was almost certain that she caught a flash of tenderness in his eyes, and certainly his voice had softened.

"You looked very pretty to-night," he said. But he passed on, and she had again the sense of rebuff with which he met all her small overtures at that time. However, he turned at the foot of the upper flight.

"I would like to talk to you, Lily. Will you come upstairs?"

She had been summoned before to those mysterious upper rooms of his, where entrance was always by request, and generally such requests presaged trouble. But she followed him light-heartedly enough then. His rare compliment had pleased and touched her.

The lamp beside his high-backed, almost throne-like chair was lighted, and in the dressing-room beyond his valet was moving about, preparing for the night. Anthony dismissed the man, and sat down under the lamp.

"You heard the discussion downstairs, to-night, Lily. Personally I anticipate no trouble, but if there is any it may be directed at this house." He smiled grimly. "I cannot rely on my personal popularity to protect me, I fear. Your mother obstinately refuses to leave your father, but I have decided to send you to your grand-aunt Caroline."

"Aunt Caroline! She doesn't care for me, grandfather. She never has."

"That is hardly pertinent, is it? The situation is this: She intends to open the Newport house early in June, and at my request she will bring you out there. Next fall we will do something here; I haven't decided just what."

There was a sudden wild surge of revolt in Lily. She hated Newport. Grand-aunt Caroline was a terrible person. She was like Anthony, domineering and cruel, and with even less control over her tongue.

"I need not point out the advantages of the plan," said Anthony suavely. "There may be trouble here, although I doubt it. But in any event you will have to come out, and this seems an excellent way."

"Is it a good thing to spend a lot of money now, grandfather, when there is so much discontent?"

Old Anthony had a small jagged vein down the center of his forehead, and in anger or his rare excitements it stood out like a scar. Lily saw it now, but his voice was quiet enough.

"I consider it vitally important to the country to continue its social life as before the war."

"You mean, to show we are not frightened?"

"Frightened! Good God, nobody's frightened. It will take more than a handful of demagogues to upset this government. Which brings me to a subject you insist on reopening, by your conduct. I have reason to believe that you are still going to that man's house."

He never called Doyle by name if he could avoid it.

"I have been there several times."

"After you were forbidden?"

His tone roused every particle of antagonism in her. She flushed.

"Perhaps because I was forbidden," she said, slowly. "Hasn't it occurred to you that I may consider your attitude very unjust?"

If she looked for an outburst from him it did not come. He stood for a moment, deep in thought.

"You understand that this Doyle once tried to assassinate me?"

"I know that he tried to beat you, grandfather. I am sorry, but that was long ago. And there was a reason for it, wasn't there?"

"I see," he said, slowly. "What you are conveying to me, not too delicately, is that you have definitely allied yourself with my enemies. That, here in my own house, you intend to defy me. That, regardless of my wishes or commands, while eating my food, you purpose to traffic with a man who has sworn to get me, sooner or later. Am I correct?"

"I have only said that I see no reason why I should not visit Aunt Elinor."

"And that you intend to. Do I understand also that you refuse to go to Newport?"

"I daresay I shall have to go, if you send me. I don't want to go."

"Very well. I am glad we have had this little talk. It makes my own course quite plain. Good-night."

He opened the door for her and she went out and down the stairs. She felt very calm, and as though something irrevocable had happened. With her anger at her grandfather there was mixed a sort of pity for him, because she knew that nothing he could do would change the fundamental situation. Even if he locked her up, and that was possible, he would know that he had not really changed things, or her. She felt surprisingly strong. All these years that she had feared him, and yet when it came to a direct issue, he was helpless! What had he but his wicked tongue, and what did that matter to deaf ears?

She found her maid gone, and Mademoiselle waiting to help her undress. Mademoiselle often did that. It made her feel still essential in Lily's life.

"A long seance!" she said. "Your mother told me to-night. It is Newport?"

"He wants me to go. Unhook me, Mademoiselle, and then run off and go to bed. You ought not to wait up like this."

"Newport!" said Mademoiselle, deftly slipping off the white and silver that was Lily's gown. "It will be wonderful, dear. And you will be a great success. You are very beautiful."

"I am not going to Newport, Mademoiselle."

Mademoiselle broke into rapid expostulation, in French. Every girl wanted to make her debut at Newport. Here it was all industry, money, dirt. Men who slaved in offices daily. At Newport was gathered the real leisure class of America, those who knew how to play, who lived. But Lily, taking off her birthday pearls before the mirror of her dressing table, only shook her head.

"I'm not going," she said. "I might as well tell you, for you'll hear about it later. I have quarreled with him, very badly. I think he intends to lock me up."

"C'est impossible!" cried Mademoiselle.

But a glance at Lily's set face in the mirror told her it was true.

She went away very soon, sadly troubled. There were bad times coming. The old peaceful quiet days were gone, for age and obstinacy had met youth and the arrogance of youth, and it was to be battle.

Chapter XVII

But there was a truce for a time. Lily came and went without interference, and without comment. Nothing more was said about Newport. She motored on bright days to the country club, lunched and played golf or tennis, rode along the country lanes with Pink Denslow, accepted such invitations as came her way cheerfully enough but without enthusiasm, and was very gentle to her mother. But Mademoiselle found her tense and restless, as though she were waiting.

And there were times when she disappeared for an hour or two in the afternoons, proffering no excuses, and came back flushed, and perhaps a little frightened. On the evenings that followed those small excursions she was particularly gentle to her mother. Mademoiselle watched and waited for the blow she feared was about to fall. She felt sure that the girl was seeing Louis Akers, and that she would ultimately marry him. In her despair she fell back on Willy Cameron and persuaded Grace to invite him to dinner. It was meant to be a surprise for Lily, but she had telephoned at seven o'clock that she was dining at the Doyles'.

It was that evening that Willy Cameron learned that Mr. Hendricks had been right about Lily. He and Grace dined alone, for Howard was away at a political conference, and Anthony had dined at his club. And in the morning room after dinner Grace found herself giving him her confidence.

"I have no right to burden you with our troubles, Mr. Cameron," Grace said, "but she is so fond of you, and she has great respect for your judgment. If you could only talk to her about the anxiety she is causing. These Doyles, or rather Mr. Doyle-the wife is Mr. Cardew's sister-are putting all sorts of ideas into her head. And she has met a man there, a Mr. Akers, and —I'm afraid she thinks she is in love with him, Mr. Cameron."

He met her eyes gravely.

"Have you tried not forbidding her to go to the Doyles?"

"I have forbidden her nothing. It is her grandfather."

"Then it seems to be Mr. Cardew who needs to be talked to, doesn't it?" he said. "I wouldn't worry too much, Mrs. Cardew. And don't hold too tight a rein."

He was very down-hearted when he left. Grace's last words placed a heavy burden on him.

"I simply feel," she said, "that you can do more with her than we can, and that if something isn't done she will ruin her life. She is too fine and wonderful to have her do that."

To picture Lily as willfully going her own gait at that period would be most unfair. She was suffering cruelly; the impulse that led her to meet Louis Akers against her family's wishes was irresistible, but there was a new angle to her visits to the Doyle house. She was going there now, not so much because she wished to go, as because she began to feel that her Aunt Elinor needed her.

There was something mysterious about her Aunt Elinor, mysterious and very sad. Even her smile had pathos in it, and she was smiling less and less. She sat in those bright little gatherings, in them but not of them, unbrilliant and very quiet. Sometimes she gave Lily the sense that like Lily herself she was waiting. Waiting for what?

Lily had a queer feeling too, once or twice, that Elinor was afraid. But again, afraid of what? Sometimes she wondered if Elinor Doyle was afraid of her husband; certainly there were times, when they were alone, when he dropped his unctuous mask and held Elinor up to smiling contempt.

"You can see what a clever wife I have," he said once. "Sometimes I wonder, Elinor, how you have lived with me so long and absorbed so little of what really counts."

"Perhaps the difficulty," Elinor had said quietly, "is because we differ as to what really counts."

Lily brought Elinor something she needed, of youth and irresponsible chatter, and in the end the girl found the older woman depending on her. To cut her off from that small solace was unthinkable. And then too she formed Elinor's sole link with her former world, a world of dinners and receptions, of clothes and horses and men who habitually dressed for dinner, of the wealth and panoply of life. A world in which her interest strangely persisted.

"What did you wear at the country club dance last night?" she would ask.

"A rose-colored chiffon over yellow. It gives the oddest effect, like an Ophelia rose."

Or:

"At the Mainwarings? George or Albert?"

"The Alberts."

"Did they ever have any children?"

One day she told her about not going to Newport, and was surprised to see Elinor troubled.

"Why won't you go? It is a wonderful house."

"I don't care to go away, Aunt Nellie." She called her that sometimes.

Elinor had knitted silently for a little. Then:

"Do you mind if I say something to you?"

"Say anything you like, of course."

"I just-Lily, don't see too much of Louis Akers. Don't let him carry you off your feet. He is good-looking, but if you marry him, you will be terribly unhappy."

"That isn't enough to say, Aunt Nellie," she said gravely. "You must have a reason."

Elinor hesitated.

"I don't like him. He is a man of very impure life."

"That's because he has never known any good women." Lily rose valiantly to his defense, but the words hurt her. "Suppose a good woman came into his life? Couldn't she change him?"

"I don't know," Elinor said helplessly. "But there is something else. It will cut you off from your family."

"You did that. You couldn't stand it, either. You know what it's like."

"There must be some other way. That is no reason for marriage."

"But-suppose I care for him?" Lily said, shyly.

"You wouldn't live with him a year. There are different ways of caring, Lily. There is such a thing as being carried away by a man's violent devotion, but it isn't the violent love that lasts."

Lily considered that carefully, and she felt that there was some truth in it. When Louis Akers came to take her home that night he found her unresponsive and thoughtful.

"Mrs. Doyle's been talking to you," he said at last. "She hates me, you know."

"Why should she hate you?"

"Because, with all her vicissitudes, she's still a snob," he said roughly. "My family was nothing, so I'm nothing."

"She wants me to be happy, Louis."

"And she thinks you won't be with me."

"I am not at all sure that I would be." She made an effort then to throw off the strange bond that held her to him. "I should like to have three months, Louis, to get a —well, a sort of perspective. I can't think clearly when you're around, and —"

"And I'm always around? Thanks." But she had alarmed him. "You're hurting me awfully, little girl," he said, in a different tone. "I can't live without seeing you, and you know it. You're all I have in life. You have everything, wealth, friends, position. You could play for three months and never miss me. But you are all I have."

In the end she capitulated

Jim Doyle was very content those days. There had been a time when Jim Doyle was the honest advocate of labor, a flaming partizan of those who worked with their hands. But he had traveled a long road since then, from dreamer to conspirator. Once he had planned to build up; now he plotted to tear down.

His weekly paper had enormous power. To the workers he had begun to preach class consciousness, and the doctrine of being true to their class. From class consciousness to class hatred was but a step. Ostensibly he stood for a vast equality, world wide and beneficent; actually he preached an inflammable doctrine of an earth where the last shall be first. He advocated the overthrow of all centralized government, and considered the wages system robbery. Under it workers were slaves, and employers of workers slave-masters. It was with such phrases that he had for months been consistently inflaming the inflammable foreign element in and around the city, and not the foreign element only. A certain percentage of American-born workmen fell before the hammer-like blows of his words, repeated and driven home each week.

He had no scruples, and preached none. He preached only revolt, and in that revolt defiance of all existing laws. He had no religion; Christ to him was a pitiful weakling, a historic victim of the same system that still crucified those who fought the established order. In his new world there would be no churches and no laws. He advocated bloodshed, arson, sabotage of all sorts, as a means to an end.

Fanatic he was, but practical fanatic, and the more dangerous for that. He had viewed the failure of the plan to capture a city in the northwest in February with irritation, but without discouragement. They had acted prematurely there and without sufficient secrecy. That was all. The plan in itself was right. And he had watched the scant reports of the uprising in the newspapers with amusement and scorn. The very steps taken to suppress the facts showed the uneasiness of the authorities and left the nation with a feeling of false security.

The people were always like that. Twice in a hundred years France had experienced the commune. Each time she had been warned, and each time she had waited too long. Ever so often in the life of every nation came these periodic outbursts of discontent, economic in their origin, and ran their course like diseases, contagious, violent and deadly.

The commune always followed long and costly wars. The people would dance, but they revolted at paying the piper.

The plan in Seattle had been well enough conceived; the city light plant was to have been taken over during the early evening of February 6, and at ten o'clock that night the city was to have gone dark. But the reign of terrorization that was to follow had revolted Jim Osborne, one of their leaders, and from his hotel bedroom he had notified the authorities. Word had gone out to "get" Osborne.

If it had not been for Osborne, and the conservative element behind him, a flame would have been kindled at Seattle that would have burnt across the nation.

Doyle watched Gompers cynically.. He considered his advocacy of patriotic cooperation between labor and the Government during the war the skillful attitude of an opportunist. Gompers could do better with public opinion behind him than without it. He was an opportunist, riding the wave which would carry him farthest. Playing both ends against the middle, and the middle, himself. He saw Gompers, watching the release of tension that followed the armistice and seeing the great child he had fathered, grown now and conscious of its power, —watching it, fully aware that it had become stronger than he.

Gompers, according to Doyle, had ceased to be a leader and become a follower, into strange and difficult paths.

The war had made labor's day. No public move was made without consulting organized labor, and a certain element in it had grown drunk with power. To this element Doyle appealed. It was Doyle who wrote the carefully prepared incendiary speeches, which were learned verbatim by his agents for delivery. For Doyle knew one thing, and knew it well. Labor, thinking along new lines, must think along the same lines. Be taught the same doctrines. Be pushed in one direction.

There were, then, two Doyles, one the poseur, flaunting his outrageous doctrines with a sardonic grin, gathering about him a small circle of the intelligentsia, and too openly heterodox to be dangerous. And the other, secretly plotting against the city, wary, cautious, practical and deadly, waiting to overthrow the established order and substitute for it chaos. It was only incidental to him that old Anthony should go with the rest.

But he found a saturnine pleasure in being old Anthony's Nemesis. He meant to be that. He steadily widened the breach between Lily and her family, and he watched the progress of her affair with Louis Akers with relish. He had not sought this particular form of revenge, but Fate had thrust it into his hands, and he meant to be worthy of the opportunity.

He was in no hurry. He had extraordinary patience, and he rather liked sitting back and watching the slow development of his plans. It was like chess; it was deliberate and inevitable. One made a move, and then sat back waiting and watching while the other side countered it, or fell, with slow agonizing, into the trap.

A few days after Lily had had her talk with Elinor, Doyle found a way to widen the gulf between Lily and her grandfather. Elinor seldom left the house, and Lily had done some shopping for her. The two women were in Elinor's bedroom, opening small parcels, when he knocked and came in.

"I don't like to disturb the serenity of this happy family group," he said, "but I am inclined to think that a certain gentleman, standing not far from a certain young lady's taxicab, belongs to a certain department of our great city government. And from his unflattering lack of interest in me, that he —"

Elinor half rose, terrified.

"Not the police, Jim?"

"Sit down," he said, in a tone Lily had never heard him use before. And to Lily, more gently: "I am not altogether surprised. As a matter of fact, I have known it for some time. Your esteemed grandfather seems to take a deep interest in your movements these days."

"Do you mean that I am being followed?"

"I'm afraid so. You see, you are a very important person, and if you will venture in the slums which surround the Cardew Mills, you should be protected. At any time, for instance, Aunt Elinor and I may despoil you of those pearls you wear so casually, and —"

"Don't talk like that, Jim," Elinor protested. She was very pale. "Are you sure he is watching Lily?"

He gave her an ugly look.

"Who else?" he inquired suavely.

Lily sat still, frozen with anger. So this was her grandfather's method of dealing with her. He could not lock her up, but he would know, day by day, and hour by hour, what she was doing. She could see him reading carefully his wicked little notes on her day. Perhaps he was watching her mail, too. Then when he had secured a hateful total he would go to her father, and together they would send her away somewhere. Away from Louis Akers. If he was watching her mail too he would know that Louis was in love with her. They would rake up all the things that belonged in the past he was done with, and recite them to her. As though they mattered now!

She went to the window and looked out. Yes, she had seen the detective before. He must have been hanging around for days, his face unconsciously impressing itself upon her. When she turned:

"Louis is coming to dinner, isn't he?"

"Yes."

"If you don't mind, Aunt Nellie, I think I'll dine out with him somewhere. I want to talk to him alone."

"But the detective —"

"If my grandfather uses low and detestable means to spy on me, Aunt Nellie, he deserves what he gets, doesn't he?"

When Louis Akers came at half-past six, he found that she had been crying, but she greeted him calmly enough, with her head held high. Elinor, watching her, thought she was very like old Anthony himself just then.

Chapter XVIII

Willy Cameron came home from a night class in metallurgy the evening after the day Lily had made her declaration of independence, and let himself in with his night key. There was a light in the little parlor, and Mrs. Boyd's fragile silhouette against the window shade.

He was not surprised at that. She had developed a maternal affection for him stronger than any she showed for either Edith or Dan. She revealed it in rather touching ways, too, keeping accounts when he accused her of gross extravagance, for she spent Dan's swollen wages wastefully; making him coffee late at night, and forcing him to drink it, although it kept him awake for hours; and never going to bed until he was safely closeted in his room at the top of the stairs.

He came in as early as possible, therefore, for he had had Doctor Smalley in to see her, and the result had been unsatisfactory.

"Heart's bad," said the doctor, when they had retired to Willy's room. "Leaks like a sieve. And there may be an aneurism. Looks like it, anyhow."

"What is there to do?" Willy asked, feeling helpless and extremely shocked. "We might send her somewhere."

"Nothing to do. Don't send her away; she'd die of loneliness. Keep her quiet and keep her happy. Don't let her worry. She only has a short time, I should say, and you can't lengthen it. It could be shortened, of course, if she had a shock, or anything like that."

"Shall I tell the family?"

"What's the use?" asked Doctor Smalley, philosophically. "If they fuss over her she'll suspect something."

As he went down the stairs he looked about him. The hall was fresh with new paper and white paint, and in the yard at the rear, visible through an open door, the border of annuals was putting out its first blossoms.

"Nice little place you've got here," he observed. "I think I see the fine hand of Miss Edith, eh?"

"Yes," said Willy Cameron, gravely.

He had made renewed efforts to get a servant after that, but the invalid herself balked him. When he found an applicant Mrs. Boyd would sit, very much the grande dame, and question her, although she always ended by sending her away.

"She looked like the sort that would be running out at nights," she would say. Or: "She wouldn't take telling, and I know the way you like your things, Willy. I could see by looking at her that she couldn't cook at all."

She cherished the delusion that he was improving and gaining flesh under her ministrations, and there was a sort of jealousy in her care for him. She wanted to yield to no one the right to sit proudly behind one of her heavy, tasteless pies, and say:

"Now I made this for you, Willy, because I know country boys like pies. Just see if that crust isn't nice."

"You don't mean to say you made it!"

"I certainly did." And to please her he would clear his plate. He rather ran to digestive tablets those days, and Edith, surprising him with one at the kitchen sink one evening, accused him roundly of hypocrisy.

"I don't know why you stay anyhow," she said, staring into the yard where Jinx was burying a bone in the heliotrope bed. "The food's awful. I'm used to it, but you're not."

"You don't eat anything, Edith."

"I'm not hungry. Willy, I wish you'd go away. What right we got to tie you up with us, anyhow? We're a poor lot. You're not comfortable and you know it. D'you know where she is now?"

"She" in the vernacular of the house, was always Mrs. Boyd.

"She forgot to make your bed, and she's doing it now."

He ran up the stairs, and forcibly putting Mrs. Boyd in a chair, made up his own bed, awkwardly and with an eye on her chest, which rose and fell alarmingly. It was after that that he warned Edith.

"She's not strong," he said. "She needs care and-well, to be happy. That's up to the three of us. For one thing, she must not have a shock. I'm going to warn Dan against exploding paper bags; she goes white every time."

Dan was at a meeting, and Willy dried the supper dishes for Edith. She was silent and morose. Finally she said:

"She's not very strong for me, Willy. You needn't look so shocked. She loves Dan and you, but not me. I don't mind, you know. She doesn't know it, but I do."

"She is very proud of you."

"That's different. You're right, though. Pride's her middle name. It nearly killed her at first to take a roomer, because she is always thinking of what the neighbors will say. That's why she hates me sometimes."

"I wish you wouldn't talk that way."

"But it's true. That fool Hodge woman at the corner came here one day last winter and filled her up with a lot of talk about me, and she's been queer to me ever since."

"You are a very good daughter."

She eyed him furtively. If only he wouldn't always believe in her! It was almost worse than to have him know the truth. But he went along with his head in the clouds; all women were good and all men meant well. Sometimes it worked out; Dan, for instance. Dan was trying to live up to him. But it was too late for her. Forever too late.

It was Willy Cameron's night off, and they went, the three of them, to the movies that evening. To Mrs. Boyd the movies was the acme of dissipation. She would, if warned in advance, spend the entire day with her hair in curlers, and once there she feasted her starved romantic soul to repletion. But that night the building was stifling, and without any warning Edith suddenly got up and walked toward the door. There was something odd about her walk and Willy followed her, but she turned on him almost fiercely outside.

"I wish you'd let me alone," she said, and then swayed a little. But she did not faint.

"I'm going home," she said. "You stay with her. And for heaven's sake don't stare at me like that. I'm all right."

Nevertheless he had taken her home, Edith obstinately silent and sullen, and Willy anxious and perplexed. At the door she said:

"Now go back to her, and tell her I just got sick of the picture. It was the smells in that rotten place. They'd turn a pig's stomach."

"I wish you'd see a doctor."

She looked at him with suspicious eyes. "If you run Smalley in on me I'll leave home."

"Will you go to bed?"

"I'll go to bed, all right."

He had found things rather more difficult after that. Two women, both ill and refusing to acknowledge it, and the prospect of Dan's being called out by the union. Try as he would, he could not introduce any habit of thrift into the family. Dan's money came and went, and on Saturday nights there was not only nothing left, but often a deficit. Dan, skillfully worked upon outside, began to develop a grievance, also, and on his rare evenings at home or at the table he would voice his wrongs.

"It's just hand to mouth all the time," he would grumble. "A fellow working for the Cardews never gets ahead. What chance has he got, anyhow? It takes all he can get to live."

Willy Cameron began to see that the trouble was not with Dan, but with his women folks. And Dan was one of thousands. His wages went for food, too much food, food spoiled in cooking. There were men, with able women behind them, making less than Dan and saving money.

"Keep some of it out and bank it," he suggested, but Dan sneered.

"And have a store bill a mile long! You know mother as well as I do. She means well, but she's a fool with money."

He counted his hours from the time he entered the mill until he left it, but he revealed once that there were long idle periods when the heating was going on, when he and the other men of the furnace crew sat and waited, doing nothing.

"But I'm there, all right," he said. "I'm not playing golf or riding in my automobile. I'm on the job."

"Well," said Willy Cameron, "I'm on the job about eleven hours a day, and I wear out more shoe leather than trouser seats at that. But it doesn't seem to hurt me."

"It's a question of principle," said Dan doggedly. "I've got no personal kick, y'understand. Only I'm not getting anywhere, and something's got to be done about it."

So, on the evening of the day after Lily had made her declaration of independence, Willy Cameron made his way rather heavily toward the Boyd house. He was very tired. He had made one or two speeches for Hendricks already, before local ward organizations, and he was working hard at his night class in metallurgy. He had had a letter from his mother, too, and he thought he read homesickness between the lines. He was not at all sure where his duty lay, yet to quit now, to leave Mr. Hendricks and the Boyds flat, seemed impossible.

He had tried to see Lily, too, and failed. She had been very gentle over the telephone, but, attuned as he was to every inflection of her voice, he had thought there was unhappiness in it. Almost despair. But she had pleaded a week of engagements.

"I'm sorry," she had said. "I'll call you up next week some time I have a lot of things I want to talk over with you."

But he knew she was avoiding him.

And he knew that he ought to see her. Through Mr. Hendricks he had learned something more about Jim Doyle, the real Doyle and not the poseur, and he felt she should know the nature of the accusations against him. Lily mixed up with a band of traitors, Lily of the white flame of patriotism, was unthinkable. She must not go to the house on Cardew Way. A man's loyalty was like a woman's virtue; it could not be questionable. There was no middle ground.

He heard voices as he entered the house, and to his amazement found Ellen in the parlor. She was sitting very stiff on the edge of her chair, her hat slightly crooked and a suit-case and brown paper bundle at her feet.

Mrs. Boyd was busily entertaining her.

"I make it a point to hold my head high," she was saying. "I guess there was a lot of talk when I took a boarder, but-Is that you, Willy?"

"Why, Miss Ellen!" he said. "And looking as though headed for a journey!"

Ellen's face did not relax. She had been sitting there for an hour, letting Mrs. Boyd's prattle pour over her like a rain, and thinking meanwhile her own bitter thoughts.

"I am, Willy. Only I didn't wait for my money and the bank's closed, and I came to borrow ten dollars, if you have it."

That told him she was in trouble, but Mrs. Boyd, amiably hospitable and reveling in a fresh audience, showed no sign of departing.

"She says she's been living at the Cardews," she put in, rocking valiantly. "I guess most any place would seem tame after that. I do hear, Miss Hart, that Mrs. Howard Cardew only wears her clothes once and then gives them away."

She hitched the chair away from the fireplace, where it showed every indication of going up the chimney.

"I call that downright wasteful," she offered.

Willy glanced at his watch, which had been his father's, and bore the inscription: "James Duncan Cameron, 1876" inside the case.

"Eleven o'clock," he said sternly. "And me promising the doctor I'd have you in bed at ten sharp every night! Now off with you."

"But, Willy —"

" —or I shall have to carry you," he threatened. It was an old joke between them, and she rose, smiling, her thin face illuminated with the sense of being looked after.

"He's that domineering," she said to Ellen, "that I can't call my soul my own."

"Good-night," Ellen said briefly.

Willy stood at the foot of the stairs and watched her going up. He knew she liked him to do that, that she would expect to find him there when she reached the top and looked down, panting slightly.

"Good-night," he called. "Both windows open. I shall go outside to see."

Then he went back to Ellen, still standing primly over her Lares and Penates.

"Now tell me about it," he said.

"I've left them. There has been a terrible fuss, and when Miss Lily left to-night, I did too."

"She left her home?"

She nodded.

"It's awful, Willy. I don't know all of it, but they've been having her followed, or her grandfather did. I think there's a man in it. Followed! And her a good girl! Her grandfather's been treating her like a dog for weeks. We all noticed it. And to-night there was a quarrel, with all of them at her like a pack of dogs, and her governess crying in the hall. I just went up and packed my things."

"Where did she go?"

"I don't know. I got her a taxicab, and she only took one bag. I went right off to the housekeeper and told her I wouldn't stay, and they could send my money after me."

"Did you notice the number of the taxicab?"

"I never thought of it."

He saw it all with terrible distinctness, The man was Akers, of course. Then, if she had left her home rather than give him up, she was really in love with him. He had too much common sense to believe for a moment that she had fled to Louis Akers' protection, however. That was the last thing she would do. She would have gone to a hotel, or to the Doyle house.

"She shouldn't have left home, Ellen."

"They drove her out, I tell you," Ellen cried, irritably. "At least that's what it amounted to. There are things no high-minded girl will stand. Can you lend me some money, Willy?"

He felt in his pocket, producing a handful of loose money.

"Of course you can have all I've got," he said. "But you must not go to-night, Miss Ellen. It's too late. I'll give you my room and go in with Dan Boyd."

And he prevailed over her protests, in the end. It was not until he saw her settled there, hiding her sense of strangeness under an impassive mask, that he went downstairs again and took his hat from its hook.

Lily must go back home, he knew. It was unthinkable that she should break with her family, and go to the Doyles. He had too little self-consciousness to question the propriety of his own interference, too much love for her to care whether she resented that interference. And he was filled with a vast anger at Jim Doyle. He saw in all this, somehow, Doyle's work; how it would play into Doyle's plans to have Anthony Cardew's granddaughter a member of his household. He would take her away from there if he had to carry her.

He was a long time in getting to the mill district, and a longer time still in finding Cardew Way. At an all-night pharmacy he learned which was the house, and his determined movements took on a sort of uncertainty. It was very late. Ellen had waited for him for some time. If Lily were in that sinister darkened house across the street, the family had probably retired. And for the first time, too, he began to doubt if Doyle would let him see her. Lily herself might even refuse to see him.

Nevertheless, the urgency to get her away from there, if she were there, prevailed at last, and a strip of light in an upper window, as from an imperfectly fitting blind, assured him that some one was still awake in the house.

He went across the street and opening the gate, strode up the walk. Almost immediately he was confronted by the figure of a man who had been concealed by the trunk of one of the trees. He lounged forward, huge, menacing, yet not entirely hostile.

"Who is it?" demanded the figure blocking his way.

"I want to see Mr. Doyle."

"What about?"

"I'll tell him that," said Willy Cameron.

"What's your name?"

"That's my business, too," said Mr. Cameron, with disarming pleasantness.

"Damn private about your business, aren't you?" jeered the sentry, still in cautious tones. "Well, you can write it down on a piece of paper and mail it to him. He's busy now."

"All I want to do," persisted Mr. William Wallace Cameron, growing slightly giddy with repressed fury, "is to ring that doorbell and ask him a question. I'm going to do it, too."

There was rather an interesting moment then, because the figure lunged at Mr. Cameron, and Mr. Cameron, stooping low and swiftly, as well as to one side, and at the same instant becoming a fighting Scot, which means a cool-eyed madman, got in one or two rather neat effects with his fists. The first took the shadow just below his breast-bone, and the left caught him at that angle of the jaw where a small cause sometimes produces a large effect. The figure sat down on the brick walk and grunted, and Mr. Cameron, judging that he had about ten seconds' leeway, felt in the dazed person's right hand pocket for the revolver he knew would be there, and secured it. The sitting figure made puffing, feeble attempts to prevent him, but there was no real struggle.

Mr. Cameron himself was feeling extremely triumphant and as strong as a lion. He was rather sorry no one had seen the affair, but that of course was sub-conscious. And he was more cheerful than he had been for some days. He had been up against so many purely intangible obstacles lately that it was a relief to find one he could use his fists on.

"Now I'll have a few words with you, my desperate friend," he said. "I've got your gun, and I am hell with a revolver, because I've never fired one, and there's a sort of homicidal beginner's luck about the thing. If you move or speak, I'll shoot it into you first and when it's empty I'll choke it down your throat and strangle you to death."

After which ferocious speech he strolled up the path, revolver in hand, and rang the doorbell. He put the weapon in his pocket then, but he kept his hand upon it. He had read somewhere that a revolver was quite useable from a pocket. There was no immediate answer to the bell, and he turned and surveyed the man under the tree, faintly distinguishable in the blackness. It had occurred to him that the number of guns a man may carry is only limited to his pockets, which are about fifteen.

There were heavy, deliberate footsteps inside, and the door was flung open. No glare of light followed it, however. There was a man there, alarmingly tall, who seemed to stare at him, and then beyond him into the yard.

"Well?"

"Are you Mr. Doyle?"

"I am."

"My name is Cameron, Mr. Doyle. I have had a small difference with your watch-dog, but he finally let me by."

"I'm afraid I don't understand. I have no dog."

"The sentry you keep posted, then." Mr. Cameron disliked fencing.

"Ah!" said Mr. Doyle, urbanely. "You have happened on one of my good friends, I see. I have many enemies, Mr. Cameron-was that the name? And my friends sometimes like to keep an eye on me. It is rather touching."

He was smiling, Mr. Cameron knew, and his anger rose afresh.

"Very touching," said Mr. Cameron, "but if he bothers me going out you may be short one friend. Mr. Doyle, Miss Lily Cardew left her home to-night. I want to know if she is here."

"Are you sent by her family?"

"I have asked you if she is here."

Jim Doyle apparently deliberated.

"My niece is here, although just why you should interest yourself—"

"May I see her?"

"I regret to say she has retired."

"I think she would see me."

A door opened into the hall, throwing a shaft of light on the wall across and letting out the sounds of voices.

"Shut that door," said Doyle, wheeling sharply. It was closed at once. "Now," he said, turning to his visitor, "I'll tell you this. My niece is here." He emphasized the "my." "She has come to me for refuge, and I intend to give it to her. You won't see her to-night, and if you come from her people you can tell them she came here of her own free will, and that if she stays it will be because she wants to. Joe!" he called into the darkness.

"Yes," came a sullen voice, after a moment's hesitation.

"Show this gentleman out."

All at once Willy Cameron was staring at a closed door, on the inner side of which a bolt was being slipped. He felt absurd and futile, and not at all like a lion. With the revolver in his hand, he went down the steps.

"Don't bother about the gate, Joe," he said. "I like to open my own gates. And-don't try any tricks, Joe. Get back to your kennel."

Fearful mutterings followed that, but the shadow retired, and he made an undisturbed exit to the street. Once on the street-car, the entire episode became unreal and theatrical, with only the drag of Joe's revolver in his coat pocket to prove its reality.

It was after midnight when, shoes in hand, he crept up the stairs to Dan's room, and careful not to disturb him, slipped into his side of the double bed. He did not sleep at all. He lay there, facing the fact that Lily had delivered herself voluntarily into the hands of the enemy of her house, and not only of her house, an enemy of the country. That conference that night was a sinister one. Brought to book about it, Doyle might claim it as a labor meeting. Organizers planning a strike might-did indeed-hold secret conferences, but they did not post armed guards. They opened business offices, and brought in the press men, and shouted their grievances for the world to hear.

This was different. This was anarchy. And in every city it was going on, this rallying of the malcontents, the idlers, the envious and the dangerous, to the red flag. Organized labor gathered together the workmen, but men like Doyle were organizing the riff-raff of the country. They secured a small percentage of idealists and pseudo-intellectuals, and taught them a so-called internationalism which under the name of brotherhood was nothing but a raid on private property, a scheme of pillage and arson. They allied with themselves imported laborers from Europe, men with everything to gain and nothing to lose, and by magnifying real grievances and inflaming them with imaginary ones, were building out of this material the rank and file of an anarchist army.

And against it, what?

On toward morning he remembered something, and sat bolt upright in bed. Edith had once said something about knowing of a secret telephone. She had known Louis Akers very well. He might have told her what she knew, or have shown her, in some braggart moment. A certain type of man was unable to keep a secret from a woman. But that would imply-For the first time he wondered what Edith's relations with Louis Akers might have been.

Chapter XIX

The surface peace of the house on Cardew Way, the even tenor of her days there, the feeling she had of sanctuary did not offset Lily's clear knowledge that she had done a cruel and an impulsive thing. Even her grandfather, whose anger had driven her away, she remembered now as a feeble old man, fighting his losing battle in a changing world, and yet with a sort of mistaken heroism hoisting his colors to the end.

She had determined, that first night in Elinor's immaculate guest room, to go back the next day. They had been right at home, by all the tenets to which they adhered so religiously. She had broken the unwritten law not to break bread with an enemy of her house. She had done what they had expressly forbidden, done it over and over.

"On top of all this," old Anthony had said, after reading the tale of her delinquencies from some notes in his hand, "you dined last night openly at the Saint Elmo Hotel with this same Louis Akers, a man openly my enemy, and openly of impure life."

"I do not believe he is your enemy."

"He is one of the band of anarchists who have repeatedly threatened to kill me."

"Oh, Lily, Lily!" said her mother.

But it was to her father, standing grave and still, that Lily replied.

"I don't believe that, father. He is not a murderer. If you would let him come here —"

"Never in this house," said old Anthony, savagely crushing notes in his hand. "He will come here over my dead body."

"You have no right to condemn a man unheard."

"Unheard! I tell you I know all about him. The man is an anarchist, a rake, a —dog."

"Just a moment, father," Howard had put in, quietly. "Lily, do you care for this man? I mean by that, do you want to marry him?"

"He has asked me. I have not given him any answer yet. I don't want to marry a man my family will not receive. It wouldn't be fair to him."

Which speech drove old Anthony into a frenzy, and led him to a bitterness of language that turned Lily cold and obstinate. She heard him through, with her father vainly trying to break in and save the situation; then she said, coldly:

"I am sorry you feel that way about it," and turned and left the room.

She had made no plan, of course. She hated doing theatrical things. But shut in her bedroom with the doors locked, Anthony's furious words came back, his threats, his bitter sneers. She felt strangely alone, too. In all the great house she had no one to support her. Mademoiselle, her father and mother, even the servants, were tacitly aligned with the opposition. Except Ellen. She had felt lately that Ellen, in her humble way, had espoused her cause.

She had sent for Ellen.

In spite of the warmth of her greeting, Lily had felt a reserve in Aunt Elinor's welcome. It was as though she was determinedly making the best of a bad situation.

"I had to do it, Aunt Elinor," she said, when they had gone upstairs. There was a labor conference, Doyle had explained, being held below.

"I know," said Elinor. "I understand. I'll pin back the curtains so you can open your windows. The night air is so smoky here."

"I am afraid mother will grieve terribly."

"I think she will," said Elinor, with her quiet gravity. "You are all she has."

"She has father. She cares more for him than for anything in the world."

"Would you like some ice-water, dear?"

Some time later Lily roused from the light sleep of emotional exhaustion. She had thought she heard Willy Cameron's voice. But that was absurd, of course, and she lay back to toss uneasily for hours. Out of all her thinking there emerged at last her real self, so long overlaid with her infatuation. She would go home again, and make what amends she could. They were wrong about Louis Akers, but they were right, too.

Lying there, as the dawn slowly turned her windows to gray, she saw him with a new clarity. She had a swift vision of what life with him would mean. Intervals of passionate loving, of boyish dependence on her, and then —a new face. Never again was she to see him with such clearness. He was incapable of loyalty to a woman, even though he loved her. He was born to be a wanderer in love, an experimenter in passion. She even recognized in him an incurable sensuous curiosity about women, that would be quite remote from his love for her. He would see nothing wrong in his infidelities, so long as she did not know and did not suffer. And he would come back to her from them, watchful for suspicion, relieved when he did not find it, and bringing her small gifts which would be actually burnt offerings to his own soul.

She made up her mind to give him up. She would go home in the morning, make her peace with them all, and never see Louis Akers again.

She slept after that, and at ten o'clock Elinor wakened her with the word that her father was downstairs. Elinor was very pale. It had been a shock to her to see her brother in her home after all the years, and a still greater one when he had put his arm around her and kissed her.

"I am so sorry, Howard," she had said. The sight of him had set her lips trembling. He patted her shoulder.

"Poor Elinor," he said. "Poor old girl! We're a queer lot, aren't we?"

"All but you."

"An obstinate, do-and-be-damned lot," he said slowly. "I'd like to see my little girl, Nellie. We can't have another break in the family."

He held Lily in much the same way when she came down, an arm around her, his big shoulders thrown back as though he would guard her against the world. But he was very uneasy and depressed, at that. He had come on a difficult errand, and because he had no finesse he blundered badly. It was some time before she gathered the full meaning of what he was saying.

"Aunt Cornelia's!" she exclaimed.

"Or, if you and your mother want to go to Europe," he put in hastily, seeing her puzzled face, "I think I can arrange about passports."

"Does that mean he won't have me back, father?"

"Lily, dear," he said, hoarse with anxiety, "we simply have to remember that he is a very old man, and that his mind is not elastic. He is feeling very bitter now, but he will get over it."

"And I am to travel around waiting to be forgiven! I was ready to go back, but-he won't have me. Is that it?"

"Only just for the present." He threw out his hands. "I have tried everything. I suppose, in a way, I could insist, make a point of it, but there are other things to be considered. His age, for one thing, and then-the strike. If he takes an arbitrary stand against me, no concession, no argument with the men, it makes it very difficult, in many ways."

"I see. It is wicked that any one man should have such power. The city, the mills, his family-it's wicked." But she was conscious of no deep anger against Anthony now. She merely saw that between them, they, she and her grandfather, had dug a gulf that could not be passed. And in Howard's efforts she saw the temporizing that her impatient youth resented.

"I am afraid it is a final break, father," she said. "And if he shuts me out I must live my own life. But I am not going to run away to Aunt Cornelia or Europe. I shall stay here."

He had to be content with that. After all, his own sister-but he wished it were not Jim Doyle's house. Not that he regarded Lily's shift toward what he termed Bolshevism very seriously; all youth had a slant toward socialism, and outgrew it. But he went away sorely troubled, after a few words with Elinor Doyle alone.

"You don't look unhappy, Nellie."

"Things have been much better the last few years."

"Is he kind to you?"

"Not always, Howard. He doesn't drink now, so that is over. And I think there are no other women. But when things go wrong I suffer, of course." She stared past him toward the open window.

"Why don't you leave him?"

"I couldn't go home, Howard. You know what it would be. Worse than Lily. And I'm too old to start out by myself. My habits are formed, and besides, I —" She checked herself.

"I could take a house somewhere for both of you, Lily and yourself," he said eagerly; "that would be a wonderful way out for everybody."

She shook her head.

"We'll manage all right," she said. "I'll make Lily comfortable and as happy as I can."

He felt that he had to make his own case clear, or he might have noticed with what care she was choosing her words. His father's age, his unconscious dependence on Grace, his certainty to retire soon from the arbitrary stand he had taken. Elinor hardly heard him. Months afterwards he was to remember the distant look in her eyes, a sort of half-frightened determination, but he was self-engrossed just then.

"I can't persuade you?" he finished.

"No. But it is good of you to think of it."

"You know what the actual trouble was last night? It was not her coming here."

"I know, Howard."

"Don't let her marry him, Nellie! Better than any one, you ought to know what that would mean."

"I knew too, Howard, but I did it."

In the end he went away not greatly comforted, to fight his own battles, to meet committees from the union, and having met them, to find himself facing the fact that, driven by some strange urge he could not understand, the leaders wished a strike. There were times when he wondered what would happen if he should suddenly yield every point, make every concession. They would only make further demands, he felt. They seemed determined to put him out of business. If only he could have dealt with the men directly, instead of with their paid representatives, he felt that he would get somewhere. But always, interposed between himself and his workmen, was this barrier of their own erecting.

It was like representative government. It did not always represent. It, too, was founded on representation in good faith; but there was not always good faith. The union system was wrong. It was like politics. The few handled the many. The union, with its all-powerful leaders, was only another form of autocracy. It was Prussian. Yet the ideal behind the union was sound enough.

He had no quarrel with the union. He puzzled it out, traveling unaccustomed mental paths. The country was founded on liberty. All men were created free and equal. Free, yes, but equal? Was not equality a long way ahead along a thorny road? Men were not equal in the effort they made, nor did equal efforts bring equal result. If there was class antagonism behind all this unrest, would there not always be those who rose by dint of ceaseless effort? Equality of opportunity, yes. Equality of effort and result, no.

To destroy the chance of gain was to put a premium on inertia; to kill ambition; to reduce the high without raising the low.

At noon on the same day Willy Cameron went back to the house on Cardew Way, to find Lily composed and resigned, instead of the militant figure he had expected. He asked her to go home, and she told him then that she had no longer a home to go to.

"I meant to go, Willy," she finished. "I meant to go this morning. But you see how things are."

He had stood for a long time, looking at nothing very hard. "I see," he said finally. "Of course your grandfather will be sorry in a day or two, but he may not swallow his pride very soon."

That rather hurt her.

"What about my pride?" she asked.

"You can afford to be magnanimous with all your life before you." Then he faced her. "Besides, Lily, you're wrong. Dead wrong. You've hurt three people, and all you've got out of it has been your own way."

"There is such a thing as liberty."

"I don't know about that. And a good many crimes have been committed in its name." Even in his unhappiness he was controversial. "We are never really free, so long as we love people, and they love us. Well—" He picked up his old felt hat and absently turned down the brim; it was raining. "I'll have to get back. I've overstayed my lunch hour as it is."

"You haven't had any luncheon?"

"I wasn't hungry," he had said, and had gone away, his coat collar turned up against the shower. Lily had had a presentiment that he was taking himself out of her life, that he had given her up as a bad job. She felt depressed and lonely, and not quite so sure of herself as she had been; rather, although she did not put it that way, as though something fine had passed her way, like Pippa singing, and had then gone on.

She settled down as well as she could to her new life, making no plans, however, and always with the stricken feeling that she had gained her own point at the cost of much suffering. She telephoned to her mother daily, broken little conversations with long pauses while Grace steadied her voice. Once her mother hung up the receiver hastily, and Lily guessed that her grandfather had come in. She felt very bitter toward him.

But she found the small oneage interesting, in a quiet way; to make her own bed and mend her stockings-Grace had sent her a trunkful of clothing; and on the elderly maid's afternoon out, to help Elinor with the supper. She seldom went out, but Louis Akers came daily, and on the sixth day of her stay she promised to marry him.

She had not meant to do it, but it was difficult to refuse him. She had let him think she would do it ultimately, for one thing. And, however clearly she might analyze him in his absences, his strange attraction reasserted itself when he was near. But her acceptance of him was almost stoical.

"But not soon, Louis," she said, holding him off. "And —I ought to tell you —I don't think we will be happy together."

"Why not?"

"Because —" she found it hard to put into words —"because love with you is a sort of selfish thing, I think."

"I'll lie down now and let you tramp on me," he said exultantly, and held out his arms. But even as she moved toward him she voiced her inner perplexity.

"I never seem to be able to see myself married to you."

"Then the sooner the better, so you can."

"You won't like being married, you know."

"That's all you know about it, Lily. I'm mad about you. I'm mad for you."

There was a new air of maturity about Lily those days, and sometimes a sort of aloofness that both maddened him and increased his desire to possess her. She went into his arms, but when he held her closest she sometimes seemed farthest away.

"I want you now."

"I want to be engaged a long time, Louis. We have so much to learn about each other."

He thought that rather childish. But whatever had been his motive in the beginning, he was desperately in love with her by that time, and because of that he frightened her sometimes. He was less sure of himself, too, even after she had accepted him, and to prove his continued dominance over her he would bully her.

"Come here," he would say, from the hearth rug, or by the window.

"Certainly not."

"Come here."

Sometimes she went, to be smothered in his hot embrace; sometimes she did not.

But her infatuation persisted, although there were times when his inordinate vitality and his caresses gave her a sense of physical weariness, times when sheer contact revolted her. He seemed always to want to touch her. Fastidiously reared, taught a sort of aloofness from childhood, Lily found herself wondering if all men in love were like that, always having to be held off.

Chapter XX

Ellen was staying at the Boyd house. She went downstairs the morning after her arrival, and found the bread-bakery bread-toasted and growing cold on the table, while a slice of ham, ready to be cooked, was not yet on the fire, and Mrs. Boyd had run out to buy some milk.

Dan had already gone, and his half-empty cup of black coffee was on the kitchen table. Ellen sniffed it and raised her eyebrows.

She rolled up her sleeves, put the toast in the oven and the ham in the frying pan, with much the same grimness with which she had sat the night before listening to Mrs. Boyd's monologue. If this was the way they looked after Willy Cameron, no wonder he was thin and pale. She threw out the coffee, which she suspected had been made by the time-saving method of pouring water on last night's grounds, and made a fresh pot of it. After that she inspected the tea towels, and getting a tin dishpan, set them to boil in it on the top of the range.

"Enough to give him typhoid," she reflected.

Ellen disapproved of her surroundings; she disapproved of any woman who did not boil her tea towels. And when Edith came down carefully dressed and undeniably rouged she formed a disapproving opinion of that young lady, which was that she was trying to land Willy Cameron, and that he would be better dead than landed.

She met Edith's stare of surprise with one of thinly veiled hostility.

"Hello!" said Edith. "When did you blow in, and where from?"

"I came to see Mr. Cameron last night, and he made me stay."

"A friend of Willy's! Well, I guess you needn't pay for your breakfast by cooking it. Mother's probably run out for something-she never has anything in the house-and is talking somewhere. I'll take that fork."

But Ellen proceeded to turn the ham.

"I'll do it," she said. "You might spoil your hands."

But Edith showed no offense.

"All right," she acceded indifferently. "If you're going to eat it you'd better cook it. We're rotten housekeepers here."

"I should think, if you're going to keep boarders, somebody would learn to cook. Mr. Cameron's mother is the best housekeeper in town, and he was raised on good food and plenty of it."

Her tone was truculent. Ellen's world, the world of short hours and easy service, of the decorum of the Cardew servants' hall, of luxury and dignity and good pay, had suddenly gone to pieces about her. She was feeling very bitter, especially toward a certain chauffeur who had prophesied the end of all service. He had made the statement that before long all people would be equal. There would be no above and below-stairs, no servants' hall.

"They'll drive their own cars, then, damn them," he had said once, "if they can get any to drive. And answer their own bells, if they've got any to ring. And get up and cook their own breakfasts."

"Which you won't have any to cook," Grayson had said irritably, from the head of the long table. "Just a word, my man. That sort of talk is forbidden here. One word more and I go to Mr. Cardew."

The chauffeur had not sulked, however. "All right, Mr. Grayson," he said affably. "But I can go on thinking, I daresay. And some of these days you'll be wishing you'd climbed on the band wagon before it's too late."

Ellen, turning the ham carefully, was conscious that her revolt had been only partially on Lily's account. It was not so much Lily's plight as the abuse of power, although she did not put it that way, that had driven her out. Ellen then had carried out her own small revolution, and where had it put her? She had lost a good home, and what could she do? All she knew was service.

Edith poured herself a cup of coffee, and taking a piece of toast from the oven, stood nibbling it. The crumbs fell on the not over-clean floor.

"Why don't you go into the dining-room to eat?" Ellen demanded.

"Got out of the wrong side of the bed, didn't you?" Edith asked. "Willy's bed, I suppose. I'm not hungry, and I always eat breakfast like this. I wish he would hurry. We'll be late."

Ellen stared. It was her first knowledge that this girl, this painted hussy, worked in Willy's pharmacy, and her suspicions increased. She had a quick vision, as she had once had of Lily, of Edith in the Cameron house; Edith reading or embroidering on the front porch while Willy's mother slaved for her; Edith on the same porch in the evening, with all the boys in town around her. She knew the type, the sort that set an entire village by the ears and in the end left home and husband and ran away with a traveling salesman.

Ellen had already got Willy married and divorced when Mrs. Boyd came in. She carried the milk pail, but her lips were blue and she sat down in a chair and held her hand to her heart.

"I'm that short of breath!" she gasped. "I declare I could hardly get back."

"I'll give you some coffee, right off."

When Willy Cameron had finished his breakfast she followed him into the parlor. His pallor was not lost on her, or his sunken eyes. He looked badly fed, shabby, and harassed, and he bore the marks of his sleepless night on his face. "Are you going to stay here?" she demanded.

"Why, yes, Miss Ellen."

"Your mother would break her heart if she knew the way you're living."

"I'm very comfortable. We've tried to get a ser —" He changed color at that. In the simple life of the village at home a woman whose only training was the town standard of good housekeeping might go into service in the city and not lose caste. But she was never thought of as a servant. " —help," he substituted. "But we can't get any one, and Mrs. Boyd is delicate. It is heart trouble."

"Does that girl work where you do?"

"Yes. Why?"

"Is she engaged to you? She calls you Willy." He smiled into her eyes.

"Not a bit of it, or thinking of it."

"How do you know what she's thinking? It's all over her. It's Willy this and Willy that-and men are such fools."

There flashed into his mind certain things that he had tried to forget; Edith at his doorway, with that odd look in her eyes; Edith never going to sleep until he had gone to bed; and recently, certain things she had said, that he had passed over lightly and somewhat uncomfortably.

"That's ridiculous, Miss Ellen. But even if it were true, which it isn't, don't you think it would be rather nice of her?" He smiled.

"I do not. I heard you going out last night, Willy. Did you find her?"

"She is at the Doyles'. I didn't see her."

"That'll finish it," Ellen prophesied, somberly. She glanced around the parlor, at the dust on the furniture, at the unwashed baseboard, at the unwound clock on the mantel shelf.

"If you're going to stay here I will," she announced abruptly. "I owe that much to your mother. I've got some money. I'll take what they'd pay some foreigner who'd throw out enough to keep another family." Then, seeing hesitation in his eyes: "That woman's sick, and you've got to be looked after. I could do all the work, if that-if the girl would help in the evenings."

He demurred at first. She would find it hard. They had no luxuries, and she was accustomed to luxury. There was no room for her. But in the end he called Edith and Mrs. Boyd, and was rather touched to find Edith offering to share her upper bedroom.

"It's a hole," she said, "cold in winter and hot as blazes in summer. But there's room for a cot, and I guess we can let each other alone."

"I wish you'd let me move up there, Edith," he said for perhaps the twentieth time since he had found out where she slept, "and you would take my room."

"No chance," she said cheerfully. "Mother would raise the devil if you tried it." She glanced at Ellen's face. "If that word shocks you, you're due for a few shocks, you know."

"The way you talk is your business, not mine," said Ellen austerely.

When they finally departed on a half-run Ellen was established as a fixture in the Boyd house, and was already piling all the cooking utensils into a wash boiler and with grim efficiency was searching for lye with which to clean them.

Two weeks later, the end of June, the strike occurred. It was not, in spite of predictions, a general walk-out. Some of the mills, particularly the smaller plants, did not go down at all, and with reduced forces kept on, but the chain of Cardew Mills was closed. There was occasional rioting by the foreign element in outlying districts, but the state constabulary handled it easily.

Dan was out of work, and the loss of his pay was a serious matter in the little house. He had managed to lay by a hundred dollars, and Willy Cameron had banked it for him, but there was a real problem to be faced. On the night of the day the Cardew Mills went down Willy called a meeting of the household after supper, around the dining room table. He had been in to see Mr. Hendricks, who had been laid up with bronchitis, and Mr. Hendricks had predicted a long strike.

"The irresistible force and the immovable body, son," he said. "They'll stay set this time. And unless I miss my guess that is playing Doyle's hand for him, all right. His chance will come when the men have used up their savings and are growing bitter. Every strike plays into the hands of the enemy, son, and they know it. The moment production ceases prices go up, and soon all the money in the world won't pay them wages enough to live on."

He had a store of homely common sense, and a gift of putting things into few words. Willy Cameron, going back to the little house that evening, remembered the last thing he had said.

"The only way to solve this problem of living," he said, "is to see how much we can work, and not how little. Germany's working ten hours a day, and producing. We're talking about six, and loafing and fighting while we talk."

So Willy went home and called his meeting, and knowing Mrs. Boyd's regard for figures, set down and added or subtracted, he placed a pad and pencil on the table before him. It was an odd group: Dan sullen, resenting the strike and the causes that had led to it; Ellen, austere and competent; Mrs. Boyd with a lace fichu pinned around her neck, now that she had achieved the dignity of hired help, and Edith. Edith silent, morose and fixing now and then rather haggard eyes on Willy Cameron's unruly hair. She seldom met his eyes.

"First of all," said Willy, "we'll take our weekly assets. Of course Dan will get something temporarily, but we'll leave that out for the present."

The weekly assets turned out to be his salary and Edith's.

"Why, Willy," said Mrs. Boyd, "you can't turn all your money over to us."

"You are all the family I have just now. Why not? Anyhow, I'll have to keep out lunch money and carfare, and so will Edith. Now as to expenses."

Ellen had made a great reduction in expenses, but food was high. And there was gas and coal, and Dan's small insurance, and the rent. There was absolutely no margin, and a sort of silence fell.

"What about your tuition at night school?" Edith asked suddenly.

"Spring term ended this week."

"But you said there was a summer one."

"Well, I'll tell you about that," Willy said, feeling for words. "I'm going to be busy helping Mr. Hendricks in his campaign. Then next fall-well, I'll either go back or Hendricks will make me chief of police, or something." He smiled around the table. "I ought to get some sort of graft out of it."

"Mother!" Edith protested. "He mustn't sacrifice himself for us. What are we to him anyhow? A lot of stones hung around his neck. That's all."

It was after Willy had declared that this was his home now, and he had a right to help keep it going, and after Ellen had observed that she had some money laid by and would not take any wages during the strike, that the meeting threatened to become emotional. Mrs. Boyd shed a few tears, and as she never by any chance carried a handkerchief, let them flow over her fichu. And Dan shook Willy's hand and Ellen's, and said that if he'd had his way he'd be working, and not sitting round like a stiff letting other people work for him. But Edith got up and went out into the little back garden, and did not come back until the meeting was both actually and morally broken up. When she heard Dan go out, and Ellen and Mrs. Boyd go upstairs, chatting in a new amiability brought about by trouble and sacrifice, she put on her hat and left the house.

Ellen, rousing on her cot in Edith's upper room, heard her come in some time later, and undress and get into bed. Her old suspicion of the girl revived, and she sat upright.

"Where I come from girls don't stay out alone until all hours," she said.

"Oh, let me alone."

Ellen fell asleep, and in her sleep she dreamed that Mrs. Boyd had taken sick and was moaning. The moaning was terrible; it filled the little house. Ellen wakened suddenly. It was not moaning; it was strange, heavy breathing, strangling; and it came from Edith's bed.

"Are you sick?" she called, and getting up, her knees hardly holding her, she lighted the gas at its unshaded bracket on the wall and ran to the other bed.

Edith was lying there, her mouth open, her lips bleached and twisted. Her stertorous breathing filled the room, and over all was the odor of carbolic acid.

"Edith, for God's sake!"

The girl was only partially conscious. Ellen ran down the stairs and into Willy's room.

"Get up," she cried, shaking him. "That girl's killed herself."

"Lily!"

"No, Edith. Carbolic acid."

Even then he remembered her mother.

"Don't let her hear anything, It will kill her," he said, and ran up the stairs. Almost immediately he was down again, searching for alcohol; he found a small quantity and poured that down the swollen throat. He roused Dan then, and sent him running madly for Doctor Smalley, with a warning to bring him past Mrs. Boyd's door quietly, and to bring an intubation set with him in case her throat should close. Then, on one of his innumerable journeys up and down the stairs he encountered Mrs. Boyd herself, in her nightgown, and terrified.

"What's the matter, Willy?" she asked. "Is it a fire?"

"Edith is sick. I don't want you to go up. It may be contagious. It's her throat."

And from that Mrs. Boyd deduced diphtheria; she sat on the stairs in her nightgown, a shaken helpless figure, asking countless questions of those that hurried past. But they reassured her, and after a time she went downstairs and made a pot of coffee. Ensconced with it in the lower hall, and milk bottle in hand, she waylaid them with it as they hurried up and down.

Upstairs the battle went on. There were times when the paralyzed muscles almost stopped lifting the chest walls, when each breath was a new miracle. Her throat was closing fast, too, and at eight o'clock came a brisk young surgeon, and with Willy Cameron's assistance, an operation was performed. After that, and for days, Edith breathed through a tube in her neck.

The fiction of diphtheria was kept up, and Mrs. Boyd, having a childlike faith in medical men, betrayed no anxiety after the first hour or two. She saw nothing incongruous in Ellen going down through the house while she herself was kept out of that upper room where Edith lay, conscious now but sullen, disfigured, silent. She was happy, too, to have her old domain hers again, while Ellen nursed; to make again her flavorless desserts, her mounds of rubberlike gelatine, her pies. She brewed broths daily, and when Edith could swallow she sent up the results of hours of cooking which Ellen cooled, skimmed the crust of grease from the top, and heated again over the gas flame.

She never guessed the conspiracy against her.

Between Ellen and Edith there was no real liking. Ellen did her duty, and more; got up at night; was gentle with rather heavy hands; bathed the girl and brushed and braided her long hair. But there were hours during that simulated quarantine when a brooding silence held in the sick-room, and when Ellen, turning suddenly, would find Edith's eyes on her, full of angry distrust. At those times Ellen was glad that Edith could not speak.

For at the end of a few days Ellen knew, and Edith knew she knew.

Edith could not speak. She wrote her wants with a stub of pencil, or made signs. One day she motioned toward a mirror and Ellen took it to her.

"You needn't be frightened," she said. "When those scabs come off the doctor says you'll hardly be marked at all."

But Edith only glanced at herself, and threw the mirror aside.

Another time she wrote: "Willy?"

"He's all right. They've got a girl at the store to take your place, but I guess you can go back if you want to." Then, seeing the hunger in the girl's eyes: "He's out a good bit these nights. He's making speeches for that Mr. Hendricks. As if he could be elected against Mr. Cardew!"

The confinement told on Ellen. She would sit for hours, wondering what had become of Lily. Had she gone back home? Was she seeing that other man? Perhaps her valiant loyalty to Lily faded somewhat during those days, because she began to guess Willy Cameron's secret. If a girl had no eyes in her head, and couldn't see that Willy Cameron was the finest gentleman who ever stepped in shoe leather, that girl had something wrong about her.

Then, sometimes, she wondered how Edith's condition was going to be kept from her mother. She had measured Mrs. Boyd's pride by that time, her almost terrible respectability. She rather hoped that the sick woman would die some night, easily and painlessly in her sleep, because death was easier than some things. She liked Mrs. Boyd; she felt a slightly contemptuous but real affection for her.

Then one night Edith heard Willy's voice below, and indicated that she wanted to see him. He came in, stooping under the sheet which Mrs. Boyd had heard belonged in the doorway of diphtheria, and stood looking down at her. His heart ached. He sat down on the bed beside her and stroked her hand.

"Poor little girl," he said. "We've got to make things very happy for her, to make up for all this!"

But Edith freed her hand, and reaching out for paper and pencil stub, wrote something and gave it to Ellen.

Ellen read it.

"Tell him."

"I don't want to, Edith. You wait and do it yourself."

But Edith made an insistent gesture, and Ellen, flushed and wretched, had to tell. He made no sign, but sat stroking Edith's hand, only he stared rather fixedly at the wall, conscious that the girl's eyes were watching him for a single gesture of surprise or anger. He felt no anger, only a great perplexity and sadness, an older-brother grief.

"I'm sorry, little sister," he said, and did the kindest thing he could think of, bent over and kissed her on the forehead. "Of course I know how you feel, but it is a big thing to bear a child, isn't it? It is the only miracle we have these days."

"A child with no father," said Ellen, stonily.

"Even then," he persisted, "it's a big thing. We would have this one come under happier circumstances if we could, but we will welcome and take care of it, anyhow. A child's a child, and mighty valuable. And," he added —"I appreciate your wanting me to know, Edith."

He stayed a little while after that, but he read aloud, choosing a humorous story and laughing very hard at all the proper places. In the end he brought a faint smile to Edith's blistered lips, and a small lift to the cloud that hung over her now, day and night.

He made a speech that night, and into it he put all of his aching, anxious soul; Edith and Dan and Lily were behind it. Akers and Doyle. It was at a meeting in the hall over the city market, and the audience a new men's non-partisan association.

"Sometimes," he said, "I am asked what it is that we want, we men who are standing behind Hendricks as an independent candidate." He was supposed to bring Mr. Hendricks' name in as often as possible. "I answer that we want honest government, law and order, an end to this conviction that the country is owned by the unions and the capitalists, a fair deal for the plain people, which is you and I, my friends. But I answer still further, we want one thing more, a greater thing, and that thing we shall have. All through this great country to-night are groups of men hoping and planning for an incredible thing. They are not great in numbers; they are, however, organized, competent, intelligent and deadly. They plow the land with discord to sow the seeds of sedition. And the thing they want is civil war.

"And against them, what? The people like you and me; the men with homes they love; the men with little businesses they have fought and labored to secure; the clerks; the preachers; the doctors, the honest laborers, the God-fearing rich. I tell you, we are the people, and it is time we knew our power.

"And this is the thing we want, we the people; the greater thing, the thing we shall have; that this government, this country which we love, which has three times been saved at such cost of blood, shall survive."

It was after that speech that he met Pink Denslow for the first time. A square, solidly built young man edged his way through the crowd, and shook hands with him.

"Name's Denslow," said Pink. "Liked what you said. Have you time to run over to my club with me and have a high-ball and a talk?"

"I've got all the rest of the night."

"Right-o!" said Pink, who had brought back a phrase or two from the British.

It was not until they were in the car that Pink said:

"I think you're a friend of Miss Cardew's, aren't you?"

"I know Miss Cardew," said Willy Cameron, guardedly. And they were both rather silent for a time.

That night proved to be a significant one for them both, as it happened. They struck up a curious sort of friendship, based on a humble admiration on Pink's part, and with Willy Cameron on sheer hunger for the society of his kind. He had been suffering a real mental starvation. He had been constantly giving out and getting nothing in return.

Pink developed a habit of dropping into the pharmacy when he happened to be nearby. He was rather wistfully envious of that year in the camp, when Lily Cardew and Cameron had been together, and at first it was the bond of Lily that sent him to the shop. In the beginning the shop irritated him, because it seemed an incongruous background for the fiery young orator. But later on he joined the small open forum in the back room, and perhaps for the first time in his idle years he began to think. He had made the sacrifice of his luxurious young life to go to war, had slept in mud and risked his body and been hungry and cold and often frightfully homesick. And now it appeared that a lot of madmen were going to try to undo all that he had helped to do. He was surprised and highly indignant. Even a handful of agitators, it seemed, could do incredible harm.

One night he and Willy Cameron slipped into a meeting of a Russian Society, wearing old clothes, which with Willy was not difficult, and shuffling up dirty stairs without molestation. They came away thoughtful.

"Looks like it's more than talk," Pink said, after a time.

"They're not dangerous," Willy Cameron said. "That's talk. But it shows a state of mind. The real incendiaries don't show their hand like that."

"You think it's real, then?"

"Some boils don't come to a head. But most do."

It was after a mob of foreigners had tried to capture the town of Donesson, near Pittsburgh, and had been turned back by a hastily armed body of its citizens, doctors, lawyers and shop-keepers, that a nebulous plan began to form in Willy Cameron's active mind.

If one could unite the plain people politically, or against a foreign war, why could they not be united against an enemy at home? The South had had a similar problem, and the result was the Ku Klux Klan.

The Chief of Police was convinced that a plan was being formulated to repeat the Seattle experiment against the city. The Mayor was dubious. He was not a strong man; he had a conviction that because a thing never had happened it never could happen.

"The mob has done it before," urged the Chief of Police one day. "They took Paris, and it was damned disagreeable."

The Mayor was a trifle weak in history.

"Maybe they did," he agreed. "But this is different. This is America."

He was rather uneasy after that. It had occurred to him that the Chief might have referred to Paris, Illinois.

Now and then Pink coaxed Willy Cameron to his club, and for those rare occasions he provided always a little group of men like themselves, young, eager, loyal, and struggling with the new problems of the day. In this environment Willy Cameron received as well as gave.

Most of the men had been in the army, and he found in them an eager anxiety to face the coming situation and combat it. In the end the nucleus of the new Vigilance Committee was formed there.

Not immediately. The idea was of slow growth even with its originator, and it only reached the point of speech when Mr. Hendricks stopped in one day at the pharmacy and brought a bundle which he slapped down on the prescription desk.

"Read that dynamite," he said, his face flushed and lowering. "A man I know got it translated for me. Read it and then tell me whether I'm an alarmist and a plain fool, or if it means trouble around here."

There was no question in Willy Cameron's mind as to which it meant.

Louis Akers had by that time announced his candidacy for Mayor, and organized labor was behind him to an alarming extent. When Willy Cameron went with Pink to the club that afternoon, he found Akers under discussion, and he heard some facts about that gentleman's private life which left him silent and morose. Pink knew nothing of Lily's friendship with Akers. Indeed, Pink did not know that Lily was in the city, and Willy Cameron had not undeceived him. It had pleased Anthony Cardew to announce in the press that Lily was making a round of visits, and the secret was not his to divulge. But the question which was always in his mind rose again. What did she see in the man? How could she have thrown away her home and her family for a fellow who was so obviously what Pink would have called "a wrong one"?

He roused, however, at a question.

"He may," he said; "with three candidates we're splitting the vote three ways, and it's hard to predict. Mr. Cardew can't be elected, but he weakens Hendricks. One thing's sure. Where's my pipe?" Silence while Mr. Cameron searched for his pipe, and took his own time to divulge the sure thing. "If Hendricks is elected he'll clear out the entire bunch of anarchists. The present man's afraid. But if Akers can hypnotize labor into voting for him, and he gets it, it will be up to the city to protect itself, for he won't. He'll let them hold their infamous meetings and spread their damnable doctrine, and-you know what they've tried to do in other places."

He explained what he had in mind then, finding them expectant and eager. There ought to be some sort of citizen organization, to supplement the state and city forces. Nothing spectacular; indeed, the least said about it the better. He harked back then to his idea of the plain people, with homes to protect.

"That needn't keep you fellows out," he said, with his whimsical smile. "But the rank and file will have to constitute the big end. We don't want a lot of busybodies, pussy-footing around with guns and looking for trouble. We had enough of that during the war. We would want some men who would answer a riot call if they were needed. That's all."

He had some of the translations Hendricks had brought him in his pocket, and they circulated around the group.

"Do you think they mean to attack the city?"

"That looks like it, doesn't it? And they are getting that sort of stuff all the time. There are a hundred thousand of them in this end of the state."

"Would you make it a secret organization?"

"Yes. I like doing things in the open myself, but you've got to fight a rat in his hole, if he won't come out."

"Would you hold office?" Pink asked.

Willy Cameron smiled.

"I'm a good bit like the boy who dug post holes in the daytime and took in washing at night to support the family. But I'll work, if that's what you mean."

"We'd better have a constitution and all that, don't you think?" Pink asked. "We can draw up a tentative one, and then fix it up at the first meeting. This is going to be a big thing. It'll go like a fire."

But Willy Cameron overruled that.

"We don't need that sort of stuff," he said, "and if we begin that we might as well put it in the newspapers. We want men who can keep their mouths shut, and who will sign some sort of a card agreeing to stand by the government and to preserve law and order. Then an office and a filing case, and their addresses, so we can get at them in a hurry if we need them. Get me a piece of paper, somebody."

Then and there, in twenty words, Willy Cameron wrote the now historic oath of the new Vigilance Committee, on the back of an old envelope. It was a promise, an agreement rather than an oath. There was a little hush as the paper passed from hand to hand. Not a man there but felt a certain solemnity in the occasion. To preserve the Union and the flag, to fight all sedition, to love their country and support it; the very simplicity of the words was impressive. And the mere putting of it into visible form crystallized their hitherto vague anxieties, pointed to a real enemy and a real danger. Yet, as Willy Cameron pointed out, they might never be needed.

"Our job," he said, "is only as a last resort. Only for real trouble. Until the state troops can get here, for instance, and if the constabulary is greatly outnumbered. It's their work up to a certain point. We'll fight if they need us. That's all."

It was very surprising to him to find the enterprise financed immediately. Pink offered an office in the bank building. Some one agreed to pay a clerk who should belong to the committee. It was practical, businesslike, and-done. And, although he had protested, he found himself made the head of the organization.

"—without title and without pay," he stipulated. "If you wish a title on me, I'll resign."

He went home that night very exalted and very humble.

Chapter XXI

For a time Lily remained hidden in the house on Cardew Way, walking out after nightfall with Louis occasionally, but shrinkingly keeping to quiet back streets. She had a horror of meeting some one she knew, of explanations and of gossip. But after a time the desire to see her mother became overwhelming. She took to making little flying visits home at an hour when her grandfather was certain to be away, going in a taxicab, and reaching the house somewhat breathless and excited. She was driven by an impulse toward the old familiar things; she was homesick for them all, for her mother, for Mademoiselle, for her own rooms, for her little toilet table, for her bed and her reading lamp. For the old house itself.

She was still an alien where she was. Elinor Doyle was a perpetual enigma to her; now and then she thought she had penetrated behind the gentle mask that was Elinor's face, only to find beyond it something inscrutable. There was a dead line in Elinor's life across which Lily never stepped. Whatever Elinor's battles were, she fought them alone, and Lily had begun to realize that there were battles.

The atmosphere of the little house had changed. Sometimes, after she had gone to bed, she heard Doyle's voice from the room across the hall, raised angrily. He was nervous and impatient; at times he dropped the unctuousness of his manner toward her, and she found herself looking into a pair of cold blue eyes which terrified her.

The brilliant little dinners had entirely ceased, with her coming. A sort of early summer lethargy had apparently settled on the house. Doyle wrote for hours, shut in the room with the desk; the group of intellectuals, as he had dubbed them, had dispersed on summer vacations. But she discovered that there were other conferences being held in the house, generally late at night.

She learned to know the nights when those meetings were to occur. On those evenings Elinor always made an early move toward bed, and Lily would repair to her hot low-ceiled room, to sit in the darkness by the window and think long, painful thoughts.

That was how she learned of the conferences. She had no curiosity about them at first. They had something to do with the strike, she considered, and with that her interest died. Strikes were a symptom, and ultimately, through great thinkers like Mr. Doyle, they would discover the cure for the disease that caused them. She was quite content to wait for that time.

Then, one night, she went downstairs for a glass of ice water, and found the lower floor dark, and subdued voices coming from the study. The kitchen door was standing open, and she closed and locked it, placing the key, as was Elinor's custom, in a table drawer. The door was partly glass, and Elinor had a fear of the glass being broken and thus the key turned in the lock by some intruder.

On toward morning there came a violent hammering at her bedroom door, and Doyle's voice outside, a savage voice that she scarcely recognized. When she had thrown on her dressing gown and opened the door he had instantly caught her by the shoulder, and she bore the imprints of his fingers for days.

"Did you lock the kitchen door?" he demanded, his tones thick with fury.

"Yes. Why not?" She tried to shake off his hand, but failed.

"None of your business why not," he said, and gave her an angry shake. "Hereafter, when you find that door open, you leave it that way. That's all."

"Take your hands off me!" She was rather like her grandfather at that moment, and his lost caution came back. He freed her at once and laughed a little.

"Sorry!" he said. "I get a bit emphatic at times. But there are times when a locked door becomes a mighty serious matter."

The next day he removed the key from the door, and substituted a bolt. Elinor made no protest.

Another night Elinor was taken ill, and Lily had been forced to knock at the study door and call Doyle. She had an instant's impression of the room crowded with strange figures. The heavy odors of sweating bodies, of tobacco, and of stale beer came through the half-open door and revolted her. And Doyle had refused to go upstairs.

She began to feel that she could not remain there very long. The atmosphere was variable. It was either cynical or sinister, and she hated them both. She had a curious feeling, too, that Doyle both wanted her there and did not want her, and that he was changing his attitude toward her Aunt Elinor. Sometimes she saw him watching Elinor from under half-closed eyelids.

But she could not fill her days with anxieties and suspicions, and she turned to Louis Akers as a flower to the open day. He at least was what he appeared to be. There was nothing mysterious about him.

He came in daily, big, dominant and demonstrative, filling the house with his presence, and demanding her in a loud, urgent voice. Hardly had the door slammed before he would call:

"Lily! Where are you?"

Sometimes he lifted her off her feet and held her to him.

"You little whiffet!" he would say. "I could crush you to death in my arms."

Had his wooing all been violent she might have tired sooner, because those phases of his passion for her tired her. But there were times when he put her into a chair and sat on the floor at her feet, his handsome face uplifted to hers in a sort of humble adoration, his arms across her knees. It was not altogether studied. He was a born wooer, but he had his hours of humility, of vague aspirations. His insistent body was always greater than his soul, but now and then, when he was physically weary, he had a spiritual moment.

"I love you, little girl," he would say.

It was in one of those moments that she extracted a promise from him. He had been, from his position on the floor, telling her about the campaign.

"I don't like your running against my father, Louis."

"He couldn't have got it, anyhow. And he doesn't want it. I do, honey. I need it in my business. When the election's over you're going to marry me."

She ignored that.

"I don't like the men who come here, Louis. I wish they were not friends of yours."

"Friends of mine! That bunch?"

"You are always with them."

"I draw a salary for being with them, honey."

"But what do you draw a salary for?" He was immediately on the alert, but her eyes were candid and unsuspicious. "They are strikers, aren't they?"

"Yes."

"Is it legal business?"

"Partly that."

"Louis, is there going to be a general strike?"

"There may be some bad times coming, honey." He bent his head and kissed her hands, lying motionless in her lap. "I wish you would marry me soon. I want you. I want to keep you safe."

She drew her hands away.

"Safe from what, Louis?"

He sat back and looked up into her face.

"You must remember, dear, that for all your theories, which are very sweet, this is a man's world, and men have rather brutal methods of settling their differences."

"And you advocate brutality?"

"Well, the war was brutal, wasn't it? And you were in a white heat supporting it, weren't you? How about another war," —he chose his words carefully —"just as reasonable and just? You've heard Doyle. You know what I mean."

"Not now!"

He was amazed at her horror, a horror that made her recoil from him and push his hands away when he tried to touch her. He got up angrily and stood looking down at her, his hands in his pockets.

"What the devil did you think all this talk meant?" he demanded. "You've heard enough of it."

"Does Aunt Elinor know?"

"Of course."

"And she approves?"

"I don't know and I don't care." Suddenly, with one of the quick changes she knew so well, he caught her hands and drawing her to her feet, put his arms around her. "All I know is that I love you, and if you say the word I'll cut the whole business."

"You would?"

He amended his offer somewhat.

"Marry me, honey," he begged. "Marry me now. Do you think I'll let anything in God's world come between us? Marry me, and I'll do more than leave them." He was whispering to her, stroking her hair. "I'll cut the whole outfit. And on the day I go into your house as your husband I'll tell your people some things they want to know. That's a promise."

"What will they do to you?"

"Your people?"

"The others."

He drew himself to his full height, and laughed.

"They'll try to do plenty, old girl," he said, "but I'm not afraid of them, and they know it. Marry me, Lily," he urged. "Marry me now. And we'll beat them out, you and I."

He gave her a sense of power, over him and over evil. She felt suddenly an enormous responsibility, that of a human soul waiting to be uplifted and led aright.

"You can save me, honey," he whispered, and kneeling suddenly, he kissed the toe of her small shoe.

He was strong. But he was weak too. He needed her. "I'll do it, Louis," she said. "You-you will be good to me, won't you?"

"I'm crazy about you."

The mood of exaltation upheld her through the night, and into the next day. Elinor eyed her curiously, and with some anxiety. It was a long time since she had been a girl, going about star-eyed with power over a man, but she remembered that lost time well.

At noon Louis came in for a hasty luncheon, and before he left he drew Lily into the little study and slipped a solitaire diamond on her engagement finger. To Lily the moment was almost a holy one, but he seemed more interested in the quality of the stone and its appearance on her hand than in its symbolism.

"Got you cinched now, honey. Do you like it?"

"It makes me feel that I don't belong to myself any longer."

"Well, you've passed into good hands," he said, and laughed his great, vibrant laugh. "Costing me money already, you mite!"

A little of her exaltation died then. But perhaps men were like that, shyly covering the things they felt deepest.

She was rather surprised when he suggested keeping the engagement a secret.

"Except the Doyles, of course," he said. "I am not taking any chances on losing you, child."

"Not mother?"

"Not unless you want to be kidnaped and taken home. It's only a matter of a day or two, anyhow."

"I want more time than that. A month, anyhow."

And he found her curiously obstinate and determined. She did not quite know herself why she demanded delay, except that she shrank from delivering herself into hands that were so tender and might be so cruel. It was instinctive, purely.

"A month," she said, and stuck to it.

He was rather sulky when he went away, and he had told her the exact amount he had paid for her ring.

Having forced him to agree to the delay, she found her mood of exaltation returning. As always, it was when he was not with he that she saw him most clearly, and she saw his real need for her. She had a sense of peace, too, now that at last something was decided. Her future, for better or worse, would no longer be that helpless waiting which had been hers for so long. And out of her happiness came a desire to do kind things, to pat children on the head, to give alms to beggars, and-to see Willy Cameron.

She came downstairs that afternoon, dressed for the street.

"I am going out for a little while, Aunt Nellie," she said, "and when I come back I want to tell you something."

"Perhaps. I can guess."

"Perhaps you can."

She was singing to herself as she went out the door.

Elinor went back heavy-hearted to her knitting. It was very difficult always to sit by and wait. Never to raise a hand. Just to wait and watch. And pray.

Lily was rather surprised, when she reached the Eagle Pharmacy, to find Pink Denslow coming out. It gave her a little pang, too; he looked so clean and sane and normal, so much a part of her old life. And it hurt her, too, to see him flush with pleasure at the meeting.

"Why, Lily!" he said, and stood there, gazing at her, hat in hand, the sun on his gleaming, carefully brushed hair. He was quite inarticulate with happiness. "I —when did you get back?"

"I have not been away, Pink. I left home-it's a long story. I am staying with my aunt, Mrs. Doyle."

"Mrs. Doyle? You are staying there?"

"Why not? My father's sister."

His young face took on a certain sternness.

"If you knew what I suspect about Doyle, Lily, you wouldn't let the same roof cover you." But he added, rather wistfully, "I wish I might see you sometimes."

Lily's head had gone up a trifle. Why did her old world always try to put her in the wrong? She had had to seek sanctuary, and the Doyle house had been the only sanctuary she knew.

"Since you feel as you do, I'm afraid that's impossible. Mr. Doyle's roof is the only roof I have."

"You have a home," he said, sturdily.

"Not now. I left, and my grandfather won't have me back. You mustn't blame him, Pink. We quarreled and I left. I was as much responsible as he was."

For a moment after she turned and disappeared inside the pharmacy door he stood there, then he put on his hat and strode down the street, unhappy and perplexed. If only she had needed him, if she had not looked so self-possessed and so ever so faintly defiant, as though she dared him to pity her, he would have known what to do. All he needed was to be needed. His open face was full of trouble. It was unthinkable that Lily should be in that center of anarchy; more unthinkable that Doyle might have filled her up with all sorts of wild ideas. Women were queer; they liked theories. A man could have a theory of life and play with it and boast about it, but never dream of living up to it. But give one to a woman, and she chewed on it like a dog on a bone. If those Bolshevists had got hold of Lily —!

The encounter had hurt Lily, too. The fine edge of her exaltation was gone, and it did not return during her brief talk with Willy Cameron. He looked much older and very thin; there were lines around his eyes she had never seen before, and she hated seeing him in his present surroundings. But she liked him for his very unconsciousness of those surroundings. One always had to take Willy Cameron as he was.

"Do you like it, Willy?" she asked. It had dawned on her, with a sort of panic, that there was really very little to talk about. All that they had had in common lay far in the past.

"Well, it's my daily bread, and with bread costing what it does, I cling to it like a limpet to a rock."

"But I thought you were studying, so you could do something else."

"I had to give up the night school. But I'll get back to it sometime."

She was lost again. She glanced around the little shop, where once Edith Boyd had manicured her nails behind the counter, and where now a middle-aged woman stood with listless eyes looking out over the street.

"You still have Jinx, I suppose?"

"Yes. I —"

Lily glanced up as he stopped. She had drawn off her gloves, and his eyes had fallen on her engagement ring. To Lily there had always been a feeling of unreality about his declaration of love for her. He had been so restrained, so careful to ask nothing in exchange, so without expectation of return, that she had put it out of her mind as an impulse. She had not dreamed that he could still care, after these months of silence. But he had gone quite white.

"I am going to be married, Willy," she said, in a low tone. It is doubtful if he could have spoken, just then. And as if to add a finishing touch of burlesque to the meeting, a small boy with a swollen jaw came in just then and demanded something to "make it stop hurting."

He welcomed the interruption, she saw. He was very professional instantly, and so absorbed for a moment in relieving the child's pain that he could ignore his own.

"Let's see it," he said in a businesslike, slightly strained voice. "Better have it out, old chap. But I'll give you something just to ease it up a bit."

Which he proceeded to do. When he came back to Lily he was quite calm and self-possessed. As he had never thought of dramatizing himself, nor thought of himself at all, it did not occur to him that drama requires setting, that tragedy required black velvet rather than tooth-brushes, and that a small boy with an aching tooth was a comedy relief badly introduced.

All he knew was that he had somehow achieved a moment in which to steady himself, and to find that a man can suffer horribly and still smile. He did that, very gravely, when he came back to Lily.

"Can you tell me about it?"

"There is not very much to tell. It is Louis Akers."

The middle-aged clerk had disappeared.

"Of course you have thought over what that means, Lily."

"He wants me to marry him. He wants it very much, Willy. And —I know you don't like him, but he has changed. Women always think they have changed men, I know. But he is very different."

"I am sure of that," he said, steadily.

There was something childish about her, he thought. Childish and infinitely touching. He remembered a night at the camp, when some of the troops had departed for over-seas, and he had found her alone and crying in her hut. "I just can't let them go," she had sobbed. "I just can't. Some of them will never come back."

Wasn't there something of that spirit in her now, the feeling that she could not let Akers go, lest worse befall him? He did not know. All he knew was that she was more like the Lily Cardew he had known then than she had been since her return. And that he worshiped her.

But there was anger in him, too. Anger at Anthony Cardew. Anger at the Doyles. And a smoldering, bitter anger at Louis Akers, that he should take the dregs of his life and offer them to her as new wine. That he should dare to link his scheming, plotting days to this girl, so wise and yet so ignorant, so clear-eyed and yet so blind.

"Do they know at home?"

"I am going to tell mother to-day."

"Lily," he said, slowly, "there is one thing you ought to do. Go home, make your peace there, and get all this on the right footing. Then have him there. You have never seen him in that environment, yet that is the world he will have to live in, if you marry him. See how he fits there."

"What has that got to do with it?"

"Think a minute. Am I quite the same to you here, as I was in the camp?"

He saw her honest answer in her eyes.

Chapter XXII

The new movement was growing rapidly, and with a surprising catholicity of range. Already it included lawyers and doctors, chauffeurs, butchers, clergymen, clerks of all sorts, truck gardeners from the surrounding county, railroad employees, and some of the strikers from the mills, men who had obeyed their union order to quit work, but had obeyed it unwillingly; men who resented bitterly the invasion of the ranks of labor by the lawless element which was fomenting trouble.

Dan had joined.

On the day that Lily received her engagement ring from Louis Akers, one of the cards of the new Vigilance Committee was being inspected with cynical amusement by two clerks in a certain suite of offices in the Searing Building. They studied it with interest, while the man who had brought it stood by.

"Where'd you pick it up, Cusick?"

"One of our men brought it into the store. Said you might want to see it."

The three men bent over it.

The Myers Housecleaning Company had a suite of three rooms. During the day two stenographers, both men, sat before machines and made a pretense of business at such times as the door opened, or when an occasional client, seeing the name, came in to inquire for rates. At such times the clerks were politely regretful. The firm's contracts were all they could handle for months ahead.

There was a constant ebb and flow of men in the office, presumably professional cleaners. They came and went, or sat along the walls, waiting. A large percentage were foreigners but the clerks proved to be accomplished linguists. They talked, with more or less fluency, with Croats, Serbs, Poles and Slavs.

There was a supply room off the office, a room filled with pails and brushes, soap and ladders. But there was a great safe also, and its compartments were filled with pamphlets in many tongues, a supply constantly depleted and yet never diminishing. Workmen, carrying out the pails of honest labor, carried them loaded down with the literature it was their only business to circulate.

Thus, openly, and yet with infinite caution, was spread the doctrine of no God; of no government, and of no church; of the confiscation of private property; of strikes and unrest; of revolution, rape, arson and pillage.

And around this social cancer the city worked and played. Its theatres were crowded, its expensive shops, its hotels. Two classes of people were spending money prodigally; women with shawls over their heads, women who in all their peasant lives had never owned a hat, drove in automobiles to order their winter supply of coal, and vast amounts of liquors were being bought by the foreign element against the approaching prohibition law, and stored in untidy cellars.

On the other hand, the social life of the city was gay with reaction from war. The newspapers were filled with the summer plans of the wealthy, and with predictions of lavish entertaining in the fall. Among the list of debutantes Lily's name always appeared.

And, in between the upper and the nether millstone, were being ground the professional and salaried men with families, the women clerks, the vast army who asked nothing but the right to work and live. They went through their days doggedly, with little anxious lines around their eyes, suffering a thousand small deprivations, bewildered, tortured with apprehension of to-morrow, and yet patiently believing that, as things could not be worse, they must soon commence to improve.

"It's bound to clear up soon," said Joe Wilkinson over the back fence one night late in June, to Willy Cameron. Joe supported a large family of younger brothers and sisters in the house next door, and was employed in a department store. "I figure it this way-both sides need each other, don't they? Something like marriage, you know. It'll all be over in six months. Only I'm thanking heaven just now it's summer, because our kids are hell on shoes."

"I hope so," said Willy Cameron. "What are you doing over there, anyhow?"

"Wait and see," said Joe, cryptically. "If you think you're going to be the only Central Park in this vicinity you've got to think again." He hesitated and glanced around, but the small Wilkinsons were searching for worms in the overturned garden mold. "How's Edith?" he asked.

"She's all right, Joe."

"Seeing anybody yet?"

"Not yet. In a day or so she'll be downstairs."

"You might tell her I've been asking about her."

There was something in Joel's voice that caught Willy Cameron's attention. He thought about Joe a great deal that night. Joe was another one who must never know about Edith's trouble. The boy had little enough, and if he had built a dream about Edith Boyd he must keep his dream. He was rather discouraged that night, was Willy Cameron, and he began to think that dreams were the best things in life. They were a sort of sanctuary to which one fled to escape realities. Perhaps no reality was ever as beautiful as one's dream of it.

Lily had passed very definitely out of his life. Sometimes during his rare leisure he walked to Cardew Way through the warm night, and past the Doyle house, but he never saw her, and because it did not occur to him that she might want to see him he never made an attempt to call. Always after those futile excursions he was inclined to long silences, and only Jinx could have told how many hours he sat in his room at night, in the second-hand easy chair he had bought, pipe in hand and eyes on nothing in particular, lost in a dream world where the fields bore a strong resemblance to the parade ground of an army camp, and through which field he and Lily wandered like children, hand in hand.

But he had many things to think of. So grave were the immediate problems, of food and rent, of Mrs. Boyd and Edith, that a little of his fine frenzy as to the lurking danger of revolution departed from him. The meetings in the back room at the pharmacy took on a political bearing, and Hendricks was generally the central figure. The ward felt that Mr. Hendricks was already elected, and called him "Mr. Mayor." At the same time the steel strike pursued a course of comparative calm. At Friendship and at Baxter there had been rioting, and a fatality or two, but the state constabulary had the situation well in hand. On a Sunday morning Willy Cameron went out to Baxter on the trolley, and came home greatly comforted. The cool-eyed efficiency of the state police reassured him. He compared them, disciplined, steady, calm with the calmness of their dangerous calling, with the rabble of foreigners who shuffled along the sidewalks, and he felt that his anxiety had been rather absurd.

He was still making speeches, and now and then his name was mentioned in the newspapers. Mrs. Boyd, now mostly confined to her room, spent much time in searching for these notices, and then in painfully cutting them out and pasting them in a book. On those days when there was nothing about him she felt thwarted, and was liable to sharp remarks on newspapers in general, and on those of the city in particular.

Then, just as he began to feel that the strike would pass off like other strikes, and that Doyle and his crowd, having plowed the field for sedition, would find it planted with healthier grain, he had a talk with Edith.

She came downstairs for the first time one Wednesday evening early in July, the scars on her face now only faint red blotches, and he placed her, a blanket over her knees, in the small parlor. Dan had brought her down and had made a real effort to be kind, but his suspicion of the situation made it difficult for him to dissemble, and soon he went out. Ellen was on the doorstep, and through the open window came the shrieks of numerous little Wilkinsons wearing out expensive shoe-leather on the brick pavement.

They sat in the dusk together, Edith very quiet, Willy Cameron talking with a sort of determined optimism. After a time he realized that she was not even listening.

"I wish you'd close the window," she said at last. "Those crazy Wilkinson kids make such a racket. I want to tell you something."

"All right." He closed the window and stood looking down at her. "Are you sure you want me to hear it?" he asked gravely.

"Yes. It is not about myself. I've been reading the newspapers while I've been shut away up there, Willy. It kept me from thinking. And if things are as bad as they say I'd better tell you, even if I get into trouble doing it. I will, probably. Murder's nothing to them."

"Who are 'them'?"

"You get the police to search the Myers Housecleaning Company, in the Searing Building."

"Don't you think you'd better tell me more than that? The police will want something definite to go on."

She hesitated.

"I don't know very much. I met somebody there, once or twice, at night. And I know there's a telephone hidden in the drawer of the desk in the back room. I swore not to tell, but that doesn't matter now. Tell them to examine the safe, too. I don't know what's in it. Dynamite, maybe."

"What makes you think the company is wrong? A hidden telephone isn't much to go on."

"When a fellow's had a drink or two, he's likely to talk," she said briefly, and before that sordid picture Willy Cameron was silent. After a time he said:

"You won't tell me the name of the man you met there?"

"No. Don't ask me, Willy. That's between him and me." He got up and took a restless turn or two about the little rooms. Edith's problem had begun to obsess him. Not for long would it be possible to keep her condition from Mrs. Boyd. He was desperately at a loss for some course to pursue.

"Have you ever thought," he said at last, "that this man, whoever he is, ought to marry you?"

Edith's face set like a flint.

"I don't want to marry him," she said. "I wouldn't marry him if he was the last man on earth."

He knew very little of Edith's past. In his own mind he had fixed on Louis Akers, but he could not be sure.

"I won't tell you his name, either," Edith added, shrewishly. Then her voice softened. "I will tell you this, Willy," she said wistfully. "I was a good girl until I knew him. I'm not saying that to let myself out. It's the truth."

"You're a good girl now," he said gravely.

Some time after he got his hat and came in to tell her he was going out.

"I'll tell what you've told me to Mr. Hendricks," he said. "And we may go on and have a talk with the Chief of Police. If you are right it may be important."

After that for an hour or two Edith sat alone, save when Ellen now and then looked in to see if she was comfortable.

Edith's mind was chaotic. She had spoken on impulse, a good impulse at that. But suppose they trapped Louis Akers in the Searing Building?

Ellen went now and then to the Cardew house, and brought back with her the news of the family. At first she had sternly refused to talk about the Cardews to Edith, but the days in the sick room had been long and monotonous, and Edith's jealousy of Lily had taken the form, when she could talk, of incessant questions.

So Edith knew that Louis Akers had been the cause of Lily's leaving home, and called her a poor thing in her heart. Quite lately she had heard that if Lily was not already engaged she probably would be, soon. Now her motives were mixed, and her emotions confused. She had wanted to tell Willy Cameron what she knew, but she wanted Lily to marry Louis Akers. She wanted that terribly. Then Lily would be out of the way, and-Willy was not like Dan; he did not seem to think her forever lost. He had always been thoughtful, but lately he had been very tender with her. Men did strange things sometimes. He might be willing to forget, after a long time. She could board the child out somewhere, if it lived. Sometimes they didn't live.

But if they arrested Louis, Lily Cardew would fling him aside like an old shoe.

She closed her eyes. That opened a vista of possibilities she would not face.

She stopped in her mother's room on her slow progress upstairs, moved to sudden pity for the frail life now wearing to its close. If that were life she did not want it, with its drab days and futile effort, its incessant deprivations, its hands, gnarled with work that got nowhere, its greatest blessing sleep and forgetfulness.

She wondered why her mother did not want to die, to get away.

"I'll soon be able to look after you a bit, mother," she said from the doorway. "How's the pain down your arm?"

"Bring me the mucilage, Edie," requested Mrs. Boyd. She was propped up in bed and surrounded by newspapers. "I've found Willy's name again. I've got fourteen now. Where's the scissors?"

Eternity was such a long time. Did she know? Could she know, and still sit among her pillows, snipping?

"I wonder," said Mrs. Boyd, "did anybody feed Jinx? That Ellen is so saving that she grudges him a bone."

"He looks all right," said Edith, and went on up to bed. Maybe the Lord did that for people, when they reached a certain point. Maybe He took away the fear of death, by showing after years of it that life was not so valuable after all. She remembered her own facing of eternity, and her dread of what lay beyond. She had prayed first, because she wanted to have some place on the other side. She had prayed to be received young and whole and without child. And her mother —

Then she had a flash of intuition. There was something greater than life, and that was love. Her mother was upheld by love. That was what the eternal cutting and pasting meant. She was lavishing all the love of her starved days on Willy Cameron; she was facing death, because his hand was close by to hold to.

For just a moment, sitting on the edge of her bed, Edith Boyd saw what love might be, and might do. She held out both hands in the darkness, but no strong and friendly clasp caught them close. If she could only have him to cling to, to steady her wavering feet along the gray path that stretched ahead, years and years of it. Youth. Middle age. Old age.

"I'd only drag him down," she muttered bitterly.

Willy Cameron, meanwhile, had gone to Mr. Hendricks with Edith's story, and together late that evening they saw the Chief of Police at his house. Both Willy Cameron and Mr. Hendricks advocated putting a watch on the offices of the Myers Housecleaning Company and thus ultimately getting the heads of the organization. But the Chief was unwilling to delay.

"Every day means more of their infernal propaganda," he said, "and if this girl's telling a straight story, the thing to do is to get the outfit now. Those clerks, for instance-we'll get some information out of them. That sort always squeals. They're a cheap lot."

"Going to ball it up, of course," Mr. Hendricks said disgustedly, on the way home. "Won't wait, because if Akers gets in he's out, and he wants to make a big strike first. I'll drop in to-morrow evening and tell you what's happened."

He came into the pharmacy the next evening, with a bundle of red-bound pamphlets under his arm, and a look of disgust on his face.

"What did I tell you, Cameron?" he demanded, breathing heavily. "Yes, they got them all right. Got a safe full of stuff so inflammable that, since I've read some of it, I'm ready to blow up myself. It's worse than that first lot I showed you. They got the two clerks, and a half-dozen foreigners, too. And that's all they got."

"They won't talk?"

"Talk? Sure they'll talk. They say they're employed by the Myers Housecleaning Company, that they never saw the inside of the vault, and they're squealing louder than two pigs under a gate about false arrest. They'll have to let them go, son. Here. You can do most everything. Can you read Croatian? No? Well, here's something in English to cut your wisdom teeth on. Overthrowing the government is where these fellows start."

It was intelligent, that propaganda. Willy Cameron thought he saw behind it Jim Doyle and other men like Doyle, men who knew the discontents of the world, and would fatten by them; men who, secretly envious of the upper classes and unable to attain to them, would pull all men to their own level, or lower. Men who cloaked their own jealousies with the garb of idealism. Intelligent it was, dangerous, and imminent.

The pamphlets spoke of "the day." It was a Prussian phrase. The revolution was Prussian. And like the Germans, they offered loot as a reward. They appealed to the ugliest passions in the world, to lust and greed and idleness.

At a signal the mass was to arise, overthrow its masters and rule itself.

Mr. Hendricks stood in the doorway of the pharmacy and stared out at the city he loved.

"Just how far does that sort of stuff go, Cameron?" he asked. "Will our people take it up? Is the American nation going crazy?"

"Not a bit of it," said Willy Cameron stoutly. "They're about as able to overthrow the government as you are to shove over the Saint Elmo Hotel."

"I could do that, with a bomb."

"No, you couldn't. But you could make a fairly sizeable hole in it. It's the hole we don't want."

Mr. Hendricks went away, vaguely comforted.

Chapter XXIII

To old Anthony the early summer had been full of humiliations, which he carried with an increased arrogance of bearing that alienated even his own special group at his club.

"Confound the man," said Judge Peterson, holding forth on the golf links one Sunday morning while Anthony Cardew, hectic with rage, searched for a lost ball and refused to drop another. "He'll hold us up all morning, for that ball, just as he tries to hold up all progress." He lowered his voice. "What's happened to the granddaughter, anyhow?"

Senator Lovell lighted a cigarette.

"Turned Bolshevist," he said, briefly.

The Judge gazed at him.

"That's a pretty serious indictment, isn't it?"

"Well, that's what I hear. She's living in Jim Doyle's house. I guess that's the answer. Hey, Cardew! D'you want these young cubs behind us to play through, or are you going to show some sense and come on?"

Howard, fighting his father tooth and nail, was compelled to a reluctant admiration of his courage. But there was no cordiality between them. They were in accord again, as to the strike, although from different angles. Both of them knew that they were fighting for very life; both of them felt that the strikers' demands meant the end of industry, meant that the man who risked money in a business would eventually cease to control that business, although if losses came it would be he, and not the workmen, who bore them. Howard had gone as far as he could in concessions, and the result was only the demand for more. The Cardews, father and son, stood now together, their backs against a wall, and fought doggedly.

But only anxiety held them together.

His father was now backing Howard's campaign for the mayoralty, but he was rather late with his support, and in private he retained his cynical attitude. He had not come over at all until he learned that Louis Akers was an opposition candidate. At that his wrath knew no bounds and the next day he presented a large check to the campaign committee.

Mr. Hendricks, hearing of it, was moved to a dry chuckle.

"Can't you hear him?" he demanded. "He'd stalk into headquarters as important as an office boy who's been sent to the bank for money, and he'd slam down his check and say just two words."

"Which would be?" inquired Willy Cameron.

"'Buy 'em'," quoted Mr. Hendricks. "The old boy doesn't know that things have changed since the 80's. This city has changed, my lad. It's voting now the way it thinks, right or wrong. That's why these foreign language papers can play the devil with us. The only knowledge the poor wretches have got of us is what they're given to read. And most of it stinks of sedition. Queer thing, this thinking. A fellow can think himself into murder."

The strike was going along quietly enough. There had been rioting through the country, but not of any great significance. It was in reality a sort of trench warfare, with each side dug in and waiting for the other to show himself in the open. The representatives of the press, gathered in the various steel cities, with automobiles arranged for to take them quickly to any disturbance that might develop, found themselves with little news for the telegraph, and time hung heavy on their hands.

On an evening in July, Howard found Grace dressing for dinner, and realized with a shock that she was looking thin and much older. He kissed her and then held her off and looked at her.

"You've got to keep your courage up, dear," he said. "I don't think it will be long now."

"Have you seen her?"

"No. But something has happened. Don't look like that, Grace. It's not —"

"She hasn't married that man?"

"No. Not that. It only touches her indirectly. But she can't stay there. Even Elinor —" he checked himself. "I'll tell you after dinner."

Dinner was very silent, although Anthony delivered himself of one speech rather at length.

"So far as I can make out, Howard," he said, "this man Hendricks is getting pretty strong. He has a young fellow talking for him who gets over pretty well. It's my judgment that Hendricks had better be bought off. He goes around shouting that he's a plain man, after the support of the plain people. Although I'm damned if I know what he means by that."

Anthony Cardew was no longer comfortable in his own house. He placed the blame for it on Lily, and spent as many evenings away from home as possible. He considered that life was using him rather badly. Tied to the city in summer by a strike, his granddaughter openly gone over to his enemy, his own son, so long his tool and his creature, merely staying in his house to handle him, an income tax law that sent him to his lawyers with new protests almost daily! A man was no longer master even in his own home. His employees would not work for him, his family disobeyed him, his government held him up and shook him. In the good old days —

"I'm going out," he said, as he rose from the table. "Grace, that chef is worse than the last. You'd better send him off."

"I can't get any one else. I have tried for weeks. There are no servants anywhere."

"Try New York."

"I have tried-it is useless."

No cooks, either. No servants. Even Anthony recognized that, with the exception of Grayson, the servants in his house were vaguely hostile to the family. They gave grudging service, worked short hours, and, the only class of labor to which the high cost of food was a negligible matter, demanded wages he considered immoral.

"I don't know what the world's coming to," he snarled. "Well, I'm off. Thank God, there are still clubs for a man to go to."

"I want to have a talk with you, father."

"I don't want to talk."

"You needn't. I want you to listen, and I want Grace to hear, too."

In the end he went unwillingly into the library, and when Grayson had brought liqueurs and coffee and had gone, Howard drew the card from his pocket.

"I met young Denslow to-day," he said. "He came in to see me. As a matter of fact, I signed a card he had brought along, and I brought one for you, sir. Shall I read it?"

"You evidently intend to."

Howard read the card slowly. Its very simplicity was impressive, as impressive as it had been when Willy Cameron scrawled the words on the back of an old envelope. Anthony listened.

"Just what does that mean?"

"That the men behind this movement believe that there is going to be a general strike, with an endeavor to turn it into a revolution. Perhaps only local, but these things have a tendency to spread. Denslow had some literature which referred to an attempt to take over the city. They have other information, too, all pointing the same way."

"Strikers?"

"Foreign strikers, with the worst of the native born. Their plans are fairly comprehensive; they mean to dynamite the water works, shut down the gas and electric plants, and cut off all food supplies. Then when they have starved and terrorized us into submission, we'll accept their terms."

"What terms?"

"Well, the rule of the mob, I suppose. They intend to take over the banks, for one thing."

"I don't believe it. It's incredible."

"They meant to do it in Seattle."

"And didn't. Don't forget that."

"They may have learned some things from Seattle," Howard said quietly.

"We have the state troops."

"What about a half dozen similar movements in the state at the same time? Or rioting in other places, carefully planned to draw the troops and constabulary away?"

In the end old Anthony was impressed, if not entirely convinced. But he had no faith in the plain people, and said so. "They'll see property destroyed and never lift a hand," he said. "Didn't I stand by in Pittsburgh during the railroad riots, and watch them smile while the yards burned? Because the railroads meant capital to them, and they hate capital."

"Precisely," said Howard, "but after twenty-four hours they were fighting like demons to restore law and order. It is" —he fingered the card —"to save that twenty-four hours that this organization is being formed. It is secret. Did I tell you that? And the idea originated with the young man you spoke about as supporting Hendricks-you met him here once, a friend of Lily's. His name is Cameron-William Wallace Cameron."

Old Anthony remained silent, but the small jagged vein on his forehead swelled with anger. After a time:

"I suppose Doyle is behind this?" he asked. "It sounds like him."

"That is the supposition. But they have nothing on him yet; he is too shrewd for that. And that leads to something else. Lily cannot continue to stay there."

"I didn't send her there."

"Actually, no. In effect-but we needn't go into that now. The situation is very serious. I can imagine that nothing could fit better into his plans than to have her there. She gives him a cachet of respectability. Do you want that?"

"She is probably one of them now. God knows how much of his rotten doctrine she has absorbed."

Howard flushed, but he kept his temper.

"His theories, possibly. His practice, no. She certainly has no idea... it has come to this, father. She must have a home somewhere, and if it cannot be here, Grace and I must make one for her elsewhere."

Probably Anthony Cardew had never respected Howard more than at that moment, or liked him less.

"Both you and Grace are free to make a home where you please."

"We prefer it here, but you must see yourself that things cannot go on as they are. We have waited for you to see that, all three of us, and now this new situation makes it imperative to take some action."

"I won't have that fellow Akers coming here."

"He would hardly come, under the circumstances. Besides, her friendship with him is only a part of her revolt. If she comes home it will be with the understanding that she does not see him again."

"Revolt?" said old Anthony, raising his eyebrows.

"That is what it actually was. She found her liberty interfered with, and she staged her own small rebellion. It was very human, I think."

"It was very Cardew," said old Anthony, and smiled faintly. He had, to tell the truth, developed a grudging admiration for his granddaughter in the past two months. He saw in her many of his own qualities, good and bad. And, more than he cared to own, he had missed her and the young life she had brought into the quiet house. Most important of all, she was the last of the Cardews. Although his capitulation when it came was curt, he was happier than he had been for weeks.

"Bring her home," he said, "but tell her about Akers. If she says that is off, I'll forget the rest."

On her way to her room that night Grace Cardew encountered Mademoiselle, a pale, unhappy Mademoiselle, who seemed to spend her time mostly in Lily's empty rooms or wandering about corridors. Whenever the three members of the family were together she would retire to her own quarters, and there feverishly with her rosary would pray for a softening of hearts. She did not comprehend these Americans, who were so kind to those beneath them and so hard to each other.

"I wanted to see you, Mademoiselle," Grace said, not very steadily. "I have good news for you."

Mademoiselle began to tremble. "She is coming? Lily is coming?"

"Yes. Will you have some fresh flowers put in her rooms in the morning?"

Suddenly Mademoiselle forgot her years of repression, and flinging her arms around Grace's neck she kissed her. Grace held her for a moment, patting her shoulder gently.

"We must try to make her very happy, Mademoiselle. I think things will be different now."

Mademoiselle stood back and wiped her eyes.

"But she must be different, too," she said. "She is sweet and good, but she is strong of will, too. The will to do, to achieve, that is one thing, and very good. But the will to go one's own way, that is another."

"The young are always headstrong, Mademoiselle."

But, alone later on, her rosary on her knee, Mademoiselle wondered. If youth were the indictment against Lily, was she not still young? It took years, or suffering, or sometimes both, to break the will of youth and chasten its spirit. God grant Lily might not have suffering.

It was Grace's plan to say nothing to Lily, but to go for her herself, and thus save her the humiliation of coming back alone. All morning housemaids were busy in Lily's rooms. Rugs were shaken, floors waxed and rubbed, the silver frames and vases in her sitting room polished to refulgence. And all morning Mademoiselle scolded and ran suspicious fingers into corners, and arranged and re-arranged great boxes of flowers.

Long before the time she had ordered the car Grace was downstairs, dressed for the street, and clad in cool shining silk, was pacing the shaded hall. There was a vague air of expectation about the old house. In a room off the pantry the second man was polishing the buttons of his livery, using a pasteboard card with a hole in it to save the fabric beneath. Grayson pottered about in the drawing room, alert for the parlor maid's sins of omission.

The telephone in the library rang, and Grayson answered it, while Grace stood in the doorway.

"A message from Miss Lily," he said. "Mrs. Doyle has telephoned that Miss Lily is on her way here."

Grace was vaguely disappointed. She had wanted to go to Lily with her good news, to bring her home bag and baggage, to lead her into the house and to say, in effect, that this was home, her home. She had felt that they, and not Lily, should take the first step.

She went upstairs, and taking off her hat, smoothed her soft dark hair. She did not want Lily to see how she had worried; she eyed herself carefully for lines. Then she went down, to more waiting, and for the first time, to a little doubt.

Yet when Lily came all was as it should have been. There was no doubt about her close embrace of her mother, her happiness at seeing her. She did not remove her gloves, however, and after she had put Grace in a chair and perched herself on the arm of it, there was a little pause. Each was preparing to tell something, each hesitated. Because Grace's task was the easier it was she who spoke first.

"I was about to start over when you telephoned, dear," she said. "I—we want you to come home to us again."

There was a queer, strained silence.

"Who wants me?" Lily asked, unsteadily.

"All of us. Your grandfather, too. He expects to find you here to-night. I can explain to your Aunt Elinor over the telephone, and we can send for your clothes."

Suddenly Lily got up and walked the length of the room. When she came back her eyes were filled with tears, and her left hand was bare.

"It nearly kills me to hurt you," she said, "but-what about this?"

She held out her hand.

Grace seemed frozen in her chair. At the sight of her mother's face Lily flung herself on her knees beside the chair.

"Mother, mother," she said, "you must know how I love you. Love you both. Don't look like that. I can't bear it."

Grace turned away her face.

"You don't love us. You can't. Not if you are going to marry that man."

"Mother," Lily begged, desperately, "let me come home. Let me bring him here. I'll wait, if you'll only do that. He is different; I know all that you want to say about his past. He has never had a real chance in all his life. He won't belong at first, but-he's a man, mother, a strong man. And it's awfully important. He can do so much, if he only will. And he says he will, if I marry him."

"I don't understand you," Grace said coldly. "What can a man like that do, but wreck all our lives?"

Resentment was rising fast in Lily, but she kept it down. "I'll tell you about that later," she said, and slowly got to her feet. "Is that all, mother? You won't see him? I can't bring him here? Isn't there any compromise? Won't you meet me half-way?"

"When you say half-way, you mean all the way, Lily."

"I wanted you so," Lily said, drearily, "I need you so just now. I am going to be married, and I have no one to go to. Aunt Elinor doesn't understand, either. Every way I look I find —I suppose I can't come back at all, then."

"Your grandfather's condition was that you never see this Louis Akers again."

Lily's resentment left her. Anger was a thing for small matters, trivial affairs. This that was happening, an irrevocable break with her family, was as far beyond anger as it was beyond tears. She wondered dully if any man were worth all this. Perhaps she knew, sub-consciously, that Louis Akers was not. All her exaltation was gone, and in its stead was a sort of dogged determination to see the thing through now, at any cost; to re-make Louis into the man he could be, to build her own house of life, and having built it, to live in it as best she could.

"That is a condition I cannot fulfill, mother. I am engaged to him."

"Then you love him more than you do any of us, or all of us."

"I don't know. It is different," she said vaguely.

She kissed her mother very tenderly when she went away, but there was a feeling of finality in them both. Mademoiselle, waiting at the top of the stairs, heard the door close and could not believe her ears. Grace went upstairs, her face a blank before the servants, and shut herself in her room. And in Lily's boudoir the roses spread a heavy, funereal sweetness over the empty room.

Chapter XXIV

The strike had been carried on with comparatively little disorder. In some cities there had been rioting, but half-hearted and easily controlled. Almost without exception it was the foreign and unassimilated element that broke the peace. Alien women spat on the state police, and flung stones at them. Here and there property was destroyed. A few bomb outrages filled the newspapers with great scare-heads, and sent troops and a small army of secret service men here and there.

In the American Federation of Labor a stocky little man grimly fought to oppose the Radical element, which was slowly gaining ground, and at the same time to retain his leadership. The great steel companies, united at last by a common danger and a common fate if they yielded, stood doggedly and courageously together, waiting for a return of sanity to the world. The world seemed to have gone mad. Everywhere in the country production was reduced by the cessation of labor, and as a result the cost of living was mounting.

And every strike lost in the end. Labor had yet to learn that to cease to labor may express a grievance, but that in itself it righted no wrongs. Rather, it turned that great weapon, public opinion, without which no movement may succeed, against it. And that to stand behind the country in war was not enough. It must stand behind the country in peace.

It had to learn, too, that a chain is only as strong as its weakest link. The weak link in the labor chain was its Radical element. Rioters were arrested with union cards in their pockets. In vain the unions protested their lack of sympathy with the unruly element. The vast respectable family of union labor found itself accused of the sins of the minority, and lost standing thereby.

At Friendship the unruly element was very strong. For a time it held its meetings in a hall. When that was closed it resorted to the open air.

On the fifteenth of July it held an incendiary meeting on the unused polo field, and the next day awakened to the sound of hammers, and to find a high wooden fence, reenforced with barbed wire, being built around the field, with the state police on guard over the carpenters. In a few days the fence was finished, only to be partly demolished the next night, secretly and noiselessly. But no further attempts were made to hold meetings there. It was rumored that meetings were being secretly held in the woods near the town, but the rendezvous was not located.

On the restored fence around the polo grounds a Red flag was found one morning, and two nights later the guard at the padlocked gate was shot through the heart, from ambush.

Then, about the first of August, out of a clear sky, sporadic riotings began to occur. They seemed to originate without cause, and to end as suddenly as they began. Usually they were in the outlying districts, but one or two took place in the city itself. The rioters were not all foreign strikers from the mills. They were garment workers, hotel waiters, a rabble of the discontented from all trades. The riots were to no end, apparently. They began with a chance word, fought their furious way for an hour or so, and ended, leaving a trail of broken heads and torn clothing behind them.

On toward the end of July one such disturbance grew to considerable size. The police were badly outnumbered, and a surprising majority of the rioters were armed, with revolvers, with wooden bludgeons, lengths of pipe and short, wicked iron bars. Things were rather desperate until the police found themselves suddenly and mysteriously reenforced by a cool-headed number of citizens, led by a tall thin man who limped slightly, and who disposed his heterogeneous support with a few words and considerable skill.

The same thin young man, stopping later in an alley way to investigate an arm badly bruised by an iron bar, overheard a conversation between two roundsmen, met under a lamppost after the battle, for comfort and a little conversation.

"Can you beat that, Henry?" said one. "Where the hell'd they come from?"

"Search me," said Henry. "D'you see the skinny fellow? Limped, too. D'you notice that? Probably hurt in France. But he hasn't forgotten how to fight, I'll tell the world."

The outbreaks puzzled the leaders of the Vigilance Committee. Willy Cameron was inclined to regard them as without direction or intention, purely as manifestations of hate, and as such contrary to the plans of their leaders. And Mr. Hendricks, nursing a black eye at home after the recent outburst, sized up the situation shrewdly.

"You can boil a kettle too hard," he said, "and then the lid pops off. Doyle and that outfit of his have been burning the fire a little high, that's all. They'll quit now, because they want to get us off guard later. You and your committee can take a vacation, unless you can set them to electioneering for me. They've had enough for a while, the devils. They'll wait now for Akers to get in and make things easy for them. Mind my words, boy. That's the game."

And the game it seemed to be. Small violations of order still occurred, but no big ones. To the headquarters in the Denslow Bank came an increasing volume of information, to be duly docketed and filed. Some of it was valueless. Now and then there came in something worth following up. Thus one night Pink and a picked band, following a vague clew, went in automobiles to the state borderline, and held up and captured two trucks loaded with whiskey and destined for Friendship and Baxter. He reported to Willy Cameron late that night.

"Smashed it all up and spilled it in the road," he said. "Hurt like sin to do it, though. Felt like the fellow who shot the last passenger pigeon."

But if the situation in the city was that of armed neutrality, in the Boyd house things were rapidly approaching a climax, and that through Dan. He was on edge, constantly to be placated and watched. The strike was on his nerves; he felt his position keenly, resented Willy Cameron supporting the family, and had developed a curious jealousy of his mother's affection for him.

Toward Edith his suspicions had now become certainty, and an open break came on an evening when she said that she felt able to go to work again. They were at the table, and Ellen was moving to and from the kitchen, carrying in the meal. Her utmost thrift could not make it other than scanty, and finally Dan pushed his plate away.

"Going back to work, are you?" he sneered. "And how long do you think you'll be able to work?"

"You keep quiet," Edith flared at him. "I'm going to work. That's all you need to know. I can't sit here and let a man who doesn't belong to us provide every bite we eat, if you can." Willy Cameron got up and closed the door, for Mrs. Boyd an uncanny ability to hear much that went on below.

"Now," he said when he came back, "we might as well have this out. Dan has a right to be told, Edith, and he can help us plan something." He turned to Dan. "It must be kept from your mother, Dan."

"Plan something!" Dan snarled. "I know what to plan, all right. I'll find the —" he broke into foul, furious language, but suddenly Willy Cameron rose, and there was something threatening in his eyes.

"I know who it is," Dan said, more quietly, "and he's got to marry her, or I'll kill him."

"You know, do you? Well, you don't," Edith said, "and I won't marry him anyhow."

"You will marry him. Do you think I'm going to see mother disgraced, sick as she is, and let you get away with it? Where does Akers live? You know, don't you? You've been there, haven't you?"

All Edith's caution was forgotten in her shame and anger.

"Yes, I know," she said, hysterically, "but I won't tell you. And I won't marry him. I hate him. If you go to him he'll beat you to death." Suddenly the horrible picture of Dan in Akers' brutal hands overwhelmed her. "Dan, you won't go?" she begged. "He'll kill you."

"A lot you'd care," he said, coldly. "As if we didn't have enough already! As if you couldn't have married Joe Wilkinson, next door, and been a decent woman. And instead, you're a —"

"Be quiet, Dan," Willy Cameron interrupted him. "That sort of talk doesn't help any. Edith is right. If you go to Akers there will be a fight. And that's no way to protect her."

"God!" Dan muttered. "With all the men in the world, to choose that rotten anarchist!"

It was sordid, terribly tragic, the three of them sitting there in the badly lighted little room around the disordered table, with Ellen grimly listening in the doorway, and the odors of cooking still heavy in the air. Edith sat there, her hands on the table, staring ahead, and recounted her wrongs. She had never had a chance. Home had always been a place to get away from. Nobody had cared what became of her. And hadn't she tried to get out of the way? Only they all did their best to make her live. She wished she had died.

Dan, huddled low in his chair, his legs sprawling, stared at nothing with hopeless eyes.

Afterwards Willy Cameron could remember nothing of the scene in detail. He remembered its setting, but of all the argument and quarreling only one thing stood out distinctly, and that was Edith's acceptance of Dan's accusation. It was Akers, then. And Lily Cardew was going to marry him. Was in love with him.

"Does he know how things are?" he asked.

She nodded. "Yes."

"Does he offer to do anything?"

"Him? He does not. And don't you go to him and try to get him to marry me. I tell you I'd die first."

He left them there, sitting in the half light, and going out into the hall picked up his hat. Mrs. Boyd heard him and called to him, and before he went out he ran upstairs to her room. It seemed to him, as he bent over her, that her lips were bluer than ever, her breath a little shallower and more difficult. Her untouched supper tray was beside her.

"I wasn't hungry," she explained. "Seems to me, Willy, if you'd let me go downstairs so I could get some of my own cooking I'd eat better. Ellen's all right, but I kind o' crave sweet stuff, and she don't like making desserts."

"You'll be down before long," he assured her. "And making me pies. Remember those pies you used to bake?"

"You always were a great one for my pies," she said, complacently.

He kissed her when he left. He had always marveled at the strange lack of demonstrativeness in the household, and he knew that she valued his small tendernesses.

"Now remember," he said, "light out at ten o'clock, and no going downstairs in the middle of the night because you smell smoke. When you do, it's my pipe."

"I don't think you hardly ever go to bed, Willy."

"Me? Get too much sleep. I'm getting fat with it."

The stale little joke was never stale with her. He left her smiling, and went down the stairs and out into the street.

He had no plan in his mind except to see Louis Akers, and to find out from him if he could what truth there was in Edith Boyd's accusation. He believed Edith, but he must have absolute certainty before he did anything. Girls in trouble sometimes shielded men. If he could get the facts from Louis Akers-but he had no idea of what he would do then. He couldn't very well tell Lily, but her people might do something. Or Mrs. Doyle.

He knew Lily well enough to know that she would far rather die than marry Akers, under the circumstances. That her failure to marry Louis Akers would mean anything as to his own relationship with her he never even considered. All that had been settled long ago, when she said she did not love him.

At the Benedict he found that his man had not come home, and for an hour or two he walked the streets. The city seemed less majestic to him than usual; its quiet by-streets were lined with homes, it is true, but those very streets hid also vice and degradation, and ugly passions. They sheltered, but also they concealed.

At eleven o'clock he went back to the Benedict, and was told that Mr. Akers had come in.

It was Akers himself who opened the door. Because the night was hot he had shed coat and shirt, and his fine torso, bare to the shoulders and at the neck, gleamed in the electric light. Willy Cameron had not seen him since those spring days when he had made his casual, bold-eyed visits to Edith at the pharmacy, and he had a swift insight into the power this man must have over women. He himself was tall; but Akers was taller, fully muscled, his head strongly set on a neck like a column. But he surmised that the man was soft, out of condition. And he had lost the first elasticity of youth.

Akers' expression had changed from one of annoyance to watchfulness when he opened the door.

"Well!" he said. "Making a late call, aren't you?"

"What I had to say wouldn't wait."

Akers had, rather unwillingly, thrown the door wide, and he went in. The room was very hot, for a small fire, littered as to its edges with papers, burned in the grate. Although he knew that Akers had guessed the meaning of his visit at once and was on guard, there was a moment or two when each sparred for an opening.

"Sit down. Have a cigarette?"

"No, thanks." He remained standing.

"Or a high-ball? I still have some fairly good whiskey."

"No. I came to ask you a question, Mr. Akers."

"Well, answering questions is one of the best little things I do."

"You know about Edith Boyd's condition. She says you are responsible. Is that true?"

Louis Akers was not unprepared. Sooner or later he had known that Edith would tell. But what he had not counted on was that she would tell any one who knew Lily. He had felt that her leaving the pharmacy had eliminated that chance. "What do you mean, her condition?"

"You know. She says she has told you."

"You're pretty thick with her yourself, aren't you?"

"I happen to live at the Boyd house."

He was keeping himself well under control, but Akers saw his hand clench, and resorted to other tactics. He was not angry himself, but he was wary now; he considered that life was unnecessarily complicated, and that he had a distinct grievance.

"I have asked you a question, Mr. Akers."

"You don't expect me to answer it, do you?"

"I do."

"If you have come here to talk to me about marrying her —"

"She won't marry you," Willy Cameron said steadily. "That's not the point I want your own acknowledgment of responsibility, that's all."

Akers was puzzled, suspicious, and yet relieved. He lighted a cigarette and over the match stared at the other man's quiet face.

"No!" he said suddenly. "I'm damned if I'll take the responsibility. She knew her way around long before I ever saw her. Ask her. She can't lie about it. I can produce other men to prove what I say. I played around with her, but I don't know whose child that is, and I don't believe she does."

"I think you are lying."

"All right. But I can produce the goods."

Willy Cameron went very pale. His hands were clenched again, and Akers eyed him warily.

"None of that," he cautioned. "I don't know what interest you've got in this, and I don't give a God-damn. But you'd better not try any funny business with me."

Willy Cameron smiled. Much the sort of smile he had worn during the rioting.

"I don't like to soil my hands on you," he said, "but I don't mind telling you that any man who ruins a girl's life and then tries to get out of it by defaming her, is a skunk."

Akers lunged at him.

Some time later Mr. William Wallace Cameron descended to the street. He wore his coat collar turned up to conceal the absence of certain articles of wearing apparel which he had mysteriously lost. And he wore, too, a somewhat distorted, grim and entirely complacent smile.

Chapter XXV

The city had taken the rioting with a weary philosophy. It was tired of fighting. For two years it had labored at high tension for the European war. It had paid taxes and bought bonds, for the war. It had saved and skimped and denied itself, for the war. And for the war it had made steel, steel for cannon and for tanks, for ships and for railroads. It had labored hard and well, and now all it wanted was to be allowed to get back to normal things. It wanted peace.

It said, in effect: "I have both fought and labored, sacrificed and endured. Give me now my rest of nights, after a day's work. Give me marriage and children. Give me contentment. Give me the things I have loved long since, and lost awhile."

And because the city craved peace, it was hard to rouse it to its danger. It was war-weary, and its weariness was not of apathy, but of exhaustion. It was not yet ready for new activity.

Then, the same night that had seen Willy Cameron's encounter with Akers, it was roused from its lethargy. A series of bomb outrages shook the downtown district. The Denslow Bank was the first to go. Willy Cameron, inspecting a cut lip in his mirror, heard a dull explosion, and ran down to the street. There he was joined by Joe Wilkinson, in trousers over his night shirt, and as they looked, a dull red glare showed against the sky. Joe went back for more clothing, but Willy Cameron ran down the street. At the first corner he heard a second explosion, further away and to the east, but apparently no fire followed it. That, he learned later, was the City Club, founded by Anthony Cardew years before.

The Denslow Bank was burning. The facade had been shattered and from the interior already poured a steady flow of flame and smoke. He stood among the crowd, while the engines throbbed and the great fire hose lay along the streets, and watched the little upper room where the precious records of the Committee were burning brightly. The front wall gone, the small office stood open to the world, a bright and shameless thing, flaunting its nakedness to the crowd below.

He wondered why Providence should so play into the hands of the enemy.

After a time he happened on Pink Denslow, wandering alone on the outskirts of the crowd.

"Just about kill the governor, this," said Pink, heavily. "Don't suppose the watchmen got out, either. Not that they'd care," he added, savagely.

"How about the vaults? I suppose they are fireproof?"

"Yes. Do you realize that every record we've got has gone? D'you suppose those fellows knew about them?"

Willy Cameron had been asking himself the same question.

"Trouble is," Pink went on, "you don't know who to trust. They're not all foreigners. Let's get away from here; it makes me sick."

They wandered through the night together, almost unconsciously in the direction of the City Club, but within a block of it they realized that something was wrong. A hospital ambulance dashed by, its gong ringing wildly, and a fire engine, not pumping, stood at the curb.

"Come on," Pink said suddenly. "There were two explosions. It's just possible —"

The club was more sinister than the burning bank; it was a mass of grim wreckage, black and gaping, with now and then the sound of settling masonry, and already dotted with the moving flash-lights of men who searched.

To Pink this catastrophe was infinitely greater than that of the bank. Men he knew had lived there. There were old club servants who were like family retainers; one or two employees were ex-service men for whom he had found employment. He stood there, with Willy Cameron's hand on his arm, with a new maturity and a vast suffering in his face.

"Before God," he said solemnly, "I swear never to rest until the fellows behind this are tried, condemned and hanged. You've heard it, Cameron."

The death list for that night numbered thirteen, the two watchmen at the bank and eleven men at the club, two of them members. Willy Cameron, going home at dawn, exhausted and covered with plaster dust, bought an extra and learned that a third bomb, less powerful, had wrecked the mayor's house. It had been placed under the sleeping porch, and but for the accident of a sick baby the entire family would have been wiped out.

Even his high courage began to waver. His records were gone; that was all to do over again. But what seemed to him the impasse was this fighting in the dark. An unseen enemy, always. And an enemy which combined with skill a total lack of any rules of warfare, which killed here, there and everywhere, as though for the sheer joy of killing. It struck at the high but killed the low. And it had only begun.

Chapter XXVI

Dominant family traits have a way of skipping one generation and appearing in the next. Lily Cardew at that stage of her life had a considerable amount of old Anthony's obstinacy and determination, although it was softened by a long line of Cardew women behind her, women who had loved, and suffered dominance because they loved. Her very infatuation for Louis Akers, like Elinor's for Doyle, was possibly an inheritance from her fore-mothers, who had been wont to overlook the evil in a man for the strength in him. Only Lily mistook physical strength for moral fibre, insolence and effrontery for courage.

In both her virtues and her faults, however, irrespective of heredity, Lily represented very fully the girl of her position and period. With no traditions to follow, setting her course by no compass, taught to think but not how to think, resentful of tyranny but unused to freedom, she moved ahead along the path she had elected to follow, blindly and obstinately, yet unhappy and suffering.

Her infatuation for Louis Akers had come to a new phase of its rapid development. She had reached that point where a woman realizes that the man she loves is, not a god of strength and wisdom, but a great child who needs her. It is at that point that one of two things happens: the weak woman abandons him, and follows her dream elsewhere. The woman of character, her maternal instinct roused, marries him, bears him children, is both wife and mother to him, and finds in their united weaknesses such strength as she can.

In her youth and self-sufficiency Lily stood ready to give, rather than to receive. She felt now that he needed her more than she needed him. There was something unconsciously patronizing those days in her attitude toward him, and if he recognized it he did not resent it. Women had always been "easy" for him. Her very aloofness, her faint condescension, her air of a young grande dame, were a part of her attraction for him.

Love sees clearly, and seeing, loves on. But infatuation is blind; when it gains sight, it dies. Already Lily was seeing him with the critical eyes of youth, his loud voice, his over-fastidious dress, his occasional grossnesses. To offset these she placed vast importance on his promise to leave his old associates when she married him.

The time was very close now. She could not hold him off much longer, and she began to feel, too, that she must soon leave the house on Cardew Way. Doyle's attitude to her was increasingly suspicious and ungracious. She knew that he had no knowledge of Louis's promise, but he began to feel that she was working against him, and showed it.

And in Louis Akers too she began to discern an inclination not to pull out until after the election. He was ambitious, and again and again he urged that he would be more useful for the purpose in her mind if he were elected first.

That issue came to a climax the day she had seen her mother and learned the terms on which she might return home. She was alarmed by his noisy anger at the situation.

"Do sit down, Louis, and be quiet," she said. "You have known their attitude all along, haven't you?"

"I'll show them," he said, thickly. "Damned snobs!" He glanced at her then uneasily, and her expression put him on his guard. "I didn't mean that, little girl. Honestly I didn't. I don't care for myself. It's you."

"You must understand that they think they are acting for my good. And I am not sure," she added, her clear eyes on him, "that they are not right. You frighten me sometimes, Louis."

But a little later he broke out again. If he wasn't good enough to enter their house, he'd show them something. The election would show them something. They couldn't refuse to receive the mayor of the city. She saw then that he was bent on remaining with Doyle until after the election.

Lily sat back, listening and thinking. Sometimes she thought that he did not love her at all. He always said he wanted her, but that was different.

"I think you love yourself more than you love me, Louis," she said, when he had exhausted himself. "I don't believe you know what love is."

That brought him to his knees, his arms around her, kissing her hands, begging her not to give him up, and once again her curious sense of responsibility for him triumphed.

"You will marry me soon, dear, won't you?" he implored her. But she thought of Willy Cameron, oddly enough, even while his arms were around her; of the difference in the two men. Louis, big, crouching, suppliant and insistent; Willy Cameron, grave, reserved and steady, taking what she now knew was the blow of her engagement like a gentleman and a soldier.

They represented, although she did not know it, the two divisions of men in love, the men who offer much and give little, the others who, out of a deep humility, offer little and give everything they have.

In the end, nothing was settled. After he had gone Lily, went up to Elinor's room. She had found in Elinor lately a sort of nervous tension that puzzled her, and that tension almost snapped when Lily told her of her visit home, and of her determination to marry Louis within the next few days. Elinor had dropped her sewing and clenched her hands in her lap.

"Not soon, Lily!" she said. "Oh, not soon. Wait a little-wait two months."

"Two months?" Lily said wonderingly. "Why two months?"

"Because, at the end of two months, nothing would make you marry him," Elinor said, almost violently. "I have sat by and waited, because I thought you would surely see your mistake. But now-Lily, do you envy me my life?"

"No," Lily said truthfully; "but you love him."

Elinor sat, her eyes downcast and brooding.

"You are different," she said finally. "You will break, where I have only bent."

But she said no more about a delay. She had been passive too long to be able to take any strong initiative now. And all her moral and physical courage she was saving for a great emergency.

Cardew Way was far from the center of town, and Lily knew nothing of the bomb outrages of that night.

When she went down to breakfast the next morning she found Jim Doyle pacing the floor of the dining room in a frenzy of rage, a newspaper clenched in his hand. By the window stood Elinor, very pale and with slightly reddened eyes. They had not heard her, and Doyle continued a furious harangue.

"The fools!" he said. "Damn such material as I have to work with! This isn't the time, and they know it. I've warned them over and over. The fools!"

Elinor saw her then, and made a gesture of warning. But it was too late. Lily had a certain quality of directness, and it did not occur to her to dissemble.

"Is anything wrong?" she asked, and went at once to Elinor. She had once or twice before this stood between them for Elinor's protection.

"Everything is as happy as a May morning," Doyle sneered. "Your Aunt Elinor has an unpleasant habit of weeping for joy."

Lily stiffened, but Elinor touched her arm.

"Sit down and eat your breakfast, Lily," she said, and left the room.

Doyle stood staring at Lily angrily. He did not know how much she had heard, how much she knew. At the moment he did not care. He had a reckless impulse to tell her the truth, but his habitual caution prevailed. He forced a cold smile.

"Don't bother your pretty head about politics," he said.

Lily was equally cold. Her dislike of him had been growing for weeks, coupled to a new and strange distrust.

"Politics? You seem to take your politics very hard."

"I do," he said urbanely. "Particularly when I am fighting my wife's family. May I pour you some coffee?"

And pour it he did, eyeing her furtively the while, and brought it to her.

"May I give you a word of advice, Lily?" he said. "Don't treat your husband to tears at breakfast-unless you want to see him romping off to some other woman."

"If he cared to do that I shouldn't want him anyhow."

"You're a self-sufficient child, aren't you? Well, the best of us do it, sometimes."

He had successfully changed the trend of her thoughts, and he went out, carrying the newspaper with him.

Nevertheless, he began to feel that her presence in the house was a menace. With all her theories he knew that a word of the truth would send her flying, breathless with outrage, out of his door. He could quite plainly visualize that home-coming of hers. The instant steps that would be taken against him, old Anthony on the wire appealing to the governor, Howard closeted with the Chief of Police, an instant closing of the net. And he was not ready for the clash.

No. She must stay. If only Elinor would play the game, instead of puling and mouthing! In the room across the hall where his desk stood he paced the floor, first angrily, then thoughtfully, his head bent. He saw, and not far away now, himself seated in the city hall, holding the city in the hollow of his hand. From that his dreams ranged far. He saw himself the head, not of the nation-there would be no nation, as such-but of the country. The very incidents of the night before, blundering as they were, showed him the ease with which the new force could be applied.

He was drunk with power.

Chapter XXVII

Lily had an unexpected visitor that afternoon, in the person of Pink Denslow. She had assumed some of Elinor's cares for the day, for Elinor herself had not been visible since breakfast. It soothed the girl to attend to small duties, and she was washing and wiping Elinor's small stock of fine china when the bell rang.

"Mr. Denslow is calling," said Jennie. "I didn't know if you'd see him, so I said I didn't know if you were in."

Lily's surprise at Pink's visit was increased when she saw him. He was covered with plaster dust, even to the brim of his hat, and his hands were scratched and rough.

"Pink!" she said. "Why, what is the matter?"

For the first time he was conscious of his appearance, and for the first time in his life perhaps, entirely indifferent to it.

"I've been digging in the ruins," he said. "Is that man Doyle in the house?"

Her color faded. Suddenly she noticed a certain wildness about Pink's eyes, and the hard strained look of his mouth.

"What ruins, Pink?" she managed to ask.

"All the ruins," he said. "You know, don't you? The bank, our bank, and the club?"

It seemed to her afterwards that she knew before he told her, saw it all, a dreadful picture which had somehow superimposed upon it a vision of Jim Doyle with the morning paper, and the thing that this was not the time for.

"That's all," he finished. "Eleven at the club, two of them my own fellows. In France, you know. I found one of them myself, this morning." He stared past her, over her head. "Killed for nothing, the way the Germans terrorized Belgium. Haven't you seen the papers?"

"No, they wouldn't let you see them, of course. Lily, I want you to leave here. If you don't, if you stay now, you're one of them, whether you believe what they preach or not. Don't you see that?"

She was not listening. Her faith was dying hard, and the mental shock had brought her dizziness and a faint nausea. He stood watching her, and when she glanced up at him it seemed to her that Pink was hard. Hard and suspicious, and the suspicion was for her. It was incredible.

"Do you believe what they preach?" he demanded. "I've got to know, Lily. I've suffered the tortures of the damned all night."

"I didn't know it meant this."

"Do you?" he repeated.

"No. You ought to know me better than that. But I don't believe that it started here, Pink. He was very angry this morning, and he wouldn't let me see the paper."

"He's behind it all right," Pink said grimly. "Maybe he didn't plant the bombs, but his infernal influence did it, just the same. Do you mean to say you've lived here all this time and don't know he is plotting a revolution? What if he didn't authorize these things last night? He is only waiting, to place a hundred bombs instead of three. A thousand, perhaps."

"Oh, no!"

"We've got their own statements. Department of Justice found them. The fools, to think they can overthrow the government! Can you imagine men planning to capture this city and hold it?"

"It wouldn't be possible, Pink?"

"It isn't possible now, but they'll make a try at it."

There was a short pause, with Lily struggling to understand. Pink's set face relaxed somewhat. All that night he had been fighting for his belief in her.

"I never dreamed of it, Pink. I suppose all the talk I've heard meant that, but I never-are you sure? About Jim Doyle, I mean."

"We know he is behind it. We haven't got the goods on him yet, but we know. Cameron knows. You ask him and he'll tell you."

"Willy Cameron?"

"Yes. He's had some vision, while the rest of us —! He's got a lot of us working now, Lily. We are on the right trail, too, although we lost some records last night that put us back a couple of months. We'll get them, all right. We'll smash their little revolution into a cocked hat." It occurred to him, then, that this house was a poor place for such a confidence. "I'll tell you about it later. Get your things now, and let me take you home."

But Lily's problem was too complex for Pink's simple remedy. She was stricken with sudden conviction; the very mention of Willy Cameron gave Pink's statements authority. But to go like that, to leave Elinor in that house, with all that it implied, was impossible. And there was her own private problem to dispose of.

"I'll go this afternoon, Pink. I'll promise you that. But I can't go with you now. I can't. You'll have to take my word, that's all. And you must believe I didn't know."

"Of course you didn't know," he said, sturdily. "But I hate like thunder to go and leave you here." He picked up his hat, reluctantly. "If I can do anything —"

Lily's mind was working more clearly now. This was the thing Louis Akers had been concerned with, then, a revolution against his country. But it was the thing, too, that he had promised to abandon. He was not a killer. She knew him well, and he was not a killer. He had got to a certain point, and then the thing had sickened him. Even without her he would never have gone through with it. But it would be necessary now to get his information quickly. Very quickly.

"Suppose," she said, hesitatingly, "suppose I tell you that I think I am going to be able to help you before long?"

"Help? I want you safe. This is not work for women."

"But suppose I can bring you a very valuable ally?" she persisted. "Some one who knows all about certain plans, and has changed his views about them?"

"One of them?"

"He has been."

"Is he selling his information?"

"In a way, yes," said Lily, slowly.

"Ware the fellow who sells information," Pink said. "But we'll be glad to have it. We need it, God knows. And-you'll leave?"

"I couldn't stay, could I?"

He kissed her hand when he went away, doing it awkwardly and self-consciously, but withal reverently. She wondered, rather dully, why she could not love Pink. A woman would be so safe with him, so sure.

She had not even then gathered the full force of what he had told her. But little by little things came back to her; the man on guard in the garden; the incident of the locked kitchen door; Jim Doyle once talking angrily over a telephone in his study, although no telephone, so far as she knew, was installed in the room; his recent mysterious absences, and the increasing visits of the hateful Woslosky.

She went back to Louis. This was what he had meant. He had known all along, and plotted with them; even if his stomach had turned now, he had been a party to this infamy. Even then she did not hate him; she saw him, misled as she had been by Doyle's high-sounding phrases, lured on by one of those wild dreams of empire to which men were sometimes given. She did not love him any more; she was sorry for him.

She saw her position with the utmost clearness. To go home was to abandon him, to lose him for those who needed what he could give, to send him back to the enemy. She had told Pink she could secure an ally for a price, and she was the price. There was not an ounce of melodrama in her, as she stood facing the situation. She considered, quite simply, that she had assumed an obligation which she must carry out. Perhaps her pride was dictating to her also. To go crawling home, bowed to the dust, to admit that life had beaten her, to face old Anthony's sneers and her mother's pity-that was hard for any Cardew.

She remembered Elinor's home-comings of years ago, the strained air of the household, the whispering servants, and Elinor herself shut away, or making her rare, almost furtive visits downstairs when her father was out of the house.

No, she could not face that.

Her own willfulness had brought her to this pass; she faced that uncompromisingly. She would marry Louis, and hold him to his promise, and so perhaps out of all this misery some good would come. But at the thought of marriage she found herself trembling violently. With no love and no real respect to build on, with an intuitive knowledge of the man's primitive violences, the reluctance toward marriage with him which she had always felt crystallized into something very close to dread.

But a few minutes later she went upstairs, quite steady again, and fully determined. At Elinor's door she tapped lightly, and she heard movements within. Then Elinor opened the door wide. She had been lying on her bed, and automatically after closing the door she began to smooth it. Lily felt a wave of intense pity for her.

"I wish you would go away from here, Aunt Elinor," she said.

Elinor glanced up, without surprise.

"Where could I go?"

"If you left him definitely, you could go home."

Elinor shook her head, dumbly, and her passivity drove Lily suddenly to desperation.

"You know what is going on," she said, her voice strained. "You don't believe it is right; you know it is wicked. Clothe it in all the fine language in the world, Aunt Elinor, and it is still wicked. If you stay here you condone it. I won't. I am going away."

"I wish you had never come, Lily."

"It's too late for that," Lily said, stonily. "But it is not too late for you to get away."

"I shall stay," Elinor said, with an air of finality. But Lily made one more effort.

"He is killing you."

"No, he is killing himself." Suddenly Elinor flared into a passionate outburst. "Don't you think I know where all this is leading? Do you believe for a moment that I think all this can lead to anything but death? It is a madness, Lily; they are all mad, these men. Don't you know that I have talked and argued and prayed, against it?"

"Then come away. You have done all you could, and you have failed, haven't you?"

"It is not time for me to go," Elinor said. And Lily, puzzled and baffled, found herself again looking into Elinor's quiet, inscrutable eyes.

Elinor had taken it for granted that the girl was going home, and together they packed almost in silence. Once Elinor looked up from folding a garment, and said:

"You said you had not understood before, but that now you do. What did you mean?"

"Pink Denslow was here."

"What does he know?"

"Do you think I ought to tell you, Aunt Elinor? It isn't that I don't trust you. You must believe that, but don't you see that so long as you stay here-he said that to me-you are one of them."

Elinor resumed her folding.

"Yes, I suppose I am one of them," she said quietly. "And you are right. You must not tell me anything. Pink is Henry Denslow's son, I suppose."

"Yes."

"Do they-still live in the old house?"

"Yes."

Elinor continued her methodical work.

Chapter XXVIII

Willy Cameron was free that evening. Although he had not slept at all the night before, he felt singularly awake and active. The Committee had made temporary quarters of his small back room at the pharmacy, and there had sat in rather depressed conclave during a part of the afternoon. Pink Denslow had come in late, and had remained, silent and haggard, through the debate.

There was nothing to do but to start again in an attempt to get files and card indexes. Greater secrecy was to be preserved and enjoined, the location of the office to be known only to a small inner circle, and careful policing of it and of the building which housed it to be established. As a further safeguard, two duplicate files would be kept in other places. The Committee groaned over its own underestimate of the knowledge of the radicals.

The two buildings chosen for destruction were, respectively, the bank building where their file was kept, and the club, where nine-tenths of the officers of the Committee were members. The significance of the double outrage was unquestionable.

When the meeting broke up Pink remained behind. He found it rather difficult to broach the matter in his mind. It was always hard for him to talk about Lily Cardew, and lately he had had a growing conviction that Willy Cameron found it equally difficult. He wondered if Cameron, too, was in love with Lily. There had been a queer look in his face on those rare occasions when Pink had mentioned her, a sort of exaltation, and an odd difficulty afterwards in getting back to the subject in hand.

Pink had developed an enormous affection and admiration for Willy Cameron, a strange, loyal, half wistful, totally unselfish devotion. It had steadied him, when the loss of Lily might have made him reckless, and had taken the form in recent weeks of finding innumerable business opportunities, which Willy Cameron cheerfully refused to take.

"I'll stay here until this other thing is settled," was Willy's invariable answer. "I have a certain amount of time here, and the fellows can drop in to see me without causing suspicion. In an office it would be different. And besides, I can't throw Mr. Davis down. His wife is in bad shape."

So, that afternoon, Pink waited until the Committee had dispersed, and then said, with some difficulty:

"I saw her, Cameron. She has promised to leave."

"To-day?"

"This afternoon. I wanted to take her away, but she had some things to do."

"Then she hadn't known before?"

"No. She thought it was just talk. And they'd kept the papers from her. She hadn't heard about last night. Well, that's all. I thought you'd want to know."

Pink started out, but Willy Cameron called him back.

"Have any of your people any influence with the Cardews?"

"No one has any influence with the Cardews, if you mean the Cardew men. Why?"

"Because Cardew has got to get out of the mayoralty campaign. That's all."

"That's a-plenty," said Pink, grinning. "Why don't you go and tell him so?"

"I'm thinking of it. He hasn't a chance in the world, but he'll defeat Hendricks by splitting the vote, and let the other side in. And you know what that means."

"I know it," Pink observed, "but Mr. Cardew doesn't, and he won't after you've told him. They've put a lot of money in, and once a Cardew has invested in a thing he holds on like death. Especially the old man. Wouldn't wonder he was the fellow who pounded the daylights out of Akers last night," he added.

Willy Cameron, having carefully filled his pipe, closed the door into the shop, and opened a window.

"Akers?" he inquired.

"Noon edition has it," Pink said. "Claims to have been attacked in his rooms by two masked men. Probably wouldn't have told it, but the doctor talked. Looks as though he could wallop six masked men, doesn't he?"

"Yes," said Willy Cameron, reflectively. "Yes; he does, rather."

He felt more hopeful than he had for days. Lily on her way home, clear once more of the poisonous atmosphere of Doyle and his associates; Akers temporarily out of the way, perhaps for long enough to let the normal influences of her home life show him to her in a real perspective; and a rather unholy but very human joy that he had given Akers a part of what was coming to him-all united to cheer him. He saw Lily going home, and a great wave of tenderness flooded him. If only they would be tactful and careful, if only they would be understanding and kind. If they would only be normal and every-day, and accept her as though she had never been away. These people were so hedged about with conventions and restrictions, they put so much emphasis on the letter and so little on the spirit. If only-God, if only they wouldn't patronize her!

His mother would have known how to receive her. He felt, that afternoon, a real homesickness for his mother. He saw her, ample and comfortable and sane, so busy with the comforts of the body that she seemed to ignore the soul, and yet bringing healing with her every matter-of-fact movement.

If only Lily could have gone back to her, instead of to that great house, full of curious eyes and whispering voices.

He saw Mr. Hendricks that evening on his way home to supper. Mr. Hendricks had lost flesh and some of his buoyancy, but he was persistently optimistic.

"Up to last night I'd have said we were done, son," he observed. "But this bomb business has settled them. The labor vote'll split on it, sure as whooping cough."

"They've bought a half-page in all the morning papers, disclaiming all responsibility and calling on all citizens to help them in protecting private property."

"Have they, now," said Hendricks, with grudging admiration. "Can you beat that? Where do they get the money, anyhow? If I lost my watch these days I'd have to do some high-finance before I'd be able to advertise for it."

"All right, see Cardew," were his parting words. "But he doesn't want this election any more than I want my right leg. He'll stick. You can talk, Cameron, I'll say it. But you can't pry him off with kind words, any more than you can a porous plaster."

Behind Mr. Hendricks' colloquialisms there was something sturdy and fine. His very vernacular made him popular; his honesty was beyond suspicion. If he belonged to the old school in politics, he had most of its virtues and few of its vices. He would take care of his friends, undoubtedly, but he was careful in his choice of friends. He would make the city a good place to live in. Like Willy Cameron, he saw it, not a center of trade so much as a vast settlement of homes. Business supported the city in his mind, not the city business.

Nevertheless the situation was serious, and it was with a sense of a desperate remedy for a desperate disease that Willy Cameron, after a careful toilet, rang the bell of the Cardew house that night. He had no hope of seeing Lily, but the mere thought that they were under one roof gave him a sense of nearness and of comfort in her safety.

Dinner was recently over, and he found both the Cardews, father and son, in the library smoking. He had arrived at a bad moment, for the bomb outrage, coming on top of Lily's refusal to come home under the given conditions, had roused Anthony to a cold rage, and left Howard with a feeling of helplessness.

Anthony Cardew nodded to him grimly, but Howard shook hands and offered him a chair.

"I heard you speak some time ago, Mr. Cameron," he said. "You made me wish I could have had your support."

"I came to talk about that. I am sorry to have to come in the evening, but I am not free at any other time."

"When we go into politics," said old Anthony in his jibing voice, "the ordinary amenities have to go. When you are elected, Howard, I shall live somewhere else."

Willy Cameron smiled.

"I don't think you will be put to that inconvenience, Mr. Cardew."

"What's that?" Old Anthony's voice was incredulous. Here, in his own house, this whipper-snapper —

"I am sure Mr. Howard Cardew realizes he cannot be elected."

The small ragged vein on Anthony's forehead was the storm signal for the family. Howard glanced at him, and said urbanely:

"Will you have a cigar, Mr. Cameron? Or a liqueur?"

"Nothing, thank you. If I can have a few minutes' talk with you —"

"If you mean that as a request for me to go out, I will remind you that I am heavily interested in this matter myself," said old Anthony. "I have put in a great deal of money. If you people are going to drop out, I want to hear it. You've played the devil with us already, with your independent candidate who can't talk English."

Willy Cameron kept his temper.

"No," he said, slowly. "It wasn't a question of Mr. Hendricks withdrawing. It was a question of Mr. Cardew getting out."

Sheer astonishment held old Anthony speechless.

"It's like this," Willy Cameron said. "Your son knows it. Even if we drop out he won't get it. Justly or unjustly-and I mean that-nobody with the name of Cardew can be elected to any high office in this city. There's no reflection on anybody in my saying that. I am telling you a fact."

Howard had listened attentively and without anger. "For a long time, Mr. Cameron," he said, "I have been urging men of-of position in the city, to go into politics. We have needed to get away from the professional politician. I went in, without much hope of election, to-well, you can say to blaze a trail. It is not being elected that counts with me, so much as to show my willingness to serve."

Old Anthony recovered his voice.

"The Cardews made this town, sir," he barked. "Willingness to serve, piffle! We need a business man to run the city, and by God, we'll get it!"

"You'll get an anarchist," said Willy Cameron, slightly flushed.

"If you want my opinion, young man, this is a trick, a political trick. And how do we know that your Vigilance Committee isn't a trick, too? You try to tell us that there is an organized movement here to do heaven knows what, and by sheer terror you build up a machine which appeals to the public imagination. You don't say anything about votes, but you see that they vote for your man. Isn't that true?"

"Yes. If they can keep an anarchist out of office. Akers is an anarchist. He calls himself something else, but that's what it amounts to. And those bombs last night were not imaginary."

The introduction of Louis Akers' name had a sobering effect on Anthony Cardew. After all, more than anything else, he wanted Akers defeated. The discussion slowly lost its acrimony, and ended, oddly enough, in Willy Cameron and Anthony Cardew virtually uniting against Howard. What Willy Cameron told about Jim Doyle fed the old man's hatred of his daughter's husband, and there was something very convincing about Cameron himself. Something of fearlessness and honesty that began, slowly, to dispose Anthony in his favor.

It was Howard who held out.

"If I quit now it will look as though I didn't want to take a licking," he said, quietly obstinate. "Grant your point, that I'm defeated. All right, I'll be defeated-but I won't quit."

And Anthony Cardew, confronted by that very quality of obstinacy which had been his own weapon for so many years, retired in high dudgeon to his upper rooms. He was living in a strange new world, a reasonable soul on an unreasonable earth, an earth where a man's last sanctuary, his club, was blown up about him, and a man's family apparently lived only to thwart him.

With Anthony gone, Howard dropped the discussion with the air of a man who has made a final stand.

"What you have said about Mr. Doyle interests me greatly," he observed, "because-you probably do not know this-my sister married him some years ago. It was a most unhappy affair."

"I do know it. For that reason I am glad that Miss Lily has come home."

"Has come home? She has not come home, Mr. Cameron. There was a condition we felt forced to make, and she refused to agree to it. Perhaps we were wrong. I —"

Willy Cameron got up.

"Was that to-day?" he asked.

"No."

"But she was coming home to-day. She was to leave there this afternoon."

"How do you know that?"

"Denslow saw her there this afternoon. She agreed to leave at once. He had told her of the bombs, and of other things. She hadn't understood before, and she was horrified. It is just possible Doyle wouldn't let her go."

"But-that's ridiculous. She can't be a prisoner in my sister's house."

"Will you telephone and find out if she is there?" Howard went to the telephone at once. It seemed to Willy Cameron that he stood there for uncounted years, and as though, through all that eternity of waiting, he knew what the answer would be. And that he knew, too, what that answer meant, where she had gone, what she had done. If only she had come to him. If only she had come to him. He would have saved her from herself. He —

"She is not there," Howard Cardew said, in a voice from which all life had gone. "She left this afternoon, at four o'clock. Of course she has friends. Or she may have gone to a hotel. We had managed to make it practically impossible for her to come home."

Willy Cameron glanced at his watch. He had discounted the worst before it came, and unlike the older man, was ready for action. It was he who took hold of the situation.

"Order a car, Mr. Cardew, and go to the hotels," he said. "And if you will drop me down-town —I'll tell you where —I'll follow up something that has just occurred to me."

Chapter XXIX

In one way Howard had been correct in his surmise. It had been Lily's idea to go to a hotel until she had made some definite plan. She would telephone Louis then, and the rest-she did not think beyond that. She called a taxi and took a small bag with her, but in the taxi-cab she suddenly realized that she could not go to any of the hotels she knew. She would be recognized at once.

She wanted a little time to herself, time to think. And before it was discovered that she had left Cardew Way she must see Louis, and judge again if he intended to act in good faith. While he was with her, reiterating his promises, she believed him, but when he was gone, she always felt, a curious doubt.

She thought then of finding a quiet room somewhere, and stopping the cab, bought a newspaper. It was when she was searching for the "rooms for rent" column that she saw he had been attacked and slightly injured.

They had got him. He had said that if they ever suspected him of playing them false they would get him, and now they had done so. That removed the last doubt of his good faith from her mind. She felt indignation and dismay, and a sort of aching consciousness that always she brought only trouble to the people who cared for her; she felt that she was going through her life, leaving only unhappiness behind her.

He had suffered, and for her.

She told the chauffeur to go to the Benedict Apartments, and sitting back read the notice again. He had been attacked by two masked men and badly bruised, after putting up a terrific resistance. They would wear masks, of course. They loved the theatrical. Their very flag was theatrical. And he had made a hard fight That was like him, too; he was a fighter.

She was a Cardew, and she loved strength. There were other men, men like Willy Cameron, for instance, who were lovable in many ways, but they were not fighters. They sat back, and let life beat them, and they took the hurt bravely and stoically. But they never got life by the throat and shook it until it gave up what they wanted.

She had never been in a bachelors' apartment house before, and she was both frightened and self-conscious. The girl at the desk eyed her curiously while she telephoned her message, and watched her as she moved toward the elevator. "Ever seen her before?" she said to the hall boy.

"No. She's a new one."

"Face's kind of familiar to me," said the telephone girl, reflectively. "Looks worried, doesn't she? Two masked men! Huh! All Sam took up there last night was a thin fellow with a limp."

The hall boy grinned.

"Then his limp didn't bother him any. Sam says y'ought to seen that place."

In the meantime, outside the door of Akers' apartment, Lily's fine courage almost left her. Had it not been for the eyes of the elevator man, fixed on her while he lounged in his gateway, she might have gone away, even then. But she stood there, committed to a course of action, and rang.

Louis himself admitted her, an oddly battered Louis, in a dressing gown and slippers; an oddly watchful Louis, too, waiting, after the manner of men of his kind the world over, to see which way the cat would jump. He had had a bad day, and his nerves were on edge. All day he had sat there, unable to go out, and had wondered just when Cameron would see her and tell her about Edith Boyd. For, just as Willy Cameron rushed him for the first time, there had been something from between clenched teeth about marrying another girl, under the given circumstances. Only that had not been the sort of language in which it was delivered.

"I just saw about it in the newspaper," Lily said. "How dreadful, Louis."

He straightened himself and drew a deep breath. The game was still his, if he played it right.

"Bad enough, dear," he said, "but I gave them some trouble, too." He pushed a chair toward her. "It was like you to come. But I don't like your seeing me all mussed up, little girl."

He made a move then to kiss her, but she drew back.

"Please!" she said. "Not here. And I can't sit down. I can't stay. I only came because I wanted to tell you something and I didn't want to telephone it. Louis, Jim Doyle knew about those bombs last night. He didn't want it to happen before the election, but-that doesn't alter the fact, does it?"

"How do you know he knew?"

"I do know. That's all. And I have left Aunt Elinor's."

"No!"

"I couldn't stay, could I?" She looked up at him, the little wistful glance that Willy always found so infinitely touching, like the appeal of a willful but lovable child, that has somehow got into trouble. "And I can't go home, Louis, unless I —"

"Unless you give me up," he finished for her. "Well?"

She hesitated. She hated making terms with him, and yet somehow she must make terms.

"Well?" he repeated. "Are you going to throw me over?"

Apparently merely putting the thought into words crystallized all his fears of the past hours; seeing her there, too, had intensified his want of her. She stood there, where he had so often dreamed of seeing her, but still holding him off with the aloofness that both chilled and inflamed him, and with a question in her eyes. He held out his arms, but she drew back.

"Do you mean what you have said, Louis, about leaving them, if I marry you, and doing all you can to stop them?"

"You know I mean it."

"Then —I'll not go home."

"You are going to marry me? Now?"

"Whenever you say."

Suddenly she was trembling violently, and her lips felt dry and stiff. He pushed her into a chair, and knelt down beside her.

"You poor little kid," he said, softly.

Through his brain were racing a hundred thoughts; Lily his, in his arms, in spite of that white-faced drug clerk with the cold eyes; himself in the Cardew house, one of them, beating old Anthony Cardew at his own cynical game; and persistently held back and often rising again to the surface, Woslosky and Doyle and the others, killers that they were, pursuing him with their vengeance over the world. They would have to be counted in; they were his price, as he, had he known it, was Lily's.

"My wife!" he said. "My wife."

She stiffened in his arms.

"I must go, Louis," she said. "I can't stay here. I felt very queer downstairs. They all stared so."

There was a clock on the mantel shelf, and he looked at it. It was a quarter before five.

"One thing is sure, Lily," he said. "You can't wander about alone, and you are right-you can't stay here. They probably recognized you downstairs. You are pretty well known."

For the first time it occurred to her that she had compromised herself, and that the net, of her own making, was closing fast about her.

"I wish I hadn't come."

"Why? We can fix that all right in a jiffy."

But when he suggested an immediate marriage she made a final struggle. In a few days, even to-morrow, but not just then. He listened, impatiently, his eyes on the clock. Beside it in the mirror he saw his own marred face, and it added to his anger. In the end he took control of the situation; went into his bedroom, changed into a coat, and came out again, ready for the street. He telephoned down for a taxicab, and then confronted her, his face grim.

"I've let you run things pretty much to suit yourself, Lily," he said. "Now I'm in charge. It won't be to-morrow or next week or next month. It will be now. You're here. You've given them a chance to talk downstairs. You've nowhere to go, and you're going to marry me at once."

In the cab he explained more fully. They would get a license, and then go to one of the hotels. There they could be married, in their own suite.

"All regularly and in order, honey," he said, and kissed her hand. She had hardly heard. She was staring ahead, not thinking, not listening, not seeing, fighting down a growing fear of the man before her, of his sheer physical proximity, of his increasing exuberance.

"I'm mad about you, girl," he said. "Mad. And now you are going to be mine, until death do us part."

She shivered and drew away, and he laughed a little. Girls were like that, at such times. They always took a step back for every two steps forward. He let her hand go, and took a careful survey of his face in the mirror of the cab. The swelling had gone down, but that bruise below his eye would last for days. He cursed under his breath.

It was after nine o'clock when one of the Cardew cars stopped not far from the Benedict Apartments, and Willy Cameron got out.

He was quite certain that Louis Akers would know where Lily was, and he anticipated the interview with a sort of grim humor. There might be another fight; certainly Akers would try to get back at him for the night before. But he set his jaw. He would learn where Lily was if he had to choke the knowledge out of that leering devil's thick white throat. His arrival in the foyer of the Benedict Apartments caused more than a ripple of excitement.

"Well, look who's here!" muttered the telephone girl, and watched his approach, with its faint limp, over the top of her desk. Behind, from his cage, the elevator man was staring with avid interest.

"I suppose Mr. Akers is in?" said Willy Cameron, politely. The girl smiled up at him.

"I'll say he ought to be, after last night! What're you going to do now? Kill him?"

In spite of his anxiety there was a faint twinkle in Willy Cameron's eyes.

"No," he said slowly. "No. I think not. I want to talk to him."

"Sam," called the telephone girl, "take this gentleman up to forty-three."

"Forty-three's out." Sam partly shut the elevator door; he had seen Forty-three's rooms the night before, and he had the discretion of his race. "Went out with a lady at quarter to five."

Willy Cameron took a step or two toward the cage.

"You don't happen to be lying, I suppose?"

"No, sir!" said Sam. "I'll take you up to look, if you like. And about an hour ago he sent a boy here with a note, to get some of his clothes. The young lady at the desk was out at the movies at the time."

"I was getting my supper, Sam."

Willy Cameron had gone very white.

"Did the boy say where he was taking the things?"

"To the Saint Elmo Hotel, sir."

On the street again Willy Cameron took himself fiercely in hand. There were a half-dozen reasons why Akers might go to the Saint Elmo. He might, for one thing, have thought that he, Cameron, would go back to the Benedict. He might be hiding from Dan, or from reporters.

But there had been, apparently, no attempt to keep his new quarters secret. If Lily was at the Saint Elmo —

He found a taxicab, and as it drew up at the curb before the hotel he saw the Cardew car moving away. It gave him his first real breath for twenty minutes. Lily was not there.

But Louis Akers was. He got his room number from a clerk and went up, still determinedly holding on to himself. Afterwards he had no clear recollection of any interval between the Benedict and the moment he found himself standing outside a door on an upper floor of the Saint Elmo. From that time on it was as clear as crystal, his own sudden calm, the overturning of a chair inside, a man's voice, slightly raised, which he recognized, and then the thin crash of a wineglass dropped or thrown to the floor.

He opened the door and went in.

In the center of the sitting room a table was set, and on it the remains of a dinner for two. Akers was standing by the table, his chair overturned behind him, a splintered glass at his feet, staring angrily at the window. Even then Willy Cameron saw that he had had too much to drink, and that he was in an ugly mood. He was in dinner clothes, but with his bruised face and scowling brows he looked a sinister imitation of a gentleman.

By the window, her back to the room, was Lily.

Neither of them glanced at the door. Evidently the waiter had been moving in and out, and Akers considered him as little as he would a dog.

"Come and sit down," he said angrily. "I've quit drinking, I tell you. Good God, just because I've had a little wine-and I had the hell of a time getting it-you won't eat and won't talk. Come here."

"I'm not hungry."

"Come here."

"Stay where you are, Lily," said Willy Cameron, from inside the closed door. "Or perhaps you'd better get your wraps. I came to take you home."

Akers had wheeled at the voice, and now stood staring incredulously. First anger, and then a grin of triumph, showed in his face. Drink had made him not so much drunk as reckless. He had lost last night, but to-day he had won.

"Hello, Cameron," he said.

Willy Cameron ignored him.

"Will you come?" he said to Lily.

"I can't, Willy."

"Listen, Lily dear," he said gravely. "Your father is searching the city for you. Do you know what that means? Don't you see that you must go home at once? You can't dine here in a private suite, like this, and not expose yourself to all sorts of talk."

"Go on," said Akers, leering. "I like to hear you."

"Especially," continued Willy Cameron, "with a man like this."

Akers took a step toward him, but he was not too sure of himself, and he knew now that the other man had a swing to his right arm like the driving rod of a locomotive. He retreated again to the table, and his hand closed over a knife there.

"Louis!" Lily said sharply.

He picked up the knife and smiled at her, his eyes cunning. "Not going to kill him, my dear," he said. "Merely to give him a hint that I'm not as easy as I was last night."

That was a slip, and he knew it. Lily had left the window and come forward, a stricken slip of a girl, and he turned to her angrily.

"Go into the other room and close the door," he ordered. "When I've thrown this fellow out, you can come back."

But Lily's eyes were fixed on Willy Cameron's face.

"It was you last night?"

"Yes."

"Why?"

"Because," Willy Cameron said steadily, "he had got a girl into trouble, and then insulted her. I wouldn't tell you, but you've got to know the truth before it's too late."

Lily threw out both hands dizzily, as though catching for support. But she steadied herself. Neither man moved.

"It is too late, Willy," she said. "I have just married him."

Chapter XXX

At midnight Howard Cardew reached home again, a tired and broken man. Grace had been lying awake in her bedroom, puzzled by his unexplained absence, and brooding, as she now did continually, over Lily's absence.

At half past eleven she heard Anthony Cardew come in and go upstairs, and for some time after that she heard him steadily pacing back and forth overhead. Sometimes Grace felt sorry for Anthony. He had made himself at such cost, and now when he was old, he had everything and yet nothing.

They had never understood women, these Cardews. Howard was gentle with them where Anthony was hard, but he did not understand, either. She herself, of other blood, got along by making few demands, but the Cardew women were as insistent in their demands as the men. Elinor, Lily-She formed a sudden resolution, and getting up, dressed feverishly. She had no plan in her mind, nothing but a desperate resolution to put Lily's case before her grandfather, and to beg that she be brought home without conditions.

She was frightened as she went up the stairs. Never before had she permitted things to come to an issue between herself and Anthony. But now it must be done. She knocked at the door.

Anthony Cardew opened it. The room was dark, save for one lamp burning dimly on a great mahogany table, and Anthony's erect figure was little more than a blur of black and white.

"I heard you walking about," she said breathlessly. "May I come in and talk to you?"

"Come in," he said, with a sort of grave heaviness. "Shall I light the other lamps?"

"Please don't."

"Will you sit down? No? Do you mind if I do? I am very tired. I suppose it is about Lily?"

"Yes. I can't stand it any longer. I can't."

Sitting under the lamp she saw that he looked very old and very weary. A tired little old man, almost a broken one.

"She won't come back?"

"Not under the conditions. But she must come back, father. To let her stay on there, in that house, after last night —"

She had never called him "father" before. It seemed to touch him.

"You're a good woman, Grace," he said, still heavily. "We Cardews all marry good women, but we don't know how to treat them. Even Howard —" His voice trailed off. "No, she can't stay there," he said, after a pause.

"But —I must tell you-she refuses to give up that man."

"You are a woman, Grace. You ought to know something about girls. Does she actually care for him, or is it because he offers the liberty she thinks we fail to give her? Or" —he smiled faintly —"is it Cardew pig-headedness?"

Grace made a little gesture of despair.

"I don't know. She wanted to come home. She begged-it was dreadful." Grace hesitated. "Even that couldn't be as bad as this, father," she said. "We have all lived our own lives, you and Howard and myself, and now we won't let her do it."

"And a pretty mess we have made of them!" His tone was grim. "No, I can't say that we offer her any felicitous examples. But the fellow's plan is transparent enough. He is ambitious. He sees himself installed here, one of us. Mark my words, Grace, he may love the child, but his real actuating motive is that. He's a Radical, because since he can't climb up, he'll pull down. But once let him get his foot on the Cardew ladder, and he'll climb, over her, over all of us."

He sat after that, his head dropped on his chest, his hands resting on the arms of his chair, in a brooding reverie. Grace waited.

"Better bring her home," he said finally. "Tell her I surrender. I want her here. Let her bring that fellow here, too, if she has to see him. But for God's sake, Grace," he added, with a flash of his old fire, "show her some real men, too."

Suddenly Grace bent over and kissed him. He put up his hand, and patted her on the shoulder.

"A good woman, Grace," he said, "and a good daughter to me. I'm sorry. I'll try to do better."

As Grace straightened she heard the door close below, and Howard's voice. Almost immediately she heard him coming up the staircase, and going out into the hall she called softly to him.

"Where are you?" he asked, looking up. "Is father there?"

"Yes."

"I want you both to come down to the library, Grace."

She heard him turn and go slowly down the stairs. His voice had been strained and unnatural. As she turned she found Anthony behind her.

"Something has happened!"

"I rather think so," said old Anthony, slowly.

They went together down the stairs.

In the library Lily was standing, facing the door, a quiet figure, listening and waiting. Howard had dropped into a chair and was staring ahead. And beyond the circle of lights was a shadowy figure, vaguely familiar, tall, thin, and watchful. Willy Cameron.

Chapter XXXI

The discovery that Lily had left his house threw Jim Doyle into a frenzy. The very manner of her going filled him with dark suspicion. Either she had heard more that morning than he had thought, or-In his cunning mind for weeks there had been growing a smoldering suspicion of his wife. She was too quiet, too acquiescent. In the beginning, when Woslosky had brought the scheme to him, and had promised it financial support from Europe, he had taken a cruel and savage delight in outlining it to her, in seeing her cringe and go pale.

He had not feared her then. She had borne with so much, endured, tolerated, accepted, that he had not realized that she might have a breaking point.

The plan had appealed to his cynical soul from the first. It was the apotheosis of cynicism, this reducing of a world to its lowest level. And it had amused him to see his wife, a gentlewoman born, bewildered before the chaos he depicted.

"But-it is German!" she had said.

"I bow before intelligence. It is German. Also it is Russian. Also it is of all nations. All this talk now, of a League of Nations, a few dull diplomats acting as God over the peoples of the earth!" His eyes blazed. "While the true league, of the workers of the world, is already in effect!"

But he watched her after that, not that he was afraid of her, but because her re-action as a woman was important. He feared women in the movement. It had its disciples, fervent and eloquent, paid and unpaid women agitators, but he did not trust them. They were invariably women without home ties, women with nothing to protect, women with everything to gain and nothing to lose. The woman in the home was a natural anti-radical. Not the police, not even the army, but the woman in the home was the deadly enemy of the great plan.

He began to hate Elinor, not so much for herself, as for the women she represented. She became the embodiment of possible failure. She stood in his path, passively resistant, stubbornly brave.

She was not a clever woman, and she was slow in gathering the full significance of a nation-wide general strike, that with an end of all production the non-producing world would be beaten to its knees. And then she waited for a world movement, forgetting that a flame must start somewhere and then spread. But she listened and learned. There was a great deal of talk about class and mass. She learned that the mass, for instance, was hungry for a change. It would welcome any change. Woslosky had been in Russia when the Kerensky regime was overthrown, and had seen that strange three days when the submerged part of the city filled the streets, singing, smiling, endlessly walking, exalted and without guile.

No problems troubled them. They had ceased to labor, and that was enough.

Had it not been for its leaders, the mass would have risen like a tide, and ebbed again.

Elinor had struggled to understand. This was not Socialism. Jim had been a Socialist for years. He had believed that the gradual elevation of the few, the gradual subjection of the many, would go on until the majority would drag the few down to their own level. But this new dream was something immediate. At her table she began to hear talk of substituting for that slow process a militant minority. She was a long time, months, in discovering that Jim Doyle was one of the leaders of that militant minority, and that the methods of it were unspeakably criminal.

Then had begun Elinor Doyle's long battle, at first to hold him back, and that failing, the fight between her duty to her husband and that to her country. He had been her one occupation and obsession too long to be easily abandoned, but she was sturdily national, too. In the end she made her decision. She lived in his house, mended his clothing, served his food, met his accomplices, and-watched.

She hated herself for it. Every fine fiber of her revolted. But as time went on, and she learned the full wickedness of the thing, her days became one long waiting. She saw one move after another succeed, strike after strike slowing production, and thus increasing the cost of living. She saw the growing discontent and muttering, the vicious circle of labor striking for more money, and by its own ceasing of activity making the very increases they asked inadequate. And behind it all she saw the ceaseless working, the endless sowing, of a grim-faced band of conspirators.

She was obliged to wait. A few men talking in secret meetings, a hidden propaganda of crime and disorder-there was nothing to strike at. And Elinor, while not clever, had the Cardew shrewdness. She saw that, like the crisis in a fever, the thing would have to come, be met, and defeated.

She had no hope that the government would take hold. Government was aloof, haughty, and secure in its own strength. Just now, too, it was objective, not subjective. It was like a horse set to win a race, and unconscious of the fly on its withers. But the fly was a gadfly.

Elinor knew Doyle was beginning to suspect her. Sometimes she thought he would kill her, if he discovered what she meant to do. She did not greatly care. She waited for some inkling of the day set for the uprising in the city, and saved out of her small house allowance by innumerable economies and subterfuges. When she found out the time she would go to the Governor of the State. He seemed to be a strong man, and she would present him facts. Facts and names. Then he must act-and quickly.

Cut off from her own world, and with no roots thrown out in the new, she had no friends, no one to confide in or of whom to ask assistance. And she was afraid to go to Howard. He would precipitate things. The leaders would escape, and a new group would take their places. Such a group, she knew, stood ready for that very emergency.

On the afternoon of Lily's departure she heard Doyle come in. He had not recovered from his morning's anger, and she heard his voice, raised in some violent reproof to Jennie. He came up the stairs, his head sagged forward, his every step deliberate, heavy, ominous. He had an evening paper in his hand, and he gave it to her with his finger pointing to a paragraph.

"You might show that to the last of the Cardews," he sneered.

It was the paragraph about Louis Akers. Elinor read it. "Who were the masked men?" she asked. "Do you know?"

"I wish to God I did. I'd—Makes him a laughing stock, of course. And just now, when- Where's Lily?"

Elinor put down the paper.

"She is not here. She went home this afternoon."

He stared at her, angrily incredulous.

"Home?"

"This afternoon."

She passed him and went out into the hall. But he followed her and caught her by the arm as she reached the top of the staircase.

"What made her go home?"

"I don't know, Jim."

"She didn't say?"

"Don't hold me like that. No."

She tried to free her arm, but he held her, his face angry and suspicious.

"You are lying to me," he snarled. "She gave you a reason. What was it?"

Elinor was frightened, but she had not lost her head. She was thinking rapidly.

"She had a visitor this afternoon, a young man. He must have told her something about last night. She came up and told me she was going."

"You know he told her something, don't you?"

"Yes." Elinor had cowered against the wall. "Jim, don't look like that. You frighten me. I couldn't keep her here. I—"

"What did he tell her?"

"He accused you."

He was eyeing her coldly, calculatingly. All his suspicions of the past weeks suddenly crystallized. "And you let her go, after that," he said slowly. "You were glad to have her go. You didn't deny what she said. You let her run back home, with what she had guessed and what you told her to-day. You—"

He struck her then. The blow was as remorseless as his voice, as deliberate. She fell down the staircase headlong, and lay there, not moving.

The elderly maid came running from the kitchen, and found him half-way down the stairs, his eyes still calculating, but his body shaking.

"She fell," he said, still staring down. But the servant faced him, her eyes full of hate.

"You devil!" she said. "If she's dead, I'll see you hang for it."

But Elinor was not dead. Doctor Smalley, making rounds in a nearby hospital and answering the emergency call, found her lying on her bed, fully conscious and in great pain, while her husband bent over her in seeming agony of mind. She had broken her leg. He sent Doyle out during the setting. It was a principle of his to keep agonized husbands out of the room.

Chapter XXXII

Life had beaten Lily Cardew. She went about the house, pathetically reminiscent of Elinor Doyle in those days when she had sought sanctuary there; but where Elinor had seen those days only as interludes in her stormy life, Lily was finding a strange new peace. She was very tender, very thoughtful, insistently cheerful, as though determined that her own ill-fortune should not affect the rest of the household.

But to Lily this peace was not an interlude, but an end. Life for her was over. Her bright dreams were gone, her future settled. Without so putting it, even to herself, she dedicated herself to service, to small kindnesses, and little thoughtful acts. She was, daily and hourly, making reparation to them all for what she had cost them, in hope.

That was the thing that had gone out of life. Hope. Her loathing of Louis Akers was gone. She did not hate him. Rather she felt toward him a sort of numbed indifference. She wished never to see him again, but the revolt that had followed her knowledge of the conditions under which he had married her was gone. She tried to understand his viewpoint, to make allowances for his lack of some fundamental creed to live by. But as the days went on, with that healthy tendency of the mind to bury pain, she found him, from a figure that bulked so large as to shut out all the horizon of her life, receding more and more.

But always he would shut off certain things. Love, and marriage, and of course the hope of happiness. Happiness was a thing one earned, and she had not earned it.

After the scene at the Saint Elmo, when he had refused to let her go, and when Willy Cameron had at last locked him in the bedroom of the suite and had taken her away, there had followed a complete silence. She had waited for some move or his part, perhaps an announcement of the marriage in the newspapers, but nothing had appeared. He had commenced a whirlwind campaign for the mayoralty and was receiving a substantial support from labor.

The months at the house on Cardew Way seemed more and more dream-like, and that quality of remoteness was accentuated by the fact that she had not been able to talk to Elinor. She had telephoned more than once during the week, but a new maid had answered. Mrs. Doyle was out. Mrs. Doyle was unable to come to the telephone. The girl was a foreigner, with something of Woslosky's burr in her voice.

Lily had not left the house since her return. During that family conclave which had followed her arrival, a stricken thing of few words and long anxious pauses, her grandfather had suggested that. He had been curiously mild with her, her grandfather. He had made no friendly overtures, but he had neither jibed nor sneered.

"It's done," he had said briefly. "The thing now is to keep her out of his clutches." He had turned to her. "I wouldn't leave the house for few days, Lily."

It was then that Willy Cameron had gone. Afterwards she thought that he must have been waiting, patiently protective, to see how the old man received her.

Her inability to reach Elinor began to dismay her, at last. There was something sinister about it, and finally Howard himself went to the Doyle house. Lily had come back on Thursday, and on the following Tuesday he made his call, timing it so that Doyle would probably be away from home. But he came back baffled.

"She was not at home," he said. "I had to take the servant's word for it, but I think the girl was lying."

"She may be ill. She almost never goes out."

"What possible object could they have in concealing her illness?" Howard said impatiently.

But he was very uneasy, and what Lily had told him since her return only increased his anxiety. The house was a hotbed of conspiracy, and for her own reasons Elinor was remaining there. It was no place for a sister of his. But Elinor for years had only touched the outer fringes of his life, and his days were crowded with other things; the increasing arrogance of the strikers, the utter uselessness of trying to make terms with them, his own determination to continue to fight his futile political campaign. He put her out of his mind.

Then, at the end of another week, a curious thing happened. Anthony and Lily were in the library. Old Anthony without a club was Old Anthony lost, and he had developed a habit, at first rather embarrassing to the others, of spending much of his time downstairs. He was no sinner turned saint. He still let the lash of his tongue play over the household, but his old zest in it seemed gone. He made, too, small tentative overtures to Lily, intended to be friendly, but actually absurdly self-conscious. Grace, watching him, often felt him rather touching. It was obvious to her that he blamed himself, rather than Lily, for what had happened.

On this occasion he had asked Lily to read to him.

"And leave out the politics," he had said, "I get enough of that wherever I go."

As she read she felt him watching her, and in the middle of a paragraph he suddenly said: "What's become of Cameron?"

"He must be very busy. He is supporting Mr. Hendricks, you know."

"Supporting him! He's carrying him on his back," grunted Anthony. "What is it, Grayson?"

"A lady —a woman-calling on Miss Cardew."

Lily rose, but Anthony motioned her back.

"Did she give any name?"

"She said to say it was Jennie, sir."

"Jennie! It must be Aunt Elinor's Jennie!"

"Send her in," said Anthony, and stood waiting Lily noticed his face twitching; it occurred to her then that this strange old man might still love his daughter, after all the years, and all his cruelty.

It was the elderly servant from the Doyle house who came in, a tall gaunt woman, looking oddly unfamiliar to Lily in a hat.

"Why, Jennie!" she said. And then: "Is anything wrong?"

"There is and there isn't," Jennie said, somberly. "I just wanted to tell you, and I don't care if he kills me for it. It was him that threw her downstairs. I heard him hit her."

Old Anthony stiffened.

"He threw Aunt Elinor downstairs?"

"That's how she broke her leg."

Sheer amazement made Lily inarticulate.

"But they said-we didn't know-do you mean that she has been there all this time, hurt?"

"I mean just that," said Jennie, stolidly. "I helped set it, with him pretending to be all worked up, for the doctor to see. He got rid of me all right. He's got one of his spies there now, a Bolshevik like himself. You can ask the neighbors."

Howard was out, and when the woman had gone Anthony ordered his car. Lily, frightened by the look on his face, made only one protest.

"You mustn't go alone," she said. "Let me go, too. Or take Grayson-anybody."

But he went alone; in the hall he picked up his hat and stick, and drew on his gloves.

"What is the house number?"

Lily told him and he went out, moving deliberately, like a man who has made up his mind to follow a certain course, but to keep himself well in hand.

Chapter XXXIII

Acting on Willy Cameron's suggestion, Dan Boyd retained his membership in the union and frequented the meetings. He learned various things, that the strike vote had been padded, for instance, and that the Radicals had taken advantage of the absence of some of the conservative leaders to secure such support as they had received. He found the better class of workmen dissatisfied and unhappy. Some of them, men who loved their tools, had resented the order to put them down where they were and walk out, and this resentment, childish as it seemed, was an expression of their general dissatisfaction with the autocracy they had themselves built up.

Finally Dan's persistent attendance and meek acquiescence, added to his war record, brought him reward. He was elected member of a conference to take to the Central Labor Council the suggestion for a general strike. It was arranged that the delegates take the floor one after the other, and hold it for as long as possible. Then they were to ask the President of the Council to put the question.

The arguments were carefully prepared. The general strike was to be urged as the one salvation of the labor movement. It would prove the solidarity of labor. And, at the Council meeting a few days later, the rank and file were impressed by the arguments. Dan, gnawing his nails and listening, watched anxiously. The idea was favorably received, and the delegates went back to their local unions, to urge, coerce and threaten.

Not once, during the meeting, had there been any suggestion of violence, but violence was in the air, nevertheless. The quantity of revolutionary literature increased greatly during the following ten days, and now it was no longer furtively distributed. It was sold or given away at all meetings; it flooded the various headquarters with its skillful compound of lies and truth. The leaders notified of the situation, pretended that it was harmless raving, a natural and safe outlet for suppressed discontents.

Dan gathered up an armful of it and took it home. On a Sunday following, there was a mass meeting at the Colosseum, and a business agent of one of the unions made an impassioned speech. He recited old and new grievances, said that the government had failed to live up to its promises, that the government boards were always unjust to the workers, and ended with a statement of the steel makers' profits. Dan turned impatiently to a man beside him.

"Why doesn't he say how much of that profit the government gets?" he demanded.

But the man only eyed him suspiciously.

Dan fell silent. He knew it was wrong, but he had no gift of tongue. It was at that meeting that for the first time he heard used the word "revolution."

Chapter XXXIV

Old Anthony's excursion to his daughter's house had not prospered. During the drive to Cardew Way he sat forward on the edge of the seat of his limousine, his mouth twitching with impatience and anger, his stick tightly clutched in his hand. Almost before the machine stopped he was out on the pavement, scanning the house with hostile eyes.

The building was dark. Paul, the chauffeur, watching curiously, for the household knew that Anthony Cardew had sworn never to darken his daughter's door, saw his erect, militant figure enter the gate and lose itself in the shadow of the house. There followed a short interval of nothing in particular, and then a tall man appeared in the rectangle of light which was the open door.

Jim Doyle was astounded when he saw his visitor. Astounded and alarmed. But he recovered himself quickly, and smiled.

"This is something I never expected to see," he said, "Mr. Anthony Cardew on my doorstep."

"I don't give a damn what you expected to see," said Mr. Anthony Cardew. "I want to see my daughter."

"Your daughter? You have said for a good many years that you have no daughter."

"Stand aside, sir. I didn't come here to quibble."

"But I love to quibble," sneered Doyle. "However, if you insist —I might as well tell you, I haven't the remotest intention of letting you in."

"I'll ask you a question," said old Anthony. "Is it true that my daughter has been hurt?"

"My wife is indisposed. I presume we are speaking of the same person."

"You infernal scoundrel," shouted Anthony, and raising his cane, brought it down with a crack on Doyle's head. The chauffeur was half-way up the walk by that time, and broke into a run. He saw Doyle, against the light, reel, recover and raise his fist, but he did not bring it down.

"Stop that!" yelled the chauffeur, and came on like a charging steer. When he reached the steps old Anthony was hanging his stick over his left forearm, and Doyle was inside the door, trying to close it. This was difficult, however, because Anthony had quietly put his foot over the sill.

"I am going to see my daughter, Paul," said Anthony Cardew. "Can you open the door?"

"Open it!" Paul observed truculently. "Watch me!"

He threw himself against the door, but it gave suddenly, and sent him sprawling inside at Doyle's feet. He was up in an instant, squared to fight, but he only met Jim Doyle's mocking smile. Doyle stood, arms folded, and watched Anthony Cardew enter his house. Whatever he feared he covered with the cynical mask that was his face.

He made no move, offered no speech.

"Is she upstairs?"

"She is asleep. Do you intend to disturb her?"

"I do," said old Anthony grimly. "I'll go first, Paul. You follow me, but I'd advise you to come up backwards."

Suddenly Doyle laughed.

"What!" he said, "Mr. Anthony Cardew paying his first visit to my humble home, and anticipating violence! You underestimate the honor you are doing me."

He stood like a mocking devil at the foot of the staircase until the two men had reached the top. Then he followed them. The mask had dropped from his face, and anger and watchfulness showed in it. If she talked, he would kill her. But she knew that. She was not a fool.

Elinor lay in the bed, listening. She had recognized her father's voice, and her first impulse was one of almost unbearable relief. They had found her. They had come to take her away. For she knew now that she was a prisoner; even without the broken leg she would have been a prisoner. The girl downstairs was one of them, and her jailer. A jailer who fed her, and gave her grudgingly the attention she required, but that was all.

Just when Doyle had begun to suspect her she did not know, but on the night after her injury he had taken pains to verify his suspicions. He had found first her little store of money, and that had angered him. In the end he had broken open a locked trinket box and found a notebook in which for months she had kept her careful records. Here and there, scattered among house accounts, were the names of the radical members of The Central Labor Council, and other names, spoken before her and carefully remembered. He had read them out to her as he came to them, suffering as she was, and she had expected death then. But he had not killed her. He had sent Jennie away and brought in this Russian girl, a mad-eyed fanatic named Olga, and from that time on he visited her once daily. In his anger and triumph over her he devised the most cunning of all punishments; he told her of the movement's progress, of its ingeniously contrived devilments in store, of its inevitable success. What buildings and homes were to be bombed, the Cardew house first among them; what leading citizens were to be held as hostages, with all that that implied; and again the Cardews headed the list.

When Doctor Smalley came he or the Russian were always present, solicitous and attentive. She got out of her bed one day, and dragging her splinted leg got to her desk, in the hope of writing a note and finding some opportunity of giving it to the doctor. Only to discover that they had taken away her pen, pencils and paper.

She had been found there by Olga, but the girl had made no comment. Olga had helped her back into bed without a word, but from that time on had spent most of her day on the upper floor. Not until Doyle came in would she go downstairs to prepare his food.

Elinor lay in her bed and listened to her father coming up the stairs. She knew, before he reached the top, that Doyle would never let her be taken away. He would kill her first. He might kill Anthony Cardew. She had a sickening sense of tragedy coming up the staircase, tragedy which took the form of her father's familiar deliberate step. Perhaps had she known of the chauffeur's presence she might have chanced it, for every fiber of her tired body was crying for release. But she saw only her father, alone in that house with Doyle and the smoldering Russian.

The key turned in the lock.

Anthony Cardew stood in the doorway, looking at her. With her long hair in braids, she seemed young, almost girlish. She looked like the little girl who had gone to dancing school in short white frocks and long black silk stockings, so many years ago.

"I've just learned about it, Elinor," he said. He moved to the bed and stood beside it, looking down, but he did not touch her. "Are you able to be taken away from here?"

She knew that Doyle was outside, listening, and she hardened her heart for the part she had to play. It was difficult; she was so infinitely moved by her father's coming, and in the dim light he, too, looked like himself of years ago.

"Taken away? Where?" she asked.

"You don't want to stay here, do you?" he demanded bluntly.

"This is my home, father."

"Good God, home! Do you mean to tell me that, with all you must know about this man, you still want to stay with him?"

"I have no other home."

"I am offering you one."

Old Anthony was bewildered and angry. Elinor put out a hand to touch him, but he drew back.

"After he has thrown you downstairs and injured you —"

"How did you hear that?"

"The servant you had here came to see me to-night, Elinor. She said that that blackguard outside there had struck you and you fell down the stairs. If you tell me that's the truth I'll break every bone in his body."

Sheer terror for Anthony made her breathless.

"But it isn't true," she said wildly. "You mustn't think that. I fell. I slipped and fell."

"Then," said Anthony, speaking slowly, "you are not a prisoner here?"

"A prisoner? I'd be a prisoner anywhere, father. I can't walk."

"That door was locked."

She was fighting valiantly for him.

"I can't walk, father. I don't require a locked door to keep me in."

He was too confused and puzzled to notice the evasion.

"Do you mean to say that you won't let me have you taken home? You are still going to stay with this man? You know what he is, don't you?"

"I know what you think he is." She tried to smile, and he looked away from her quickly and stared around the room, seeing nothing, however. Suddenly he turned and walked to the door; but he stopped there, his hand on the knob, and us face twitching.

"Once more, Elinor," he said, "I ask you if you will let me take you back with me. This is the last time. I have come, after a good many years of bad feeling, to make my peace with you and to offer you a home. Will you come?"

"No."

Her courage almost failed her. She lay back, her eyes closed and her face colorless. The word itself was little more than a whisper.

Her father opened the door and went out. She heard him going down the stairs, heard other footsteps that followed him, and listened in an agony of fear that Doyle would drop him in the hall below. But nothing happened. The outside door closed, and after a moment she opened her eyes. Doyle was standing by the bed.

"So," he said, "you intend to give me the pleasure of your society for some time, do you?"

She said nothing. She was past any physical fear for herself.

"You liar!" he said softly. "Do you think I don't understand why you want to remain here? You are cleverer than I thought you were, but you are not as clever as I am. You'd have done better to have let him take you away."

"You would have killed him first."

"Perhaps I would." He lighted a cigarette. "But it is a pleasant thought to play with, and I shall miss it when the thing is fait accompli. I see Olga has left you without ice water. Shall I bring you some?"

He was still smiling faintly when he brought up the pitcher, some time later, and placed it on the stand beside the bed.

Chapter XXXV

In the Boyd house things went on much as before, but with a new heaviness. Ellen, watching keenly, knew why the little house was so cheerless and somber. It had been Willy Cameron who had brought to it its gayer moments, Willy determinedly cheerful, slamming doors and whistling; Willy racing up the stairs with something hot for Mrs. Boyd's tray; Willy at the table, making them forget the frugality of the meals with campaign anecdotes; Willy, lamenting the lack of a chance to fish, and subsequently eliciting a rare smile from Edith by being discovered angling in the kitchen sink with a piece of twine on the end of his umbrella.

Rather forced, some of it, but eminently good for all of them. And then suddenly it ceased. He made an effort, but there was no spontaneity in him. He came in quietly, never whistled, and ate very little. He began to look almost gaunt, too, and Edith, watching him with jealous, loving eyes, gave voice at last to the thought that was in her mind.

"I wish you'd go away," she said, "and let us fight this thing out ourselves. Dan would have to get something to do, then, for one thing."

"But I don't want to go away, Edith."

"Then you're a fool," she observed, bitterly. "You can't help me any, and there's no use hanging mother around your neck."

"She won't be around any one's neck very long, Edith dear."

"After that, will you go away?"

"Not if you still want me."

"Want you!"

Dan was out, and Ellen had gone up for the invalid's tray. They were alone together, standing in the kitchen doorway.

Suddenly Edith, beside him, ran her hand through his arm.

"If I had been a different sort of girl, Willy, do you think-could you ever have cared for me?"

"I never thought about you that way," he said, simply. "I do care for you. You know that."

She dropped her hand.

"You are in love with Lily Cardew. That's why you don't —I've known it all along, Willy. I used to think you'd get over it, never seeing her and all that. But you don't, do you?" She looked up at him. "The real thing lasts, I suppose. It will with me. I wish to heaven it wouldn't."

He was most uncomfortable, but he drew her hand within his arm again and held it there.

"Don't get to thinking that you care anything about me," he said. "There's not as much love in the world as there ought to be, and we all need to hold hands, but-don't fancy anything like that."

"I wanted to tell you. If I hadn't known about her I wouldn't have told you, but-you said it when you said there's not as much love as there ought to be. I'm gone, but I guess my caring for you hasn't hurt me any. It's the only reason I'm alive to-day."

She freed her hand, and stood staring out over the little autumn garden. There was such brooding trouble in her face that he watched her anxiously.

"I think mother suspects," she said at last.

"I hope not, Edith."

"I think she does. She watches me all the time, and she asked to see Dan to-night. Only he didn't come home."

"You must deny it, Edith," he said, almost fiercely. "She must not know, ever. That is one thing we can save her, and must save her."

But, going upstairs as usual before he went out, he realized that Edith was right, and that matters had reached a crisis. The sick woman had eaten nothing, and her eyes were sunken and anxious. There was an unspoken question in them, too, as she turned them on him. Most significant of all, the little album was not beside her, nor the usual litter of newspapers on the bed.

"I wish you weren't going out, Willy," she said querulously. "I want to talk to you about something."

"Can't we discuss it in the morning?"

"I won't sleep till I get it off my mind, Willy." But he could not face that situation then. He needed time, for one thing. Surely there must be some way out, some way to send this frail little woman dreamless to her last sleep, life could not be so cruel that death would seem kind.

He spoke at three different meetings that night, for the election was close at hand. Pink Denslow took him about in his car, and stood waiting for him at the back of the crowd. In the intervals between hall and hall Pink found Willy Cameron very silent and very grave, but he could not know that the young man beside him was trying to solve a difficult question. Which was: did two wrongs ever make a right?

At the end of the last meeting Willy Cameron decided to walk home.

"I have some things to think over. Pink," he said. "Thanks for the car. It saves a lot of time."

Pink sat at the wheel, carefully scrutinizing Willy. It struck him then that Cameron looked fagged and unhappy.

"Nothing I can do, I suppose?"

"Thanks, no."

Pink knew nothing of Lily's marriage, nor of the events that had followed it. To his uninquiring mind all was as it should be with her; she was at home again, although strangely quiet and very sweet, and her small world was at peace with her. It was all right with her, he considered, although all wrong with him. Except that she was strangely subdued, which rather worried him. It was not possible, for instance, to rouse her to one of their old red-hot discussions on religion, or marriage, or love.

"I saw Lily Cardew this afternoon, Cameron."

"Is she all right?" asked Willy Cameron, in a carefully casual tone.

"I don't know." Pink's honest voice showed perplexity. "She looks all right, and the family's eating out of her hand.. But she's changed somehow. She asked for you."

"Thanks. Well, good-night, old man."

Willy Cameron was facing the decision of his life that night, as he walked home. Lily was gone, out of his reach and out of his life. But then she had never been within either. She was only something wonderful and far away, like a star to which men looked and sometimes prayed. Some day she would be free again, and then in time she would marry. Some one like Pink, her own sort, and find happiness.

But he knew that he would always love her, to the end of his days, and even beyond, in that heaven in which he so simply believed. All the things that puzzled him would be straightened out there, and perhaps a man who had loved a woman and lost her here would find her there, and walk hand in hand with her, through the bright days of Paradise.

Not that that satisfied him. He was a very earthly lover, with the hungry arms of youth. He yearned unspeakably for her. He would have died for her as easily as he would have lived for her, but he could do neither.

That was one side of him. The other, having put her away in that warm corner of his heart which was hers always, was busy with the practical problem of the Boyds. He saw only one way out, and that way he had been seeing with increasing clearness for several days. Edith's candor that night, and Mrs. Boyd's suspicions, clearly pointed to it. There was one way by which to save Edith and her child, and to save the dying woman the agony of full knowledge.

Edith was sitting on the doorstep, alone. He sat down on the step below her, rather silent, still busy with his problem. Although the night was warm, the girl shivered.

"She's not asleep. She's waiting for me to go up, Willy. She means to call me in and ask me."

"Then I'd better say what I have to say quickly. Edith, will you marry me?"

She drew off and looked at him.

"I'd better explain what I mean," he said, speaking with some difficulty. "I mean-go through the ceremony with me. I don't mean actual marriage. That wouldn't be fair to either of us, because you know that I care for some one else."

"But you mean a real marriage?"

"Of course. Your child has the right to a name, dear. And, if you don't mind telling a lie to save our souls, and for her peace of mind, we can say that it took place some time ago."

She gazed at him dazedly. Then something like suspicion came into her face.

"Is it because of what I told you to-night?"

"I had thought of it before. That helped, of course."

It seemed so surprisingly simple, put into words, and the light on the girl's face was his answer. A few words, so easily spoken, and two lives were saved. No, three, for Edith's child must be considered.

"You are like God," said Edith, in a low voice. "Like God." And fell to soft weeping. She was unutterably happy and relieved. She sat there, not daring to touch him, and looked out into the quiet street. Before her she saw all the things that she had thought were gone; honor, a place in the world again, the right to look into her mother's eyes; she saw marriage and happy, golden days. He did not love her, but he would be hers, and perhaps in His own good time the Manager of all destinies would make him love her. She would try so hard to deserve that.

Mrs. Boyd was asleep when at last Edith went up the staircase, and Ellen, lying sleepless on her cot in the hot attic room, heard the girl softly humming to herself as she undressed, and marveled.

Chapter XXXVI

When Lily had been at home for some time, and Louis Akers had made no attempt to see her, or to announce the marriage, the vigilance of the household began to relax. Howard Cardew had already consulted the family lawyer about an annulment, and that gentleman had sent a letter to Akers, which had received no reply.

Then one afternoon Grayson, whose instructions had been absolute as to admitting Akers to the house, opened the door to Mrs. Denslow, who was calling, and found behind that lady Louis Akers himself. He made an effort to close the door behind the lady, but Akers was too quick for him, and a scene at the moment was impossible.

He ushered Mrs. Denslow into the drawing room, and coming out, closed the doors.

"My instructions, sir, are to say to you that the ladies are not at home."

But Akers held out his hat and gloves with so ugly a look that Grayson took them.

"I have come to see my wife," he said. "Tell her that, and that if she doesn't see me here I'll go upstairs and find her."

When Grayson still hesitated he made a move toward the staircase, and the elderly servant, astounded at the speech and the movement, put down the hat and faced him.

"I do not recognize any one in the household by that name, sir."

"You don't, don't you? Very well. Tell Miss Cardew I am here, and that either she will come down or I'll go up. I'll wait in the library."

He watched Grayson start up the stairs, and then went into the library. He was very carefully dressed, and momentarily exultant over the success of his ruse, but he was uneasy, too, and wary, and inclined to regard the house as a possible trap. He had made a gambler's venture, risking everything on the cards he held, and without much confidence in them. His vanity declined to believe that his old power over Lily was gone, but he had held a purely physical dominance over so many women that he knew both his strength and his limitations.

What he could not understand, what had kept him awake so many nights since he had seen her, was her recoil from him on Willy Cameron's announcement. She had known he had led the life of his sort; he had never played the plaster saint to her. And she had accepted her knowledge of his connection with the Red movement, on his mere promise to reform. But this other, this accident, and she had turned from him with a horror that made him furious to remember. These silly star-eyed virgins, who accepted careful abstractions and then turned sick at life itself, a man was a fool to put himself in their hands.

Mademoiselle was with Lily in her boudoir when Grayson came up, a thin, tired-faced, suddenly old Mademoiselle, much given those days to early masses, during which she prayed for eternal life for the man who had ruined Lily's life, and that soon. To Mademoiselle marriage was a final thing and divorce a wickedness against God and His establishment on earth.

Lily, rather like Willy Cameron, was finding on her spirit at that time a burden similar to his, of keeping up the morale of the household.

Grayson came in and closed the door behind him. Anger and anxiety were in his worn old face, and Lily got up quickly. "What is it, Grayson?"

"I'm sorry, Miss Lily. He was in the vestibule behind Mrs. Denslow, and I couldn't keep him out. I think he had waited for some one to call, knowing I couldn't make a scene."

Mademoiselle turned to Lily.

"You must not see him," she said in rapid French. "Remain here, and I shall telephone for your father. Lock your door. He may come up. He will do anything, that man."

"I am going down," Lily said quietly. "I owe him that. You need not be frightened. And don't tell mother; it will only worry her and do no good."

Her heart was beating fast as she went down the stairs. From the drawing room came the voices of Grace and Mrs. Denslow, chatting amiably. The second man was carrying in tea, the old silver service gleaming. Over all the lower floor was an air of peace and comfort, the passionless atmosphere of daily life running in old and easy grooves.

When Lily entered the library she closed the door behind her. She had, on turning, a swift picture of Grayson, taking up his stand in the hall, and it gave her a sense of comfort. She knew he would remain there, impassively waiting, so long as Akers was in the house.

Then she faced the man standing by the center table. He made no move toward her, did not even speak at once. It left on her the burden of the opening, of setting the key of what was to come. She was steady enough now.

"Perhaps it is as well that you came, Louis," she said. "I suppose we must talk it over some time."

"Yes," he agreed, his eyes on her. "We must. I have married a wife, and I want her, Lily."

"You know that is impossible."

"Because of something that happened before I knew you? I never made any pretensions about my life before we met. But I did promise to go straight if you'd have me, and I have. I've lived up to my bargain. What about you?"

"It was not a part of my bargain to marry you while you —I have thought and thought, Louis. There is only one thing to be done. You will have to divorce me, and marry her."

"Marry her? A girl of the streets, who chooses to say that I am the father of her child! It's the oldest trick in the word. Besides —" He played his best card —"she won't marry me. Ask Cameron, who chose to make himself so damned busy about my affairs. He's in love with her. Ask him."

In spite of herself Lily winced. Out of the wreckage of the past few weeks one thing had seemed to remain, something to hold to, solid and dependable and fine, and that had been Willy Cameron. She had found, in these last days, something infinitely comforting in the thought that he cared for her. It was because he had cared that he had saved her from herself. But, if this were true —

"I am not going back to you, Louis. I think you know that. No amount of talking about things can change that."

"Why don't you face life and try to understand it?" he demanded, brutally. "Men are like that. Women are like that-sometimes. You can't measure human passions with a tape line. That's what you good women try to do, and you make life a merry little hell." He made an effort, and softened his voice. "I'll be true to you, Lily, if you'll come back."

"No," she said, "you would mean to be, but you would not. You have no foundation to build on."

"Meaning that I am not a gentleman."

"Not that. I know you, that's all. I understand so much that I didn't before. What you call love is only something different. When that was gone there would be the same thing again. You would be sorry, but I would be lost."

Her coolness disconcerted him. Two small triangular bits of color showed in his face. He had been prepared for tears, even for a refusal to return, but this clear-eyed appraisal of himself, and the accuracy of it, confused him. He took refuge in the only method he knew; he threw himself on her pity; he made violent, passionate love to her, but her only expression was one of distaste. When at last he caught her to him she perforce submitted, a frozen thing that told him, more than any words, how completely he had lost her. He threw her away from him, then, baffled and angry.

"You little devil!" he said. "You cold little devil!"

"I don't love you. That's all. I think now that I never did."

"You pretended damned well."

"Don't you think you'd better go?" Lily said wearily. "I don't like to hurt you. I am to blame for a great deal. But there is no use going on, is there? I'll give you your freedom as soon as I can. You will want that, of course."

"My freedom! Do you think I am going to let you go like that? I'll fight you and your family in every court in the country before I give you up. You can't bring Edith Boyd up against me, either. If she does that I'll bring up other witnesses, other men, and she knows it."

Lily was very pale, but still calm. She made a movement toward the bell, but he caught her hand before she could ring it.

"I'll get your Willy Cameron, too," he said, his face distorted with anger. "I'll get him good. You've done a bad thing for your friends and your family to-day, Lily. I'll go the limit on getting back at them. I've got the power, and by God, I'll use it."

He flung out into the hall, and toward the door. There he encountered Grayson, who reminded him of his hat and gloves, or he would have gone without them.

Grayson, going into the library a moment later, found Lily standing there, staring ahead and trembling violently. He brought her a cup of tea, and stood by, his old face working, while she drank it.

Chapter XXXVII

The strike had apparently settled down to the ordinary run of strikes. The newspaper men from New York were gradually recalled, as the mill towns became orderly, and no further acts of violence took place. Here and there mills that had gone down fired their furnaces again and went back to work, many with depleted shifts, however.

But the strikers had lost, and knew it. Howard Cardew, facing the situation with his customary honesty, saw in the gradual return of the men to work only the urgency of providing for their families, and realized that it was not peace that was coming, but an armed neutrality. The Cardew Mills were still down, but by winter he was confident they would be open again. To what purpose? To more wrangling and bickering, more strikes? Where was the middle ground? He was willing to give the men a percentage of the profits they made. He did not want great wealth, only an honest return for his invested capital. But he wanted to manage his own business. It was his risk.

The coal miners were going out. The Cardews owned coal mines. The miners wanted to work a minimum day for a maximum wage, but the country must have coal. Shorter hours meant more men for the mines, and they would have to be imported. But labor resented the importation of foreign workers.

Again, what was the answer?

Still, he was grateful for peace. The strike dragged on, with only occasional acts of violence. From the hill above Baxter a sniper daily fired with a long range rifle at the toluol tank in the center of one of the mills, and had so far escaped capture, as the tank had escaped damage. But he knew well enough that a long strike was playing into the hands of the Reds. It was impossible to sow the seeds of revolution so long as a man's dinner-pail was full, his rent paid, and his family contented. But a long strike, with bank accounts becoming exhausted and credit curtailed, would pave the way for revolution.

Old Anthony had had a drastic remedy for strikes.

"Let all the storekeepers, the country over, refuse credit to the strikers, and we'd have an end to this mess," he said.

"We'd have an end to the storekeepers, too," Howard had replied, grimly.

One good thing had come out of the bomb outrages. They had had a salutary effect on the honest labor element. These had no sympathy with such methods and said so. But a certain element, both native and foreign born, secretly gloated and waited.

One thing surprised and irritated Howard. Public sentiment was not so much with the strikers, as against the mill owners. The strike worked a hardship to the stores and small businesses dependent on the great mills; they forgot the years when the Cardews had brought them prosperity, had indeed made them possible, and they felt now only bitter resentment at the loss of trade. In his anger Howard saw them as parasites, fattening on the conceptions and strength of those who had made the city. They were men who built nothing, originated nothing. Men who hated the ladder by which they had climbed, who cared little how shaky its foundation, so long as it stood.

In September, lured by a false security, the governor ordered the demobilization of the state troops, save for two companies. The men at the Baxter and Friendship plants, owned by the Cardews, had voted to remain out, but their leaders appeared to have them well in hand, and no trouble was anticipated. The agents of the Department of Justice, however, were still suspicious. The foreigners had plenty of money. Given as they were to hoarding their savings in their homes, the local banks were unable to say if they were drawing on their reserves or were being financed from the outside.

Shortly before the mayoralty election trouble broke out in the western end of the state, and in the north, in the steel towns. There were ugly riotings, bombs were sent through the mails, the old tactics of night shootings and destruction of property began. In the threatening chaos Baxter and Friendship, and the city nearby, stood out by contrast for their very orderliness. The state constabulary remained in diminished numbers, a still magnificent body of men but far too few for any real emergency, and the Federal agents, suspicious but puzzled, were removed to more turbulent fields.

The men constituting the Vigilance Committee began to feel a sense of futility, almost of absurdity. They had armed and enrolled themselves-against what? The growth of the organization slowed down, but it already numbered thousands of members. Only its leaders retained their faith in its ultimate necessity, and they owed perhaps more than they realized to Willy Cameron's own conviction.

It was owing to him that the city was divided into a series of zones, so that notification of an emergency could be made rapidly by telephone and messenger. Owing to him, too, was a new central office, with some one on duty day and night. Rather ironically, the new quarters were the dismantled rooms of the Myers Housecleaning Company.

On the day after his proposal to Edith, Willy Cameron received an unexpected holiday. Mrs. Davis, the invalid wife of the owner of the Eagle Pharmacy, died and the store was closed. He had seen Edith for only a few moments that morning, but it was understood then that the marriage would take place either that day or the next.

He had been physically so weary the night before that he had slept, but the morning found him with a heaviness of spirit that he could not throw off. The exaltation of the night before was gone, and all that remained was a dogged sense of a duty to be done. Although he smiled at Edith, his face remained with her all through the morning.

"I'll make it up to him," she thought, humbly. "I'll make it up to him somehow."

Then, with Ellen out doing her morning marketing, she heard the feeble thump of a cane overhead which was her mother's signal. She was determined not to see her mother again until she could say that she was married, but the thumping continued, and was followed by the crash of a broken glass.

"She's trying to get up!" Edith thought, panicky. "If she gets up it will kill her."

She stood at the foot of the stairs, scarcely breathing, and listened. There was a dreadful silence above. She stole up, finally, to where she could see her mother. Mrs. Boyd was still in her bed, but lying with open eyes, unmoving.

"Mother," she called, and ran in. "Mother."

Mrs. Boyd glanced at her.

"I thought that glass would bring you," she said sharply, but with difficulty. "I want you to stand over there and let me look at you."

Edith dropped on her knees beside the bed, and caught her mother's hand.

"Don't! Don't talk like that, mother," she begged. "I know what you mean. It's all right, mother. Honestly it is. I—I'm married, mother."

"You wouldn't lie to me, Edith?"

"No. I'm telling you. I've been married a long time. You-don't you worry, mother. You just lie there and quit worrying. It's all right."

There was a sudden light in the sick woman's eyes, an eager light that flared up and died away again.

"Who to?" she asked. "If it's some corner loafer, Edie —" Edith had gained new courage and new facility. Anything was right that drove the tortured look from her mother's eyes.

"You can ask him when he comes home this evening."

"Edie! Not Willy?"

"You've guessed it," said Edith, and burying her face in the bed clothing, said a little prayer, to be forgiven for the lie and for all that she had done, to be more worthy thereafter, and in the end to earn the love of the man who was like God to her.

There are lies and lies. Now and then the Great Recorder must put one on the credit side of the balance, one that has saved intolerable suffering, or has made well and happy a sick soul.

Mrs. Boyd lay back and closed her eyes.

"I haven't been so tickled since the day you were born," she said.

She put out a thin hand and laid it on the girl's bowed head. When Edith moved, a little later, her mother was asleep, with a new look of peace on her face.

It was necessary before Ellen saw her mother to tell her what she had done. She shrank from doing it. It was one thing for Willy to have done it, to have told her the plan, but Edith was secretly afraid of Ellen. And Ellen's reception of the news justified her fears.

"And you'd take him that way!" she said, scornfully. "You'd hide behind him, besides spoiling his life for him! It sounds like him to offer, and it's like you to accept."

"It's to save mother," said Edith, meekly.

"It's to save yourself. You can't fool me. And if you think I'm going to sit by and let him do it, you can think again."

"It's as good as done," Edith flashed. "I've told mother."

"That you're going to be, or that you are?"

"That we are married."

"All right," Ellen said triumphantly. "She's quiet and peaceful now, isn't she? You don't have to get married now, do you? You take my advice, and let it go at that."

It was then that Edith realized what she had done. He would still marry her, of course, but behind all his anxiety to save her had been the real actuating motive of his desire to relieve her mother's mind. That was done now. Then, could she let him sacrifice himself for her?

She could. She could and she would. She set her small mouth firmly, and confronted the future; she saw herself, without his strength to support her, going down and down. She remembered those drabs of the street on whom she had turned such cynical eyes in her virtuous youth, and she saw herself one of that lost sisterhood, sodden, hectic, hopeless.

When Willy Cameron left the pharmacy that day it was almost noon. He went to the house of mourning first, and found Mr. Davis in a chair in a closed room, a tired little man in a new black necktie around a not over-clean collar, his occupation of years gone, confronting a new and terrible leisure that he did not know how to use.

"You know how it is, Willy," he said, blinking his reddened eyelids. "You kind of wish sometimes that you had somebody to help you bear your burden, and then it's taken away, but you're kind of bent over and used to it. And you'd give your neck and all to have it back."

Willy Cameron pondered that on his way up the street.

There was one great longing in him, to see Lily again. In a few hours now he would have taken a wife, and whatever travesty of marriage resulted, he would have to keep away from Lily. He meant to play square with Edith.

He wondered if it would hurt Lily to see him, remind her of things she must be trying to forget. He decided in the end that it would hurt her, so he did not go. But he walked, on his way to see Pink Denslow at the temporary bank, through a corner of the park near the house, and took a sort of formal and heart-breaking farewell of her.

Time had been when life had seemed only a long, long trail, with Lily at the end of it somewhere, like water to the thirsty traveler, or home to the wanderer; like a camp fire at night. But now, life seemed to him a broad highway, infinitely crowded, down which he must move, surrounded yet alone.

But at least he could walk in the middle of the road, in the sunlight. It was the weaklings who were crowded to the side. He threw up his head.

It had never occurred to him that he was in any, danger, either from Louis Akers or from the unseen enemy he was fighting. He had a curious lack of physical fear. But once or twice that day, as he went about, he happened to notice a small man, foreign in appearance and shabbily dressed. He saw him first when he came out of the marriage license office, and again when he entered the bank.

He had decided to tell Pink of his approaching marriage and to ask him to be present. He meant to tell him the facts. The intimacy between them was now very close, and he felt that Pink would understand. He neither wanted nor expected approval, but he did want honesty between them. He had based his life on honesty.

Yet the thing was curiously hard to lead up to. It would be hard to set before any outsider the conditions at the Boyd house, or his own sense of obligation to help. Put into everyday English the whole scheme sounded visionary and mock-heroic.

In the end he did not tell Pink at all, for Pink came in with excitement written large all over him.

"I sent for you," he said, "because I think we've got something at last. One of our fellows has just been in, that storekeeper I told you about from Friendship, Cusick. He says he has found out where they're meeting, back in the hills. He's made a map of it. Look, here's the town, and here's the big hill. Well, behind it, about a mile and a half, there's a German outfit, a family, with a farm. They're using the barn, according to this chap."

"The barn wouldn't hold very many of them."

"That's the point. It's the leaders. The family has an alibi. It goes in to the movies in the town on meeting nights. The place has been searched twice, but he says they have a system of patrols that gives them warning. The hills are heavily wooded there, and he thinks they have rigged up telephones in the trees."

There was a short silence. Willy Cameron studied the rug.

"I had to swear to keep it to ourselves," Pink said at last. "Cusick won't let the Federal agents in on it. They've raided him for liquor twice, and he's sick as a poisoned pup."

"How about the county detectives?"

"You know them. They'll go in and fight like hell when the time comes, but they're likely to gum the game where there's any finesse required. We'd better find out for ourselves first."

Willy Cameron smiled.

"What you mean is, that it's too good a thing to throw to the other fellow. Well, I'm on, if you want me. But I'm no detective."

Pink had come armed for such surrender. He produced a road map of the county and spread it on the desk.

"Here's the main road to Friendship," he said, "and here's the road they use. But there's another way, back of the hills. Cusick said it was a dirt lane, but dry. It's about forty miles by it to a point a mile or so behind the farm. He says he doesn't think they use that road. It's too far around."

"All right," said Willy Cameron. "We use that road, and get to the farm, and what then? Surrender?"

"Not on your life. We hide in the barn. That's all."

"That's enough. They'll search the place, automatically. You're talking suicide, you know."

But his mind was working rapidly. He was a country boy, and he knew barns. There would be other outbuildings, too, probably a number of them. The Germans always had plenty of them. And the information was too detailed to be put aside lightly.

"When does he think they will meet again?"

"That's the point," Pink said eagerly. "The family has been all over the town this morning. It is going on a picnic, and he says those picnics of theirs last half the night. What he got from the noise they were making was that they were raising dust again, and something's on for to-night."

"They'll leave somebody there. Their stock has to be looked after."

"This fellow says they drop everything and go. The whole outfit. They're as busy raising an alibi as the other lot is raising the devil."

But Willy Cameron was a Scot, and hard-headed.

"It looks too simple, Pink," he said reflectively. He sat for some time, filling and lighting his pipe, and considering as he did so. He was older than Pink; not much, but he felt extremely mature and very responsible.

"What do we know about Cusick?" he asked, finally.

"One of the best men we've got. They've fired his place once, and he's keen to get them."

"You're anxious to go?"

"I'm going," said Pink, cheerfully.

"Then I'd better go along and look after you. But I tell you how I see it. After I've done that I'll go as far as you like. Either there is nothing to it and we're fools for our pains, or there's a lot to it, and in that case we are a pair of double-distilled lunatics to go there alone."

Pink laughed joyously.

Life had been very dull for him since his return from France. He had done considerable suffering and more thinking than was usual with him, but he had had no action. But behind his boyish zest there was something more, something he hid as he did the fact that he sometimes said his prayers; a deep and holy thing, that always gave him a lump in his throat at Retreat, when the flag came slowly down and the long lines of men stood at attention. Something he was half ashamed and half proud of, love of his country.

At the same time another conversation was going on in the rear room of a small printing shop in the heart of the city. It went on to the accompaniment of the rhythmic throb of the presses, and while two printers, in their shirt sleeves, kept guard both at the front and rear entrances.

Doyle sat with his back to the light, and seated across from him, smoking a cheap cigar, was the storekeeper from Friendship, Cusick. In a corner on the table, scowling, sat Louis Akers.

"I don't know why you're so damned suspicious, Jim," he was saying. "Cusick says the stall about the Federal agents went all right."

"Like a house a-fire," said Cusick, complacently.

"I think, Akers," Doyle observed, eyeing his subordinate, "that you are letting your desire to get this Cameron fellow run away with your judgment. If we get him and Denslow, there are a hundred ready to take their places."

"Cameron is the brains of the outfit," Akers said sulkily.

"How do you know Cameron will go?"

Akers rose lazily and stretched himself.

"I've got a hunch. That's all."

A girl came in from the composing room, a bundle of proofs in her hand. With one hand Akers took the sheets from her; with the other he settled his tie. He smiled down at her.

Chapter XXXVIII

Ellen was greatly disturbed. At three o'clock that afternoon she found Edith and announced her intention of going out.

"I guess you can get the supper for once," she said ungraciously.

Edith looked up at her with wistful eyes.

"I wish you didn't hate me so, Ellen."

"I don't hate you." Ellen was slightly mollified. "But when I see you trying to put your burdens on other people —"

Edith got up then and rather timidly put her arms around Ellen's neck.

"I love him so, Ellen," she whispered, "and I'll try so hard to make him happy."

Unexpected tears came into Ellen's eyes. She stroked the girl's fair hair.

"Never mind," she said. "The Good Man's got a way of fixing things to suit Himself. And I guess He knows best. We do what it's foreordained we do, after all."

Mrs. Boyd was sleeping. Edith went back to her sewing. She had depended all her life on her mother's needle, and now that that had failed her she was hastily putting some clothing into repair. In the kitchen near the stove the suit she meant to be married in was hung to dry, after pressing. She was quietly happy.

Willy Cameron found her there. He told her of Mrs. Davis' death, and then placed the license on the table at her side.

"I think it would be better to-morrow, Edith," he said. He glanced down at the needle in her unaccustomed fingers; she seemed very appealing, with her new task and the new light in her eyes. After all, it was worth while, even if it cost a lifetime, to take a soul out of purgatory.

"I had to tell mother, Willy."

"That's all right Did it cheer her any?"

"Wonderfully. She's asleep now."

He went up to his room, and for some time she heard him moving about. Then she heard the scraping of his chair as he drew it to his desk, and vaguely wondered. When he came down he had a sealed envelope in his hand.

"I am going out, Edith," he said. "I shall be late getting back, and —I am going to ask you to do something for me."

She loved doing things for him. She flushed slightly.

"If I am not back here by two o'clock to-night," he said, "I want you to open that letter and read it. Then go to the nearest telephone, and call up the number I've written down. Ask for the man whose name is given, and read him the message."

"Willy!" she gasped. "You are doing something dangerous!"

"What I really expect," he said, smiling down at her, "is to be back, feeling more or less of a fool, by eleven o'clock. I'm providing against an emergency that will almost surely never happen, and I am depending on the most trustworthy person I know."

Very soon after that he went away. She sat for some time after he had gone, fingering the blank white envelope and wondering, a little frightened but very proud of his trust.

Dan came in and went up the stairs. That reminded her of the dinner, and she sat down in the kitchen with a pan of potatoes on her knee. As she pared them she sang. She was still singing when Ellen came back.

Something had happened to Ellen. She stood in the kitchen, her hat still on, drawing her cotton gloves through her fingers and staring at Edith without seeing her.

"You're not sick, are you, Ellen?"

Ellen put down her gloves and slowly took off her hat, still with the absorbed eyes of a sleep-walker.

"I'm not sick," she said at last. "I've had bad news."

"Sit down and I'll make you a cup of tea. Then maybe you'll feel like talking about it."

"I don't want any tea. Do you know that that man Akers has married Lily Cardew?"

"Married her!"

"The devil out of hell that he is." Ellen's voice was terrible. "And all the time knowing that you-She's at home, the poor child, and Mademoiselle just sat and cried when she told me. It's a secret," she added, fiercely. "You keep your mouth shut about it. She never lived with him. She left him right off. I wouldn't know it now but the servants were talking about the house being forbidden to him, and I went straight to Mademoiselle. I said: 'You keep him away from Miss Lily, because I know something about him.' It was when I told her that she said they were married."

She went out and up the stairs, moving slowly and heavily. Edith sat still, the pan on her knee, and thought. Did Willy know? Was that why he was willing to marry her? She was swept with bitter jealousy, and added to that came suspicion. Something very near the truth flashed into her mind and stayed there. In her bitterness she saw Willy telling Lily of Akers and herself, and taking her away, or having her taken. It must have been something like that, or why had she left him?

But her anger slowly subsided; in the end she began to feel that the new situation rendered her own position more secure, even justified her own approaching marriage. Since Lily was gone, why should she not marry Willy Cameron? If what Ellen had said was true she knew him well enough to know that he would deliberately strangle his love for Lily. If it were true, and if he knew it.

She moved about the kitchen, making up the fire, working automatically in that methodless way that always set Ellen's teeth on edge, and thinking. But subconsciously she was listening, too. She had heard Dan go into his mother's room and close the door. She was bracing herself against his coming down.

Dan was difficult those days, irritable and exacting. Moody, too, and much away from home. He hated idleness at its best, and the strike was idleness at its worst. Behind the movement toward the general strike, too, he felt there was some hidden and sinister influence at work, an influence that was determined to turn what had commenced as a labor movement into a class uprising.

That very afternoon, for the first time, he had heard whispered the phrase: "when the town goes dark." There was a diabolical suggestion in it that sent him home with his fists clenched.

He did not go to his mother's room at once. Instead, he drew a chair to his window and sat there staring out on the little street. When the town went dark, what about all the little streets like this one?

After an hour or so of ominous quiet Edith heard him go into his mother's room. Her hands trembled as she closed her door.

She heard him coming down at last, and suddenly remembering the license, hid it in a drawer. She knew that he would destroy it if he saw it. And Dan's face justified the move. He came in and stood glowering at her, his hands in his pockets.

"What made you tell that lie to mother?" he demanded.

"She was worried, Dan. And it will be true to-morrow. You-Dan, you didn't tell her it was a lie, did you?"

"I should have, but I didn't. What do you mean, it will be true to-morrow?"

"We are going to be married to-morrow."

"I'll lock you up first," he said, angrily. "I've been expecting something like that. I've watched you, and I've seen you watching him. You'll not do it, do you hear? D'you think I'd let you get away with that? Isn't it enough that he's got to support us, without your coaxing him to marry you?"

She made no reply, but went on with a perfunctory laying of the table. Her mouth had gone very dry.

"The poor fish," Dan snarled. "I thought he had some sense. Letting himself in for a nice life, isn't he? We're not his kind, and you know it. He knows more in a minute than you'll know all your days. In about three months he'll hate the very sight of you, and then where'll you be?"

When she made no reply, he called to the dog and went out into the yard. She saw him there, brooding and sullen, and she knew that he had not finished. He would say no more to her, but he would wait and have it out with Willy himself.

Supper was silent. No one ate much, and Ellen, coming down with the tray, reported Mrs. Boyd as very tired, and wanting to settle down early.

"She looks bad to me," she said to Edith. "I think the doctor ought to see her."

"I'll go and send him."

Edith was glad to get out of the house. She had avoided the streets lately, but as it was the supper hour the pavements were empty. Only Joe Wilkinson, bare-headed, stood in the next doorway, and smiled and flushed slightly when he saw her.

"How's your mother?" he asked.

"She's not so well. I'm going to get the doctor."

"Do you mind if I get my hat and walk there with you?"

"I'm going somewhere else from there, Joe."

"Well, I'll walk a block or two, anyhow."

She waited impatiently. She liked Joe, but she did not want him then. She wanted to think and plan alone and in the open air, away from the little house with its odors and its querulous thumping cane upstairs; away from Ellen's grim face and Dan's angry one.

He came out almost immediately, followed by a string of little Wilkinsons, clamoring to go along.

"Do you mind?" he asked her. "They can trail along behind. The poor kids don't get out much."

"Bring them along, of course," she said, somewhat resignedly. And with a flash of her old spirit: "I might have brought Jinx, too. Then we'd have had a real procession."

They moved down the street, with five little Wilkinsons trailing along behind, and Edith was uncomfortably aware that Joe's eyes were upon her.

"You don't look well," he said at last. "You're wearing yourself out taking care of your mother, Edith."

"I don't do much for her."

"You'd say that, of course. You're very unselfish."

"Am I?" She laughed a little, but the words touched her. "Don't think I'm better than I am, Joe."

"You're the most wonderful girl in the world. I guess you know how I feel about that."

"Don't Joe!"

But at that moment a very little Wilkinson fell headlong and burst into loud, despairing wails. Joe set her on her feet, brushed her down with a fatherly hand, and on her refusal to walk further picked her up and carried her. The obvious impossibility of going on with what he had been saying made him smile sheepishly.

"Can you beat it?" he said helplessly, "these darn kids —!" But he held the child close.

At the next corner he turned toward home. Edith stopped and watched his valiant young back, his small train of followers. He was going to be very sad when he knew, poor Joe, with his vicarious fatherhood, his cluttered, noisy, anxious life.

Life was queer. Queer and cruel.

From the doctor's office, the waiting room lined with patient figures, she went on. She had a very definite plan in mind, but it took all her courage to carry it through. Outside the Benedict Apartments she hesitated, but she went in finally, upheld by sheer determination.

The chair at the telephone desk was empty, but Sam remembered her.

"He's out, miss," he said. "He's out most all the time now, with the election coming on."

"What time does he usually get in?"

"Sometimes early, sometimes late," said Sam, watching her. Everything pertaining to Louis Akers was of supreme interest those days to the Benedict employees. The beating he had received, the coming election, the mysterious young woman who had come but once, and the black days that had followed his return from the St. Elmo-out of such patchwork they were building a small drama of their own. Sam was trying to fit in Edith's visit with the rest.

The Benedict was neither more moral nor less than its kind. An unwritten law kept respectable women away, but the management showed no inclination to interfere where there was no noise or disorder. Employees were supposed to see that no feminine visitors remained after midnight, that was all.

"You might go up and wait for him," Sam suggested. "That is, if it's important."

"It's very important."

He threw open the gate of the elevator hospitably.

At half past ten that night Louis Akers went back to his rooms. The telephone girl watched him sharply as he entered.

"There's a lady waiting for you, Mr. Akers."

He swung toward her eagerly.

"A lady? Did she give any name?"

"No. Sam let her in and took her up. He said he thought you wouldn't mind. She'd been here before."

The thought of Edith never entered Akers' head. It was Lily, Lily miraculously come back to him. Lily, his wife.

Going up in the elevator he hastily formulated a plan of action. He would not be too ready to forgive; she had cost him too much. But in the end he would take her in his arms and hold her close. Lily! Lily!

It was the bitterness of his disappointment that made him brutal. Wicked and unscrupulous as he was with men, with women he was as gentle as he was cruel. He put them from him relentlessly and kissed them good-by. It was his boast that any one of them would come back to him if he wanted her.

Edith, listening for his step, was startled at the change in his face when he saw her.

"You!" he said thickly. "What are you doing here?"

"I've been waiting all evening. I want to ask you something."

He flung his hat into a chair and faced her.

"Well?"

"Is it true that you are married to Lily Cardew?"

"If I am, what are you going to do about it?" His eyes were wary, but his color was coming back. He was breathing more easily.

"I only heard it to-day. I must know, Lou. It's awfully important."

"What did you hear?" He was watching her closely.

"I heard you were married, but that she had left you."

It seemed to him incredible that she had come there to taunt him, she who was responsible for the shipwreck of his marriage. That she could come there and face him, and not expect him to kill her where she stood.

He pulled himself together.

"It's true enough." He swore under his breath. "She didn't leave me. She was taken away. And I'll get her back if I —You little fool, I ought to kill you. If you wanted a cheap revenge, you've got it."

"I don't want revenge, Lou."

He caught her by the arm.

"Then what brought you here?"

"I wanted to be sure Lily Cardew was married."

"Well, she is. What about it?"

"That's all."

"That's not all. What about it?"

She looked up at him gravely.

"Because, if she is, I am going to marry Mr. Cameron tomorrow." At the sight of his astounded face she went on hastily: "He knows, Lou, and he offered anyhow."

"And what," he said slowly, "has my wife to do with that?"

"I wanted to be fair to him. And I think he is —I think he used to be terribly in love with her."

Quite apart from his increasing fear of Willy Cameron and his Committee, there had been in Akers for some time a latent jealousy of him. In a flash he saw the room at the Saint Elmo, and a cold-eyed man inside the doorway. The humiliation of that scene had never left him, of his own maudlin inadequacy, of hearing from beyond a closed and locked door, the closing of another door behind Lily and the man who had taken her away from him. A mad anger and jealousy made him suddenly reckless.

"So," he said, "he is terribly in love with my wife, and he intends to marry you. That's — interesting. Because, my sweet child, he's got a damn poor chance of marrying you, or anybody."

"Lou!"

"Listen," he said deliberately. "Men who stick their heads into the lion's jaws are apt to lose them. Our young friend Cameron has done that. I'll change the figure. When a man tries to stop a great machine by putting his impudent fingers into the cog wheels, the man's a fool. He may lose his hand, or he may lose his life."

Fortunately for Edith he moved on that speech to the side table, and mixed himself a highball. It gave her a moment to summon her scattered wits, to decide on a plan of action. Her early training on the streets, her recent months of deceit, helped her now. If he had expected any outburst from her it did not come.

"If you mean that he is in danger, I don't believe it."

"All right, old girl. I've told you."

But the whiskey restored his equilibrium again.

"That is," he added slowly, "I've warned you. You'd better warn him. He's doing his best to get into trouble."

She knew him well, saw the craftiness come back into his eyes, and met it with equal strategy.

"I'll tell him," she said, moving toward the door. "You haven't scared me for a minute and you won't scare him. You and your machine!"

She dared not seem to hurry.

"You're a boaster," she said, with the door open. "You always were. And you'll never lay a hand on him. You're like all bullies; you're a coward!"

She was through the doorway by that time, and in terror for fear, having told her so much, he would try to detain her. She saw the idea come into his face, too, just as she slipped outside. He made a move toward her.

"I think —" he began.

She slammed the door and ran down the hallway toward the stairs. She heard him open the door and come out into the hall, but she was well in advance and running like a deer.

"Edith!" he called.

She stumbled on the second flight of stairs and fell a half-dozen steps, but she picked herself up and ran on. At the bottom of the lower flight she stopped and listened, but he had gone back. She heard the slam of his door as he closed it.

But the insistent need of haste drove her on, headlong. She shot through the lobby, past the staring telephone girl, and into the street, and there settled down into steady running, her elbows close to her sides, trying to remember to breathe slowly and evenly. She must get home somehow, get the envelope and follow the directions inside. Her thoughts raced with her. It was almost eleven o'clock and Willy had been gone for hours. She tried to pray, but the words did not come.

Chapter XXXIX

At something after seven o'clock that night Willy Cameron and Pink Denslow reached that point on the Mayville Road which had been designated by the storekeeper, Cusick. They left the car there, hidden in a grove, and struck off across country to the west. Willy Cameron had been thoughtful for some time, and as they climbed a low hill, going with extreme caution, he said:

"I'm still skeptical about Cusick, Pink. Do you think he's straight?"

"One of the best men we've got," Pink replied, confidently. "He's put us on to several things."

"He's foreign born, isn't he?"

"That's his value. They don't suspect him for a minute."

"But-what does he get out of it?"

"Good citizen," said Pink, with promptness. "You've got to remember, Cameron, that a lot of these fellows are better Americans than we are. They're like religious converts, stronger than the ones born in the fold. They're Americans because they want to be. Anyhow, you ought to be strong for him, Cameron. He said to tell you, but no one else."

"I'll tell you how strong I am for him later," Willy Cameron said, grimly. "Just at this minute I'm waiting to be shown."

They advanced with infinite caution, for the evening was still light. Going slowly, it was well after eight and fairly dark before they came within sight of the farm buildings in the valley below. Long unpainted, they were barely discernable in the shadows of the hills. The land around had been carefully cleared, and both men were dismayed at the difficulty of access without being seen.

"Doesn't look very good, does it?" Pink observed. "I will say this, for seclusion and keeping away unwanted visitors, it has it all over any dug-out I ever saw in France."

"Listen!" Willy Cameron said, tensely.

They stood on the alert, but only the evening sounds of country and forest rewarded them.

"What was it?" Pink inquired, after perhaps two minutes of waiting.

"Plain scare on my part, probably. I don't so much mind this little excursion, Pink, as I hate the idea that a certain gentleman named Cusick may have a chance to come to our funerals and laugh himself to death."

When real darkness had fallen, they had reached the lower fringe of the woods. Pink had the fault of the city dweller, however, of being unable to step lightly in the dark, and their progress had been less silent than it should have been. In spite of his handicap, Willy Cameron made his way with the instinctive knowledge of the country bred boy, treading like a cat.

"Pretty poor," Pink said in a discouraged whisper, after a twig had burst under his foot with a report like the shot of a pistol. "You travel like a spook, while I —"

"Listen, Pink. I'm going in alone to look around. Stop muttering and listen to me. It's poor strategy not to have a reserve somewhere, isn't it?"

"I'm a poor prune at the best," Pink said stubbornly, "but I am not going to let you go into that place alone. You can rave all you want."

"Very well. Then we'll both stay here. You are about as quiet as a horse going through a corn patch."

After some moments Pink spoke again.

"If you insist on stealing the whole show," he said, sulkily, "what am I to do? Run to town for help, if you need it?"

"I'm not going to round up the outfit, if there is one. I haven't lost my mind. I'll see what is going on, or about to go on. Then I'll come back."

"Here?"

Cameron considered.

"Better meet at the machine," he decided, after a glance at the sky. "In half an hour you won't be able to see your hand in front of you. Wait here for a half-hour or so, and then start back, and for heaven's sake don't shoot at anything you see moving. As a matter of fact, I might as well have your revolver. I won't need it, but it may avoid any accidental shooting by a youth I both love and admire!"

"If I hear any shooting, I'll come in," Pink said, still sulky.

"Come in and welcome," said Willy Cameron, and Pink knew he was smiling.

He took the revolver and slipped away into the darkness, leaving Pink both melancholy and disturbed. Unaccustomed to night in the woods, he found his nerves twitching at every sound. In the war there had been a definite enemy, definitely placed. Even when he had gone into that vile strip between the trenches, there had been a general direction for the inimical. Here —

He moved carefully, and stood with his back against a tree.

Not a sound came from the farm buildings. Willy Cameron's progress, too, was noiseless. With no way to tell the lapse of time, and gauging it by his war experience, when an hour had apparently passed by, he knew that Cameron had been gone about ten minutes.

Time dragged on. A cow, unmilked, lowed plaintively once or twice. A September night breeze set the dying leaves on the trees to rustling, and stirred the dried ones about his feet. Pink's mind, gradually reassured, turned to other things. He thought of Lily Cardew, for one. Like Willy Cameron, he knew he would always love her, but unlike Willy, the first pain of her loss was gone. He was glad that time was over. He was glad that she was at home again, safe from those-Some one was moving near him, passing within twenty feet. Whoever it was was stepping cautiously but blunderingly. It was not Cameron, then. He was a footfall only, not even an outline. Before Pink could decide on a line of action, the sound was lost.

Every sense acute, he waited. He had decided that if the incident were repeated, he would make an effort to get the fellow from behind, but there was no return. The wind had died again, and there was no longer even the rustling of the leaves to break the utter stillness.

Suddenly he saw a red flash near the barn, and an instant later heard the report of a pistol. Came immediately after that a brief fusillade of shots, a pause, then two or three scattering ones.

With the first shot Pink started running. He was vaguely conscious of other steps near him, running also, but he could see nothing. His whole mind was set on finding Willy Cameron. Alone he had not a chance, but two of them together could put up a fight. He pelted along, stumbling, recovering, stumbling again.

Another shot was fired. They hadn't got him yet, or they wouldn't be shooting. He raised his voice in a great call.

"Cameron! Here! Cameron!"

He ran into a low fence then, and it threw him. He had hardly got to his knees before the other running figure had hurled itself on him, and struck him with the butt of a revolver. He dropped flat and lay still.

———————————————————

For weeks Woslosky had known of the growing strength of the Vigilance Committee, and that it was arming steadily.

It threatened absolutely the success of his plans. Even the election of Akers and the changes he would make in the city police; even the ruse of other strikes and machine-made riotings to call away the state troops, —none of these, or all of them, would be effectual against an organized body of citizens, duly called to the emergency.

And such an organization was already effected. Within a week, when the first card reached his hands, it had grown to respectable proportions. Woslosky went to Doyle, and they made their counter-moves quickly. No more violence. A seemingly real but deceptive orderliness. They were dealing with inflammatory material, however, and now and then it got out of hand. Unlike Doyle the calculating, who made each move slowly and watched its results with infinite zest, the Pole chafed under delay.

"We can't hold them much longer," he complained, bitterly. "This thing of holding them off until after the election-and until Akers takes office-it's got too many ifs in it."

"It was haste lost Seattle," said Doyle, as unmoved as Woslosky was excited.

Woslosky did not like Louis Akers. What was more important, he distrusted him. When he heard of his engagement to Lily Cardew he warned Doyle about him.

"He's in this thing for what he can get out of it," he said. "He'll go as far as he can, with safety, to be accepted by the Cardews."

"Exactly," was Doyle's dry comment, "with safety, you said. Well, he knows you and he knows me, and he'll he straight because he's afraid not to be."

"When there's a woman in it!" said the Pole, skeptically.

But Doyle only smiled. He had known many women and loved none of them, and he was temperamentally unable to understand the type of man who saw the world through a woman's eyes and in them.

So Woslosky was compelled to watch the growth of Willy Cameron's organization, and to hold in check the violent passions he had himself roused, and to wait, gnawing his nails with inaction and his heart with rage. But these certain things he discovered:

That the organization's growth was coincident with a new interest in local politics, as though some vital force had wakened the plain people to a sense of responsibility.

That a drug clerk named Cameron was the founder and moving spirit of the league, and that he was, using Hendricks' candidacy as a means, rousing the city to a burning patriotic activity that Mr. Woslosky regarded as extremely pernicious.

And that this same Willy Cameron had apparently a knowledge of certain plans, which was rather worse than pernicious. Mr. Woslosky's name for it was damnable.

For instance, there were the lists of the various city stores and their estimated contents, missing from Mr. Woslosky's own inconspicuous trunk in a storage house. On that had been based the plan for feeding the revolution, by the simple expedient of exchanging by organized pillage the contents of the city stores for food stuffs from the farmers in outlying districts.

Revolution, according to Mr. Woslosky, could only be starved out. He had no anxiety as to troops which would be sent against them, because he had a cynical belief that a man's country was less to him than various other things, including his stomach. He believed that all armies were riddled with sedition and fundamentally opposed to law.

Copies of other important matters, too, were missing. Lists of officials for the revolutionary city government and of deputies to take the places of the disbanded police, plans for manning, by the radicals, the city light, water and power plants; a schedule of public eating houses to take the place of the restaurants.

Woslosky began to find this drug clerk with the ridiculous given name getting on his nerves. He considered him a dangerous enemy to progress, that particular form of progress which Mr. Woslosky advocated, and he suspected him of a lack of ethics regarding trunks in storage. Mr. Woslosky had the old-world idea that the best government was a despotism tempered by assassination. He thought considerably about Willy Cameron.

But the plan concerning the farm house was, in the end, devised by Louis Akers. Woslosky was skeptical. It was true that Cameron might stick his head into the lion's jaws, but precautions had been known to be taken at such times to prevent their closing. However, the Pole was desperate.

He took six picked men with him that afternoon to the farm, and made a strategic survey of the situation. The house was closed and locked, but he was not concerned with the house. Cusick had told Denslow the meetings were held late at night in the barn, and to the barn Woslosky repaired, sawed-off shotgun under his coat and cigarette in mouth, and inspected it with his evil smile. Two men, young and reckless, might easily plan to conceal themselves under the hay in the loft, and —

Woslosky put down his gun and went down into the cow barn below, whistling softly to himself. He began to enjoy the prospect. He gathered some eggs from the feed boxes, carrying them in his hat, and breaking the lock of the kitchen door he and his outfit looted the closet there and had an early supper, being careful to extinguish the fire afterwards.

Not until dusk was falling did he post his men, three outside among the outbuildings, one as a sentry near the woods, and two in the barn itself. He himself took up his station inside the barn door, sitting on the floor with his gun across his knees. Looking out from there, he saw the sharp flash of a hastily extinguished match, and snarled with anger. He had forbidden smoking.

"I've got to go out," he said cautiously. "Don't you fools shoot me when I come back."

He slipped out into what was by that time complete blackness.

Some five minutes later he came back, still noiselessly, and treading like a cat. He could only locate the barn door by feeling for it, and above the light scraping of his fingers he could hear, inside, cautious footsteps over the board floor. He scowled again. Damn this country quiet, anyhow! But he had found the doorway, and was feeling his way through when he found himself caught and violently thrown. The fall and the surprise stunned him. He lay still for an infuriated helpless second, with a knee on his chest and both arms tightly held, to hear one of his own men above him saying:

"Got him, all right. Woslosky, you've got the rope, haven't you?"

"You fool!" snarled Woslosky from the floor, "let me up. You've half killed me. Didn't I tell you I was going out?"

He scrambled to his feet, and to an astounded silence.

"But you came in a couple of minutes ago. Somebody came in. You heard him, Cusick, didn't you?"

Woslosky whirled and closed and fastened the barn doors, and almost with the same movement drew a searchlight and flashed it over the place. It was apparently empty.

The Pole burst into blasphemous anger, punctuated with sharp questions. Both men had heard the cautious entrance they had taken for his own, both men had remained silent and unsuspicious, and both were positive whoever had come in had not gone out again.

He stationed one man at the door, and commenced a merciless search. The summer's hay filled one end, but it was closely packed below and offered no refuge. Armed with the shotgun, and with the flash in his pocket, Woslosky climbed the ladder to the loft, going softly. He listened at the top, and then searched it with the light, holding it far to the left for a possible bullet. The loft was empty. He climbed into it and walked over it, gun in one hand and flash in the other, searching for some buried figure. But there was nothing. The loft was fragrant with the newly dried hay, sweet and empty. Woslosky descended the ladder again, the flash extinguished, and stood again on the barn floor, considering. Cusick was a man without imagination, and he had sworn that some one had come in. Then —

Suddenly there was a whirr of wings outside and above, excited flutterings first, and then a general flight of the pigeons who roosted on the roof. Woslosky listened and slowly smiled.

"We've got him, boys," he said, without excitement. "Outside, and call the others. He's on the roof."

Cusick whistled shrilly, and as the Pole ran out he met the others coming pell-mell toward him. He flung a guard of all five of them around the barn, and himself walked off a hundred feet or so and gazed upward. The very outline of the ridge pole was indistinguishable, and he swore softly. In the hope of drawing an answering flash he fired, but without result. The explosion echoed and reechoed, died away.

He called to Cusick, and had him try the same experiment, following the line of the gutter as nearly as possible in the darkness, on that side, and emptying his revolver. Still silence.

Woslosky began to doubt. The pigeons might have seen his flashlight, might have heard his own stealthy movements. He was intensely irritated. The shooting, if the alarm had been false, had ruined everything. He saw, as in a vision, Doyle's sneering face when he told him. Beside him Cusick was reloading his revolver in the darkness.

Then, out of the night, came a call from the direction of the woods, and unintelligible at that distance.

"What's that?" Cusick said hoarsely.

Woslosky made no reply. He was listening. Some one was approaching, now running, now stopping as though confused. Woslosky held his gun ready, and waited. Then, from a distance, he heard his name called.

He stepped inside the door of the barn and showed the light for a moment. Soon after the sentry floundered in, breathless and excited.

"I got one of them," he gasped. "Hit him with my gun. He's lying back by the stone fence."

"Did you call out, or did he?"

"He did. That's how I knew it wasn't one of our fellows. He called Cameron, so he's the other one."

Woslosky drew a deep breath. Then it was Cameron on the roof. It was Cameron they wanted.

"He'll sleep for an hour or two, if he ever wakes up," Pink's assailant boasted. But Woslosky was taking no chances that night. He sent two men after Pink, and began to pace the floor thoughtfully. If he could have waited for daylight it would have been simple enough, but he did not know how much time he had. He did not underestimate young Cameron's intelligence, and it had occurred to him that that young Scot might cannily have provided against his failure to return. Then, too, the state constabulary had an uncomfortable habit of riding lonely back roads at night, and shots could be heard a long distance off.

He had never surveyed the barn roof closely, but he knew that it was steeply pitched. Cameron, then, was probably braced somewhere in the gutter. The departure of the two men had left him short-handed, and he waited impatiently for their return. With a ladder, provided it could be quietly placed, a man could shoot from a corner along two sides of the roof. With two ladders, at diagonal corners, they could get him. But a careful search discovered no ladders on the place.

He went out, and standing close against the wall for protection, called up.

"We know you're there, Cameron," he said. "If you come down we won't hurt you. If you don't, we'll get you, and you know it."

But he received no reply.

Soon after that the two men carried in Pink Denslow, and laid him on the floor of the barn. Then Woslosky tried again, more reckless this time with anger. He stood out somewhat from the wall and called:

"One more chance, Cameron, or we'll put a bullet through your friend here. Come down, or we'll —"

Something struck him heavily and he fell, with a bullet in the shoulder. He struggled to his feet and gained the shelter of the wall, his face twisted with pain.

"All right," he said, "if that's the way you feel about it!"

He regained the barn and had his arm supported in an extemporized sling. Then he ordered Pink to be tied, and fighting down his pain considered the situation. Cameron was on the roof, and armed. Even if he had no extra shells he still had five shots in reserve, and he would not waste any of them. Whoever tried to scale the walls would be done in at once; whoever attempted to follow him to the roof by way of the loft would be shot instantly. And his own condition demanded haste; the bullet, striking from above, had broken his arm. Every movement was torture.

He thought of setting fire to the barn. Then Cameron would have the choice of two things, to surrender or to be killed. He might get some of them first, however. Well, that was a part of the game.

He delivered a final ultimatum from the shelter of the doorway.

"I've just thought of something, Cameron," he called. "We're going to fire the barn. Your young friend is here, tied, and we'll leave him here. Do you get that? Either throw down that gun of yours, and come down, or I'm inclined to think you'll be up against it. I'll give you a minute or so to think it over."

At half-past eleven o'clock that night the first of four automobiles drove into Friendship. It was driven by a hatless young man in a raincoat over a suit of silk pajamas, and it contained four County detectives and the city Chief of Police. Behind it, but well outdistanced, came the other cars, some of them driven by leading citizens in a state of considerable deshabille.

At a cross street in Friendship the lead car drew up, and flashlights were turned on a road map in the rear of the car. There was some argument over the proper road, and a member of the state constabulary, riding up to investigate, showed a strong inclination to place them under arrest.

It took a moment to put him right.

"Wish I could go along," he said, wistfully. "The place you want is back there. I can't leave the town, but I'll steer you out. You'll probably run into some of our fellows back there."

He rode on ahead, his big black horse restive in the light from the lamps behind him. At the end of a lane he stopped.

"Straight ahead up there," he said. "You'll find —"

He broke off and stared ahead to where a dull red glare, reflected on the low hanging clouds, had appeared over the crest of the hill.

"Something doing up there," he called suddenly. "Let's go."

He jerked his revolver free, dug his heels into the flanks of his horse, and was off on a dead run. Half way up the hill the car passed him, the black going hard, and its rider's face, under the rim of his uniform hat, a stern profile. His reins lay loose on the animal's neck, and he was examining his gun.

The road mounted to a summit, and dipped again. They were in a long valley, and the burning barn was clearly outlined at the far end of it. One side was already flaming, and tongues of fire leaped out through the roof. The men in the car were standing now, doors open, ready to leap, while the car lurched and swayed over the uneven road. Behind them they heard the clatter of the oncoming horse.

As they drew nearer they could see three watching figures against the burning building, and as they turned into the lane which led to the barnyard a shot rang out and one of the figures dropped and lay still. There was a cry of warning from somewhere, and before the detectives could leap from the car, the group had scattered, running wildly. The state policeman threw his horse back on its hunches, and fired without apparently taking aim at one of the running shadows. The man threw up his arms and fell. The state policeman galloped toward him, dismounted and bent over him.

Firing as they ran, detectives leaped out of the car and gave chase, and so it was that the young gentleman in bedroom slippers and pajamas, standing in his car and shielding his eyes against the glare, saw a curious thing.

First of all, the roof blazed up brightly, and he perceived a human figure, hanging by its hands from the eaves and preparing to drop. The young gentleman in pajamas was feeling rather out of things by that time, so he made a hasty exit from his car toward the barn, losing a slipper as he did so, and yelling in a slightly hysterical manner. It thus happened that he and the dropping figure reached the same spot at almost the same moment, one result of which was that the young gentleman in pajamas found himself struck a violent blow with a doubled-up fist, and at the same moment his bare right foot was tramped on with extreme thoroughness.

The young gentleman in pajamas reeled back dizzily and gave tongue, while standing on one foot. The person he addressed was the state constable, and his instructions were to get the fugitive and kill him. But the fugitive here did a very strange thing. Through the handkerchief which it was now seen he wore tied over his mouth, he told the running policeman to go to perdition, and then with seeming suicidal intent rushed into the burning barn. From it he emerged a moment later, dragging a figure bound hand and foot, blackened with smoke, and with its clothing smoldering in a dozen places; a figure which alternately coughed and swore in a strangled whisper, but which found breath for a loud whoop almost immediately after, on its being immersed, as it promptly was, in a nearby horse-trough.

Very soon after that the other cars arrived. They drew up and men emerged from them, variously clothed and even more variously armed, but all they saw was the ruined embers of the barn, and in the glow five figures. Of the five one lay, face up to the sky, as though the prostrate body followed with its eyes the unkillable traitor soul of one Cusick, lately storekeeper at Friendship. Woslosky, wounded for the second time, lay on an automobile rug on the ground, conscious but sullenly silent. On the driving seat of an automobile sat a young gentleman with an overcoat over a pair of silk pajamas, carefully inspecting the toes of his right foot by the light of a match, while another young gentleman with a white handkerchief around his head was sitting on the running board of the same car, dripping water and rather dazedly staring at the ruins.

And beside him stood a gaunt figure, blackened of face, minus eyebrows and charred of hair, and considerably torn as to clothing. A figure which seemed disinclined to talk, and which gave its explanations in short, staccato sentences. Having done which, it relapsed into uncompromising silence again.

Some time later the detectives returned. They had made no further captures, for the refugees had known the country, and once outside the light from the burning barn search was useless. The Chief of Police approached Willy Cameron and stood before him, eyeing him severely.

"The next time you try to raid an anarchist meeting, Cameron," he said, "you'd better honor me with your confidence. You've probably learned a lesson from all this."

Willy Cameron glanced at him, and for the first time that night, smiled.

"I have," he said; "I'll never trust a pigeon again." The Chief thought him slightly unhinged by the night's experience.

Chapter XL

Edith Boyd's child was prematurely born at the Memorial Hospital early the next morning. It lived only a few moments, but Edith's mother never knew either of its birth or of its death.

When Willy Cameron reached the house at two o'clock that night he found Dan in the lower hall, a new Dan, grave and composed but very pale.

"Mother's gone, Willy," he said quietly. "I don't think she knew anything about it. Ellen heard her breathing hard and went in, but she wasn't conscious." He sat down on the horse-hair covered chair by the stand. "I don't know anything about these things," he observed, still with that strange new composure. "What do you do now?"

"Don't worry about that, Dan, just now. There's nothing to do until morning."

He looked about him. The presence of death gave a new dignity to the little house. Through the open door he could see in the parlor Mrs. Boyd's rocking chair, in which she had traveled so many conversational miles. Even the chair had gained dignity; that which it had once enthroned had now penetrated the ultimate mystery.

He was shaken and very weary. His mind worked slowly and torpidly, so that even grief came with an effort. He was grieved; he knew that. Some one who had loved him and depended on him was gone; some one who loved life had lost it. He ran his hand over his singed hair.

"Where is Edith?"

Dan's voice hardened.

"She's out somewhere. It's like her, isn't it?"

Willy Cameron roused himself.

"Out?" he said incredulously. "Don't you know where she is?"

"No. And I don't care."

Willy Cameron was fully alert now, and staring down at Dan.

"I'll tell you something, Dan. She probably saved my life to-night. I'll tell you how later. And if she is still out there is something wrong."

"She used to stay out to all hours. She hasn't done it lately, but I thought —"

Dan got up and reached for his hat.

"Where'll I start to look for her?"

But Willy Cameron had no suggestion to make. He was trying to think straight, but it was not easy. He knew that for some reason Edith had not waited until midnight to open the envelope. She had telephoned her message clearly, he had learned, but with great excitement, saying that there was a plot against his life, and giving the farmhouse and the message he had left in full; and she had not rung off until she knew that a posse would start at once. And that had been before eleven o'clock.

Three hours. He looked at his watch. Either she had been hurt or was a prisoner, or-he came close to the truth then. He glanced at Dan, standing hat in hand.

"We'll try the hospitals first, Dan," he said. "And the best way to do that is by telephone. I don't like Ellen being left alone here, so you'd better let me do that."

Dan acquiesced unwillingly. He resumed his seat in the hail, and Willy Cameron went up-stairs. Ellen was moving softly about, setting in order the little upper room. The windows were opened, and through them came the soft night wind, giving a semblance of life and movement under it to the sheet that covered the quiet figure on the bed.

Willy Cameron stood by it and looked down, with a great wave of thankfulness in his heart. She had been saved much, and if from some new angle she was seeing them now it would be with the vision of eternity, and its understanding. She would see how sometimes the soul must lose here to gain beyond. She would see the world filled with its Ediths, and she would know that they too were a part of the great plan, and that the breaking of the body sometimes freed the soul.

He was shy of the forms of religion, but he voiced a small inarticulate prayer, standing beside the bed while Ellen straightened the few toilet articles on the dresser, that she might have rest, and then a long and placid happiness. And love, he added. There would be no Heaven without love.

Ellen was looking at him in the mirror.

"Your hair looks queer, Willy," she said. "And I declare your clothes are a sight." She turned, sternly. "Where have you been?"

"It's a long story, Ellen. Don't bother about it now. I'm worried about Edith."

Ellen's lips closed in a grim line.

"The less said about her the better. She came back in a terrible state about something or other, ran in and up to your room, and out again. I tried to tell her her mother wasn't so well, but she looked as if she didn't hear me."

It was four o'clock in the morning when Willy Cameron located Edith. He had gone to the pharmacy and let himself in, intending to telephone, but the card on the door, edged with black, gave him a curious sense of being surrounded that night by death, and he stood for a moment, unwilling to begin for fear of some further tragedy. In that moment, what with reaction from excitement and weariness, he had a feeling of futility, of struggling to no end. One fought on, and in the last analysis it was useless.

"So soon passeth it away, and we are gone."

He saw Mr. Davis, sitting alone in his house; he saw Ellen moving about that quiet upper room; he saw Cusick lying on the ground beside the smoldering heap that had been the barn, and staring up with eyes that saw only the vast infinity that was the sky. All the struggling and the fighting, and it came to that.

He picked up the telephone book at last, and finding the hospital list in the directory began his monotonous calling of numbers, and still the revolt was in his mind. Even life lay through the gates of death; daily and hourly women everywhere laid down their lives that some new soul be born. But the revulsion came with that, a return to something nearer the normal. Daily and hourly women lived, having brought to pass the miracle of life.

At half-past four he located Edith at the Memorial, and learned that her child had been born dead, but that she was doing well. He was suddenly exhausted; he sat down on a stool before the counter, and with his arms across it and his head on them, fell almost instantly asleep. When he waked it was almost seven and the intermittent sounds of early morning came through the closed doors, as though the city stirred but had not wakened.

He went to the door and opened it, looking out. He had been wrong before. Death was a beginning and not an end; it was the morning of the spirit. Tired bodies lay down to sleep and their souls wakened to the morning, rested; the first fruits of them that slept.

From the chimneys of the houses nearby small spirals of smoke began to ascend, definite promise of food and morning cheer behind the closed doors, where the milk bottles stood like small white sentinels and the morning paper was bent over the knob. Morning in the city, with children searching for lost stockings and buttoning little battered shoes; with women hurrying about, from stove to closet, from table to stove; with all burdens a little lighter and all thoughts a little kinder. Morning.

Chapter XLI

In her bed in the maternity ward Edith at first lay through the days, watching the other women with their babies, and wondering over the strange instinct that made them hover, like queer mis-shaped ministering angels, over the tiny quivering bundles. Some of them were like herself, or herself as she might have been, bearing their children out of wedlock. Yet they faced their indefinite futures impassively, content in relief from pain, in the child in their arms, in present peace and security. She could not understand.

She herself felt no sense of loss. Having never held her child in her arms she did not feel them empty.

She had not been told of her mother's death; men were not admitted to the ward, but early on that first morning, when she lay there, hardly conscious but in an ecstasy of relief from pain, Ellen had come. A tired Ellen with circles around her eyes, and a bag of oranges in her arms.

"How do you feel?" she had asked, sitting down self-consciously beside the bed. The ward had its eyes on her.

"I'm weak, but I'm all right. Last night was awful, Ellen."

She had roused herself with an effort. Ellen reminded her of something, something that had to do with Willy Cameron. Then she remembered, and tried to raise herself in the bed.

"Willy!" she gasped. "Did he come home? Is he all right?"

"He's all right. It was him that found you were here. You lie back now; the nurse is looking."

Edith lay down and closed her eyes, and the ecstasy of relief and peace gave to her pale face an almost spiritual look. Ellen saw it, and patted her arm with a roughened hand.

"You poor thing!" she said. "I've been as mean to you as I knew how to be. I'm going to be different, Edith. I'm just a cross old maid, and I guess I didn't understand."

"You've been all right," Edith said.

Ellen kissed her when she went away.

So for three days Edith lay and rested. She felt that God had been very good to her, and she began to think of God as having given her another chance. This time He had let her off, but He had given her a warning. He had said, in effect, that if she lived straight and thought straight from now on He would forget this thing she had done. But if she did not —

Then what about Willy Cameron? Did He mean her to hold him to that now? Willy did not love her. Perhaps he would grow to love her, but she was seeing things more clearly than she had before, and one of the things she saw was that Willy Cameron was a one-woman man, and that she was not the woman.

"But I love him so," she would cry to herself.

The ward moved in its orderly routine around her. The babies were carried out, bathed and brought back, their nuzzling mouths open for the waiting mother-breast. The nurses moved about, efficient, kindly, whimsically maternal. Women went out when their hour came, swollen of feature and figure, and were wheeled back later on, etherealized, purified as by fire, and later on were given their babies. Their faces were queer then, frightened and proud at first, and later watchful and tenderly brooding.

For three days Edith's struggle went on. She had her strong hours and her weak ones. There were moments when, exhausted and yet exalted, she determined to give him up altogether, to live the fiction of the marriage until her mother's death, and then to give up the house and never see him again. If she gave him up she must never see him again. At those times she prayed not to love him any longer, and sometimes, for a little while after that, she would have peace. It was almost as though she did not love him.

But there were the other times, when she lay there and pictured them married, and dreamed a dream of bringing him to her feet. He had offered a marriage that was not a marriage, but he was a man, and human. He did not want her now, but in the end he would want her; young as she was she knew already the strength of a woman's physical hold on a man.

Late on the afternoon of the third day Ellen came again, a swollen-eyed Ellen, dressed in black with black cotton gloves, and a black veil around her hat. Ellen wore her mourning with the dogged sense of duty of her class, and would as soon have gone to the burying ground in her kitchen apron as without black. She stood in the doorway of the ward, hesitating, and Edith saw her and knew.

Her first thought was not of her mother at all. She saw only that the God who had saved her had made her decision for her, and that now she would never marry Willy Cameron. All this time He had let her dream and struggle. She felt very bitter.

Ellen came and sat down beside her.

"She's gone. Edith," she said; "we didn't tell you before, but you have to know sometime. We buried her this afternoon."

Suddenly Edith forgot Willy Cameron, and God, and Dan, and the years ahead. She was a little girl again, and her mother was saying:

"Brush your teeth and say your prayers, Edie. And tomorrow's Saturday. So you don't need to get up until you're good and ready."

She lay there. She saw her mother growing older and more frail, the house more untidy, and her mother's bright spirit fading to the drab of her surroundings. She saw herself, slipping in late at night, listening always for that uneasy querulous voice. And then she saw those recent months, when her mother had bloomed with happiness; she saw her struggling with her beloved desserts, cheerfully unconscious of any failure in them; she saw her, living like a lady, as she had said, with every anxiety kept from her. There had been times when her thin face had been almost illuminated with her new content and satisfaction.

Suddenly grief and remorse overwhelmed her.

"Mother!" she said, huskily. And lay there, crying quietly, with Ellen holding her hand. All that was hard and rebellious in Edith Boyd was swept away in that rush of grief, and in its place there came a new courage and resolution. She would meet the future alone, meet it and overcome it. But not alone, either; there was always —

It was a Sunday afternoon, and the nurse had picked up the worn ward Bible and was reading from it, aloud. In their rocking chairs in a semi-circle around her were the women, some with sleeping babies in their arms, others with tense, expectant faces.

"Let not your heart be troubled," read the nurse, in a grave young voice. "Ye believe in God. Believe also in Me. In my Father's house —"

There was always God.

Edith Boyd saw her mother in the Father's house, pottering about some small celestial duty, and eagerly seeking and receiving approval. She saw her, in some celestial rocking chair, her tired hands folded, slowly rocking and resting. And perhaps, as she sat there, she held Edith's child on her knee, like the mothers in the group around the nurse. Held it and understood at last.

Chapter XLII

It was at this time that Doyle showed his hand, with his customary fearlessness. He made a series of incendiary speeches, the general theme being that the hour was close at hand for putting the fear of God into the exploiting classes for all time to come. His impassioned oratory, coming at the psychological moment, when the long strike had brought its train of debt and evictions, made a profound impression. Had he asked for a general strike vote then, he would have secured it.

As it was, it was some time before all the unions had voted for it. And the day was not set. Doyle was holding off, and for a reason. Day by day he saw a growth of the theory of Bolshevism among the so-called intellectual groups of the country. Almost every university had its radicals, men who saw emerging from Russia the beginning of a new earth. Every class now had its Bolshevists. They found a ready market for their propaganda, intelligent and insidious as it was, among a certain liberal element of the nation, disgruntled with the autocracy imposed upon them by the war.

The reaction from that autocracy was a swinging to the other extreme, and, as if to work into the hands of the revolutionary party, living costs remained at the maximum. The cry of the revolutionists, to all enough and to none too much, found a response not only in the anxious minds of honest workmen, but among an underpaid intelligentsia. Neither political party offered any relief; the old lines no longer held, and new lines of cleavage had come. Progressive Republicans and Democrats had united against reactionary members of both parties. There were no great leaders, no men of the hour.

The old vicious cycle of empires threatened to repeat itself, the old story of the many led by the few. Always it had come, autocracy, the too great power of one man; then anarchy, the overthrow of that power by the angry mob. Out of that anarchy the gradual restoration of order by the people themselves, into democracy. And then in time again, by that steady gravitation of the strong up and the weak down, some one man who emerged from the mass and crowned himself, or was crowned. And there was autocracy again, and again the vicious circle.

But such movements had always been, in the last analysis, the work of the few. It had always been the militant minority which ruled. Always the great mass of the people had submitted. They had fought, one way or the other when the time came, but without any deep conviction behind them. They wanted peace, the right to labor. They warred, to find peace. Small concern was it, to the peasant plowing his field, whether one man ruled over him or a dozen. He wanted neither place nor power.

It came to this, then, Willy Cameron argued to himself. This new world conflict was a struggle between the contented and the discontented. In Europe, discontent might conquer, but in America, never. There were too many who owned a field or had the chance to labor. There were too many ways legitimately to aspire. Those who wanted something for nothing were but a handful to those who wanted to give that they might receive.

Three days before the election, Willy Cameron received a note from Lily, sent by hand.

"Father wants to see you to-night," she wrote, "and mother suggests that as you are busy, you try to come to dinner. We are dining alone. Do come, Willy. I think it is most important."

He took the letter home with him and placed it in a locked drawer of his desk, along with a hard and shrunken doughnut, tied with a bow of Christmas ribbon, which had once helped to adorn the Christmas tree they had trimmed together. There were other things in the drawer; a postcard photograph, rather blurred, of Lily in the doorway of her little hut, smiling; and the cigar box which had been her cash register at the camp.

He stood for some time looking down at the post card; it did not seem possible that in the few months since those wonderful days, life could have been so cruel to them both. Lily married, and he himself —

Ellen came up when he was tying his tie. She stood behind him, watching him in the mirror.

"I don't know what you've done to your hair, Willy," she said; "it certainly looks queer."

"It usually looks queer, so why worry, heart of my heart?" But he turned and put an arm around her shoulders. "What would the world be without women like you, Ellen?" he said gravely.

"I haven't done anything but my duty," Ellen said, in her prim voice. "Listen, Willy. I saw Edith again to-day, and she told me to do something."

"To go home and take a rest? That's what you need."

"No. She wants me to tear up that marriage license."

He said nothing for a moment. "I'll have to see her first."

"She said it wouldn't be any good, Willy. She's made up her mind." She watched him anxiously. "You're not going to be foolish, are you? She says there's no need now, and she's right."

"Somebody will have to look after her."

"Dan can do that. He's changed, since she went." Ellen glanced toward Mrs. Boyd's empty room. "You've done enough, Willy. You've seen them through, all of them. I —isn't it time you began to think about yourself?"

He was putting on his coat, and she picked a bit of thread from it, with nervous fingers.

"Where are you going to-night, Willy?"

"To the Cardews. Mr. Cardew has sent for me."

She looked up at him.

"Willy, I want to tell you something. The Cardews won't let that marriage stand, and you know it. I think she cares for you. Don't look at me like that. I do."

"That's because you are fond of me," he said, smiling down at her. "I'm not the sort of man girls care about, Ellen. Let's face that. The General Manager said when he planned me, 'Here's going to be a fellow who is to have everything in the world, health, intelligence, wit and the beauty of an Adonis, but he has to lack something, so we'll make it that'."

But Ellen, glancing up swiftly, saw that although his tone was light, there was pain in his eyes.

He reflected on Edith's decision as he walked through the park toward the Cardew house. It had not surprised him, and yet he knew it had cost her an effort. How great an effort, man-like, he would never understand, but something of what she had gone through he realized. He wondered vaguely whether, had there never been a Lily Cardew in his life, he could ever have cared for Edith. Perhaps. Not the Edith of the early days, that was certain. But this new Edith, with her gentleness and meekness, her clear, suffering eyes, her strange new humility.

She had sent him a message of warning about Akers, and from it he had reconstructed much of the events of the night she had taken sick.

"Tell him to watch Louis Akers," she had said. "I don't know how near Willy was to trouble the other night, Ellen, but they're going to try to get him."

Ellen had repeated the message, watching him narrowly, but he had only laughed.

"Who are they?" she had persisted.

"I'll tell you all about it some day," he had said. But he had told Dan the whole story, and, although he did not know it, Dan had from that time on been his self-constituted bodyguard. During his campaign speeches Dan was always near, his right hand on a revolver in his coat pocket, and for hours at a time he stood outside the pharmacy, favoring every seeker for drugs or soap or perfume with a scowling inspection. When he could not do it, he enlisted Joe Wilkinson in the evenings, and sometimes the two of them, armed, policed the meeting halls.

As a matter of fact, Joe Wilkinson was following him that night. On his way to the Cardews Willy Cameron, suddenly remembering the uncanny ability of Jinx to escape and trail him, remaining meanwhile at a safe distance in the rear, turned suddenly and saw Joe, walking sturdily along in rubber-soled shoes, and obsessed with his high calling of personal detective.

Joe, discovered, grinned sheepishly.

"Thought that looked like your back," he said. "Nice evening for a walk, isn't it?"

"Let me look at you, Joe," said Willy Cameron. "You look strange to me. Ah, now I have it. You look like a comet without a tail. Where's the family?"

"Making taffy. How-is Edith?"

"Doing nicely." He avoided the boy's eyes.

"I guess I'd better tell you. Dan's told me about her. I —" Joe hesitated. Then: "She never seemed like that sort of a girl," he finished, bitterly.

"She isn't that sort of girl, Joe."

"She did it. How could a fellow know she wouldn't do it again?"

"She has had a pretty sad sort of lesson."

Joe, his real business forgotten, walked on with eyes down and shoulders drooping.

"I might as well finish with it," he said, "now I've started. I've always been crazy about her. Of course now —I haven't slept for two nights."

"I think it's rather like this, Joe," Willy Cameron said, after a pause. "We are not one person, really. We are all two or three people, and all different. We are bad and good, depending on which of us is the strongest at the time, and now and then we pay so much for the bad we do that we bury that part. That's what has happened to Edith. Unless, of course," he added, "we go on convincing her that she is still the thing she doesn't want to be."

"I'd like to kill the man," Joe said. But after a little, as they neared the edge of the park, he looked up.

"You mean, go on as if nothing had happened?"

"Precisely," said Willy Cameron, "as though nothing had happened."

Chapter XLIII

The atmosphere of the Cardew house was subtly changed and very friendly. Willy Cameron found himself received as an old friend, with no tendency to forget the service he had rendered, or that, in their darkest hour, he had been one of them.

To his surprise Pink Denslow was there, and he saw at once that Pink had been telling them of the night at the farm house. Pink was himself again, save for a small shaved place at the back of his head, covered with plaster.

"I've told them, Cameron," he said. "If I could only tell it generally I'd be the most popular man in the city, at dinners."

"Pair of young fools," old Anthony muttered, with his sardonic smile. But in his hand-clasp, as in Howard's, there was warmth and a sort of envy, envy of youth and the adventurous spirit of youth.

Lily was very quiet. The story had meant more to her than to the others. She had more nearly understood Pink's reference to the sealed envelope Willy Cameron had left, and the help sent by Edith Boyd. She connected that with Louis Akers, and from that to Akers' threat against Cameron was only a step. She was frightened and somewhat resentful, that this other girl should have saved him from a revenge that she knew was directed at herself. That she, who had brought this thing about, had sat quietly at home while another woman, a woman who loved him, had saved him.

She was puzzled at her own state of mind.

Dinner was almost gay. Perhaps the gayety was somewhat forced, with Pink keeping his eyes from Lily's face, and Howard Cardew relapsing now and then into abstracted silence. Because of the men who served, the conversation was carefully general. It was only in the library later, the men gathered together over their cigars, that the real reason for Willy Cameron's summons was disclosed.

Howard Cardew was about to withdraw from the contest. "I'm late in coming to this decision," he said. "Perhaps too late. But after a careful canvas of the situation, I find you are right, Cameron. Unless I withdraw, Akers" —he found a difficulty in speaking the name —"will be elected. At least it looks that way."

"And if he is," old Anthony put in, "he'll turn all the devils of hell loose on us."

It was late; very late. The Cardews stood ready to flood the papers with announcements of Howard's withdrawal, and urging his supporters to vote for Hendricks, but the time was short. Howard had asked his campaign managers to meet there that night, and also Hendricks and one or two of his men, but personally he felt doubtful.

And, as it happened, the meeting developed more enthusiasm than optimism. Cardew's withdrawal would be made the most of by the opposition. They would play it up as the end of the old regime, the beginning of new and better things.

Before midnight the conference broke up, to catch the morning editions. Willy Cameron, detained behind the others, saw Lily in the drawing-room alone as he passed the door, and hesitated.

"I have been waiting for you, Willy," she said.

But when he went in she seemed to have nothing to say. She sat in a low chair, in a soft dark dress which emphasized her paleness. To Willy Cameron she had never seemed more beautiful, or more remote.

"Do you remember how you used to whistle 'The Long, Long Trail,' Willy?" she said at last. "All evening I have been sitting here thinking what a long trail we have both traveled since then."

"A long, hard trail," he assented.

"Only you have gone up, Willy. And I have gone down, into the valley. I wish" —she smiled faintly —"I wish you would look down from your peak now and then. You never come to see me."

"I didn't know you wanted me," he said bluntly.

"Why shouldn't I want to see you?"

"I couldn't help reminding you of things."

"But I never forget them, anyhow. Sometimes I almost go mad, remembering. It isn't quite as selfish as it sounds. I've hurt them all so. Willy, do you mind telling me about the girl who opened that letter and sent you help?"

"About Edith Boyd? I'd like to tell you, Lily. Her mother is dead, and she lost her child. She is in the Memorial Hospital."

"Then she has no one but you?"

"She has a brother."

"Tell me about her sending help that night. She really saved your life, didn't she?"

While he was telling her she sat staring straight ahead, her fingers interlaced in her lap. She was telling herself that all this could not possibly matter to her, that she had cut herself off, finally and forever, from the man before her; that she did not even deserve his friendship.

Quite suddenly she knew that she did not want his friendship. She wanted to see again in his face the look that had been there the night he had told her, very simply, that he loved her. And it would never be there; it was not there now. She had killed his love. All the light in his face was for some one else, another girl, a girl more unfortunate but less wicked than herself.

When he stopped she was silent. Then:

"I wonder if you know how much you have told me that you did not intend to tell?"

"That I didn't intend to tell? I have made no reservations, Lily."

"Are you sure? Or don't you realize it yourself?"

"Realize what?" He was greatly puzzled.

"I think, Willy," she said, quietly, "that you care a great deal more for Edith Boyd than you think you do."

He looked at her in stupefaction. How could she say that? How could she fail to know better than that? And he did not see the hurt behind her careful smile.

"You are wrong about that. I —" He made a little gesture of despair. He could not tell her now that he loved her. That was all over.

"She is in love with you."

He felt absurd and helpless. He could not deny that, yet how could she sit there, cool and faintly smiling, and not know that as she sat there so she sat enshrined in his heart. She was his saint, to kneel and pray to; and she was his woman, the one woman of his life. More woman than saint, he knew, and even for that he loved her. But he did not know the barbarous cruelty of the loving woman.

"I don't know what to say to you, Lily," he said, at last. "She-it is possible that she thinks she cares, but under the circumstances —"

"Ellen told Mademoiselle you were going to marry her. That's true, isn't it?"

"Yes."

"You always said that marriage without love was wicked, Willy."

"Her child had a right to a name. And there were other things. I can't very well explain them to you. Her mother was ill. Can't you understand, Lily? I don't want to throw any heroics." In his excitement he had lapsed into boyish vernacular. "Here was a plain problem, and a simple way to solve it. But it is off now, anyhow; things cleared up without that."

She got up and held out her hand.

"It was like you to try to save her," she said.

"Does this mean I am to go?"

"I am very tired, Willy."

He had a mad impulse to take her in his arms, and holding her close to rest her there. She looked so tired. For fear he might do it he held his arms rigidly at his sides.

"You haven't asked me about him," she said unexpectedly.

"I thought you would not care to talk about him. That's over and done, Lily. I want to forget about it, myself."

She looked up at him, and had he had Louis Akers' intuitive knowledge of women he would have understood then.

"I am never going back to him, Willy. You know that, don't you?"

"I hoped it, of course."

"I know now that I never loved him."

But the hurt of her marriage was still too fresh in him for speech. He could not discuss Louis Akers with her.

"No," he said, after a moment, "I don't think you ever did. I'll come in some evening, if I may, Lily. I must not keep you up now."

How old he looked, for him! How far removed from those busy, cheerful days at the camp! And there were new lines of repression in his face; from the nostrils to the corners of his mouth. Above his ears his hair showed a faint cast of gray.

"You have been having rather a hard time, Willy, haven't you'?" she said, suddenly.

"I have been busy, of course."

"And worried?"

"Sometimes. But things are clearing up now."

She was studying him with the newly opened eyes of love. What was it he showed that the other men she knew lacked? Sensitiveness? Kindness? But her father was both sensitive and kind. So was Pink, in less degree. In the end she answered her own question, and aloud.

"I think it is patience," she said. And to his unspoken question: "You are very patient, aren't you?"

"I never thought about it. For heaven's sake don't turn my mind in on myself, Lily. I'll be running around in circles like a pup chasing his tail."

He made a movement to leave, but she seemed oddly reluctant to let him go.

"Do you know that father says you have more influence than any other man in the city?"

"That's more kind than truthful."

"And —I think he and grandfather are planning to try to get you, when the mills reopen. Father suggested it, but grandfather says you'd have the presidency of the company in six months, and he'd be sharpening your lead pencils."

Suddenly Willy Cameron laughed, and the tension was broken.

"If he did it with his tongue they'd be pretty sharp," he said.

For just a moment, before he left, they were back to where they had been months ago, enjoying together their small jokes and their small mishaps. The present fell away, with its hovering tragedy, and they were boy and girl together. Exaltation and sacrifice were a part of their love, as of all real and lasting passion, but there was always between them also that soundest bond of all, liking and comradeship.

"I love her. I like her. I adore her," was the cry in Willy Cameron's heart when he started home that night.

Chapter XLIV

Elinor Doyle was up and about her room. She walked slowly and with difficulty, using crutches, and she spent most of the time at her window, watching and waiting. From Lily there came, at frequent intervals, notes, flowers and small delicacies. The flowers and food Olga brought to her, but the notes she never saw. She knew they came. She could see the car stop at the curb, and the chauffeur, his shoulders squared and his face watchful, carrying a white envelope up the walk, but there it ended.

She felt more helpless than ever. The doctor came less often, but the vigilance was never relaxed, and she had, too, less and less hope of being able to give any warning. Doyle was seldom at home, and when he was he had ceased to give her his taunting information. She was quite sure now of his relations with the Russian girl, and her uncertainty as to her course was gone. She was no longer his wife. He held another woman in his rare embraces, a traitor like himself. It was sordid. He was sordid.

Woslosky had developed blood poisoning, and was at the point of death, with a stolid policeman on guard at his bedside. She knew that from the newspapers she occasionally saw. And she connected Doyle unerringly with the tragedy at the farm behind Friendship. She recognized, too, since that failure, a change in his manner to her. She saw that he now both hated her and feared her, and that she had become only a burden and a menace to him. He might decide to do away with her, to kill her. He would not do it himself; he never did his own dirty work, but the Russian girl-Olga was in love with Jim Doyle. Elinor knew that, as she knew many things, by a sort of intuition. She watched them in the room together, and she knew that to Doyle the girl was an incident, the vehicle of his occasional passion, a strumpet and a tool. He did not even like her; she saw him looking at her sometimes with a sort of amused contempt. But Olga's somber eyes followed him as he moved, lit with passion and sometimes with anger, but always they followed him.

She was afraid of Olga. She did not care particularly about death, but it must not come before she had learned enough to be able to send out a warning. She thought if it came it might be by poison in the food that was sent up, but she had to eat to live. She took to eating only one thing on her tray, and she thought she detected in the girl an understanding and a veiled derision.

By Doyle's increasing sullenness she knew things were not going well with him, and she found a certain courage in that, but she knew him too well to believe that he would give up easily. And she drew certain deductions from the newspapers she studied so tirelessly. She saw the announcement of the unusual number of hunting licenses issued, for one thing, and she knew the cover that such licenses furnished armed men patrolling the country. The state permitted the sale of fire-arms without restriction. Other states did the same, or demanded only the formality of a signature, never verified.

Would they never wake to the situation?

She watched the election closely. She knew that if Akers were elected the general strike and the chaos to follow would be held back until he had taken office and made the necessary changes in the city administration, but that if he went down to defeat the Council would turn loose its impatient hordes at once.

She waited for election day with burning anxiety. When it came it so happened that she was left alone all day in the house. Early in the morning Olga brought her a tray and told her she was going out. She was changed, the Russian; she had dropped the mask of sodden servility and stood before her, erect, cunningly intelligent and oddly powerful.

"I am going to be away all day, Mrs. Doyle," she said, in her excellent English. "I have work to do."

"Work?" said Elinor. "Isn't there work to do here?"

"I am not a house-worker. I came to help Mr. Doyle. To-day I shall make speeches."

Elinor was playing the game carefully. "But-can you make speeches?" she asked.

"Me? That is my work, here, in Russia, everywhere. In Russia it is the women who speak, the men who do what the women tell them to do. Here some day it will be the same."

Always afterwards Elinor remembered the five minutes that followed, for Olga, standing before her, suddenly burst into impassioned oratory. She cited the wrongs of the poor under the old regime. She painted in glowing colors the new. She was excited, hectic, powerful. Elinor in her chair, an aristocrat to the finger-tips, was frightened, interested, thrilled.

Long after Olga had gone she sat there, wondering at the real conviction, the intensity of passion, of hate and of revenge that actuated this newest tool of Doyle's. Doyle and his associates might be actuated by self-interest, but the real danger in the movement lay not with the Doyles of the world, but with these fanatic liberators. They preached to the poor a new religion, not of creed or of Church, but of freedom. Freedom without laws of God or of man, freedom of love, of lust, of time, of all responsibility. And the poor, weighted with laws and cares, longed to throw off their burdens.

Perhaps it was not the doctrine itself that was wrong. It was its imposition by force on a world not yet ready for it that was wrong; its imposition by violence. It might come, but not this way. Not, God preventing, this way.

There was a polling place across the street, in the basement of a school house. The vote was heavy and all day men lounged on the pavements, smoking and talking. Once she saw Olga in the crowd, and later on Louis Akers drove up in an open automobile, handsome, apparently confident, and greeted with cheers. But Elinor, knowing him well, gained nothing from his face.

Late that night she heard Doyle come in and move about the lower floor. She knew every emphasis of his walk, and when in the room underneath she heard him settle down to steady, deliberate pacing, she knew that he was facing some new situation, and, after his custom, thinking it out alone.

At midnight he came up the stairs and unlocked her door. He entered, closing the door behind him, and stood looking at her. His face was so strange that she wondered if he had decided to do away with her.

"To-morrow," he said, in an inflectionless voice, "you will be moved by automobile to a farm I have selected in the country. You will take only such small luggage as the car can carry."

"Is Olga going with me?"

"No. Olga is needed here."

"I suppose I am to understand from this that Louis has been defeated and there is no longer any reason for delay in your plans."

"You can understand what you like."

"Am I to know where I am going?"

"You will find that out when you get there. I will tell you this: It is a lonely place, without a telephone. You'll be cut off from your family, I am afraid."

She gazed at him. It seemed unbelievable to her that she had once lain in this man's arms.

"Why don't you kill me, Jim? I know you've thought about it."

"Yes, I've thought of it. But killing is a confession of fear, my dear. I am not afraid of you."

"I think you are. You are afraid now to tell me when you are going to try to put this wild plan into execution."

He smiled at her with mocking eyes.

"Yes," he agreed again. "I am afraid. You have a sort of diabolical ingenuity, not intelligence so much as cunning. But because I always do the thing I'm afraid to do, I'll tell you. Of course, if you succeed in passing it on —" He shrugged his shoulders. "Very well, then. With your usual logic of deduction, you have guessed correctly. Louis Akers has been defeated. Your family-and how strangely you are a Cardew! —lost its courage at the last moment, and a gentleman named Hendricks is now setting up imitation beer and cheap cigars to his friends."

Behind his mocking voice she knew the real fury of the man, kept carefully in control by his iron will.

"As you have also correctly surmised," he went on, "there is now nothing to be gained by any delay. A very few days, three or four, and —" His voice grew hard and terrible —"the first stone in the foundation of this capitalistic government will go. Inevitable law, inevitable retribution —" His voice trailed off. He turned like a man asleep and went toward the door. There he stopped and faced her.

"I've told you," he said darkly. "I am not afraid of you. You can no more stop this thing than you can stop living by ceasing to breathe. It has come."

She heard him in his room for some time after that, and she surmised from the way he moved, from closet to bed and back again, that he was packing a bag. At two o'clock she heard Olga coming in; the girl was singing in Russian, and Elinor had a sickening conviction that she had been drinking. She heard Doyle send her off to bed, his voice angry and disgusted, and resume his packing, and ten minutes later she heard a car draw up on the street, and knew that he was off, to begin the mobilization of his heterogeneous forces.

Ever since she had been able to leave her bed Elinor had been formulating a plan of escape. Once the door had been left unlocked, but her clothing had been removed from the room, and then, too, she had not learned the thing she was waiting for. Now she had clothing, a dark dressing gown and slippers, and she had the information. But the door was securely locked.

She had often thought of the window, In the day time it frightened her to look down, although it fascinated her, too. But at night it seemed much simpler. The void below was concealed in the darkness, a soft darkness that hid the hard, inhospitable earth. A darkness one could fall into and onto.

She was not a brave woman. She had moral rather than physical courage. It was easier for her to face Doyle in a black mood than the gulf below the window-sill, but she knew now that she must get away, if she were to go at all. She got out of bed, and using her crutches carefully moved to the sill, trying to accustom herself to the thought of going over the edge. The plaster cast on her leg was a real handicap. She must get it over first. How heavy it was, and unwieldy!

She found her scissors, and, stripping the bed, sat down to cut and tear the bedding into strips. Prisoners escaped that way; she had read about such things. But the knots took up an amazing amount of length. It was four o'clock in the morning when she had a serviceable rope, and she knew it was too short. In the end she tore down the window curtains and added them, working desperately against time.

She began to suspect, too, that Olga was not sleeping. She smelled faintly the odor of the long Russian cigarettes the girl smoked. She put out her light and worked in the darkness, a strange figure of adventure, this middle-aged woman with her smooth hair and lined face, sitting in her cambric nightgown with her crutches on the floor beside her.

She secured the end of the rope to the foot of her metal bed, pushing the bed painfully and cautiously, inch by inch, to the window. And in so doing she knocked over the call-bell on the stand, and almost immediately she heard Olga moving about.

The girl was coming unsteadily toward the door. If she opened it —

"I don't want anything, Olga," she called, "I knocked the bell over accidentally."

Olga hesitated, muttered, moved away again. Elinor was covered with a cold sweat.

She began to think of the window as a refuge. Surely nothing outside could be so terrible as this house itself. The black aperture seemed friendly; it beckoned to her with friendly hands.

She dropped her crutches. They fell with two soft thuds on the earth below and it seemed to her that they were a long time in falling. She listened after that, but Olga made no sign. Then slowly and painfully she worked her injured leg over the sill, and sat there looking down and breathing with difficulty. Then she freed her dressing gown around her, and slid over the edge.

Chapter XLV

Election night found various groups in various places. In the back room of the Eagle Pharmacy was gathered once again the neighborhood forum, a wildly excited forum, which ever and anon pounded Mr. Hendricks on the back, and drank round after round of soda water and pop. Doctor Smalley, coming in rather late found them all there, calling Mr. Hendricks "Mr. Mayor" or "Your Honor," reciting election anecdotes, and prophesying the end of the Reds. Only Willy Cameron, sitting on a table near the window, was silent.

Mr. Hendricks, called upon for a speech, rose with his soda water glass in his hand.

"I've got a toast for you, boys," he said. "You've been talking all evening about my winning this election. Well, I've been elected, but I didn't win it. It was the plain people of this town who elected me, and they did it because my young friend on the table yonder told them to." He raised his glass. "Cameron!" he said.

"Cameron! Cameron!" shouted the crowd. "Speech! Cameron!"

But Willy shook his head.

"I haven't any voice left," he said, "and you've heard me say all I know a dozen times. The plain truth is that Mr. Hendricks got the election because he was the best man, and enough people knew it. That's all."

To Mr. Hendricks the night was one of splendid solemnity. He felt at once very strong and very weak, very proud and very humble. He would do his best, and if honesty meant anything, the people would have it, but he knew that honesty was not enough. The city needed a strong man; he hoped that the Good Man who made cities as He made men, both evil and good, would lend him a hand with things. As prayer in his mind was indissolubly connected with church, he made up his mind to go to church the next Sunday and get matters straightened out.

At the same time another group was meeting at the Benedict.

Louis Akers had gone home early. By five o'clock he knew that the chances were against him, but he felt a real lethargy as to the outcome. He had fought, and fought hard, but it was only the surface mind of him that struggled. Only the surface mind of him hated, and had ambitions, dreamed revenge. Underneath that surface mind was a sore that ate like a cancer, and that sore was his desertion by Lily Cardew. For once in his life he suffered, who had always inflicted pain.

At six o'clock Doyle had called him on the telephone and told him that Woslosky was dead, but the death of the Pole had been discounted in advance, and already his place had been filled by a Russian agent, who had taken the first syllable of his name and called himself Ross. Louis Akers heard the news apathetically, and went back to his chair again.

By eight o'clock he knew that he had lost the election, but that, too, seemed relatively unimportant. He was not thinking coherently, but certain vague ideas floated through his mind. There was a law of compensation in the universe: it was all rot to believe that one was paid or punished in the hereafter for what one did. Hell was real, but it was on earth and its place was in a man's mind. He couldn't get away from it, because each man carried his own hell around with him. It was all stored up there; nothing he had done was left out, and the more he put into it the more he got out, when the time came.

This was his time.

Ross and Doyle, with one or two others, found him there at nine o'clock, an untasted meal on the table, and the ends of innumerable cigarettes on the hearth. In the conference that followed he took but little part. The Russian urged immediate action, and Doyle by a saturnine silence tacitly agreed with him. But Louis only half heard them. His mind was busy with that matter of hell. Only once he looked up. Ross was making use of the phrase: "Militant minority."

"Militant minority!" he said scornfully, "you overwork that idea, Ross. What we've got here now is a militant majority, and that's what elected Hendricks. You're licked before you begin. And my advice is, don't begin."

But they laughed at him.

"You act like a whipped dog," Doyle said, "crawling under the doorstep for fear somebody else with a strap comes along."

"They're organized against us. We could have put it over six months ago. Not now."

"Then you'd better get out," Doyle said, shortly.

"I'm thinking of it."

But Doyle had no real fear of him. He was sulky. Well, let him sulk.

Akers relapsed into silence. His interest in the conspiracy had always been purely self-interest; he had never had Woslosky's passion, or Doyle's cold fanaticism. They had carried him off his feet with their promises, but how much were they worth? They had failed to elect him. Every bit of brains, cunning and resource in their organization had been behind him, and they had failed.

This matter of hell, now? Suppose one put by something on the other account? Suppose one turned square? Wouldn't that earn something? Suppose that one went to the Cardews and put all his cards on the table, asking nothing in return? Suppose one gave up the by-paths of life, and love in a hedgerow, and did the other thing? Wouldn't that earn something?

He roused himself and took a perfunctory part in the conversation, but his mind obstinately returned to itself. He knew every rendezvous of the Red element in the country; he knew where their literature was printed; he knew the storehouses of arms and ammunition, and the plans for carrying on the city government by the strikers after the reign of terrorization which was to subdue the citizens.

Suppose he turned informer? Could he set a price, and that price Lily? But he discarded that. He was not selling now, he was earning. He would set himself right first, and-provided the government got the leaders before those leaders got him, as they would surely try to do-he would have earned something, surely.

Lily had come to him once when he called. She might come again, when he had earned her.

Doyle sat back in his chair and watched him. He saw that he had gone to pieces under defeat, and men did strange things at those times. With uncanny shrewdness he gauged Akers' reaction; his loss of confidence and, he surmised, his loyalty. He would follow his own interest now, and if he thought that it lay in turning informer, he might try it. But it would take courage.

When the conference broke up Doyle was sure of where his man stood. He was not worried. They did not need Akers any longer. He had been a presentable tool, a lay figure to give the organization front, and they had over-rated him, at that. He had failed them. Doyle, watching him contemptuously, realized in him his own fallacious judgment, and hated Akers for proving him wrong.

Outside the building Doyle drew the Russian aside, and spoke to him. Ross started, then grinned.

"You're wrong," he said. "He won't try it. But of course he may, and we'll see that he doesn't get away with it."

From that time on Louis Akers was under espionage.

Chapter XLVI

Doctor Smalley was by way of achieving a practice. During his morning and evening office hours he had less and less time to read the papers and the current magazines in his little back office, or to compare the month's earnings, visit by visit, with the same month of the previous year.

He took to making his hospital rounds early in the morning, rather to the outrage of various head nurses, who did not like the staff to come a-visiting until every counterpane was drawn stiff and smooth, every bed corner a geometrical angle, every patient washed and combed and temperatured, and in the exact center of the bed.

Interns were different. They were like husbands. They came and went, seeing things at their worst as well as at their best, but mostly at their worst. Like husbands, too, they developed a sort of philosophy as to the early morning, and would only make occasional remarks, such as:

"Cyclone struck you this morning, or anything?"

Doctor Smalley, being a bachelor, was entirely blind to the early morning deficiencies of his wards. Besides, he was young and had had a cold shower and two eggs and various other things, and he saw the world at eight A.M. as a good place. He would get into his little car, whistling, and driving through the market square he would sometimes stop and buy a bag of apples for the children's ward, or a bunch of fall flowers. Thus armed, it was impossible for the most austere of head nurses to hate him.

"We're not straightened up yet, doctor," they would say.

"Looks all right to me," he would reply cheerfully, and cast an eager eye over the ward. To him they were all his children, large and small, and if he did not exactly carry healing in his wings, having no wings, he brought them courage and a breath of fresh morning air, slightly tinged with bay rum, and the feeling that this was a new day. A new page, on which to write such wonderful things (in the order book) as: "Jennie may get up this afternoon." Or: "Lizzie Smith, small piece of beef steak."

On the morning after the election Doctor Smalley rose unusually early, and did five minutes of dumb bells, breathing very deep before his window, having started the cold water in the tub first. At the end of that time he padded in his bare feet to the top of the stairs and called in a huge, deep-breathing voice:

"Ten minutes."

These two cryptic words seeming to be perfectly understood below, followed the sound of a body plunging into water, a prolonged "Wow!" from the bathroom, and noisy hurried splashing. Dressing was a rapid process, due to a method learned during college days, which consists of wearing as little as possible, and arranging it at night so that two thrusts (trousers and under-drawers), one enveloping gesture (shirt and under-shirt), and a gymnastic effort of standing first on one leg and then on the other (socks and shoes), made a fairly completed toilet.

While putting on his collar and tie the doctor stood again by the window, and lustily called the garage across the narrow street.

"Jim!" he yelled. "Annabelle breakfasted yet?"

Annabelle was his shabby little car.

Annabelle had breakfasted, on gasoline, oil and water. The doctor finished tying his tie, singing lustily, and went to the door. At the door he stopped singing, put on a carefully professional air, restrained an impulse to slide down the stair-rail, and descended with the dignity of a man with a growing practice and a possible patient in the waiting-room.

At half-past seven he was on his way to the hospital. He stopped at the market and bought three dozen oranges out of a ten-dollar bill he had won on the election, and almost bought a live rabbit because it looked so dreary in its slatted box. He restrained himself, because his housekeeper had a weakness for stewed rabbit, and turned into Cardew Way. He passed the Doyle house slowly, inspecting it as he went, because he had a patient there, and because he had felt that there was something mysterious about the household, quite aside from the saturnine Doyle himself. He knew all about Doyle, of course; all, that is, that there was to know, but he was a newcomer to the city, and he did not know that Doyle's wife was a Cardew. Sometimes he had felt that he was under a sort of espionage all the time he was in the house. But that was ridiculous, wasn't it? Because they could not know that he was on the Vigilance Committee.

There was something curious about one of the windows. He slowed Annabelle and gazed at it. That was strange; there was a sort of white rope hanging from Mrs. Doyle's window.

He stopped Annabelle and stared. Then he drew up to the curb and got out of the car. He was rather uneasy when he opened the gate and started up the walk, but there was no movement of life in the house. At the foot of the steps he saw something, and almost stopped breathing. Behind a clump of winter-bare shrubbery was what looked like a dark huddle of clothing.

It was incredible.

He parted the branches and saw Elinor Doyle lying there, conscious and white with pain. Perhaps never in his life was Doctor Smalley to be so rewarded as with the look in her eyes when she saw him.

"Why, Mrs. Doyle!" was all he could think to say.

"I have broken my other leg, doctor," she said, "the rope gave way."

"You come down that rope?"

"I tried to. I was a prisoner. Don't take me back to the house, doctor. Don't take me back!"

"Of course I'll not take you back," he said, soothingly. "I'll carry you out to my car. It may hurt, but try to be quiet. Can you get your arms around my neck?"

She managed that, and he raised her slowly, but the pain must have been frightful, for a moment later he felt her arms relax and knew that she had fainted. He got to the car somehow, kicked the oranges into the gutter, and placed her, collapsed, on the seat. It was only then that he dared to look behind him, but the house, like the street, was without signs of life. As he turned the next corner, however, he saw Doyle getting off a streetcar, and probably never before had Annabelle made such speed as she did for the next six blocks.

Hours later Elinor Cardew wakened in a quiet room with gray walls, and with the sickening sweet odor of ether over everything. Instead of Olga a quiet nurse sat by her bed, and standing by a window, in low-voiced conversation, were two men. One she knew, the doctor. The other, a tall young man with a slight limp as he came toward her, she had never seen before. A friendly young man, thin, and grave of voice, who put a hand over hers and said:

"You are not to worry about anything, Mrs. Doyle. You understand me, don't you? Everything is all right. I am going now to get your people."

"My husband?"

"Your own people," he said. "I have already telephoned to your brother. And the leg's fixed. Everything's as right as rain."

Elinor closed her eyes. She felt no pain and no curiosity. Only there was something she had to do, and do quickly. What was it? But she could not remember, because she felt very sleepy and relaxed, and as though everything was indeed as right as rain.

It was evening when she looked up again, and the room was dark. The doctor had gone, and the grave young man was still in the room. There was another figure there, tall and straight, and at first she thought it was Jim Doyle.

"Jim!" she said. And then: "You must go away, Jim. I warn you. I am going to tell all I know."

But the figure turned, and it was Howard Cardew, a tense and strained Howard Cardew, who loomed amazingly tall and angry, but not with her.

"I'm sorry, Nellie dear," he said, bending over her. "If we'd only known-can you talk now?"

Her mind was suddenly very clear.

"I must. There is very little time."

"I want to tell you something first, Nellie. I think we have located the Russian woman, but we haven't got Doyle."

Howard was not very subtle, but Willy Cameron saw her face and understood. It was strange beyond belief, he felt, this loyalty of women to their men, even after love had gone; this feeling that, having once lain in a man's arms, they have taken a vow of protection over that man. It was not so much that they were his as that he was theirs. Jim Doyle had made her a prisoner, had treated her brutally, was a traitor to her and to his country, but-he had been hers. She was glad that he had got away.

Chapter XLVII

It was dark when Howard Cardew and Willy Cameron left the hospital. Elinor's information had been detailed and exact. Under cover of the general strike the radical element intended to take over the city. On the evening of the first day of the strike, armed groups from the revolutionary party would proceed first to the municipal light plant, and, having driven out any employees who remained at their posts, or such volunteers as had replaced them, would plunge the city into darkness.

Elinor was convinced that following this would come various bomb outrages, perhaps a great number of them, but of this she had no detailed information. What she did know, however, was the dependence that Doyle and the other leaders were placing in the foreign element in the nearby mill towns and from one or two mining districts in the county.

Around the city, in the mill towns, there were more than forty thousand foreign laborers. Subtract from that the loyal aliens, but add a certain percentage of the native-born element, members of seditious societies and followers of the red flag, and the Reds had a potential army of dangerous size.

As an actual fighting force they were much less impressive. Only a small percentage, she knew and told them, were adequately armed. There were a few machine guns, and some long-range rifles, but by far the greater number had only revolvers. The remainder had extemporized weapons, bars of iron, pieces of pipe, farm implements, lances of wood tipped with iron and beaten out on home forges.

They were a rabble, not an army, without organization and with few leaders. Their fighting was certain to be as individualistic as their doctrines. They had two elements in their favor only, numbers and surprise.

To oppose them, if the worst came, there were perhaps five thousand armed men, including the city and county police, the state constabulary, and the citizens who had signed the cards of the Vigilance Committee. The local post of the American Legion stood ready for instant service, and a few national guard troops still remained in the vicinity. "What they expect," she said, looking up from her pillows with tragic eyes, "is that the police and the troops will join them. You don't think they will, do you?"

They reassured her, and after a time she slept again. When she wakened, at midnight, the room was empty save for a nurse reading under a night lamp behind a screen. Elinor was not in pain. She lay there, listening to the night sounds of the hospital, the watchman shuffling along the corridor in slippers, the closing of a window, the wail of a newborn infant far away.

There was a shuffling of feet in the street below, the sound of many men, not marching but grimly walking, bent on some unknown errand. The nurse opened the window and looked out.

"That's queer!" she said. "About thirty men, and not saying a word. They walk like soldiers, but they're not in uniform."

Elinor pondered that, but it was not for some days that she knew that Pink Denslow and a picked number of volunteers from the American Legion had that night, quite silently and unemotionally, broken into the printing office where Doyle and Akers had met Cusick, and had, not so silently but still unemotionally, destroyed the presses and about a ton of inflammatory pamphlets.

Chapter XLVIII

There was a little city, and few men within it; And there came a great king against it, and besieged it, And built great bulwarks against it; Now there was found in it a Poor Wise Man, And he by his wisdom delivered the city. —Ecclesiastes IX:14, 15.

The general strike occurred two days later, at mid-day. During the interval a joint committee representing the workers, the employers and the public had held a protracted sitting, but without result, and by one o'clock the city was in the throes of a complete tie-up. Laundry and delivery wagons were abandoned where they stood. Some of the street cars had been returned to the barns, but others stood in the street where the crews had deserted them.

There was no disorder, however, and the city took its difficulties with a quiet patience and a certain sense of humor. Bulletins similar to the ones used in Seattle began to appear.

"Strikers, the world is the workers' for the taking, and the workers are the vast majority in society. Your interests are paramount to those of a small, useless band of parasites who exploit you to their advantage. You have nothing to lose but your chains and you have a world to gain. The world for the workers."

There was one ray of light in the darkness, however. The municipal employees had refused to strike, and only by force would the city go dark that night. It was a blow to the conspirators. In the strange psychology of the mob, darkness was an essential to violence, and by three o'clock that afternoon the light plant and city water supply had been secured against attack by effectual policing. The power plant for the car lines was likewise protected, and at five o'clock a line of street cars, stalled on Amanda Street, began to show signs of life.

The first car was boarded by a half dozen youngish men, unobtrusively ready for trouble, and headed by a tall youth who limped slightly and wore an extremely anxious expression. He went forward and commenced a series of experiments with levers and brake, in which process incidentally he liberated a quantity of sand onto the rails. A moment later the car lurched forward, and then stopped with a jerk.

Willy Cameron looked behind him and grinned. The entire guard was piled in an ignoble mass on the floor.

By six o'clock volunteer crews were running a number of cars, and had been subjected to nothing worse than abuse. Strikers lined the streets and watched them, but the grim faces of the guards kept them back. They jeered from the curbs, but except for the flinging of an occasional stone they made no inimical move.

By eight o'clock it was clear that the tie-up would be only partial. Volunteers from all walks of life were in line at the temporary headquarters of the Vigilance Committee and were being detailed, for police duty, to bring in the trains with the morning milk, to move street cars and trucks. The water plant and the reservoirs were protected. Willy Cameron, abandoning his car after the homeward rush of the evening, found a line before the Committee Building which extended for blocks down the street.

Troops had been sent for, but it took time to mobilize and move them. It would be morning before they arrived. And the governor, over the long distance wire to the mayor, was inclined to be querulous.

"We'll send them, of course," he said. "But if the strikers are keeping quiet —I don't know what the country's coming to. We're holding a conference here now. There's rioting breaking out all over the state."

There was a conference held in the Mayor's office that night: Cameron and Cardew and one or two others of the Vigilance Committee, two agents of the government secret service, the captains of the companies of state troops and constabulary, the Chief of Police, the Mayor himself, and some representatives of the conservative element of organized labor. Quiet men, these last, uneasy and anxious, as ignorant as the others of which way the black cat, the symbol of sabotage and destruction, would jump. The majority of their men would stand for order, they declared, but there were some who would go over. They urged, to offset that reflection on their organization that the proletariat of the city might go over, too.

But, by midnight, it seemed as though the situation was solving itself. In the segregated district there had been a small riot, and another along the river front, disturbances quickly ended by the police and the volunteer deputies. The city had not gone dark. The bombs had not exploded. Word came in that by back roads and devious paths the most rabid of the agitators were leaving town. And before two o'clock Howard Cardew and some of the others went home to bed.

At three o'clock the Cardew doorbell rang, and Howard, not asleep, flung on his dressing gown and went out into the hall. Lily was in her doorway, intent and anxious.

"Don't answer it, father," she begged. "You don't know what it may be."

Howard smiled, but went back and got his revolver. The visitor was Willy Cameron.

"I don't like to waken you," he said, "but word has come in of suspicious movements at Baxter and Friendship, and one or two other places. It looks like concerted action of some sort."

"What sort of concerted action?"

"They still have one card to play. The foreign element outside hasn't been heard from. It looks as though the fellows who left town to-night have been getting busy up the river."

"They wouldn't be such fools as to come to the city."

"They've been made a lot of promises. They may be out of hand, you know."

While Howard was hastily dressing, Willy Cameron waited below. He caught a glimpse of himself in the big mirror and looked away. His face was drawn and haggard, his eyes hollow and his collar a wilted string. He was dusty and shabby, too, and to Lily, coming down the staircase, he looked almost ill.

Lily was in a soft negligee garment, her bare feet thrust into slippers, but she was too anxious to be self-conscious.

"Willy," she said, "there is trouble after all?"

"Not in the city. Things are not so quiet up the river."

She placed a hand on his arm.

"Are you and father going up the river?"

He explained, after a momentary hesitation. "It may crystallize into something, or it may not," he finished.

"You think it will, don't you?"

"It will be nothing more, at the worst, than rioting."

"But you may be hurt!"

"I may have one chance to fight for my country," he said, rather grimly. "Don't begrudge me that." But he added: "I'll not be hurt. The thing will blow up as soon as it starts."

"You don't really believe that, do you?"

"I know they'll never get into the city."

But as he moved away she called him back, more breathlessly than ever, and quite white.

"I don't want you to go without knowing-Willy, do you remember once that you said you cared for me?"

"I remember." He stared straight ahead.

"Are you-all over that?"

"You know better than that, don't you?"

"But I've done so many things," she said, wistfully. "You ought to hate me." And when he said nothing, for the simple reason that he could not speak: "I've ruined us both, haven't I?"

Suddenly he caught up her hand and, bending over it, held it to his lips.

"Always," he said, huskily, "I love you, Lily. I shall always love you."

Chapter XLIX

Howard went back to the municipal building, driving furiously through the empty streets. The news was ominous. Small bodies of men, avoiding the highways, were focusing at different points in the open country. The state police had been fired at from ambush, and two of them had been killed. They had ridden into and dispersed various gatherings in the darkness, but only to have them re-form in other places. The enemy was still shadowy, elusive; it was apparently saving its ammunition. It did little shooting, but reports of the firing of farmhouses and of buildings in small, unprotected towns began to come in rapidly.

In a short time the messages began to be more significant, indicating that the groups were coalescing and that a revolutionary army, with the city its objective, was coming down the river, evidently making for the bridge at Chester Street.

"They've lighted a fire they can't put out," was Howard's comment. His mouth was very dry and his face twitching, for he saw, behind the frail barrier of the Chester Street bridge, the quiet houses of the city, the sleeping children. He saw Grace and Lily, and Elinor. He was among the first to reach the river front.

All through the dawn volunteers labored at the bridge head. Members of the Vigilance Committee, policemen and firemen, doctors, lawyers, clerks, shop-keepers, they looted the river wharves with willing, unskillful hands. They turned coal wagons on their sides, carried packing cases and boxes, and, under the direction of men who wore the Legion button, built skillfully and well. Willy Cameron toiled with the others. He lifted and pulled and struggled, and in the midst of his labor he had again that old dream of the city. The city was a vast number of units, and those units were homes. Behind each of those men there was, somewhere, in some quiet neighborhood, a home. It was for their homes they were fighting, for the right of children to play in peaceful streets, for the right to go back at night to the rest they had earned by honest labor, for the right of the hearth, of lamp-light and sunlight, of love, of happiness.

Then, in the flare of a gasoline torch, he came face to face with Louis Akers. The two men confronted each other, silently, with hostility. Neither moved aside, but it was Akers who spoke first.

"Always busy, Cameron," he said. "What'd the world do without you, anyhow?"

"Aren't you on the wrong side of this barricade?"

"Smart as ever," Akers observed, watching him intently. "As it happens, I'm here because I want to be, and because I can't get where I ought to be."

For a furious moment Willy Cameron thought he was referring to his wife, but there was something strange in Akers' tone.

"I could be useful to you fellows," he was saying, "but it seems you don't want help. I've been trying to see the Mayor all night."

"What do you want to see him about?"

"I'll tell him that."

Willy Cameron hesitated.

"I think it's a trick, Akers."

"All right. Then go to the devil!"

He turned away sullenly, leaving Willy Cameron still undecided. It would be like the man as he knew him, this turning informer when he saw the strength of the defense, and Cameron had a flash of intuition, too, that Akers might see, in this new role, some possible chance to win back with Lily Cardew. He saw how the man's cheap soul might dramatize itself.

"Akers!" he called.

Akers stopped, but he did not turn.

"I've got a car here. If you mean what you say, and it's straight, I'll take you."

"Where's the car?"

On their way to it, threading in and out among the toiling crowd, Willy Cameron had a chance to observe the change in the other man, his drooping shoulders and the almost lassitude of his walk. He went ahead, charging the mass and going through it by sheer bulk and weight, his hands in his coat pockets, his soft hat pulled low over his face. Neither of them noticed that one of the former clerks of the Myers Housecleaning Company followed close behind, or that, holding to a tire, he rode on the rear of the Cardew automobile as it made its way into the center of the city.

In the car Akers spoke only once.

"Where is Howard Cardew?" he asked.

"With the Mayor, probably. I left him there."

It seemed to him that Akers found the answer satisfactory. He sat back in the deep seat, and lighted a cigarette.

The Municipal Building was under guard. Willy Cameron went up the steps and spoke to the sentry there. It was while his back was turned that the sharp crack of a revolver rang out, and he whirled, in time to see Louis Akers fall forward on his face and lie still.

The shadowy groups through the countryside had commenced to coalesce. Groups of twenty became a rabble of five hundred. The five hundred grew, and joined other five hundreds. From Baxter alone over two thousand rioters, mostly foreigners, started out, and by daylight the main body of the enemy reached the outskirts of the city, a long, irregular line of laughing, jostling, shouting men, constantly renewed at the rear until the procession covered miles of roadway. They were of all races and all types; individually they were, many of them, like boys playing truant from school, not quite certain of themselves, smiling and yet uneasy, not entirely wicked in intent. But they were shepherded by men with cunning eyes, men who knew well that a mob is greater than the sum of its parts, more wicked than the individuals who compose it, more cruel, more courageous.

As it marched it laughed. It was like a lion at play, ready to leap at the first scratch that brought blood.

Where the street car line met the Friendship Road the advance was met by the Chief of Police, on horseback and followed by a guard of mounted men, and ordered back. The van hesitated, but it was urged ahead, pushed on by the irresistible force behind it, and it came on no longer singing, but slowly, inevitably, sullenly protesting and muttering. Its good nature was gone.

As the Chief turned his horse was shot under him. He took another horse from one of his guard, and they retired, moving slowly and with drawn revolvers. There was no further shooting at that time, nothing but the irresistible advance. The police could no more have held the armed rabble than they could have held the invading hordes in Belgium. At the end of the street the Chief stopped and looked back. They had passed over his dead horse as though it were not there.

In the mill district, which they had now reached, they received reenforcements, justifying the judgment of the conference that to have erected their barricades there would have been to expose the city's defenders to attack from the rear. And the mill district suffered comparatively little. It was the business portion of the city toward which they turned their covetous eyes, the great stores, the hotels and restaurants, the homes of the wealthy.

Pleased by the lack of opposition the mob grew more cheerful. The lion played. They pressed forward, wanton and jeering, firing now and then at random, breaking windows as they passed, looting small shops which they stripped like locusts. Their pockets bulging, and the taste of pillage forecasting what was to come, they moved onward more rapidly, shooting at upper windows or into the air, laughing, yelling, cursing, talking. From the barricades, long before the miles-long column came into view, could be heard the ominous far-off muttering of the mob.

It was when they found the bridge barricaded on the far side, however, that the lion bared its teeth and snarled. Temporarily checked by the play of machine guns which swept the bridge and kept it clear for a time, they commenced wild, wasteful firing, from the bridge-head and from along the Cardew wharves. Their leaders were prepared, and sent snipers into the bridge towers, but the machine guns continued to fire.

That the struggle would be on the bridge Doyle and his Council had anticipated from the reports of the night before. They were prepared to take a heavy loss on the bridges, but they had not prepared for the thing that defeated them; that as the mob is braver than the individual, so also it is more cowardly.

Pushed forward from the rear and unable to retreat through the dense mass behind that was every moment growing denser, a few hundreds found themselves facing the steady machine-gun fire from behind the barricades, and unable either to advance or to retire. Thus trapped, they turned on their own forces behind them, and tried to fight their way to safety, but the inexorable pressure kept on, and the defenders, watching and powerless, saw men fling themselves from the bridges and disappear in the water below, rather than advance into the machine-gun zone. The guns were not firing into the rioters, but before them, to hold them back, and into that leaden stream there were no brave spirits to hurl themselves.

The trapped men turned on their own and battled for escape. With the same violence which had been directed toward the city they now fought each other, and the bridge slowly cleared. But the mob did not disperse.

It spread out on the bank across, a howling, frustrated, futile mass, disorganized and demoralized, which fired its useless guns across the river, which seethed and tossed and struggled, and spent itself in its own wild fury. And all the time cool-eyed men, on the wharves across, watched and waited for the time to attack.

"They're sick at their stomachs now," said an old army sergeant, watching, to Willy Cameron. "The dirty devils! They'll be starting their filthy work over there soon, and that's the zero hour."

Willy Cameron nodded. He had seen one young Russian boy with a child-like face venture forward alone into the fire zone and drop. He still lay there, on the bridge. And all of Willy Cameron was in revolt. What had he been told, that boy, that had made him ready to pour out his young life like wine? There were others like him in that milling multitude on the river bank across, young men who had come to America with a dream in their hearts, and America had done this to them. Or had she? She had taken them in, but they were not her own, and now, since she would not take them, they would take her. Was that it? Was it that America had made them her servants, but not her children? He did not know.

Robbed of the city proper, the mob turned on the mill district it had invaded. Its dream of lust and greed was over, but it could still destroy.

Like a battle charge, as indeed it was, the mounted city and state police crossed the bridge. It was followed by the state troops on foot, by city policemen in orderly files, and then by the armed citizens. The bridge vibrated to the step of marching men, going out to fight for their homes. The real battle was fought there, around the Cardew mills, a battle where the loyalists were greatly outnumbered, and where the rioters fought, according to their teaching, with every trick they could devise. Posted in upper windows they fired down from comparative safety; ambulances crossed and re-crossed the bridges. The streets were filled with rioting men, striking out murderously with bars and spikes. Fires flamed up and burned themselves out. In one place, eight blocks of mill-workers' houses, with their furnishings, went in a quarter of an hour.

Willy Cameron was fighting like a demon. Long ago his reserve of ammunition had given out, and he was fighting with the butt end of his revolver. Around him had rallied some of the men he knew best, Pink and Mr. Hendricks, Doctor Smalley, Dan and Joe Wilkinson, and they stayed together as, street by street, the revolutionists were driven back. There were dead and wounded everywhere, injured men who had crawled into the shelter of doorways and sat or lay there, nursing their wounds.

Suddenly, to his amazement, Willy saw old Anthony Cardew. He had somehow achieved an upper window of the mill office building, and he was showing himself fearlessly, a rifle in his hands; in his face was a great anger, but there was more than that. Willy Cameron, thinking it over later, decided that it was perplexity. He could not understand.

He never did understand. For other eyes also had seen old Anthony Cardew. Willy Cameron, breasting the mob and fighting madly toward the door of the building, with Pink behind him, heard a cheer and an angry roar, and, looking up, saw that the old man had disappeared. They found him there later on, the rifle beside him, his small and valiant figure looking, with eyes no longer defiant, toward the Heaven which puts, for its own strange purpose, both evil and good into the same heart.

By eleven o'clock the revolution was over. Sodden groups of men, thoroughly cowed and frightened, were on their way by back roads to the places they had left a few hours before. They had no longer dreams of empire. Behind them they could see, on the horizon, the city itself, the smoke from its chimneys, the spires of its churches. Both, homes and churches, they had meant to destroy, but behind both there was the indestructible. They had failed.

They turned, looked back, and went on.

On the crest of a hill-top overlooking the city a man was standing, looking down to where the softened towers of the great steel bridges rose above the river mist like fairy towers. Below him lay the city, powerful, significant, important.

The man saw the city only as a vast crucible, into which he had flung his all, and out of which had come only defeat and failure. But the city was not a crucible. The melting pot of a nation is not a thing of cities, but of the human soul.

The city was not a melting pot. It was a sanctuary. The man stood silent and morose, his chin dropped on his chest, and stared down.

Beside and somewhat behind him stood a woman, a somber, passionate figure, waiting passively. His eyes traveled from the city to her, and rested on her, contemptuous, thwarted, cynical.

"You fool," he said, "I hate you, and you know it."

But she only smiled faintly. "We'd better get away now, Jim," she said.

He got into the car.

Chapter L

Late that afternoon Joe Wilkinson and Dan came slowly up the street, toward the Boyd house. The light of battle was still in Dan's eyes, his clothes were torn and his collar missing, and he walked with the fine swagger of the conqueror.

"Y'ask me," he said, "and I'll tell the world this thing's done for. It was just as well to let them give it a try, and find out it won't work."

Joe said nothing. He was white and very tired, and a little sick.

"If you don't mind I'll go in your place and wash up," he remarked, as they neared the house. "I'll scare the kids to death if they see me like this."

Edith was in the parlor. She had sat there almost all day, in an agony of fear. At four o'clock the smallest Wilkinson had hammered at the front door, and on being admitted had made a shameless demand.

"Bed and thugar," she had said, looking up with an ingratiating smile.

"You little beggar!"

"Bed and thugar."

Edith had got the bread and sugar, and, having lured the baby into the parlor, had held her while she ate, receiving now and then an exceedingly sticky kiss in payment. After a little the child's head began to droop, and Edith drew the small head down onto her breast. She sat there, rocking gently, while the chair slowly traveled, according to its wont, about the room.

The child brought her comfort. She began to understand those grave rocking figures in the hospital ward, women who sat, with eyes that seemed to look into distant places, with a child's head on their breasts.

After all, that was life for a woman. Love was only a part of the scheme of life, a means to an end. And that end was the child.

For the first time she wished that her child had lived.

She felt no bitterness now, and no anger. He was dead. It was hard to think of him as dead, who had been so vitally alive. She was sorry he had had to die, but death was like love and children, it was a part of some general scheme of things. Suppose this had been his child she was holding? Would she so easily have forgiven him? She did not know.

Then she thought of Willy Cameron. The bitterness had strangely gone out of that, too. Perhaps, vaguely, she began to realize that only young love gives itself passionately and desperately, when there is no hope of a return, and that the agonies of youth, although terrible enough, pass with youth itself.

She felt very old.

Joe found her there, the chair displaying its usual tendency to climb the chimney flue, and stood in the doorway, looking at her with haunted, hungry eyes. There was a sort of despair in Joe those days, and now he was tired and shaken from the battle.

"I'll take her home in a minute," he said, still with the strange eyes.

He came into the room, and suddenly he was kneeling beside the chair, his head buried against the baby's warm, round body. His bent shoulders shook, and Edith, still with the maternal impulse strong within her, put her hand on his bowed head.

"Don't, Joe!"

He looked up.

"I loved you so, Edith!"

"Don't you love me now?"

"God knows I do. I can't get over it. I can't. I've tried, Edith."

He sat back on the floor and looked at her.

"I can't," he repeated. "And when I saw you like that just now, with the kid in your arms —I used to think that maybe you and I —"

"I know, Joe. No decent man would want me now."

She was still strangely composed, peaceful, almost detached.

"That!" he said, astonished. "I don't mean that, Edith. I've had my fight about that, and got it over. That's done with. I mean —" he got up and straightened himself. "You don't care about me."

"But I do care for you. Perhaps not quite the way you care, Joe, but I've been through such a lot. I can't seem to feel anything terribly. I just want peace."

"I could give you that," he said eagerly.

Edith smiled. Peace, in that noisy house next door, with children and kittens and puppies everywhere! And yet it would be peace, after all, a peace of the soul, the peace of a good man's love. After a time, too, there might come another peace, the peace of those tired women in the ward, rocking.

"If you want me, I'll marry you," she said, very simply. "I'll be a good wife, Joe. And I want children. I want the right to have them."

He never noticed that the kiss she gave him, over the sleeping baby, was slightly tinged with granulated sugar.

Chapter LI

Old Anthony's body had been brought home, and lay in state in his great bed. There had been a bad hour; death seems so strangely to erase faults and leave virtues. Something strong and vital had gone from the house, and the servants moved about with cautious, noiseless steps. In Grace's boudoir, Howard was sitting, his arms around his wife, telling her the story of the day. At dawn he had notified her by telephone of Akers' murder.

"Shall I tell Lily?" she had asked, trembling.

"Do you want to wait until I get back?"

"I don't know how she will take it, Howard. I wish you could be here, anyhow."

But then had come the battle and his father's death, and in the end it was Willy Cameron who told her. He had brought back all that was mortal of Anthony Cardew, and, having seen the melancholy procession up the stairs, had stood in the hall, hating to intrude but hoping to be useful. Howard found him there, a strange, disheveled figure, bearing the scars of battle, and held out his hand.

"It's hard to thank you, Cameron," he said; "you seem to be always about when we need help. And" —he paused —"we seem to have needed it considerably lately."

Willy Cameron flushed.

"I feel rather like a meddler, sir."

"Better go up and wash," Howard said. "I'll go up with you."

It happened, therefore, that it was in Howard Cardew's opulent dressing-room that Howard first spoke to Willy Cameron of Akers' death, pacing the floor as he did so.

"I haven't told her, Cameron." He was anxious and puzzled. "She'll have to be told soon, of course. I don't know anything about women. I don't know how she'll take it."

"She has a great deal of courage. It will be a shock, but not a grief. But I have been thinking—" Willy Cameron hesitated. "She must not feel any remorse," he went on. "She must not feel that she contributed to it in any way. If you can make that clear to her —"

"Are you sure she did not?"

"It isn't facts that matter now. We can't help those. And no one can tell what actually led to his change of heart. It is what she is to think the rest of her life."

Howard nodded.

"I wish you would tell her," he said. "I'm a blundering fool when it comes to her. I suppose I care too much."

He caught rather an odd look in Willy Cameron's face at that, and pondered over it later.

"I will tell her, if you wish."

And Howard drew a deep breath of relief. It was shortly after that he broached another matter, rather diffidently.

"I don't know whether you realize it or not, Cameron," he said, "but this thing to-day might have been a different story if it had not been for you. And-don't think I'm putting this on a reward basis. It's nothing of the sort-but I would like to feel that you were working with me. I'd hate like thunder to have you working against me," he added.

"I am only trained for one thing."

"We use chemists in the mills."

But the discussion ended there. Both men knew that it would be taken up later, at some more opportune time, and in the meantime both had one thought, Lily.

So it happened that Lily heard the news of Louis Akers' death from Willy Cameron. She stood, straight and erect, and heard him through, watching him with eyes sunken by her night's vigil and by the strain of the day. But it seemed to her that he was speaking of some one she had known long ago, in some infinitely remote past.

"I am sorry," she said, when he finished. "I didn't want him to die. You know that, don't you? I never wished him-Willy, I say I am sorry, but I don't really feel anything. It's dreadful."

Before he could catch her she had fallen to the floor, fainting for the first time in her healthy young life.

An hour later Mademoiselle went down to the library door. She found Willy Cameron pacing the floor, a pipe clenched in his teeth, and a look of wild despair in his eyes.

Mademoiselle took a long breath. She had changed her view-point somewhat since the spring. After all, what mattered was happiness. Wealth and worldly ambition were well enough, but they brought one, in the end, to the thing which waited for all in some quiet upstairs room, with the shades drawn and the heavy odors of hot-house flowers over everything.

"She is all right, quite, Mr. Cameron," she said. "It was but a crisis of the nerves, and to be expected. And now she demands to see you."

Grayson, standing in the hall, had a swift vision of a tall figure, which issued with extreme rapidity from the library door, and went up the stairs, much like a horse taking a series of hurdles. But the figure lost momentum suddenly at the top, hesitated, and apparently moved forward on tiptoe. Grayson went into the library and sniffed at the unmistakable odor of a pipe. Then, having opened a window, he went and stood before a great portrait of old Anthony Cardew. Tears stood in the old man's eyes, but there was a faint smile on his lips. He saw the endless procession of life. First, love. Then, out of love, life. Then death. Grayson was old, but he had lived to see young love in the Cardew house. Out of love, life. He addressed a little speech to the picture.

"Wherever you are, sir," he said, "you needn't worry any more. The line will carry on, sir. The line will carry on."

Upstairs in the little boudoir Willy Cameron knelt beside the couch, and gathered Lily close in his arms.

Chapter LII

Thanksgiving of the year of our Lord 1919 saw many changes. It saw, slowly emerging from the chaos of war, new nations, like children, taking their first feeble steps. It saw a socialism which, born at full term might have thrived, prematurely and forcibly delivered, and making a valiant but losing fight for life. It saw that war is never good, but always evil; that war takes everything and gives nothing, save that sometimes a man may lose the whole world and gain his own soul.

It saw old Anthony Cardew gone to his fathers, into the vast democracy of heaven, and Louis Akers passed through the Traitors' Gate of eternity to be judged and perhaps reprieved. For a man is many men, good and bad, and the Judge of the Tower of Heaven is a just Judge.

It saw Jim Doyle a fugitive, Woslosky dead, and the Russian, Ross, bland, cunning and eternally plotting, in New England under another name. And Mr. Hendricks ordering a new suit for the day of taking office. And Doctor Smalley tying a bunch of chrysanthemums on Annabelle, against a football game, and taking a pretty nurse to see it.

It saw Ellen roasting a turkey, and a strange young man in the Eagle Pharmacy, a young man who did not smoke a pipe, and allowed no visitors in the back room. And it saw Willy Cameron in the laboratory of the reopened Cardew Mills, dealing in tons instead of grains and drams, and learning to touch any piece of metal in the mill with a moistened fore-finger before he sat down upon it.

But it saw more than that.

On the evening of Thanksgiving Day there was an air of repressed excitement about the Cardew house. Mademoiselle, in a new silk dress, ran about the lower floor, followed by an agitated Grayson with a cloth, for Mademoiselle was shifting ceaselessly and with trembling hands vases of flowers, and spilling water at each shift. At six o'clock had arrived a large square white box, which the footman had carried to the rear and there exhibited, allowing a palpitating cook, scullery maid and divers other excitable and emotional women to peep within.

After which he tied it up again and carried it upstairs.

At seven o'clock Elinor Cardew, lovely in black satin, was carried down the stairs and placed in a position which commanded both the hall and the drawing-room. For some strange reason it was essential that she should see both.

At seven-thirty came in a rush:

(a) —Mr. Alston Denslow, in evening clothes and gardenia, and feeling in his right waist-coat pocket nervously every few minutes.

(b) —An excited woman of middle age, in a black silk dress still faintly bearing the creases of five days in a trunk, and accompanied by a mongrel dog, both being taken upstairs by Grayson, Mademoiselle, Pink, and Howard Cardew. ("He said Jinx was to come," she explained breathlessly to her bodyguard. "I never knew such a boy!")

(c) —Mr. Davis, in a frock coat and white lawn tie, and taken upstairs by Grayson, who mistook him for the bishop.

(d) —Aunt Caroline, in her diamond dog collar and purple velvet, and determined to make the best of things.

(e) —The real bishop this time, and his assistant, followed by a valet with a suitcase, containing the proper habiliments for a prince of the church while functioning. (A military term, since the Bishop had been in the army.)

(f) —A few unimportant important people, very curious, and the women uncertain about the proper garb for a festive occasion in a house of mourning.

(g) —Set of silver table vases, belated.

(h) —Mr. and Mrs. Hendricks, Mayor and Mayoress-elect. Extremely dignified.

(i) —An overfull taxicab, containing inside it Ellen, Edith, Dan and Joe. The overflow, consisting of a tall young man, displaying repressed excitement and new evening clothes, with gardenia, sat on the seat outside beside the chauffeur and repeated to himself a sort of chant accompanied by furious searchings of his pockets. "Money. Checkbook. Tickets. Trunk checks," was the burden of his song.

(j) —Doctor Smalley and Annabelle. He left Annabelle outside.

The city moved on about its business. In thousands of homes the lights shone down on little family groups, infinitely tender little groups. The workers of the city were there, the doors shut, the fires burning. To each man the thing he had earned, not the thing that he took. To all men the right to labor, to love, and to rest. To children, the right to play. To women, the hearth, and the peace of the hearth. To lovers, love, and marriage, and home.

The city moved on about its business, and its business was homes.

At the great organ behind the staircase the organist sat. In stiff rows near him were the Cardew servants, marshaled by Grayson and in their best.

Grayson stood, very rigid, and waited. And as he waited he kept his eyes on the portrait of old Anthony, in the drawing-room beyond. There was a fixed, rapt look in Grayson's eyes, and there was reassurance. It was as though he would say to the portrait: "It has all come out very well, you see, sir. It always works out somehow. We worry and fret, we old ones, but the young come along, and somehow or other they manage, sir."

What he actually said was to tell a house maid to stop sniveling.

Over the house was the strange hush of waiting. It had waited before this, for birth and for death, but never before —

The Bishop was waiting also, and he too had his eyes fixed on old Anthony's portrait, a straight, level-eyed gaze, as of man to man, as of prince of the church to prince of industry. The Bishop's eyes said: "All shall be done properly and in order, and as befits the Cardews, Anthony."

The Bishop was as successful in his line as Anthony Cardew had been in his. He cleared his throat.

The organist sat at the great organ behind the staircase, waiting. He was playing very softly, with his eyes turned up. He had played the same music many times before, and always he felt very solemn, as one who makes history. He sighed. Sometimes it seemed to him that he was only an accompaniment to life, to which others sang and prayed, were christened, confirmed and married. But what was the song without the music? He wished the scullery maid would stop crying.

Grayson touched him on the arm.

"All ready, sir," he said.

Willy Cameron stood at the foot of the staircase, looking up.